RETURN OF THE WOLF

by

Steven A. McKay

Book 5 in

THE FOREST LORD CHRONICLES

Dedicated to all the bands who provide the soundtrack for my writing sessions, particularly Norway's Enslaved.

emeralds, and a broken sword that was said to have belonged to one of King Arthur's knights – were safely stored in the wagons that creaked and groaned through the area known locally as The Wash.

In truth, there was not a great deal of worth within the baggage train, for John's fortune had rapidly dwindled over the years as he was beset by his own barons. Most of the space in the wagons Giselbrecht and his Flemish mercenaries guarded was taken up by food, tents, and weaponry. In its own way, this cargo was valuable, but it was the jewellery and other treasure that Giselbrecht was really being paid to look after. He had seen some of it, like the rings and exquisite clasp, but not all of it, for King John was a secretive, distrustful man. Giselbrecht had heard him talk about some of the pieces though, and most intriguing to the mercenary knight was a golden goblet that the king believed dated back to the time of Christ Himself.

Giselbrecht would dearly like to see that goblet – a golden cup dating back to the time of the Last Supper? What devout Christian would not want to see such a treasure? Could it be the very cup used by Christ at that final, sacred meal? Perhaps. Many holy relics were scattered throughout Europe, and such a priceless artefact as the fabled Holy Grail must be somewhere. No peasant could possibly own it; only a monarch, or the pope himself could afford something so valuable. There was a legend that said Joseph of Arimathea had brought the sacred chalice to England, so why should it not have come into the hands of King John?

"Did you see the state of that fool this morning before he left us?"

Giselbrecht, forced to abandon his holy reverie, turned to his captain, Pieter, and nodded. "I did. He looked terrible."

"No wonder," Pieter snorted. "Did you notice how much cider he downed last night?"

3

Giselbrecht nodded again. "And a whole basket of peaches as well. Not a healthy combination I'd think." Indeed, he had gone to empty his bladder during the feast at Bishop's Lynn the night before and seen the king outside the hall, vomiting forcefully as a great, silvery full moon looked down upon them. It was a truly degrading state for a king to be in. "He indulged far too much last evening, it's true, but there was more to his sickness today than a simple hangover."

The captain murmured agreement. "I think our time here in England is drawing to an end, my lord, one way or another. John is not a well man."

Giselbrecht did not answer. What was there to say? Either King John would be defeated by the barons and Prince Louis or, as seemed more likely, he would die before he could even reach Lincolnshire. It was quite possible he was already dead, and the news hadn't come back to the baggage train yet.

"We have not been paid," Pieter said in a low voice, and Giselbrecht turned, frowning, to look at him.

"Are you suggesting we take what we're owed from the wagons?"

His captain shrugged. "Only if we hear King John has died. If we don't do so, I doubt anyone will ever pay us."

They had been paid regularly until then; Giselbrecht could have no complaints about that. But they were owed their most recent payment, and it seemed certain that giving money to a group of Flemish mercenaries would be the last thing on any Englishman's mind when their king died and the country was thrown into even more chaos.

"Well, John is still alive, as far as we know," the knight said firmly. "And we are men of honour, not common thieves. For now, we guard these wagons with our lives, as we swore to do."

Pieter accepted that and the men rode on in companionable silence as the clouds grew even heavier and it began to rain.

It was low tide – it had to be, or the route they were traversing would be impassable. Known locally as the Wash Way, Giselbrecht had hired a guide to see them safely along this shortcut to Swineshead Abbey in Lincolnshire. The guide, a man called Paul, had earned his wages so far, as his route had saved the wagons from going all the way around a large bay, allowing them to pass straight through it instead.

"How much farther, Paul?" the knight called to the guide, who was walking at the front of the column.

Glancing over his shoulder, the man shouted back in an accent so thick that the Flemish nobleman could hardly translate it, "Not much longer now, lord! Don't fret, we'll be long gone by the time the tide comes back in."

"What did he say?" Pieter asked, brow furrowed.

"No idea," Giselbrecht admitted, laughing. "But he seems happy enough, so I won't worry."

The rain grew steadily heavier, relentlessly pelting down on them in great, fat drops as the wind picked up alarmingly. It was frigid too, England being even colder than Flanders at this time of the year.

Ahead of them, the guide turned his head and looked to the east, towards the sea. He was no longer smiling.

A chill ran down Giselbrecht's back, and it was not from the weather.

"Something's wrong," he said, instinctively riding closer to the wagon nearest them. This wagon held the most valuable items belonging to King John, and Giselbrecht would not let anything happen to it, not while he still had breath in his body.

Pieter was looking all around, frowning, irritated, for there seemed to be no enemies nearby to account for his superior's obvious anxiety. "What"— he began, and then there was a scream from ahead, and something struck them from the side.

Giselbrecht felt his horse collapse, and he opened his mouth to cry out. Immediately, it was filled with icy water, and he tried desperately not to swallow any of it, his mind whirling, screaming silently, God save me from whatever this is! Had the rain been so heavy? Of course not, this was not some downpour that had submerged them, it was a wave.

How could a wave have appeared so suddenly, from out of nowhere?

His head broke free of the water and he spat out what was in his mouth, gasping in air, turning to look back at the many wagons, riders, and infantrymen in the column behind. Terror filled him, for he could see the monstrous wave had swept almost everything away. He was still, miraculously, on his horse's back, and the animal struggled to stand and catch its breath as crying and pleas for help filled the air.

"What's happening?" Pieter shouted in desperation.

"I don't know," Giselbrecht called back. The wagon he'd been riding beside was sinking into the sand, and he thought of the treasures held within its wooden walls, sucked under, never to be seen again. He thought of the golden goblet that had been used by Christ himself at the Last Supper, and knew he could not let it be lost. "Help me!" he ordered Pieter, jumping down from his shaky horse's saddle and trudging through the sodden sand to the wagon.

The chest that he knew contained the holy chalice had been knocked loose by the sudden wave, and it stuck out from amongst the others surrounding it. Giselbrecht grabbed it and pulled, and it fell immediately onto the wet ground.

Pieter appeared beside him then, and they opened the box, since it was far too heavy to carry away on horseback.

For one desperate moment Giselbrecht van Zottegem thought they had salvaged the wrong chest, for it was a sword with a broken tip that he saw before him. But then he spotted the golden cup, seeming to shine in some Heavenly light, and he grabbed it, staring in wonder.

"I'll take the sword," Pieter gasped, and then they were both thrown backwards as another great wave struck them before they could rescue any more of the treasure from the wooden box.

Slightly less panicked this time, Giselbrecht held his breath and prayed silently until the water receded and he was able to push himself onto his feet again. "God be praised," he breathed, seeing his loyal horse was somehow still with him, terrified, but seeming uninjured. "Are you alright, Pieter?"

His captain looked stunned and Giselbrecht guessed he must have the same look on his own face.

"We should get away from here before another wave comes," the knight commanded, weakly hauling himself up onto his horse. Pieter's mount was also alive, although further away, and he was forced to run to it, feet squelching and casting up clods of sand and water as he moved with a frightening lack of speed.

Giselbrecht kicked his heels in and his horse shot forwards, westwards, away from the direction of the sea. He looked back and saw his captain following him, mounted, and gripping the broken sword beneath his right arm.

Not a single other soul could be seen, and, as Giselbrecht galloped further away from the danger, he saw another wave come crashing in, terrifying in its eldritch power, sweeping away all remnants of King John's crown jewels, and the men, beasts, and wagons that had been travelling peacefully there just moments before.

CHAPTER ONE

Yorkshire, England
February, AD 1331

It was raining. Again. The rider tried to adjust the hood he wore so the rivulets of water wouldn't run straight down into his eyes but it did little good for the material was completely soaked through.

"How much farther is it, John?" he called to his companion as they rode beneath a copse of trees that formed a crude, natural roof, and offered at least a moment's respite from the downpour.

"D'you not remember?" John Little called back over his shoulder, surprise in his voice. "We've come this way dozens of times over the years."

Robert Hood, better known as Robin, looked around at the leafless, bland trees and shook his head, amazed that he'd forgotten so many of the lands, rivers, and roads around Wakefield. He'd left the village five years before and taken his burgeoning family to live in Scotland, only returning two months ago.

His mind wandered back to that reunion, and he smiled at the memory. He'd been so nervous about seeing his friends again for they all believed him dead, and he truly wasn't sure how they'd react when they saw him. So he'd sat alone in a corner of Wakefield's alehouse, hood drawn up, watching as patrons came and go and, at last John, Friar Tuck, and Will Scaflock came in. They had a tale to tell, all about some exciting adventure they'd shared in the lead up to Christmas, and they entertained the alehouse patrons with the story, enjoying one another's company as well as several rounds of drinks before, at last, Robin had worked up the courage to reveal himself to them.

"Robin!" Friar Tuck had exclaimed when recognition finally dawned on him. "It's Robin Hood. You've come home to Wakefield at last!"

Tuck had risen then to embrace the 'prodigal son', with John and Will soon joining in, tears of joy in their eyes as they realised their young friend and leader had not died after all.

Robin felt a lump in his throat as he recalled that snowy Christmas night. He'd missed his friends desperately, and it was evident they'd felt the same. The tears of joy eventually dried up however, and then there were angry recriminations, particularly from volatile Will Scaflock, as his friends berated Robin for letting them believe he was dead and buried. They'd all attended his 'funeral' after all, and carried the burden of grief ever since.

"I'm sorry," he'd said repeatedly, doing his best to explain his motives for faking his death. Eventually, the bad feeling had passed and the atmosphere in the alehouse grew suitably festive as Christmas Day reached its conclusion. In the weeks since, Robin's old friendships had been rekindled, falling back into the familiar ways they'd all shared in the years before. To an extent, at least. Five years was a long time to be apart, and the other three had remained firm friends in that time, so Robin found himself something of an outsider, uncertain about his place within the group, and suspecting John, Tuck, and Will in particular, still harboured feelings of anger and resentment over his deceit.

Five years was a long time, as Robin kept reminding himself, but he was sure that he would be fully accepted back into the fold eventually.

"Look, there's that tree that blew down in the storm of 1325, d'you not remember that?" Little John brought Robin back to the present as he pointed at the trunk of an old birch that was almost completely covered now by the undergrowth. "It's still alive, even though it's on its side.

The branches just started growing up from the trunk instead of out to the side."

Robin had assumed his memory of the lands surrounding his childhood home would remain clear in his mind when he returned. He was only twenty-seven after all, hardly a doddering old greybeard. Yet he had absolutely no recollection of that fallen birch, or this stretch of road, or how much farther it was to their destination, and he admitted all that to his friend.

"Notton is seven miles from Wakefield," John said, slowing his horse so it was trotting beside Robin's. "So we're nearly there." He looked at his companion as if he feared for the younger man's sanity. "Are you all right? We had a camp at Notton when we were outlaws. You knew this whole area like the back of your own hand. We spoke about that tree when we came by here after the storm."

Robin shrugged. "Funny how your memory fades, isn't it? I expect it'll all come back to me eventually. Maybe if I could see farther ahead I'd recognise landmarks, but it's been raining for days now. All I see before us are grey clouds, mud, and sodden trees."

John laughed. "Could be worse," he said, reaching up to squeeze rain from his grizzled beard. "It could be snowing, frosty, and windy."

Robin wasn't sure if that really would be worse but his old friend's positivity made him smile, just as it always had when he'd been an outlaw – a wolf's head. It was a hard life that, camping outdoors in all weathers, knowing that the sheriff's men could find them at any moment and kill them or take them away to be hanged in front of a laughing, baying mob. Thankfully most of the other outlaws in their gang were good company: jovial Tuck; quick-tempered but fiercely loyal Will; the musician, Allan a Dale; Robin's childhood friend, Much; Stephen the Hospitaller sergeant-at-arms; and all the others who'd lived – and sometimes died – alongside them.

Little John had always been Robin's closest confidant during those years, and, over time, his second-in-command. Standing almost seven feet tall and built like the side of a barn, John was the ideal man to have beside you in a fight. Being seven years older than Robin, he also had more experience surviving in the greenwood, and the two had formed a close bond as they adventured around Northern England together before the gang had all won pardons and been allowed to return to their homes to live a normal life.

Things had not turned out exactly like that, of course. Will Scaflock became a farmer of sorts, while Robin and John became lawmen, performing duties for the Sheriff of Nottingham and Yorkshire, Sir Henry de Faucumberg. They had made powerful enemies during their time as outlaws, however. One of them, Prior John de Monte Martini, had Robin Hood declared a wolf's head again and, seeing no other way out, Robin faked his own death and took his family north, to Scotland, rather than returning to life as a fugitive.

Little John had continued to act as a sort of roving bailiff for the sheriff after that, travelling to the towns and villages of northern England to deal with dangerous criminals that regular lawmen struggled to bring to justice. Even the most dangerous of men would think twice about fighting when confronted by Little John, a towering giant of a man with a reputation as a brutal warrior, well earned during his time as an outlaw.

Now, as the rain mercifully lessened to a drizzle and the lowering clouds lifted to reveal the village of Notton ahead, Robin wondered what the day would bring.

John had been asked by Sir Henry de Faucumberg to ride here and collect an outstanding fine from a tanner named Simon. The man had broken into a neighbour's house, assaulting the couple who lived there. The tanner was ordered to pay a fine of five shillings for his crime but, instead of paying, he'd returned to the neighbour's home and attacked him again. The local bailiff had claimed to have tried his best to collect the fine and bring the tanner to heel, but there were rumours that Simon had ties to the notorious Coterel family.

The Coterels were actually minor nobility, but it was well known they engaged in all sorts of illegal activity. Their name struck terror into the hearts of people all across England so it was no great surprise that Notton's bailiff was too afraid to deal with the violent tanner.

John was not afraid of anyone – not the tanner, nor the Coterels, and he'd readily agreed to come to Notton when the sheriff asked. He was also not a fool, though, and Robin expected his huge friend to deal with the situation sensibly. No point in getting on the wrong side of one of the most notorious families in all of England after all.

Robin knew that Little John was well suited to this life. He was calm, and fair, and empathetic, but if attacked would readily retaliate with fearsome skill and strength. The big fellow was a better lawman than Robin had been, no doubt about it.

Realising his sodden hood was only making him feel cold Robin took it off and wrung it out, smiling wryly at the amount of water that dribbled out of it. Ah, Yorkshire, he thought. I've missed you. That only made his smile even broader – it was hardly as if Scotland was any drier!

He thought back to his time as a lawman and his smile faded. It had been a decent life at first, doing much the same as John still did. But Robin, young and idealistic at the time, had found himself taking bribes from the people he was sent to collect fines from and it had taken a stern talking-to from Friar Tuck to make him realise he was becoming the kind of man he despised. When Sheriff de Faucumberg had told them of a new, brutal gang of outlaws in the area and asked Robin to bring them down, he'd jumped at the chance to do good again. With his friends by his side they had eventually destroyed those outlaws who were led by a vicious lunatic named Philip Groves, but it had been a true war of attrition between the two groups and, by the end of it, Robin lay at death's door with a fearful wound that should really have killed him.

If he'd survived those horrific injuries Prior John de Monte Martini would have seen Robin executed, but, to his astonishment, Sir Henry had killed the prior, running the corrupt clergyman through with his sword. That was a dark secret only the sheriff, Robin, and Little John knew about.

Still, even with the powerful, vindictive churchman dead, Robin had already been declared an outlaw so, given he truly was terribly wounded, faking his death seemed the best way to remain a free man while avoiding repercussions from surviving members of Philip Groves's gang. It also meant he could be blamed for the prior's death, allowing the sheriff's part in it all to remain a secret. So Robin had secretly taken Matilda and their son, Arthur, to Scotland, where she had given birth to a second son, Henry, and life had been good.

"We're here," John said, bringing Robin back to the present with a start.

The young man stretched himself up in the saddle, rolling his massive archer's shoulders, trying to work out the stiffness that had settled in them during the damp ride from Wakefield.

"Remember, I'm the bailiff. You're just here for moral support, Robin. Don't be getting yourself worked up if this tanner turns out to be an arsehole. You're still, I suppose, an outlaw." He frowned, evidently trying to work out what Robin's actual status was, then shrugged. "Don't draw attention to yourself until we meet in person with the sheriff and see what can be done about having you pardoned."

"You think this is a good idea, bearing all that in mind?"

John shrugged. "You refuse to remain indoors in Wakefield, so it's likely word has got around the whole of England that you've miraculously returned from the grave.

Just don't draw unwanted attention to yourself here is all I'm saying."

Robin nodded, smiling. "I'll do my best."

John rolled his eyes and dismounted, tying his horse to the post beside one of Notton's alehouses.

Now that he was in the village, the memories came back to Robin and he gazed around, nostalgia making him both happy and melancholic in equal measure. There had been some good times when they camped near this place, and some not so good as well.

"The tannery is over there," John noted, jerking his head to the left, but Robin was already moving in that direction.

"I know, I remember that at least," he said, touching the hilt of his sword as he led the way towards their destination. There should be no need for the oiled steel blade, but it would not hurt to have it ready.

John, as usual, had his sword too, but his favoured weapon was a quarterstaff almost as big as him. A cruder weapon than a fancy blade, but quite deadly when wielded by someone as skilled as the giant bailiff.

The ground was sodden and they stepped carefully towards the tannery which was beside the dyke and built a fair distance away from the main part of the village thanks to the stench that emanated from it.

"God's bollocks," John murmured as they approached the complex of rough, wooden buildings, not taking the road but working their way through the surrounding undergrowth so as not to alert their quarry of their approach. "You could easily find this place in the dark, the smell is so strong."

Robin sniffed the air, squinting as he did so. Dung and urine were the most obvious scents, heady and pungent even in the damp, cold air, and he pulled his hood back on, this time using the material to cover the bottom part of his face rather than the top. It was wet and uncomfortable, but went some way to blocking out the rising stink.

Had Robin been in charge, as he had been in the old days, he might have suggested they split up, but John was the leader and he did not seem to care for clever tactics, instead moving forward without hesitation towards the buildings.

Animal hides hung from wooden frames in the courtyard outside, lending the place a somewhat sinister air that was not improved by the appearance of a heavyset man coming out of a building with a tall chimney.

"Here, who the fuck are you two?" the man called, rubbing his hands on the leather apron he wore. His skin was pale and he was almost completely bald with a pronounced underbite, while his eyebrows were thick and shockingly ginger as they came together in a furious glare that moved from Robin to John. "What are you doing here?" he demanded and, as Robin watched, the man's expression changed from anger to recognition.

"I'm John Little," said the bailiff, unnecessarily for it was clear that the man knew fine well who the towering warrior was. "Are you the tanner? Simon?"

For a long moment the man simply stared malevolently at them, his fiery brows seeming to form an even deeper V in his forehead, and then, with an oath, the man sprinted into the building he'd emerged from and slammed the door behind him.

"Shit," John muttered, trying the door but finding it locked.

"I can hear him calling out to someone," Robin said, fingering the pommel of his sword again as he looked around at the cluster of dilapidated buildings. "He's not alone in there, and he knows the layout of the place while we don't."

"Oh well," said John, a wry smile appearing on his bearded face. "Looks like this isn't going to be as easy as we'd hoped. Ready? Just like old times." And, with that, he leaned back and slammed his massive boot against the tannery door.

CHAPTER TWO

"Christ's bones, it stinks in here!" John had led the way into the tannery but he pulled up, almost gagging as the fumes accosted them.

"Pull up your tunic," Robin advised. "Come on." He drew his sword for it was clear the tanner had no intentions of co-operating without a fight, and moved past the bailiff, eyes scanning the gloomy interior of the room.

The shouting had intensified when they first stormed into the building, but it had died away and now a sinister, forbidding silence fell across the place. Robin had instinctively taken charge, and John did not complain. As the pair moved forward, past more wooden frames and towards the back of the chamber, the years seemed to fall away and the near-telepathy they had once shared as outlaws returned.

A scream of rage suddenly split the air and a dark figure appeared from behind one of the wooden frames. Robin saw a knife, designed for scraping animal hides but just as useful as a weapon, scything through the gloom towards Little John's back. In one fluid motion Robin's sword flashed out, parrying the tanning knife, and then he brutally kicked the attacker in the side. There was a grunt of pain as the man slammed into a barrel filled with vile smelling liquid, and then Robin's right fist hammered into his jaw and he slumped to the ground.

Little John had a second enemy to deal with, a rat-faced, slim man with a wispy beard and barely a tooth in the mouth that opened to issue a war cry as he swung at the bailiff with his tanning knife. The tool had two handles, one at either end, so – lacking a point – it was no use as a thrusting weapon, but the blade itself was sharp and heavy enough that it could likely sever a limb and John dodged away from it desperately.

The attacker stumbled forward and John brought up his staff, catching the man beneath the chin. It was a lucky strike but it smashed the enemy's mouth shut and he reeled back, grasping his jaw, eyes screwed shut in pain. They did not open again, as John's staff came around once more, this time cracking against the thin man's head.

"That the lot?" Robin wondered.

"Can't be," John said, eyeing the unconscious tanners. "Neither of these two are the one we met outside. He's still around somewhere."

Robin bent, picking up both the tanning knives and dropping them into the nearest barrel. "You can fish them out of the piss and shit, you pair of useless bastards." He chuckled nastily as he moved past the tanners, leading the way towards the rear of the workshop again.

"Are you all right?" Robin glanced quickly back over his shoulder, concerned for his friend for John was now wheezing and his eyes were red and watering.

"I'll be fine when we get the hell out of here. The fumes are killing me. How the fuck can anyone work in this place all day?"

"You get used to it!"

Robin looked upward and saw the first man they'd met, Simon presumably, standing on a platform overhead.

"Get out of the way!" Little John's great bellow filled the building as he lunged at Robin, the full weight of his near-seven-feet physique cannoning into the younger man as a huge tanning frame dropped from the platform above.

The wooden frame struck a barrel right beside Robin and John and there was a terrific crack as the thing shattered, hitting both of them with splinters and broken sections of wood. Robin thanked God for John's hasty intervention, but he was not quite so thankful a moment later when the barrel that had been struck splintered at the seams. The iron hoops holding it together were ancient and rusted and now they gave way as Robin and John were just struggling back to their feet. The entire barrel full of urine, faeces and God-knew what else exploded across the floor.

"Bastard!" John roared. He had just been about to stand up, but his foot slipped and his face hit the filthy floor.

Robin fared only a little better, finding his breeches and his sleeves covered in filth before he was able to get up. Above them, Simon Tanner was roaring with laughter, tears streaking his cheeks as he watched his two hunters slipping and sliding around in shit and piss. The tanner's amusement soon faded, however, when he saw the murderous rage on the faces of Hood and Little John.

"Get the bastard!"

Robin didn't need to be told twice; he was already running towards the rickety old steps that would carry him up to their quarry and he was glad he'd brought his sword for he had no intention of letting Simon Tanner leave the building alive.

The floor above fed out through a large set of doors which Robin guessed must be for supplies to be lifted in and out of the tannery. There was a sturdy rope to facilitate this, and Simon used it now to escape, sliding down with an infuriating cackle that quickly changed to a yelp of pain as his hands were burned by the friction.

"Back! Go back!" Robin was leading the way but he turned now as the fugitive disappeared outside, bumping into John who almost fell down the stairs before he righted himself. "Hurry up, he's getting away!"

They thundered back down the steps and out of the back door into the dreary afternoon with its cloudy sky and leafless trees, cursing as they saw the tanner disappearing into the woods.

"Come on," John cried, cloak flying behind him as he sprinted after the fleeing man. "Don't let the whoreson get too far into the trees or we'll never find him!"

Robin ran, faster than he had done since he'd left Wakefield five years before. He was soaked from the rain, and now he stank from the disgusting contents that had been in the shattered barrel, yet, incredibly, he found himself grinning like a wolf as he sprinted through the long grass behind the tannery and into the woods. Just like old times right enough.

"Take care," he shouted to John. "He might be waiting to attack us again."

"Not if he's got any sense," the bailiff called. "Look! There!"

Robin saw the foliage springing back into place just ahead as their quarry desperately tried to evade them.

Simon must have known he could not outrun his fitter, more athletic pursuers who both had fewer years, and longer strides than he had. As Robin charged through the trees he barely registered the heavy branch that came towards him, only ducking at the very last instant as it whistled over his head and clattered against one of the trees.

John had not slowed, and his enormous frame came barrelling through the undergrowth directly beside Robin, slamming straight into the wide-eyed tanner. They went down in a heap and Robin, absolutely enraged by everything that had happened, fell onto one knee and grasped the struggling tanner by the throat.

"You think that was funny, dropping that wooden frame on us? You could have killed us, you ugly bastard!"

"I wish I had," Simon gasped, eyes bulging, fists hammering against Robin's heavily muscled arms as he tried to free himself. "Get off me," he choked, fear replacing the anger in his eyes as Robin pressed ever harder on his neck.

"God's blood, man, get off him! We're not here to kill him!"

Robin felt the inexorable weight of Little John dragging him backwards and, finally realising that he was close to murdering the tanner, he released his grip.

"You're…" the tanner tried to speak but his words came out only as a tortured rasp. "You're…. fucking insane!" he finally ground out, before rolling over into a foetal position and coughing so much that he eventually vomited.

Robin was breathing heavily, more from the excitement of the chase than exhaustion, but he saw John giving him a worried look and spread his hands wide in…what? He wasn't even sure. Apology? For what? The tanner deserved what he got, and more.

"We're lawmen," Little John reminded him quietly. "Control yourself."

"Aye, control yourself, you big oaf," the tanner croaked, flinching as John made as if to kick him. "What do you even want with me?"

"You know very well what we want," John replied, becoming business-like as he glared down at Simon. "You were supposed to pay a fine to your neighbour. Punishment for attacking him. Twice! You haven't paid up, so I'm here to collect."

The tanner struggled slowly to his feet, massaging his throat and eyeing Robin warily the entire time. "What if I don't have it?" he growled.

"Oh, I think you do have it," John said. "But, if you don't, well I'll take some of your equipment to the value of the fine. Your neighbour can then sell it. Those knives your workers attacked us with must be worth a few coins I'd guess. What's it to be?"

They stared at one another for a time and then, spitting in disgust, Simon headed back to his workshop. When they reached it the two men that had been left lying injured were both on their feet, but they made no move to attack Robin or John as Simon led the way to a wooden chest set against one of the tannery walls.

There was a crude but sturdy padlock on the chest and Simon produced a key from his purse. With another disgusted look at John he released the lock and opened the chest.

Robin's eyes widened for there were a lot of silver coins within that box – far more than one would expect a simple tanner to have in his workshop.

"How much was the fine again?" Simon asked smugly, clearly enjoying Robin and John's surprise at his apparent wealth.

"Five shillings," John replied.

"Here." The tanner counted out the sum and gave it to the bailiff, still with the self-satisfied smirk on his face.

"You're clearly not short of money," John noted, nodding down at the chest. "Why didn't you just pay the damn fine and save all this trouble?"

"Because usually no one comes to collect unpaid fines from me," Simon told him. "Or, if they do, I soon send them on their way. D'you idiots not know who my friends are?"

Robin glanced across at the sullen, beaten men who were still standing amongst the spilled contents of the broken barrel.

"Not them!" Simon snapped. "I mean my powerful friends."

"No," John said. "Who might that be?"

Simon examined the towering bailiff's face, as if he knew John was lying. Eventually he shrugged. "Never mind. If you don't know who they are, I'm sure you'll find out at some point. Especially if you keep being a nuisance to me and... my *friends*."

"Don't go attacking people," John told him in a low, dangerous voice. "And I won't have to come back here being a nuisance. You understand me?" He moved in closer to the tanner and stared down at him, the promise of violence emanating from him like a physical force. "And don't ever threaten me again, you little sack of shit, or next time I won't stop my friend here from killing you – I'll help him dispose of your battered body!"

Simon leaned back but, with the coin chest behind him he had nowhere to go. He looked utterly terrified and Robin couldn't resist smiling. Little John might be an upstanding member of society nowadays, but he remained as frightening as he'd been when he was a wolf's head.

"Come on, let's go," the bailiff said, turning away and leading Robin towards the front door without another word to the men in the tannery.

"Well, that was interesting," Robin said as they walked back to Notton, this time taking the road rather than forging through the undergrowth. "Where do you think he got all that money? Do tanners earn that much?"

"No, they don't. I'll wager the money has something to do with the Coterels."

Robin nodded. The Coterel gang had fingers in all sorts of pies, and if the people of Notton were all aware of Simon's relationship with them, they would leave the tannery alone. Common thieves might be tempted by the presence of such a large sum of money in the workshop, but it would be a brave thief who raided the tannery and crossed the Coterels.

"Do you think there'll be repercussions from what we've done here?" Robin wondered as they reached the main road through Notton and went to meet the headman so they could give him the tanner's fine for delivery to the neighbour he'd assaulted.

"From the Coterels?" John thought about the possibility. "I doubt it. They've got enough to worry about without getting on the wrong side of us."

"I hope so," Robin said. "I didn't come back to Yorkshire just to get into another war with a gang of dangerous outlaws."

"Don't worry about the Coterels." John laughed, completely at ease. "They're no threat to us, they have bigger issues to take up their time. What I'm more worried about is just how badly we smell! What are we going to do about our clothes? I can't go home to Amber stinking of piss and shit."

"Will she even notice a difference?"

"Hey, I had a bath just last month!"

"God's blood, we're going to have to buy new clothes, aren't we?" Robin cursed. "We should have taken some of that bastard tanner's coins to cover the cost."

"I'm not throwing away my clothes," John retorted indignantly. "I like these clothes. Ideally we'd visit a public bath, or stew, but there's none near here. So…"

"You can't be serious? The Calder? In this weather?"

"Aye, a nice dip in the river and we'll be as good as new. Come on, let's get this fine to the headman – look, there he is there! – and get back home for some clean clothes to change into after our bath."

"Satan's balls," Robin groaned, fully regretting his decision to accompany Little John to Notton that day. "Now I remember why I gave up life as a bailiff."

"Ach, stop moaning. At least we won't have to pay for our drinks in the alehouse later, not with this story to entertain everyone!"

CHAPTER THREE

"Another ale, Robin?"

"Go on then, you've twisted my arm!"

John's prediction that they'd enjoy free drinks in Wakefield's alehouse that night proved correct, although Robin had no intention of imbibing too much and stumbling back to Matilda's parents' house where his family were staying for now. Henry and Mary Fletcher were kind enough to take their daughter's family in; they didn't need Robin falling about the dwelling completely drunk.

"Don't worry, I'll be good," he said to Matilda who had happily accompanied Robin and John to the alehouse after they'd endured a thorough wash in the nearby River Calder and changed into fresh clothes. She'd been angry at first when she saw the state of her husband but their tale proved so entertaining that she quickly forgave Robin and helped him get cleaned and warmed up. It had not been at all pleasant bathing in the freezing February waters, but the free drinks and the crackling fire in the alehouse were quickly lifting his mood again.

John had done most of the storytelling for, although Robin had grown up in Wakefield and knew most of the people there, he'd been living in Scotland for some time while John, his wife Amber, and their adult son, also called John, lived in the town and were well known and liked there. Robin had always enjoyed listening to his big friend telling stories anyway. John had a deep, soothing voice – unless he was angry – and his easy smile meant things were generally kept light, even when his tales took a dark turn.

"There's never a dull moment around here with you boys," Alexander Gilbert, proprietor of the alehouse said as he delivered another round of drinks to the tables by the hearth. "If it's not you and Robin, John, it's Brother Tuck or Will Scarlet getting up to some wild antics."

"Speak of the devil!"

Will Scaflock, far better known as Scarlet thanks to his incendiary temper that had only slightly diminished now that he was in his mid-forties, came in the door at that moment, scowling around at the other patrons who all cheered his arrival.

"What are you bastards laughing at?" he demanded, bringing further cheers from the villagers.

"We're all happy to see you, Will," said Matilda, shaking her head with a wry smile at Robin and John and standing up to beckon the newcomer across to join them.

Friar Tuck found a stool and handed it to Will who took it with, for him, good grace, although he shook his fist at one inebriated villager who laughed just a little too loudly beside him.

"Where's Elspeth?" wondered Robin, who'd expected to see Will's wife with him.

"At home watching over Blase. We don't all have in-laws to take care of our children while we spend hours in the alehouse you know."

That, of course, brought more hoots of laughter but Robin and Matilda took the jibe well. Both their little boys were at the Fletchers, who were more than happy to spend time with their grandchildren.

With the story of Simon Tanner now over the other villagers returned to their own smaller groups, chattering amongst themselves, while some made their way home for it was getting late and there would be early starts for most of them on the morrow, working in the fields and nearby greenwood.

Robin, Matilda, Little John, Tuck, and Scarlet found themselves left alone beside the fire, everyone with a drink in their hand, making small talk just as they'd all done so often when they'd lived together as outlaws in the greenwood. As they spoke, Alexander brought over some bowls of pottage for Will and Tuck, who were both huge fans of the proprietor's food.

"Why *have* you come back to Wakefield after all this time, Robin?" Alexander asked. "If you don't mind me asking, that is. It was quite a shock to see you alive, when we all thought you'd died. Your funeral was a sad affair; I remember it like yesterday."

The man had run the alehouse for many years and Robin knew him well. He did not mind the question at all, although he bowed his head, acknowledging the sadness his fake death had brought to so many people, not just in Wakefield, but all over northern England.

"We got a message saying my mother was terribly ill," Matilda spoke up. "Our parents were the only ones who knew we were living in Scotland, and that Robin was alive." That wasn't entirely true – the sheriff had helped fake Robin's death, but there was no need for the alehouse patrons to know that.

"When Matilda heard about her ma's illness," Robin said, "she wanted to come back and see her."

"I thought she was dying, and I couldn't bear the thought of her not seeing our second son, Henry." Matilda swallowed back tears, overcome by the memory of the feelings that fearful message had engendered in her.

"So we packed up and headed home," Robin said, brown eyes shining as he gave his wife an affectionate hug. "And, by the time we got here, Matilda's ma was all better!"

"Praise God," the young woman said, wiping her eyes and grinning.

"Scotland is a fine place though," Robin continued, smiling up at Alexander from his stool. "And we enjoyed living there, didn't we?"

Matilda nodded. "Aye, we did. But it wasn't home."

"We missed all this," Robin agreed, holding up his hands and looking around the room at the other patrons. "We missed our mothers and fathers, our friends, and, to be honest, there's been so much strife between the Scots and

27

us English in recent years that we always felt like outsiders up there, so we were happy to come home."

"And we wanted Arthur and Henry to grow up here in Wakefield." Matilda was beaming, face flushed from both happiness at being back in her childhood home, and the ale she'd downed. "I'm so glad you're all well. Five years is a long time to be away."

"I always hoped you were alive," Will said to Robin. "I saw someone climbing into Matilda's wagon when she left here that day, bound for Scotland. I thought it must be you. I prayed it was."

"Aye, he told us about that," John agreed.

"And it made sense," added Tuck while chewing a mouthful of steaming pottage. "Didn't seem likely that Matilda would travel away to Scotland with Arthur, and no one to protect her on the road or help her set up a home once they got there."

Robin and Matilda looked at one another, surprised.

"Everyone else believed it though, didn't they?"

"Aye," Will said in reply to Robin's question. "I think everyone was too wrapped up in grief to look into things too much, including us."

Robin sighed, taken back to that whole period five years ago, when Philip Groves and his gang had wreaked so much death and destruction across Yorkshire. Good people had been killed, raped, and tortured, including members of Robin's own former gang. Friends. It had rocked them all to the core, and Robin had been glad to escape to Scotland with his family and live in relative peace and safety for a time.

A lot had changed in England during those five years, with King Edward II's reign ending in a rebellion led by the baron, Roger Mortimer and the king's own wife, Isabella, who forced her husband to give up his throne to their son, Edward III. Isabella and Mortimer then acted as regents, killing many noblemen who'd been loyal to the old king.

28

Young Edward soon grew tired of Mortimer disrespecting him though, and ordered the regent captured at Nottingham Castle. When Mortimer was executed soon after, Edward took full control of England's throne himself despite being just seventeen at the time.

After all that, surely everyone would have forgotten about Robin being declared an outlaw five years before? So he'd reasoned, and Matilda agreed. They'd packed up their belongings on the same wagon they'd used to transport them originally to Scotland, said goodbye to their few neighbours, and headed south once more.

"Where did you live in Scotland?" Will asked, contentedly shovelling steaming pottage into his mouth.

"We didn't want to go too far north," Matilda said. "But we had to move past Berwick. There's always trouble there between the Scots and English."

"Aye, and we were trying to avoid trouble!" Robin agreed with a laugh. "So we ended up in a little town called Longformacus. The locals were wary at first, but when they found out Matilda was a fletcher they welcomed us. There's always call for arrows around the border settlements, thanks to all the fighting that goes on."

"Aye," Matilda sighed. "If it's not armies battling one another, it's the damned Schavaldours. That's a fancy name for the bandits that plague the borders."

"We made a steady living selling arrows," Robin said. "Our house was a fair way off from the main village so we were mostly left to ourselves, and the locals would take our arrows to the markets in the bigger towns and sell them for us. "

"Sounds like Matilda was doing all the work!" Will noted. Robin did not rise to the bait, but Matilda defended her husband, replying in a stern tone.

"Robin made longbows, and he trained the villagers how to use them too. He also hunted, selling anything we didn't need for ourselves. Trust me, Will Scaflock," her eyebrows came together in a stern frown, "a man of Robin's talents is never a burden. Either to his wife, or to his community."

"All right, all right, calm down!" Will returned, holding his hands up and laughing at her spirited defence of her spouse.

"What have you been doing while we were away?" Matilda demanded, smiling but clearly unwilling to let Scarlet off the hook just yet. "Sitting around with these two doing precious little no doubt."

Little John and Friar Tuck protested the accusation and then regaled Matilda and Robin with stories of all their adventures in recent years, dealing with religious cults, murderous noblemen, haunted marshes, necromancers masquerading as Benedictines, drunken pedlars, and, to Robin's complete amazement, Will Scarlet becoming a monk, if only for a while. By the time the tales were finished it was very late and the friends were the last ones in the alehouse.

"Come on, it's time I was abed," Alexander chided them good-naturedly, refusing Tuck's request for another bowl of pottage. "Some of us have to be up early in the morning, you know."

"Aye, we know," Will protested. "I've to be up at dawn myself, milking the cows and…" He trailed off, too drunk to remember what else a farmer did every day. "Other stuff," he finished lamely as Little John threw open the alehouse door and they all filed out into the cold night.

For a moment, as the air hit them and they drew up their cloaks and put on hoods, they were silent, eyeing each other in inebriated amusement.

"You glad you came home then?" Friar Tuck asked, reaching out to give Matilda a fatherly hug before moving on to do the same with Robin.

"Aye, we are," Matilda said, taking her husband's arm in hers and beaming widely, eyes bright in the light of a crescent moon.

"Indeed," Robin nodded. "We've missed you all. It's good to be back."

"Amen," Tuck said, clasping his hands in thanks to God.

They went their separate ways then, weaving along the silent streets of Wakefield to their homes.

Aye, it truly is good to be back, thought Robin as Matilda huddled into him for warmth. *I just hope we can live in peace, without any more wild adventures, or trouble from Schavaldours, outlaws, bounty hunters, or any of the other bastards we've had to deal with over the past ten years!*

CHAPTER FOUR

Simon Tanner and his two labourers had spent a great deal of time clearing up the mess left by their encounter with Robin Hood and the bailiff, John Little. The whole affair still rankled even a week later, for it had been quite a task mending or replacing the tanning frames, knives, barrels, and other equipment damaged during the altercation. Simon's business lost money as result of the whole affair, and, to top it all off, the coins he'd used to pay the fine had come from the Coterel gang's coffers.

The Coterels, led by the three brothers, James, Nicholas, and John were, ostensibly, like any other criminal gang who used the greenwood to hide out in. There were many such groups, including the similarly notorious Folville's and, formerly, Robin Hood's infamous band, but the Coterels were not simple thieves who stole from corrupt, wealthy nobles and clergymen, they were far more brutal than that. Over the past few years, their gang had been responsible for extortion, cattle thefts, rapes, murders, kidnappings, and many other acts of extreme violence.

One of their major sources of income was the protection rackets they operated in various areas such as Derbyshire, Nottingham, and sections of Yorkshire, including Notton.

At first, Simon Tanner did not have to terrorise his own neighbours in the village – other members of the Coterel gang did that, viciously assaulting the local tailor, butcher, baker, and blacksmith who all then agreed it would be prudent to pay their attackers a regular amount to be left in peace. Later, when payments were not made in time, Simon and his two workers discovered that throwing their weight around, bullying and attacking their neighbours in the name of the Coterel gang, was a greatly empowering pastime, and they went about the task with vicious relish.

The frightened villagers' payments were always brought to the tannery, and Simon would then deliver the money to the Coterel leaders wherever they commanded. Usually he was just a go between, for the highest-ranking members of the gang did not generally camp out in Barnsdale, preferring to remain further south.

Simon had set out that morning on his wagon with the chest of silver, bound for Barnsley. James Coterel and his brothers were, he had heard, staying further south in Stainsby at the moment, so they'd sent lackeys to collect Simon's chest from an inn named the Lame Jackdaw in Barnsley. The tanner was greatly surprised and dismayed then to walk into the common room of the inn and find John Coterel himself sitting in front of the fire supping warmed wine. The youngest of the Coterel siblings was not sitting at the table alone either, as an even younger man with the hooked nose that all the Coterel family shared was with him.

"John!" the tanner exclaimed, doing his best to mask his discomfort. He'd only ever met the gang leaders once before and greatly feared them so, although it was a cold March day, perspiration immediately coated his brow and he hastily wiped it with his sleeve, praying the Coterels hadn't noticed.

"Simon," John grunted. "You're finally here, by Christ. My nephew, Matthew, and I have been waiting hours for you to turn up."

"I'm sorry, sirs," the tanner replied, wringing his cloth cap in his hands like a naughty child. "The roads are not in good condition after the long winter. My wagon got bogged down in a couple of places and—"

"Enough of your excuses, you oaf," John broke in, more disinterested than angry, Simon thought with a hint of relief. "Have you brought all our money?" Before the tanner could answer, the gang leader held up a warning finger, a hard stare on his face. "Remember, we know exactly how much should be there, so don't try to palm us off with less, or it'll go very badly for you."

Simon bridled at being spoken to in such a disrespectful manner, but he knew better than to complain.

John was the youngest of the three Coterel brothers, not being quite thirty years old yet. He was of average height and build with a neat beard, intelligent green eyes and the pronounced hooked nose that seemed to be a trait of all the Coterel men. The siblings were from good stock, with their father being a minor nobleman of wealth and means – a privileged upbringing had given the three brothers an inflated sense of their own self-importance, and a belief that they were entitled to take whatever they wanted, by force if necessary.

Despite their character flaws, though, they were generally well respected or at least feared by others of the noble class, with even some high-ranking but evidently crooked clergymen going out of their way to help the Coterels when it came to issues with the law.

Simon, on the other hand, was a poor, working tanner who had no idea how politics worked, or any interest in learning. All he knew was that it would be an extremely bad idea to ever anger John Coterel, either of his brothers, or, indeed, the young man named Matthew who sat beside John exuding all the arrogant confidence of his older relatives.

With all that in his mind, the tanner bobbed his head ingratiatingly. "All the money is there, sirs, you can trust me. Every penny."

"And yet," John said, piercing gaze boring into the nervous tanner. "We heard that you took some of the coins out of our chest. To pay a fine, was it?"

Simon felt as if someone had thrown a bucket of ice water down his back and he struggled to keep the shock from his face. How the hell did John know? One of Simon's own labourers must have told the Coterels. It was a sobering thought, that even in his own workshop he was being watched, his actions reported on. Damn it, he'd even drunkenly boasted to his labourers that he planned on

34

leaving Notton eventually to strike out on his own, extorting people in other towns and taking all the proceeds for himself!

The tanner swallowed, finally understanding just how wide the Coterels' influence really was. From the lowest villein, to bailiffs, reeves, and even Members of Parliament, the criminal family had all levels of society at their beck and call. He prayed his imprudent, drunken words had not been reported to his masters. Damn it, but he had a big mouth when he was in his cups!

"Well?" Matthew Coterel snapped, breaking Simon's reverie. "Did you take money from us?"

"No!" the tanner replied quickly. "Well, aye, but I put it all back in from my own wages, once I had it. You can count it, sirs, it's all there, as it should be. You know I'm trustworthy." Simon despised the wheedling tone of his voice as he stood wringing his cap, brow coated once more in sweat, but what could he do? He was as much under the Coterels' thumb as any of the other reputed fifty or so members of the gang, and he had to keep on their good side or…

"Why didn't you just pay the fine in the first place?"

Simon blinked at Matthew's question. "Usually, if I don't pay fines, the bailiff comes looking for it and I tell him to fuck off." He shrugged, forcing a sickly smile on his heavily lined face. "I thought it would be the same this time."

"But it wasn't," Matthew stated, still staring at him in a most unsettling manner. "The sheriff sent a different bailiff. One who wasn't afraid to use violence." His voice became even colder then, if that was possible. "One who did not care that you were an acquaintance of ours."

"That's right," Simon agreed, eager to divert Matthew's ire onto this new target. "John Little. He turned up with his friend Robin Hood and they—"

"We know what happened," John Coterel interrupted, waving a hand dismissively. "We've heard all about it. You may go. Next time you get into trouble with the law, pay the fine before the bailiffs come sniffing around the tannery, eh? It's bad enough that you had a bailiff there, but to let him see the chest with our money in it? You're a bloody fool. Get out, and be more careful in future."

"Yes, sir," Simon said, nodding vigorously, relieved to be leaving with his life, and all his body parts intact. "Will you be doing anything to get Hood and Little back?"

John Coterel turned his steely gaze back on the tanner, making Simon wish he'd kept his mouth shut and just fled when he had the chance. "Why would we do that? Their issue was with you. The money they took belonged to you, not us. No, at the moment I see no need to do anything against those men, it would only attract the wrong kind of attention just as we're really beginning to grow in power." He waved his hand towards the door again, this time more forcefully. "Now, get out and get back to your tannery, and do what we're paying you for."

Simon did not hesitate this time; bowing his head as if he was in the presence of the king himself, the tanner hurried from the room, face flushing as the two burly guards at the door smirked when they let him out. When he was in the street he stood and took deep breaths to steady his nerves, thanking God for his continued existence.

John might be the youngest of the Coterel gang leaders, but tales abounded about his cruelty and his willingness to use extreme violence against those who got on the wrong side of him. The other one the tanner had just met, Matthew, was not previously known to him at all, but, if anything, he seemed even more deranged than his uncle John.

Still, Simon had emerged from the Lame Jackdaw safely and he was free to go home to Notton and continue working for the gang. He walked to his wagon and thought back to John Coterel's murderous look when the subject of Robin

Hood and John Little had been broached. The Coterels might have said they would not go after the bailiff and his friend Robin Hood, but Simon had seen the dark expression on both their faces and guessed it was only a matter of time.

Eventually, Hood or the bailiff would come up against another of the Coterels' lackeys and then they would get what was coming to them. Simon might be able to brutalise the simple folk of Notton but he could not stand up to Hood or Little John. The Coterels could though, and the tanner looked forward to hearing all about it when the day finally came.

* * *

The falcon soared majestically overhead, gliding on its impressive wings before lancing downwards like an arrow and slamming into the wood pigeon that had been flying happily along, oblivious to the danger above. There was no sound, no explosion of feathers as the falcon brought its prey to the ground.

"Is it already dead?" a young noblewoman asked in grim fascination.

"Looks like it," Sir Henry de Faucumberg, Sheriff of Nottingham and Yorkshire, replied proudly. "Neck will be broken most likely. That's what makes birds of prey such useful hunters. Imagine what an arrow would do to the pigeon's body if one of these two shot it down." He gestured at Little John and Robin Hood who were visiting the town that day as guests of his. "The carcass would be damaged, meat wasted. Whereas my falcon kills the pigeon quickly, cleanly, with no mess, and we can cook it for a fine meal later."

The noblewoman nodded, smiling in appreciation at de Faucumberg's explanation. She watched with interest as the sheriff walked towards the two birds and gave a low whistle. The falcon was remarkably well trained, and it immediately came to his gloved hand, perching easily there and accepting a treat as a reward for its work.

"Come on," the sheriff said, putting a hood over his prized falcon's head. "Let's get back to the castle – the feast must be about to start."

It was not a special occasion but feasts were regularly enjoyed in Nottingham Castle, as the sheriff entertained the noblemen and -women who lived in the surrounding areas, as well as high-ranking officials and visitors from further afield. He'd invited John and Robin to join the festivities, but neither man really felt comfortable in such a setting. They were not from noble stock, and much preferred the company of yeomen and villeins.

When they reached the castle, de Faucumberg's servants took the falcon away while his steward ushered the rest of the group into the hall where some guests were already enjoying fine food and drink. The sheriff excused himself, promising he would join them in the hall soon, and then he led John and Robin to his own private chamber, where he did much of his administrative work.

"Take a seat, lads," he said, gesturing to the chairs on one side of the desk while he fell into his own. "Are you sure you don't want to join us in the hall? There's a delicious menu on offer. We have goose, suckling pig, mortrews, and even Leche Lombard."

Robin glanced at John, mouth watering although he had no idea what 'Leche Lombard' even was, but both men shook their heads. They were not interested in attempting small talk with the noble guests. From past experience, both knew they would be viewed as strange novelties, out of place amongst the higher-class guests who would smirk at their poor etiquette and rough manners.

"No thanks, Sir Henry," John replied.

"Very well." The sheriff nodded with an understanding smile. "Let's get down to business then. I asked you to visit me because, well, your return to Wakefield was a surprise, Robin, and not a particularly pleasant one."

Robin swallowed, not sure how to respond.

"Don't misunderstand me," de Faucumberg said, leaning back in his chair and falling silent as a servant knocked on the door and then stepped in carrying a jug of ale and three cups. When the men were all furnished with drinks, and the servant had left with a nod of thanks, the sheriff continued. "I like you, Robin. I always did, and I was sad when you asked me to help you fake your death. It was a good solution to our problems though, and we managed to work it well."

John snorted. "Aye, you certainly did. Keeping it all a secret even from those of us who were closest to Robin."

"Indeed, and I'm sorry about that," the sheriff said, sipping his ale slowly. "But for the scheme to work everyone had to truly believe Robin was dead."

"I suppose so," the bailiff conceded. "The arsehole Prior de Monte Martini wasted no time in letting everyone know that Robin had been declared an outlaw again, and after his funeral some of the king's men did come asking questions about what had happened."

"And, if Edward's men suspected Robin was still alive, they would have searched for him until they found him. They would also have looked more into what exactly happened that fateful day when de Monte Martini died."

Robin swallowed some of his ale, finding it to be of the very best quality, as expected since Nottingham Castle boasted some of the finest brewers in England. "Things turned out perfectly for all of us," he said.

"The problem is," de Faucumberg went on. "You're still officially an outlaw, Robin. When the new king finds out that you're still alive he may demand your arrest. Or, since he has so much else occupying him at the moment, having not long taken control of the throne, he might just send someone to hunt you down."

"Or, since he does have more important things to deal with – as you say yourself – he might just forget all about it."

The sheriff held up his palms and gave a noncommittal nod in reply to John's suggestion. "He might. Had it been the old king, I would have been happier to believe that. Edward, second king of that name, liked you two, but his son has never met you."

Robin smiled, remembering the occasions when he and John had spent time in King Edward II's company, first when they'd posed as Franciscan friars, and later when Robin fought Sir Guy of Gisbourne to the death in Wakefield. The monarch had been impressed by their daring, their martial prowess, and by John's prodigious size, even asking the giant to join the royal rowing team.

King Edward II had been dead for four years though, and now his son ruled in England. Would he give a damn about one outlaw in Yorkshire, when gangs like the Coterels and the Folvilles were operating so openly, and often with the backing of some of the king's own noblemen?

"What should we do?" Robin asked, emptying his cup and placing it on the table with a sigh. When he returned to Wakefield he had hoped everyone would have forgotten his status as an outlaw – it had been five years after all! – but perhaps it was not to be.

"For now, nothing. Just go about your business, whatever that may be – I can't take you on as a bailiff again, even if you wanted me to, not while you're classed as a wolf's head."

Robin had no desire to be a bailiff again anyway. Those days were gone. No, he still had plenty of money from his days robbing rich folk in the greenwood and he could easily fill his days helping his friends and family – Will Scarlet's farm always had plenty of jobs needing done, and Tuck and John would welcome an extra travelling companion when they went about the local towns and villages on their own business.

"You'll have to be careful," the sheriff cautioned. "Just in case the king does send someone after you, like the old one did when he sent Gisbourne."

"I shall," Robin agreed. "Thank you, sheriff."

"Don't mention it. Despite your return bringing possible issues, I'm glad to see you again. And you, John, as always. Now, I best join my guests in the hall, they'll be wondering where I am."

"We should be off home too," John said, rising.

"Not yet," de Faucumberg said, smiling at them. "I know you don't want to join the feast, but you can share the refreshments. I'll have some sent in here for you. Take your time and enjoy yourselves before you leave."

With that, the sheriff left them and, true to his word, a short time later servants brought trenchers laden with roast pork, duck, vegetables, cheese, bread, and more ale.

"Ah, this is wonderful," John exclaimed as he set about the food with gusto. "A private feast, just for us! I bet you're glad you came home now."

"Damn right," Robin laughed as he washed down a piece of perfectly marinated meat with a large swallow of ale. As they ate and drank, however, his mind was already going over the sheriff's words. He did not want to spend his days looking over his shoulder, waiting for another Guy of Gisbourne to come looking for him. If possible, he would have to find a way to be pardoned again.

For now though, he had a trencher piled high with the finest food he'd eaten in years and the company of his best friend, and he meant to enjoy every moment and every mouthful.

CHAPTER FIVE

"The weather's been strange for a while now, don't you think?"

Friar Tuck shrugged at Will Scarlet's observation. They were sitting beneath a sprawling yew tree in St Mary's churchyard in Wakefield, sheltering from the oppressive heat. "People always say that," the clergyman avowed. "They claim the weather was better, or worse, or just different when they were young."

Will yawned loudly, clearly drowsy from the warmth even in the shade cast by the yew. "Nah, it definitely is different nowadays. The winters are hard and wet, the summers are unbearably hot and dry. It's not just my memory, I've heard other people saying it. Have you not noticed the change, Robin?"

The young archer shrugged, idly pulling the bark from a small twig. "Dunno."

"Pah, what about you, Tuck?" Scarlet persisted. "You've been around longer than us."

Tuck pursed his lips and gave an expansive shrug. "Maybe. I don't know. I have a lot to remember, without trying to recall the weather from decades ago."

"Pfft," Will snorted, giving Tuck a mocking look. "The only thing you like to remember is which baker sells the best savouries, and which alewife brews the strongest ale in each town."

"I'm deeply hurt and offended by your insults, Will," the friar returned gravely. "Don't you have a fence to mend on your farm or something?"

Scarlet's wry smile was quickly replaced by an angry glare. "I fixed it the other day."

"Aye, but you always do such a terrible job of it that the thing invariably falls down as soon as a crow lands on it, or one of your sheep farts beside it, or someone glances in its direction."

Scarlet had to laugh at his old friend's claim, delivered in such a deadpan, earnest manner. "Aye, you're probably right," he conceded. "The damn thing probably has collapsed already. Ah well, it's so hot the sheep won't even bother wandering off."

"What are you three jesters doing?" A new, loud voice came to them across the wall around the churchyard and its owner peered in at them. "Sitting around telling knob and fart jokes no doubt, while the rest of us are busy earning a living."

Tuck chuckled, somewhat shamed by the accuracy of Little John's guess. "No, we were discussing theology," he retorted.

"Aye, we're arguing about the Council of Nicaea," called Will, while adding to Tuck in a quieter tone, "See, I did learn a few things when I was a monk."

"Stop bellowing at us like an angry bull," Robin drawled languidly. "And come in and join us."

Without bothering to walk to the gate, Little John stepped across the dry-stone wall and came to sit beside them beneath the tree, the familiar smile visible within his grizzled beard.

"We were just saying how weird the weather's been for a few years now," Will said, and Robin didn't bother to mention that he and Tuck had not actually agreed with the claim. It was, after all, far too hot to get into an argument over such a trivial matter.

"Aye, it has that," John said, pushing a lock of matted hair from his forehead. "I don't remember it ever being as hot as this, or for so long. When did it last rain?"

"Three weeks ago," Will told him.

"What was the weather like in Scotland?" Tuck asked Robin.

"Much like here. Rained a lot, bit windy, snowed in the winters." He shrugged. "All I know is, if it doesn't rain soon, the crops will be ruined and there'll be another famine."

That brought the mood of the conversation down. They'd all lived through famines in their lives, and Robin's own sister, Rebekah, had died of hunger during the famine of 1315. She'd only been seven years old, and the experience had deeply affected Robin and been one of the things that drove him to steal from the wealthy nobles and redistribute their wealth to the poor when he'd become an outlaw. Although that famine had been caused by too much rain destroying the crops, not enough rain would have the same effect.

Tuck laid a reassuring hand on Robin's arm. "Don't worry," he said. "God will provide for us. Your children will not go hungry." He did not mention Rebekah, there was no need. They all knew the story.

They all knew every story about one another, in fact. The days spent living together in the greenwood had taught them each other's backstory, motivations, dreams, fears, and much more. It had been a hard time, but it had formed an iron-hard bond of brotherhood between them all.

"My children may have enough to eat," sighed Robin. "But plenty others will not if the crops fail. Pray for rain, Tuck, and beg God to end this drought before it's too late."

"It won't just be food that's scarce," John put in, leaning his head back and squinting through the yew's branches at the dazzling yellow orb overhead. "Without water there won't be any ale."

"Hell on Earth," Will murmured softly and Robin felt particularly sorry for him. Will Scarlet may not be the best farmer in Yorkshire, but he cared deeply for his animals, and the thought of his sheep, dogs, and cattle dying from thirst must have been preying on his mind. Any available water would be used by the people, so the beasts would be the first to die if it came to it.

"What are you planning on doing with yourself in the coming weeks, Robin?" asked Tuck, steering everyone's thoughts in a new direction.

"I'm not sure," Robin said, standing up and pulling his tunic down around his waist. A couple of passing young washerwomen, on the way to the river for water, called over lasciviously at the sight of his tanned, rippling torso. He pretended not to hear them and, in fact, flushed in embarrassment, turning even redder when John laughed at his discomfort. His chiseled features, muscular build, and easy smile had always made him popular with the women of Wakefield, but he'd only ever been interested in Matilda. "I was planning on training the men in the village how to use a longbow each Sunday," he said, pointedly focusing his attention on Tuck. "It pays quite well, and I enjoy doing it. But, with everyone fearing water supplies will run out, Patrick has decided there'll be no unnecessary physical activity, at least until it rains."

Patrick Prudhomme was Wakefield's headman, and the tasks of training and organising the village's militia fell to him. The men, young and old, were all expected to be proficient with a longbow so that, if the king needed to call upon them to join his army, they would at least be useful. Putting such training, which would require huge amounts of drinking water or ale in this heat, on hold for a time was a prudent decision.

"You know what you could do?" Will drawled, eyes closed, head tilted upwards as he reclined against the tree. "Go looking for the missing treasure of King John."

"Eh?" Robin was so hot that he wondered if his mind wasn't working properly and he'd misheard Scarlet. He wasn't the only one either, as both Tuck and Little John turned astonished glances on the drowsing Will.

"You know, old Softsword," Scarlet said, using one of King John's epithets, granted to him either because he'd made peace with France or because he was a coward who

45

ran from battles he wasn't confident of winning, depending on who you believed. "He lost England's crown jewels just before he died, down in the Fens when a great wave appeared and washed it all away, never to be seen again. Or so the story goes."

Robin did not learn much history when he was a child, and he was only vaguely aware of King John. He didn't think Little John would know much either, so he turned to the most learned member of the group – Friar Tuck.

"He's right," the clergyman nodded, reaching up to wipe perspiration from his tonsured scalp with a scrap of linen. "All that treasure – jewels, gold, valuable weapons, coins – lies hidden beneath the sand, or the marshland, in the Wash."

The friends sat in silence, pondering this and trying to calculate just how much such a hoard would be worth, as bees buzzed around them and laughing children made the most of the sunshine by chasing one another along the street that ran past the churchyard.

Eventually, John whistled through dry lips. "Anyone finding all that would instantly be one of the richest men in England."

"It'll all be scattered about the place though," Will argued. "You might find one or two pieces, but not the whole lot."

"Even one piece," John returned, "would be enough to make you wealthy."

"You're already wealthy."

"Aye, so I am." John laughed at Tuck's dry observation. "But it would still be nice to find something like a crown, don't you think? Besides, I'm not that rich, or I wouldn't be living in Wakefield with the likes of you."

"Oh, he thinks he's better than us," Will exclaimed, but it was a half-hearted attempt at mock outrage. Even the volatile Scarlet couldn't work up a good, righteous anger in this weather. John simply grinned and lay back on the grass.

Robin watched it all with pleasure. This – the silly humour, the banter between longtime friends – had been missing from his life for the past five years, and it felt good to be amongst it again. He frowned though, turning to Will once more.

"What the hell has King John's missing treasure got to do with me?" he asked, baffled by his friend even bringing up the topic, never mind suggesting he get involved in some way.

"Well, you said you needed something to do," Scarlet replied, as if it should be obvious.

"So I should head to the Fens, or the Wash, wherever that is, and just start looking for a load of stuff that's been missing for over a hundred years?"

"Aye."

Robin chuckled, bemused, and wondering if his old friend had taken too many blows to the head during his life as a mercenary and outlaw.

"I'm not an idiot," Scarlet stated then, propping himself up on his elbows.

"Yes you are," John grinned.

"No, listen," Will said, standing and walking across to Robin who had to shade his eyes to look up at him for the sunshine was blindingly bright through the tree's branches. "Where did the treasure go missing? Around a marsh, right? Well, what happens to marshes during a drought?"

Robin shrugged. "They dry out?"

"Exactly!" Will gazed down at him triumphantly. "The treasure has never been found before now because it's always too damp in the Fens. But, with this dry weather – three weeks without rain, and no end in sight…"

A smile formed on Robin's face as he thought about Will's suggestion, but then a thought struck him. "If it's that easy, someone else must have done it already," he said. "This can't be the first drought there's been in the past hundred years."

"If anyone had found any of the treasure already, it would be known about," Will argued. "That would be a tale in itself, wouldn't it? But no one's ever found any of it, so it must all still be there."

"What else was in his treasure, Tuck?" John rumbled, evidently finding himself interested in the discussion too. "Anything someone like me might be interested in?"

The friar thought about it, lips pursed, and then said, "A polished steel mirror."

"A mirror?" Will demanded, laughing incredulously. "Why would someone as ugly as John want to look at himself in a mirror? That's the last thing he needs! No offence, John."

"Some taken," John replied dryly, and Robin watched them, feeling as if he was witnessing some mummer's comedy and loving every moment.

"A sword, then?" Tuck asked. "The king was said to own Tristan's Sword, which originally belonged to one of King Arthur's knights. It was used in coronations, and had a broken blade."

"Not much use to me then," John scoffed. "Not if the blade's broken."

"It's been lying in mud for over a century," Robin reminded him. "It wouldn't be much use to anyone, broken blade or no. It would still be wonderful to find it though, don't you think? And I'd bet King Edward would pay the finder a small fortune to get it back."

The others pondered this, and then Tuck raised an eyebrow and said to Robin, "A small fortune? He might even pardon an outlaw if they were to bring him Tristan's Sword, or, indeed, any part of the lost treasure…"

"So we just turn up in the Fens with shovels, and start digging?" Robin demanded. "We wouldn't know where to start."

"You're still a wealthy man, aren't you?" Tuck asked. "As are John and Will from all the raids we conducted as outlaws. You can put some money together and we'll hire some of the locals down in the Fens to help us search. Think about it! There must be hundreds of items scattered about that marsh, but all you have to do is find one of them, and a pardon could be yours!"

It was stiflingly hot in the lee of the yew tree, and yet, even so, Robin felt a cold thrill run through him at the friar's words, and a grin split his face as he looked at his friends.

"You're right!" He laughed. "So I had better start making preparations for my journey. To the Wash, lads! Who's with me?"

CHAPTER SIX

As it turned out, only Friar Tuck was able to make the journey to the Fens with Robin. Little John asked his wife, Amber, but, as she pointed out, with the drought and possibility of famine there may be a breakdown in law and order as people strove to take water, ale, food, or whatever else they could from their neighbours. A bailiff like John would prove useful in and around Wakefield. Will Scarlet also refused to travel with Robin, afraid the harsh weather might affect his animals and his crops. At least if he was at home he might be able to manage things without too much loss or damage. So Tuck, who had no official ties to Wakefield, being after all a mendicant friar, had gladly offered to accompany his young friend to the east coast in search of the legendary lost treasure.

Matilda, quite to Robin's surprise, was happy for him to go off on his adventure, especially with the hardy Tuck to look out for him, both physically and spiritually.

"Honestly," she'd said when he explained to her what he hoped to achieve. "I think it's a good idea. I doubt the king cares about you – the old king sent Gisbourne after us because you and the others were outlaws, and causing all sorts of trouble for the sheriff in the forests of Barnsdale and Sherwood. You're no danger now – far from it. But you just never know, and if people find out you're still a wolf's head old enemies might crawl out of the woodwork to take advantage of the chance to kill you without fear of legal retribution."

Robin had nodded at that. The same thoughts had crossed his mind too.

"So, if you can find some of this lost treasure and win a pardon through it, I'd say it's worth a try. Me and the children are quite safe with my ma and da to take care of us, and your ma and da, and John and Will are always around if any trouble flares up. We'll be fine until you return."

"You don't think it's a wild goose chase then?" he'd asked, somewhat sheepishly, for the more he'd thought about the entire scheme the more ridiculous it seemed.

"Probably," his wife had chuckled, giving him a quick hug as though she'd seen his uncertainty and wanted to reassure him, as she would do for one of their boys. "But you're not doing anything else around here at the moment so…Go, my love. Go, and win another pardon, that we may live free, and in peace."

He'd laughed at her grand speech which she delivered with a flourish, and they kissed one another with abandon, young lovers as well as a married couple who'd been together for years.

Matilda made sure Robin and Tuck had plenty of provisions for their journey, packing some ale that had been freshly brewed by her mother, salted meat, bread, and cheese, and scolded both men when she realised they'd forgotten to pack hats, a necessity in the hot weather if travellers didn't want to get sunstroke, especially Tuck with his tonsured head.

"Are you sure you'll be all right while I'm away?" Robin had asked more than once, a nagging feeling of guilt growing within as the moment came to ride southeast.

"All right? I'll be perfectly fine, Robin," Matilda had assured him as the boys, Arthur and Henry, gave their father heartfelt, and rather earnest hugs of goodbye.

Robin had looked at them all with a heart bursting with love, and pride. Yet, as he mounted his horse and rode to meet Tuck, his family's farewells ringing in his ears, he had felt a little anxious to be leaving. For the past five years he had been around Matilda and the boys almost every day – now, with the prospect of a journey that might see him away from them for a couple of weeks or more, he had found himself feeling homesick even before they'd left Wakefield.

Being on the road with the friar had soon put him at ease, however. Tuck was a fine travelling companion, with a seemingly inexhaustible store of tales and anecdotes – either biblical, or from his own chequered past. He was also a good listener, and knew his business when it came time to erect their camps each night. Robin was just sorry that he'd spent so long living in Scotland, without the companionship of such excellent friends as Tuck, John, and Will.

Their destination in the Fens, as vague as that was when they'd set out, was roughly one hundred miles away. Their horses were from good stock, young and fit, and they made decent time although the riders did not push the animals hard, for fear of harming them in the baking sun. They rested in shade often, particularly in the middle of the day when the heat was at its peak, and made the most of any rivers, dykes, and streams that had not completely dried up yet, allowing the horses to drink their fill while the men refilled their waterskins if the water appeared clean enough.

Despite the heat, which wasn't blistering but maddeningly persistent and dry, the miles passed quickly for Robin, undoubtedly because he was enjoying Tuck's company so much. The ale that Matilda's mother had brewed proved rather strong and, on the first couple of nights the men's camp was filled with laughter and even song as they fell easily back into the old relationship that had once been theirs living together in the greenwood. Of his three friends, Tuck was the most forgiving – as one would expect from a man of God – and Robin saw none of the repressed resentment that was sometimes evident on the faces of John or Will when they remembered his faked death.

As they drew nearer to their destination Robin imagined what they would find there. He had never been to the Fens, or the area within it known as the Wash. Not many people in England travelled extensively, with most inhabitants of a village like Wakefield rarely travelling more than a few miles from their own home. Robin, of course, had lived a rather more adventurous life than most, visiting London, and Scotland, as well as many of the towns and cities around Yorkshire. The eastern coast of the country was unknown territory to him though, and Tuck had never been there either, at least as far as the friar could remember. In Robin's mind, the Fens would be damp, swampy grassland for most of the time, but now, after almost a month of little rain, they would be dry, and as arid as the deserts from the exotic ballads sung by minstrels.

Obviously, the ground being parched would not make it easy to find treasure buried beneath a century of shifting sands and soil and silt, but it would be a far more manageable task than when the place was submerged in water.

"I hope you've been praying for the success of this mission," the young archer asked Tuck as the town of Longa Sutton came into view on the horizon. It looked to be a medium-sized village and, with the River Nene nearby there should be some ale on offer to slake their thirst, in spite of the dry weather.

"I certainly have," Tuck replied, touching the wooden pectoral cross he habitually wore around his neck. "But, even if this venture comes to naught, God will provide for you, Robin, don't worry. Remember that word we used to hold onto when darkness threatened?"

Robin did remember. "Hope," he said, nodding thoughtfully, images of bleak past times flooding his memory. Times when he'd thought he would die, would never see Matilda or his friends again, would never be free. Hope had become a word for him to cling to, almost a talisman like the cross Tuck wore, and it had proved powerful had it not? He was still alive, and although still officially an outlaw, he'd lived well enough in recent years, raising a family and now restoring old relationships in Wakefield.

"You're right, as always," he said to the jovial friar who beamed and bowed his head in acknowledgement as Robin continued. "But we'll find King John's lost treasure, Tuck, or some of it at least. I can feel it! We're on the right path here, and, by Christ and all the Saints, I shall win another pardon."

They rode into Longa Sutton, smiling reassuringly at the villagers who watched suspiciously as they passed.

"Think they get many visitors here?" Robin asked the more worldly Tuck.

"Should do. The place is on a busy road after all, and there's a couple of rivers not far away so there'll be trade as well as travellers. We're probably getting dark looks because of you."

"Me?" Robin laughed.

"Aye, you. You appear a lot more dangerous than I do with your sword and longbow."

"If only the poor fools of Longa Sutton knew about that cudgel hidden beneath your cassock, eh? Or the numerous heads you've cracked with that or your quarterstaff."

Tuck theatrically made the sign of the cross, eyes turned Heavenwards. "Anyway," he said. "It looks like there's a decent sized tavern just ahead. We can stable the horses there, and find some decent sustenance for ourselves I'd say."

The Three Moons was, as Tuck guessed, a tavern rather than an inn, offering only food and drink without lodgings. There was a stable though, and the horses seemed happy to stand in the shade while a young lad rubbed them down and took care of them as their riders went indoors for an ale or two.

The place was not very busy since it was mid-afternoon and the villagers would mostly be out at work. There were a couple of men in one corner, well-dressed and groomed, and Robin took them to be travelling merchants or the like. They barely glanced at the newcomers and Tuck led the way to the tavern keeper who was watching them with a broad, expectant smile, plainly looking forward to selling a goodly amount of drink to the parched pair. Most taverns sold mainly wine, but Robin was pleased to see the other patrons had mugs of ale at their table. He was not much of a wine drinker.

"God give you good day," the friar said, powerful baritone filling the room easily, as did his cheery grin. "Two ales please, taverner. And—" he raised an eyebrow and absentmindedly patted his round belly "—do you have any food available?"

"I certainly do!" the tavern keeper replied, nodding vigorously. His accent was thick and hard for the travellers to understand, and he seemed to recognise the fact for he slowed his speech as he went on. "Vegetable stew? Made with the finest local ingredients, gathered in the garden out back by my own children. Or perhaps a leg of the finest mutton? Cooked to perfection by my wife, and only three pence to you, friar."

Robin raised a sardonic eyebrow, not believing the man's claims for a moment. He'd heard a similar sales pitch from countless taverners and inn-keepers over the years and nine times out of ten the fare they provided was hardly fit for a dog. Maybe that was a reflection on the establishments Robin frequented, he had to admit, tossing a few small coins on the counter. "A leg of lamb, then, and two bowls of pottage. Is that enough?"

The taverner scooped up the coins with such speed that even a court jester trained in sleight-of-hand would have been impressed. "Aye, that's enough, friend. Take a seat and I'll bring your food and drink to you."

While they waited the pair simply sat in silence, looking around at the building which appeared to be at least a hundred years old. Robin liked to see such places, and it was good to be inside, away from the sunshine for a time. Before long, the tavern keeper appeared from the back room carrying a trencher with their food and drinks. He gingerly placed the lot down on the table and straightened, beaming from Tuck to Robin and back again, as though waiting to hear what they thought of his wares.

Robin's mouth was watering from the smell of the mutton, but he took a sip of the ale first and, pleased, gave a low moan of exaggerated pleasure. It was certainly good stuff, and he felt the taverner deserved the reaction.

"Good, eh?" the man practically demanded, puffing out his chest proudly. "I only serve the best in the Three Moons. Try the food, go on."

Tuck did not need to be told twice, he was already using his knife to cut the mutton and his eyes lit up as he chewed some, licking his fingers when he finished. "Wonderful," he announced, as though the king's own cook had made the meal.

"And the pottage?" he taverner said, looking once more to Robin and gesturing at the bowl.

"I'll let it cool a little first," the archer said with a smile. "While we wait, why don't you sit with us? Pour yourself a drink, on me."

"Very kind of you, sir!" The tavern keeper, although much wider around the waist than even Tuck, made it to a jug of wine in the blink of an eye, filling a cup and returning to sit beside the travellers with a cheery, "Thank you."

Robin helped himself to some of the mutton before his friend polished off the lot, and he nodded in satisfaction as he chewed. It smelled delicious, and tasted even better. Apparently the taverner's wife was quite an accomplished cook, using just the right amount of salt, herbs, and butter. It might well have been the best meat Robin had ever eaten while travelling and, from the taverner's pleased expression, the man knew it.

"What brings you here to Longa Sutton?" the taverner asked, sipping his wine and watching Tuck devour more of the mutton with relish. "A man of God, and a man who makes his living with a sword and a longbow judging by the size of your shoulders. Are you his guard?"

Robin smirked and dipped a spoon into the pottage. "Trust me, the friar needs no guard, he can look after himself."

"We're heading to the Fens," Tuck said.

"We heard King John lost a load of treasure there," Robin said, trying a mouthful of pottage and finding it almost as delicious as the mutton.

"Aye, so he did," the taverner confirmed. "It's said he lost it just a few miles southwest of here, near the River Nene. Jewels, coins, crowns, weapons, all sorts! Must be worth a bloody fortune, my lads, I tell you."

"Well, we're hoping to find some of it," Robin said, already halfway through his bowl of pottage.

"Aren't we all!" the taverner chuckled, and then, seeing his customers were deadly serious, he gazed at them in clear amazement. "Have you travelled far?" he asked. "By your speech I'd say you're a Yorkshire lad?"

Robin nodded. "Wakefield."

The taverner had hardly stopped smiling since the two travellers had come into his establishment, but the smile now seemed to change, from welcoming to… Robin wasn't entirely sure what the man's expression betrayed. Mockery? Pity? Amusement? Disbelief? A mixture of all four perhaps, and it made the archer self-conscious and quite irritated. He was not used to being laughed at.

"What's so funny?" he demanded, and the tone of his voice was almost enough to wipe the grin from the taverner's red face.

"Why, sir," the man replied, still smiling but with his hands up in a gesture of appeasement as, clearly, he sensed the danger this tall, massively built man posed. "If you've come here thinking you'd find Softsword's treasure, you'll be sorely disappointed."

"Why?" Tuck asked. His tone was level, his eyes curious, but he'd stopped eating, a sure sign that he was alarmed.

"Aye," Robin demanded. "Why shouldn't we find it? It's not rained for weeks, has it? The rivers are drying up, and the land all around. Wherever King John's treasure lies, the marshes that have hidden it for a hundred years will be easy to search, surely? And we have money to hire locals to help us, it won't just be the me and the friar."

The tavern keeper's look of amazement seemed to deepen as he listened to Robin, but he shook his head and grew deadly serious. "You've come all this way for nothing, my friends," he said. "There might be a drought at the moment, but, well, the thing is…The fens are right beside the sea, and the Wash is an estuary of it."

"So what?" Robin asked.

"Well, the rivers might dry up, sir, but the sea never does, at least not for as long as I've been alive, and I'm nearly fifty!"

"What are you saying?" Robin asked, knowing he was being foolish, but unable to get the image of a dry, arid land out of his mind – one that was ripe for digging and littered with plunder.

"I'm saying," the taverner replied, and his earlier amusement was replaced completely by pity. "That Softsword's treasure is impossible to find, and you've wasted a journey coming here."

CHAPTER SEVEN

"Don't feel too bad," Friar Tuck said to Robin as they sat at the table nursing another round of drinks and another helping of pottage. "At least our road here was pleasant."

Robin did not reply. He drained his mug and irritably gestured to the taverner for a refill. He could hardly believe he'd wasted his time riding over a hundred miles for nothing. Had Will Scarlet known he was sending them on a wild goose chase? Was that why Scarlet hadn't travelled with them? It was humiliating, Robin thought. Coming all this way, expecting to find a parched landscape, only to discover the Wash was fed by the sea and never dried up, even during the harshest of droughts.

It was obvious now, Robin thought. Of course the treasure would not be easy to find simply because the rest of the country was dried out – this was not the first drought England had suffered in the past hundred and fifteen years, by Christ! If it was so easy to locate the king's missing jewels someone else would have done it long ago. He felt a complete fool, and Tuck's good humour was not helping. It was all a big joke to the taverner and the friar, for they were not outlaws searching for a way to a pardon.

His refill was placed on the table before him but he did not look up, he could not bear to see the look in the taverner's eyes. The man's earlier amusement was better than the concern that replaced it. For some reason the tavern keeper thought this whole ludicrous scheme was Robin's fault.

Sighing, he lifted the ale and murmured a, "thank you". He was acting like a child, he knew. Sulking in a manner that he would rebuke his own boys for, should they ever behave in such a way.

"Eat your pottage," Tuck said, shoving the bowl towards him. "And don't give up hope. We'll find another way to win you a pardon."

Robin did manage a smile then. Tuck had always been the kind of friend who could make even the direst of circumstances seem like a minor bump in the trail.

Hope.

He laughed and set about the second bowl of pottage, savouring every mouthful. What had they lost? Other than the – wildly optimistic – chance at a pardon, Robin had not lost anything. In fact, he had greatly enjoyed spending time on the road with his old friend and gained yet another story to tell his friends and family back in Wakefield, albeit an embarrassing one. Scarlet had not sent them here knowing it was a fool's errand, Will simply had no better understanding of the topography of this area than they did.

"Perhaps we should have found someone in Wakefield who knows the Fens, and asked them about it before we came all this way," he said to Tuck through a mouthful of pottage.

"Aye, that seems obvious now," said the friar. "What a pair of idiots we are, eh? We should look for employment as fools after this."

"What will you do now, lads?" The tavern keeper, noticing the thawing in Robin's frosty demeanour, came over to stand beside their table. "There's a tavern in—"

"No, we don't need a tavern," Robin interrupted. "We're happy enough in a tent, friend. I'm not keen on sharing a bed with strangers. But it's a long way we've come, seems a waste just to turn around and go home, eh, Tuck?"

The friar nodded and the taverner sat down beside them again. "Absolutely," he agreed. "You should go and see the Wash anyway. There's some nice views around here, even if the land is mostly flat."

"Then that's what we'll do," the big archer decided. "We'll take a look around the Fens, see the Wash, and speak with some of the other locals. It'll be interesting."

"A fine idea," said Tuck. He leaned back on his stool and gazed at the taverner. "Well, if we're continuing along the road, we're going to need more supplies. I don't suppose you could refill our packs with some of your fine fare, my good fellow?"

Grinning, the taverner accepted the proffered packs which Tuck had brought in from the horses and hurried off, promising his wife would sort them out with the very best food and drink for their journey onwards.

* * *

Little John was not an anxious man, usually. Being so much bigger than the vast majority of other people meant he was rarely threatened physically – of course, there would always be the odd troublemaker who sought to make a name for himself by besting the massive bailiff, but those folk were thankfully rare. So he did not worry too much about being harmed, and he was no pauper so he did not have the stress of wondering where his next meal would come from, or how he would afford a new winter cloak. In general, John was one of the most contented men in Yorkshire, stoically accepting all that life could throw at him.

Today though, riding towards another job on the Sheriff's behalf, he did not feel quite as confident as he usually did, for he was going once again to Notton.

When Sir Henry de Faucumberg sent the messenger with the details of this particular job, John listened with mounting dismay. He'd just been to Notton, and, although he'd collected the fine he was supposed to, the whole experience with Simon Tanner had not been a pleasant one. Being soaked in piss and shit was not even the worst of it – the tanner's connection with the Coterel gang was more concerning.

So concerning that John had asked Will Scarlet to come with him to Notton this time.

"You really think those Coterel arseholes will come after you?" Will asked as they rode into the village, drawing looks of interest and even concern from the locals who recognised them.

"I don't know," John said, dismounting and tying up his horse at the alehouse. "Maybe. If I become too much of a nuisance. They've gone after other bailiffs in the past."

"But people know what happens to anyone who crosses a member of Robin Hood's old gang," Will growled, throwing a dark look at a middle-aged lounger who was staring rather too intently at them.

"True," John agreed. "But the Coterels have plenty of men on their payroll. Money can tempt people to do things they might otherwise think are too dangerous. Besides, there's not many of our old gang left, Will."

The man who had been watching them slunk off in the opposite direction as John led the way towards the blacksmith's forge, which was situated at the far end of the street. Of all the buildings in a settlement the smithy, with its super-heated forge, was the one most likely to cause a fire, so, like the noxious tannery, it was always located a safe distance away from the rest of the houses and workshops.

John knew the blacksmith quite well, as did Will. The man had supplied them with arrowheads, nails, horseshoes, and other much needed supplies during their outlaw days. He was not exactly a friend, but the bailiff appreciated the smith for selling his wares to them, and even, once or twice, mending damaged weapons for their companions, so this was not going to be a pleasant job.

The smith was sitting outside his workshop, sweat beading his forehead, dark moustache bristling on his ruddy face. He saw them approaching and managed a smile, although he did not rise to greet them. "John," he said, nodding to the bailiff, before glancing at Will and nodding at him too.

"God give you good day, Alfred," said John, resting on his great quarterstaff as he squinted up at the sky. "Taking a rest?"

"Aye. Too damn hot in there," the smith told them. "Too damn hot out here as well, but at least there's a bit of a breeze. What brings you to Notton, lads? You looking for some arrowheads for the fletcher in Wakefield?"

John shifted from one foot to the other, looked at Will, then, at last, said to the blacksmith, "No, Alfred. I'm here on the sheriff's business." He forged on as the smith's expression grew cold. "You were found guilty of selling poor quality horseshoes to one of the noblemen in York."

"That's a bloody lie!"

"It's not a lie," John insisted calmly. "You were found guilty."

"That may be true, but the charges were a lie. Those horseshoes were perfectly good. That snooty bastard, John le Sauvage, made up a story about them being brittle and damaging his horses' hooves. I was ordered to pay back the money he gave me for making them, as well as extra for injuring his animals. And I was given a fine!"

His face had been red when they first met him, but now the smith's face looked as if it might actually burst into flames, so incandescent was the man.

"Calm down," said Scarlet.

"Calm down? That's rich, coming from you," the smith retorted. "What the fuck are you doing here anyway? You're no lawman. I hear you're a farmer nowadays, and a shit one at that."

John stepped between them as the burly smith got to his feet and Scarlet moved forward. "That's enough!" the bailiff, ground out, huge arms pushing both men back. "I'm not here to discuss Will's farming skills," he said to Alfred. "I'm here because you haven't paid your fines."

"What's it got to do with you?" the smith demanded, turning his ire on John again. "You're not our bailiff. You were a blacksmith like me once, you're no better than I am."

"Your bailiff is too scared of the Coterels to come here and do his fucking job," Scarlet said, earning a warning look from John who had not wanted the criminal gang mentioned at all. "That's why we're here."

"Oh, really?" The smith's eyebrows lifted, and he sneered at John. "You're not afraid of them though, are you? Big, hard, John Little, once a wolf's head, now a tax collector."

John found himself growing angry as well, and forced himself to remain calm. "Look, Alfred, I agreed to come here for the sheriff because I know you. I thought you'd listen to me without there having to be any trouble." In truth, he was wishing he'd refused to come – he always had that option, working for de Faucumberg only out of choice rather than necessity. The sheriff was happy with the arrangement, and John was starting to think he should be more selective in the jobs he took on, for this was not the kind of thing he wanted to spend his days doing. Alfred was a good man, he knew that, and the charges against him could very well be false. John had been unhappy when he and Robin first became bailiffs and Robin performed his duties with rather too much zeal, going after people that John did not believe deserved to be persecuted. He had vowed never to do that himself, and now he was seriously wondering if he should tell the sheriff he wasn't doing this anymore.

"Listen, bailiff," the blacksmith growled, muscles flexing in his meaty arms as he glared up at John. "Those horseshoes were good ones, but I would have paid my fines. You know me, I'm a law-abiding man."

"Then why didn't you?" John asked reasonably.

"I can't bloody afford it!"

"Why not?" Will said, gesturing at the man's workshop. "You've always been busy with work for as long as we've known you."

"Aye, and I still am," Alfred said, and all the rage seemed to flow out of him in a great, gusty sigh. He sat back down and stared into the middle distance, absently scratching a midge bite on the side of his neck.

"What's going on?"

John was surprised to see Will lift a stool out of the forge and sit down beside the smith. From wanting to kill one another, the two men now began chatting like old friends and it was clear that Alfred – a widower – had needed someone to talk to for quite some time. The words gushed like the Calder after a rainstorm and his message was clear: He was being forced to pay for 'protection' by the Coterels and, on top of that, Alfred was convinced the nobleman he'd sold the supposedly faulty horseshoes to, John le Sauvage, was in league with the Coterels.

"Wait," Will said, holding up a hand as the smith's tale of woe came at last to an end. "You're saying the Coterels and le Sauvage set out to ruin you?"

Alfred frowned in obvious surprise. "No, nothing like that. If I was ruined, who would pay them for protection? I don't think they had any master plan to do me out of money, at least not in any…" He paused, searching for the right word before finishing, "Conspiratorial way."

"Then it's just a coincidence that le Sauvage is part of the Coterel gang?"

"I think so," Alfred agreed, nodding, sweat dripping down into one eye which he rubbed irritably as it began to water. "It's just made things even harder to bear, knowing I'm being fleeced by two parts of the same gang. I don't deserve it, lads, by Christ and all the saints, I don't."

"No," John muttered, sitting down on the ground, for there didn't seem to be any more stools available. "I don't think you do."

The three sat in thoughtful silence for a long time, the sounds of men calling out to one another in the nearby fields, and a dog barking in the distance doing nothing to disturb their gloomy reverie.

"What will you do?" the blacksmith asked at last, apparently resigned to his fate, whatever that might be.

"Your fine isn't a large one," John replied.

"Isn't large? Maybe not to you, but it is to me, when I've just had to pay a shilling to that fucking tanner so the Coterels won't break my legs." He spread his hands wide, almost pleading to the bailiff. "I've no money left, John. Not enough to pay the fines anyway. I won't have for a while, until I've completed some of the work I've got lined up in there." He jerked a thumb back over his shoulder, at the gently smouldering forge that awaited him returning to pump the bellows and bring the fires to life again.

John stood up, legs becoming cramped from sitting on the hard ground, and arched his back as he looked out across the fields. The crops did not show visible signs of failing yet, despite the drought, but he knew it couldn't be long before they dried up and then…He pushed the bleak thoughts aside and returned to the matter at hand. What could he do? Ideally, he would like to get to the bottom of Alfred's claims – find out if John le Sauvage really was making false claims about the horseshoes he'd been supplied with, and then smash the Coterels' protection racket. Oh, it would give John great pleasure to sort out that fucking tanner properly, it truly would!

But John did not have the power to do such things. He might be well known all across Yorkshire, but he was no king, no baron, not even a sheriff. And he could not solve all the problems in Notton.

He could, however, solve this.

"Forget the fines," the bailiff said to Alfred, who eyed him and Will sceptically, as though he suspected he was the butt of some joke.

"You'll give me more time to pay them?" he asked hopefully.

"Just forget them," John said. "I'll see they're written off. But a word of advice, Alfred: don't make any more horseshoes for John le Sauvage!"

* * *

As they headed back for their horses, Will Scarlet remained silent until they were halfway along the road, well out of the blacksmith's earshot, and then he said, "You're going to pay his fine yourself, aren't you?"

John shrugged. "Like I said to him, it's not that much. What else can I do, Will? He's a good man; he was good to us when we needed him. It's not fair that he should be persecuted, and made a pauper, because some noble wanker made false allegations against him, and another bunch of noble arseholes are extorting protection money from him."

"I get that," Will murmured, waving to an elderly man sweeping the dusty path outside his house. "But this is like, I don't know, tying a bandage around a mortal injury. What happens the next time something like this happens to someone? You can't afford to keep paying everyone's fines when they give you a sob story."

John's face flushed red. He knew Will was right, but he'd just done a good thing and expected his friend to appreciate that. "Maybe not," he spat. "But at least I've helped one man. That's all I can do for now."

They approached the alehouse and Will gestured at the doorway which had been left open, no doubt by the owner in hopes of letting in some cool air.

"Come on," said Scarlet. "Let's at least get a drink before we go home."

John shook his head. He was not in the mood to sit in a sweltering hot building, downing ale that would undoubtedly be old, its sour taste masked ineffectually by

67

the alewife's herbs and spices. Before he could say as much, however, three men came around the side of the alehouse and stopped, staring at the towering bailiff with expressions ranging from surprise to naked hatred.

"Who're they?" Will asked in a low voice, hand falling to the knife he wore on his belt. "I don't think they like you much."

John snorted. "No, I don't think they do either. That's the tanner and his apprentices."

"We're not apprentices," one of the men retorted. "Do I look like a fucking child?"

He was small, but his rat-face face and rotten teeth suggested he was at least in his thirties.

"No," Will admitted. "You don't look like a child, but you do look like an ugly little twat."

The tanner grabbed hold of the man who'd stepped forward as though he would attack Scarlet. "Ignore them," he said, not having to try very hard to restrain his apprentice, or helper, or whatever he was. "They can't touch us. If they do…" He trailed off, and, predictably to Little John, Will spoke up again.

"'If they do', what? What'll you do?"

"I won't do anything," Simon Tanner retorted, and a nasty smile tugged at the corners of his mouth. "It's not me you need to be worried about. John and Matthew Coterel are already angry at you, bailiff, for disturbing my work here in Notton."

"John and Matthew Coterel can take a fuck to themselves," Scarlet growled. "And so can you."

He walked straight up to the tanner and John didn't try to stop him. He wanted to see exactly how this would all play out and, if it came to another fight, he would gladly make sure Simon and his mates came off even worse than they had the last time he'd come up against them with Robin.

68

"Ignore him," the tanner warned his companions again, blinking nervously as Will Scarlet stopped in front of him. Fury radiated from the former outlaw as his eyes swept across the three men.

"If any of you go near the blacksmith again," Scarlet said, hand caressing the hilt of his knife menacingly. "Even the Coterels won't be able to protect you. Do you hear me?"

Scarlet may not have had the prodigious height of Little John but he was every bit as threatening when roused. The tanner and his friends remained silent and, with anxious backward glances, walked into the alehouse, one of them closing and latching the door behind them.

"Are you sure you don't want a drink?" Will demanded, turning back to John, his eyes practically begging the bailiff to lead them into the alehouse.

"No." John grinned. "I think we've done enough for one day without destroying Notton's only alehouse. Come on, let's ride. When we get back to Wakefield I'll buy you a drink at Alexander's."

With obvious reluctance, Will gave in and they collected their horses, throwing the extremely young stableboy a coin for his trouble although he was so short John didn't think he could have properly groomed the animals. The bailiff wondered if the alehouse proprietor was being forced to pay for 'protection' by the tanner as well. If he was, it was not John's business to deal with it. The Sheriff would have to sort things out, if he had the will, or the manpower, or the political clout to go up against the Coterels. John doubted at least two of those were true, and, feeling somewhat depressed, he urged his mount into a trot and followed Will along the road to Wakefield.

He had been unusually anxious while travelling to Notton that day and, now that they were leaving, his fears had not abated. Simon Tanner's words echoed in his mind. 'John Coterel is already angry at you,' the man had claimed, and the thought was not a pleasant one.

Little John was not a coward, but neither was he a reckless fool. He wondered just how much more interference the Coterels would take in their business before they retaliated against him and his friends...

CHAPTER EIGHT

There were heavy grey clouds overhead and Robin gazed at them hopefully. Now that his plans to dig in the hard-baked ground of the Fens had been dashed he looked forward to the rains those thunderheads might carry, washing the land clean and restoring the rivers and wells to their usual levels.

It did not take long for them to reach the place the tavern keeper had claimed to be the legendary site of King John's lost treasure and, when they arrived, Robin felt even more of a fool than before.

"I see what he meant," Tuck said, shaking his head, clearly sharing his young friend's embarrassment. "The ground here is as marshy as ever. Look," he pointed at various spots all around them. "Pools of water, and what seems to be quicksand. We should be very careful."

"Ach, what's the point?" Robin returned dolefully. "We're not likely to stumble upon St Tristan's sword even if we were to spend a month walking and riding around this swamp. Still," he trailed off, shading his eyes with his hand and gazing out at the horizon. "It is a nice view. And the air here is cooler, thanks to the closeness of the sea."

They sat atop their horses, well back from what looked like the most sodden parts of the land, observing men and women they guessed must be collecting reeds for thatching which they would then take to weave into baskets and other items.

One of the women wandered past, and Tuck called a hearty greeting to her. She smiled uncertainly, her eyes moving from the friar to his warrior-like companion.

"Busy here today," said Tuck. His cheery nature did its work, thawing the woman's reticence and she returned his smile, if a little shyly.

"Today we collect reeds," she told him. "Tomorrow, we use them to makc things."

71

"Ever find anything else amongst your reeds?" Robin asked, doing his best to come across as pleasantly as the friar.

"Like what?"

"Treasure," Tuck replied.

The woman laughed, but she did not seem to be mocking them. Perhaps if she'd found them with shovels in their hands, digging amongst the silt, she would have doubled over at the hilarity of it, but, for now, she simply shook her head. "No. I wish I could. There are old tales of people stumbling across a trinket here and there, but I've never personally known anyone to find anything."

"We had hoped to find this area all dried out from the lack of rain," Robin admitted sheepishly.

"Never dries out here," she stated. "If it ever does we'll be in trouble, for it'll mean the sea's gone. And what could make a whole sea dry up?"

Robin grunted, taking her point. The Wash was visible from where they sat, salty air ruffling his closely cropped hair. It would take an even greater natural disaster to make this area completely dry; he understood that now. With a start, he realised he was daydreaming, and the woman was still talking.

"What was that?" he broke in. "Sorry, lady, I didn't catch that last thing you said."

She frowned, but repeated herself as requested. "I don't think there's any treasure here. That's what I said, and I stand by it. I don't care what anyone says, there's people who've lived and worked here their whole lives know the truth."

"The truth?" Tuck peered down at her, wiping a sleeve across his tonsured, perspiring scalp. "What truth?"

"The treasure was all taken by John's soldiers," said the woman, much to Robin's surprise.

"If that's the case, why do the old stories say John lost all the treasure?"

"Because he did, brother," she replied, nodding vigorously up at Tuck. "It was washed away by a big wave – they can come out of nowhere when you least expect it here. I know. A big wave came in, probably right around here, and drowned the men and animals in the king's retinue, while the treasure was all lost."

Robin shared a sceptical look with Tuck, but neither man challenged her account, and she continued, clearly relishing the chance to share her well-worn tale with a new audience.

"King John travelled on, and he was told about what had happened. Then he died – some say because he was upset at losing so much wealth, although I doubt that. He was a king, wasn't he? He could just have gone and taken someone else's treasure, or taxed the people more." She shrugged. "But anyway, when he was dead, a couple of his Flemish mercenaries rode back here and, before the treasure was completely covered by the sand, and stones, and silt, they recovered it."

Robin was not very familiar with the story of John and his missing treasure, but Tuck had some knowledge of it, and his face betrayed his surprise. Clearly the friar had never heard this particular version of the tale before.

"Flemish?" he repeated. "Did the king have Flemish guards?"

"So people say. Maybe the Flemish were better fighters than his own English knights." She waved a hand, unable to add more, and not interested enough in that aspect of the story to even attempt it.

"And these foreign soldiers somehow found the treasure before it was completely lost, and…Then what?"

"Why, they carried it away with them, brother," she replied, as if he was as no smarter than the bundle of reeds lying in her basket. "What else would men do with treasure?"

"If everyone knows about these foreign knights finding the treasure," Robin began, but the woman cut him off before he could finish the sentence.

"Everyone doesn't know. I know because my great-granda saw the knights here, scrabbling about in the sand when the wave first hit them. Later, he tried to tell folk about it, but he was a sot, and no one believed him."

"You believe him, though?"

"I don't know," she said, shrugging. "He died before I was born. My ma says he stuck to his tale all his life though, and he had been a soldier so he could recognise the language those Flemish knights spoke." She shook her head and gave a little shrug. "Who knows?"

"Hoi, you lazy cow! Are you going to stand there all day, blabbering to them two, or are you going to do some damn work?"

The woman turned at the shout and made an extremely crude gesture towards the man who'd berated her. His face turned crimson with anger but the woman simply cackled and called out, "I'll collect my quota, you smelly old turnip, don't you worry about that, so fuck off and get on with your own work." She looked back at Friar Tuck and, without a hint of shame or embarrassment, said, "I'm sorry, brother, forgive my language. It's the only way to talk to the likes of him."

"That's quite alright," Tuck smiled. "I've heard worse."

"Not much," Robin muttered, then, as her steely eyes fixed on him, he asked, "Where did these Flemish knights take the treasure? If it was returned to the king, or his people, surely the legend about his lost crown jewels being here in the Fens would never have sprung up."

"I don't know," she said. For all her bluster and bravado she'd obviously taken the man's shouted rebuke to heart and was wandering off, looking down at the clumped undergrowth for more reeds to collect. "They carried it off, and who knows where to? So, you see," she glanced back at them one last time. "The treasure really is lost, but not here in the Fens!"

* * *

Sir Henry de Faucumberg was a man of vast experience. Born to a wealthy father, he fell on hard times as a young man and was convicted of stealing wood from old Lord Warenne, was later held in contempt of court, and then once more fined for theft. He had good connections through his family however, and managed to get his affairs in order before King Edward II, an old friend of his father, promoted him to the lofty position of Sheriff of Nottingham. He had held that position more than once in the intervening years, as well as being Sheriff of Yorkshire and, sometimes, as now, holding both offices in the same period. As the king's representative he was responsible for taxes being collected on time, protecting the tax collectors and royal messengers, and ensuring there was no unrest in the lands he oversaw. In principle, he was the highest authority in the area, although, in reality, he had little control over the wealthy barons and their noble associates.

One of whom was in Nottingham Castle that very day, and, thus far, it had not been a pleasant experience for Sir Henry de Faucumberg.

"Look, Coterel, what do you expect me to do?" he demanded. "My bailiffs have their duties to carry out. Would you have me tell them not to bother – stop collecting fines, just allow lawbreakers free rein in these lands? The king would soon find a new sheriff if I were to do that, and I rather like my position here!" He seethed quietly, trying his best to hide his anger behind a cup of wine which he slowly upended into his mouth. How dare this bloody oaf come here to his castle and demand he stop persecuting the people of Notton!

De Faucumberg knew he could not afford to get on the wrong side of John Coterel, though. Outlaw gangs – like the one Robin Hood had been part of, and the Contrariant foot soldiers that had fled into the greenwood after the Battle of Boroughbridge in 1322 – could be dealt with harshly, as long as they could be found. The Coterels were another matter entirely though, thanks to their powerful connections. They might not openly strike a sheriff, but they could not simply be dismissed out of hand.

"I understand you must be seen to uphold law and order," John Coterel said reasonably. Or so he seemed, at least. "But you are employing bailiffs who overstep their authority by harassing regular God-fearing workers."

"Like the tanner in Notton," the sheriff grunted, trying not to sound sarcastic. He knew very well that Simon Tanner was one of the low-ranking lackeys of the Coterels.

"Exactly. He's a hard-working fellow who simply wants to be left in peace. He paid his fine, and that should be the end of it. But your bailiff, John Little, has been threatening him. And, as if that wasn't bad enough, he takes along the likes of William Scaflock – an intimidating, rage-fuelled oaf as far as I understand – to back him up."

The sheriff smirked at that. He knew Will, and the man was certainly angry and intimidating. It gave de Faucumberg great pleasure to imagine John and Will Scarlet putting Simon Tanner in his place.

His smile faded soon enough though, as John Coterel continued. "Your bailiff even took a wolf's head with him when he went to collect that fine from the tanner. Did you know that?"

The sheriff did not reply, sipping his wine again and staring at his uninvited guest over the rim of the cup. He did not like where this was going.

"Robert Hood of Wakefield," said Coterel venomously. "An infamous outlaw, Sir Henry. I'm sure you know who I mean – you had several run-ins with him a few years back."

"I know him. He was once in my service. The *king's service.*"

Coterel nodded knowingly, eyes never once moving away from the sheriff. "Aye, you employed him when he was pardoned, but then, as such men are prone to do, he got himself in trouble again, didn't he? Attacked a prior and his retinue, doing all sorts of horrible things to them and being outlawed again."

Sir Henry shifted uncomfortably in his seat. This damn fool knew far too much.

Coterel was not finished though. "Apparently Robert, or Robin Hood as the folk tales would have it, was mortally wounded at Kirklees Priory. He, along with the prior I mentioned, both died there."

The sheriff felt a bead of sweat run down his back but tried his best to ignore it. Did the Coterels know what had happened that day at the priory? Did they know that he, Sir Henry, had killed Prior de Monte Martini, and helped Robin Hood fake his death?

No. No one knew about that, other than a handful of people the sheriff did not believe had ever talked. By Christ, even Hood's closest friends Little John, Friar Tuck, and Will Scaflock, had believed Robin was dead, and buried in St Mary's graveyard! How could someone like John Coterel know the truth of that, or of the prior's true killer?

Meeting the man's hard gaze, de Faucumberg decided he was being paranoid. His secret was safe, even if Coterel might have suspicions about what really transpired on that infamous day.

"Robin Hood is not, in fact, dead, is he?" John Coterel drawled, leaning back in his chair and swirling the wine in his cup before he drained it and slammed it down on the desk between them.

"Apparently not," the sheriff admitted uncomfortably.

"Apparently? I've been told that you have actually met with the outlaw, Sir Henry. Here, in this very room, not so long ago!"

Damn it, the sheriff raged inwardly. How did this bastard know so much? Out loud, he said, "That is true. I was as shocked as anyone when I heard that he'd turned up, alive, in Wakefield. He was stabbed by an outlaw named Philip Groves – I saw the wound, and I was as convinced as everyone else that it would prove fatal." He shook his head at that, and his expression of astonishment was not faked – he had genuinely thought Robin would die from that horrific injury. Yet, somehow, he had not.

John Coterel stared at him, eyes boring right into him, clearly trying to decide whether the sheriff was being truthful or not. At last, he sat forward, refilled his and the sheriff's cups from the wine jug on the desk as though this was his castle, and then sat back again, smiling, all trace of belligerence gone.

"Look, Sir Henry, we're both men of the world. We know how things work. I understand why you didn't arrest Robin Hood when he came here: he's your friend."

The sheriff's eyes blazed at that but he held his temper in check. "I did not arrest him because I did not even know if he was still an outlaw. His supposed crime was committed years ago, and, I can tell you categorically, he was not guilty! Prior John de Monte Martini made false accusations because he had an irrational hatred for Robin Hood. It was Philip Groves who attacked the clergymen, and trust me, the bastard was brought to justice for his crimes." He leaned forward, feeling it was high time he took control of the situation and put this Coterel upstart in his place. "If we're talking about arresting outlaws, perhaps I should start with you. What do you say to that? Everyone in England knows about your family's activities, Coterel."

At first John Coterel's face turned stony, and he chewed the side of his cheek as he glared murderously at de

Faucumberg, but, eventually, he smiled and spread his hands wide. "It's true," he admitted jovially. "My family do get up to some unruly antics."

"Unruly! Members of your band have murdered, raped, assaulted, stolen from, and extorted many innocent people. Aye, extorted – and I know very well that this is what's been going on in Notton."

Coterel did not deny it, he simply lifted his wine and drank it slowly as he waited for the sheriff to continue his tirade.

"You're right," said de Faucumberg. "We are both men of the world, and we both understand how things work. The king has never commanded me to hunt down your gang, Coterel, and, in fact, I have been subtly advised – warned, even – to turn a blind eye to your activities."

This admission did bring a reaction from the gang member, as he smirked at the sheriff who went on in a resigned tone, bored of the conversation now.

"I have ignored your gang's transgressions," said de Faucumberg. "And, since I know what's good for me, I will continue to do so." Now, he stood up and stared menacingly down at John Coterel. Although the sheriff was not a particularly large man, he had an unmistakable air of authority from years of commanding others. He knew how to speak to the likes of the Coterels. "If you threaten me however, or try to make trouble for those I class as friends, I might decide that turning a blind eye to you and your family is no longer the wisest course of action. Do you understand me?"

His voice had grown softer and yet somehow even more threatening as he spoke, and this last question was ground out through gritted teeth, hand resting firmly on the hilt of his sword, a statement of intent that the other man could not fail to notice.

"Oh, I understand you well enough." John Coterel stood up as well then. "But remember, Sir Henry – you may be safe within Nottingham Castle for now, surrounded by your guards, but you will not always be sheriff. You'd do well to seek our friendship, or, at the very least, don't get in our way. Do you understand?" Without waiting for a reply, Coterel turned and stalked towards the door. Just as he was leaving, he looked over his shoulder and snarled, "Oh, and by the way, Robert Hood of Wakefield *is* still an outlaw. We've checked the records. So that means he's fair game, and any man in England can slay the wolf's head without repercussions. Farewell, sheriff, for now."

De Faucumberg watched the gang leader go, blood thundering in his veins as though his body had been prepared for a physical fight, which he might actually have welcomed. Blowing out a heavy breath, he sat down and pressed his head against the back of the chair. It would have felt good to do to John Coterel what he had done to Prior de Monte Martini, but it would only bring great trouble upon the sheriff.

Lifting his cup, he drank a mouthful and sat in silence, trying to calm his racing thoughts and come to terms with the unsavoury fact that he would need to co-exist with the damn Coterels, whether he liked it or not.

CHAPTER NINE

It had not been an overly pleasant return to Wakefield for Robin and Friar Tuck. The ribbing they'd faced when they walked into Alexander Gilbert's alehouse and shame-facedly admitted how their mission turned out had been humiliating. Everyone, including the village headman, the priest, and even the children they passed later in the street roundly mocked them. Tuck even chased after a few of the cat-callers – not just youths, but grown men as well – cassock flying behind him, cudgel in hand as he roared threats. In truth, the banter was not mean-spirited, and both men did take it in good spirit, despite Tuck's pretend fury, but that was not the only discomfort they'd had to deal with as they returned home from the Fens.

The rains that everyone in England had been praying for finally came, and they barely let up for the travellers' entire journey back to Wakefield. What had been a pleasant, if uncomfortably hot, ride down to the Fens was an entirely different prospect on the return leg. Thankfully, both men had packed their woollen cloaks, and hoods and hats as well, but even those could not keep the riders completely dry, so intense were the showers. They had been happy to camp out in their tent on the outward journey, but chose to stay the nights at inns when they could on the way back to Wakefield, allowing men and horses a chance to rest under proper shelter, with some fresh food and drink before taking to the flooded roads again. There was even a terrific storm one afternoon that saw the pair galloping desperately for the safety of the nearest village, stabling their horses and sheltering in the adjoining tavern as thunder shook the building and lightning lit up the gloomy interior.

They were happy to reach their journey's end, but Robin was dismayed when he spoke with Little John. The bailiff came to the Fletchers' house on the evening of his friend's return, apologising as he shook the rain from his cloak and hung it up to dry.

Martha Fletcher, Matilda's mother, brought ale for them, and went about her work in the moderately sized home, leaving the three friends to talk alone.

"I heard you took quite a bit of abuse from the folk in the village earlier," the bailiff said, smiling as he tried to wring the rain from his grizzled beard. "Your mission was unsuccessful."

"Aye," Robin admitted ruefully. "The Wash never dries out as I'd imagined. It's right beside the sea."

John nodded, eyes twinkling with amusement, but he soon grew serious, looking from Robin to Matilda as he said, "I have some bad news."

The couple eyed one another with some alarm, and Matilda blurted, "What?" as though she feared the worst.

"I've had word from the sheriff. One of the Coterels visited him in Nottingham. They're not happy with us, Robin, and what we did at the tannery."

Robin felt a knot form in his guts as the implications began to grow within his imagination.

"The Coterels know you're still an outlaw," John continued. "And they've threatened to come after you in particular."

Matilda groaned, and rubbed her eyes tiredly. Outside, the rain hammered on the ground and their two boys could be heard running about, playing cheerfully despite the weather. "What are we going to do?" she asked, staring up at the ceiling.

Robin sat in silence for a long moment, mind racing, wondering what to tell her. He had not expected this at all. What could Robin do, should such a well-connected outlaw family decide to come after him?

"Who was it that went to the sheriff?" he asked.

"John Coterel."

Robin nodded. He did not know a great deal about the members of the gang, but he had heard of the leaders, and he knew John to be the youngest and, perhaps, the most reckless.

"Then I'll have to visit him."

"Visit him?" Matilda demanded, angry and visibly frightened. "Are you mad, Robin? The Coterels are killers!"

"Exactly," he replied, trying to speak calmly although anxiety was rising within him. "So I'll have to kill John Coterel first, before he gets me."

"No! No, no, no, Robin." Matilda stood up and walked to the open door, gazing out at the rain and the two happy children. They had made a makeshift 'boat' from a plank of wood and were attempting to sail it across a wide puddle. It did not seem to be working very well, but Arthur and Henry were greatly enjoying themselves, yelling at each other and squealing in mock fear when their 'boat' tipped them out into the puddle. "I didn't return to Wakefield just to go back to living the life we had before we went to Scotland." She turned to look at Robin, her face set hard, mouth a thin line. "We left all that behind. The killing, the running from the law and other dangerous folk. You cannot start a war with the Coterels, Robin. By Christ, they'll destroy this entire village!"

"Don't be so dramatic," Robin replied. "Plenty of folk have stood up to them. There might be a lot of them in the gang, but they're spread across different towns and cities – there's not an army of them that'll turn up in Wakefield and start raping and pillaging because I killed one of their leaders."

Matilda gaped at him as though he'd lost his mind.

"She's right, Robin." John spoke up now, shaking his head gloomily. "It wouldn't be a good idea to hunt down the Coterels. They know who you are, where you live, where Matilda and the boys are living. They might not command an army, but it wouldn't take an army to cause terrible harm, just a couple of trained men. And I'm sure they have some of those to call upon."

"The boys!" Matilda gasped, and, without bothering to find her cloak, she ran out into the downpour, splashing across the grass behind the house. "Arthur!" she cried, gesturing at the older child. "Get back in the house. Hurry! Henry, come here! Come on!"

The boys stared at her, unmoving, until Matilda reached them and bent down to scoop up little Henry. "Get back in the house," she called to Arthur, hurrying back through the rain.

Robin went to the door and lifted a couple of linen towels, one of which he handed to Matilda when she came back inside, the other he used to dry Arthur's soaking wet hair.

"What's wrong, Ma?" Arthur asked, looking up at Matilda, head shaking from side to side as Robin dried him off. "We were having fun. I know it's raining, but it's warm."

"I know," Matilda replied with a tight smile that was obviously forced. She finished drying Henry and pulled both boys into a fierce hug, murmuring to them of how much she loved them. Eventually she let go of the bemused children and straightened, shooing them away with her hand. "Go on now, play in the other room there, stay inside for the rest of the evening, all right? And change into dry clothes or you'll catch a chill!"

The boys were already gone, and Matilda hurried to the house door, slamming it shut and throwing the bolt across.

"This is terrible," she said, pacing up and down, staring at the floor and biting her lip. "What if the Coterels do something to the boys, Robin? John? Everyone knows James Coterel murdered Sir William Knyveton in Derby. And there was another man he killed too. They're bloody animals, Robin!"

"Calm down, Matilda." It was Little John who spoke. He stood up, towering over the young woman. "Robin can take care of you and the children, and I'm not far away if you need help. Will and Tuck are always nearby as well, and your da can handle himself if it comes to it." He held up a hand as she opened her mouth to protest. "I know what you say about the Coterels is true. They are dangerous men, but they have bigger problems to worry about. I don't think they'll waste their time coming here to harm Robin."

"Then why—"

"They went to the sheriff because they knew he would warn us," John said before she had a chance to finish the question. "That's all this is: a warning not to meddle any more in their affairs. Certainly, I've not heard of anyone putting a price on Robin's head, and that's the first thing the Coterels would do if they were serious about killing him. He's an outlaw, so anyone can kill him without facing repercussions from the law."

Robin went to Matilda. Her earlier anger had evaporated and she looked like a frightened child. He took her in his great arms and held her close. "We'll be all right," he murmured, stroking her strawberry-blonde hair. "You'll see. Please don't worry."

"I can't help it," she replied, looking up at him, eyes wet with tears. "As long as you're an outlaw you are in terrible danger. Why did you have to go with John to Notton that day? Why do you always find trouble?" She trailed off, staring at the floor again and then, at last, she sighed and pulled away, returning to her seat and taking a long swallow of ale. "You must win a pardon, Robin," she told him firmly. "You must, or we'll have to go back to Longformacus and live there again. At least we were safe in Scotland, and no one knew who you were."

Robin and John also took their seats once more and the three of them sat nursing their drinks, pondering the dilemma.

"If only you could have found that old king's treasure," Matilda muttered, shaking her head sadly. She'd believed the expedition to the Fens to be as good an idea as Robin had, and even allowed herself to believe he would find some marvellous crown, or sword, or other priceless trinket that King Edward would gladly take from Robin in return for a pardon.

"What exactly happened in the Fens anyway?" John asked. He'd not been in the alehouse when Robin and Tuck visited earlier so had not heard the full story of their adventure, merely second-hand hearsay from other villagers.

Robin told the tale again while the bailiff listened, not laughing or mocking his friend for he too had believed the Wash would dry up with the lack of rain. When Robin had finished, however, John frowned thoughtfully and asked, "What about these Flemish knights that the woman claimed took the treasure? Could that be true? Why would the King of England have knights from Flanders guarding him?"

Robin shrugged. "I've no idea, and neither did Tuck. Her whole story was garbled, and it seems fanciful to think a couple of knights carried off full wagon loads of treasure, don't you think?"

"Aye, that's clearly impossible. But maybe they managed to save one or two pieces and, if that's the case, there could still be a chance of finding it. All you'd have to do would be find out who those knights were, and where they went after King John's death."

"Is that all?" Robin asked sarcastically. "How would I do that?"

"He's right," Matilda broke in, excitement in her voice and her expression. "There must be records of who was in the king's retinue. That kind of thing would be written down."

"And you know who's good at poring over old records?" John asked, grinning.

"Go and find him," Matilda said to Robin, grabbing his arm and practically dragging him towards the door. "Go to St Mary's and find Tuck right now." She was smiling, hopeful again, fears of the Coterels easing for now at least.

"Wait," Robin protested, laughing himself.

"Wait for what?" Matilda demanded.

"Well," said Robin, unbolting the door and pulling it open to reveal the downpour that continued unabated outside. "Can I at least get my cloak?"

* * *

Little John did not have much work from the sheriff over the next few weeks, probably because Sir Henry de Faucumberg didn't want to antagonise the Coterels any more than was necessary. The crime family had their claws in more villages and towns than just Notton, after all. The sheriff probably didn't want to put John in unnecessary danger either, and that suited the bailiff – he had no great desire to stand against the powerful outlaw gang and its brutal leaders unless he was forced into it. So Robin and John helped out around Wakefield, mostly at Will Scaflock's farm and in training the men and young lads of the village in the use of the longbow – now that the rains had come, the headman had reinstated the training and so everyone had plenty to keep them occupied, and out of trouble, throughout the rest of May and into June.

Robin and his friends had not forgotten about the lost treasure of King John though. Friar Tuck spent some time travelling to the nearest abbeys and monasteries, searching their libraries for any information that might be helpful in locating the mythical treasure. From the Minster in York, which he was very familiar with, to smaller places like Haltemprice Priory, and Kirkstall Abbey, he spent many long hours trying to uncover any piece of information, usually accompanied by one of his three friends. They would then reconvene in the alehouse in Wakefield, or in one of their homes, and discuss what the friar had discovered.

"You've done well, Tuck," Robin congratulated the friar as it approached the middle of June and the weather seemed to have settled into a more natural, less extreme rhythm than the previous months. "Let's go over everything you've found."

Will and John were with them and they were enjoying a couple of hours fishing in the sun by the River Calder, although none of the men had managed to catch a thing so far.

"Well, it seems that what we were told by the woman at Longa Sutton was true," the friar said, leaving go of his fishing pole and taking out a piece of parchment which he'd used to scribble down notes. He looked up from the parchment to Robin, saying, "King John really did employ foreign mercenaries, including Flemish knights."

Will frowned. "Why, though?" he demanded, in a tone of voice that suggested he was personally offended by Tuck's revelation. "I was a mercenary in my younger days. Why would an English king need to employ foreigners?"

"Well, as we know, John was not a very popular king. Names like 'Softsword' and 'Lackland' show that." Tuck squinted at the parchment, apparently trying to decipher his own writing, or perhaps simply finding it hard to see in the harsh glare of the sun. "Maybe he didn't trust his own English soldiers to support him with the loyalty a king demands. And, on top of that, John had lost lands in Normandy to the King of France, and he wanted them back. For that, he needed to enlist a large army, and hiring foreign mercenaries was a quick way to do it."

Robin listened with interest, eyes turning to his own fishing pole which seemed to jerk as though it had snagged something before settling back to gentle inactivity again.

"Did you find anything about Flemish knights in particular, Tuck?" he asked.

"I did," the friar reported proudly. "It took me a long time, poring over dozens of old texts, most of them saying the same things, until, at last, I found a chronicle written by Roger of Wendover." He put down the parchment on the grass and lifted his aleskin from where it lay in the cool river water. Pressing the chilled leather against his forehead he reclined with his eyes closed for a time as Robin watched, amused by the sight. Then the friar took a long drink, belched softly, and returned the aleskin to its previous place in the river. "It was little more than a fragment of text that I found," he went on at last. "Roger died almost a hundred years ago, so the record was very old – there must have been more to it at one point, but all that remained was mention of King John employing Flemish knights as his own personal guard."

Little John whistled and shook his great head. "He must have really mistrusted his own people if he had to hire foreigners as his personal guard."

"Was there anything else?" Robin persisted. "Who were those knights? We need something more to follow, Tuck, if we're to find out where these Flemish knights went when Softsword died."

Tuck beamed and, although he was lying on the grass resting on one arm, he seemed to preen as he returned Robin's gaze. "I have a name," he said proudly. "Giselbrecht van Zottegem."

"Zottegem?" John repeated uncertainly. "Is that a place? Sounds like it's far away."

"Don't worry," Will laughed. "I doubt old Giselbrecht is still alive! I don't think there's much point in going to Flanders to find him."

"Then are we any further ahead?" Robin asked, feeling his voice become petulant and doing his best to force a smile at Tuck. "You've done incredibly well, old friend, and this is all really interesting. Dead kings, missing treasure, foreign knights…But how does it help win me a pardon?"

Tuck nodded and raised one hand, finger outstretched in mild admonishment. "Well, we don't know yet, do we? This is just the beginning of our quest."

"Oh, it's a quest now," Will Scarlet drawled, then sat bolt upright on the warm grass as his fishing pole gave a tug in his hands. "Hold on, I have a more pressing quest to deal with. Move out the way!" he cried, gently lifting the snagged fish from the river. He grinned as he saw it was no tiddler, and turned to the right, bringing the struggling carp to shore. When he set it down it continued to struggle but Little John was there with a mallet and he soon dealt with the fish quickly and efficiently.

Will placed his pole down on the river bank and gazed around at the others as though he was some kind of noble lord. "Well, that's my dinner sorted. You lot will need to try harder."

"Well done," Robin congratulated his friend, pleased that at least one of them had managed to catch something that day.

"Aye, well done," Tuck grunted. He was a big fan of carp, as he was of most foods, and he peered at his own static fishing pole in clear disappointment. "Hopefully there's a few more of those swimming around here for the rest of us. But, anyway, as I was saying before Will rudely interrupted with his bellowing, Giselbrecht van Zottegem was known to have ties to the Knights Hospitaller."

"Not really a surprise, is it?" Will said with a shrug of his wide shoulders. He seemed to be done fishing for he lay down on the grass and stared up at the near-cloudless sky with the air of a contented hound. "Lots of noblemen have connections with the likes of the Hospitallers, or the Teutonic Knights, or the Templars before they were disbanded."

"Aye," Tuck agreed, throwing up the hood on his cassock as the skin on his tonsured head was turning red. "But we don't know any Teutonic Knights, or Templars, do we?"

"We don't know any…" Will began, and then trailed off.

"Yes, we do know a Hospitaller," Robin said. "Stephen." He took his pole out of the water, bored with fishing, and lifted his bow, bending it down expertly with his leg so he could attach the string. "D'you think he might somehow be able to help us, Tuck? Could he find out more about this Giselbrecht fellow? Maybe lead us closer to King John's missing booty?"

"I think it's worth a try," the friar replied. "The Hospitallers will have records that are not available in the abbeys and monasteries I searched. Their priory in Clerkenwell might well have a library containing details on Giselbrecht van Zottegem that no one's ever thought to look for."

"This all seems a bit far-fetched," Little John grumbled. "If we've managed to come up with this, how come no one else ever did it before us?"

"No one was looking," Robin returned somewhat irritably. "They all believed the treasure was lost in the Wash, covered by the marshes forever. It was just chance that led to us meeting that woman at Longa Sutton, guiding our search in a new direction."

"Chance," murmured the friar with a look skywards. "Or divine intervention?"

The friends all fell silent at that, thoughtfully gazing at the river, or the blue sky, wondering if perhaps they were being guided by the hand of God to locate King John's treasure. It seemed preposterous, but they had all been involved in so many strange adventures over the years that nothing could be ruled out. It did sometimes appear like these four friends had some kind of guardian angel watching

91

over them, protecting them from Guy of Gisbourne, Philip Groves, and, hopefully, the notorious Coterel gang.

Robin gripped his freshly strung bow and stared at the trees behind their fishing spot, reminded of the not-so veiled threat John Coterel had made against him to the sheriff. There could be a killer lurking in those very woods, hidden amongst the thick summer undergrowth with an arrow nocked to a longbow much like the one in Robin's hands...

There was a rustle from the leaves directly where he was looking and, in an instant, he'd pulled an arrow from his belt and had it pointed at the trees, blood pounding.

His friends watched in amazement as Matilda, Arthur, Henry, and Robin's sister Marjorie pushed through the foliage, eyes bright, cheery smiles on all their faces. Those happy expressions faded, replaced by bemusement or even fear as they saw the young archer pointing his bow at them.

"What are you doing?" Matilda demanded, panic in her voice, grabbing her children and drawing them protectively in against her.

"Sorry!" Robin called out, forcing a laugh and lowering his weapon to beckon the newcomers forward. "I was stringing my bow when I heard you lot charging through the bushes. I was hoping you might turn out to be a deer and we'd have a venison feast tonight!"

He could feel Tuck, John, and Will's eyes upon him, wondering what had come over him, but he continued to act nonchalantly, ignoring the angry frown Matilda cast upon him as she walked over to the water's edge. Arthur and Henry ran to Will as he pointed at the carp he'd caught, and Marjorie – twenty-one now, and athletic, no longer the skinny child she'd once been – went to tease John and Tuck for not catching any fish. Her mastiff, Sam, came charging out of the undergrowth as well, tail wagging as he too joined the group.

"I was just about to go hunting," Robin told Matilda as she approached him, face taut. "We've not done very well with the fishing today."

"You looked like you were about to kill us," she murmured, softly, so the others wouldn't hear.

"I was stringing the bow, and the Coterels came into my mind," he admitted. "Then I heard the bushes moving and thought it might be one of them, come to find me, or one of their lackeys at least."

"This is no way to live, Robin," she told him sadly. "Is there nothing we can do? Can't the sheriff pardon you?"

"He doesn't have the authority, unfortunately. He could petition the king on my behalf, but that might just draw unwanted attention to both of us."

"Then we must do something else," she insisted, looking over her shoulder to make sure no one had noticed the intense conversation between them.

Robin led her a short distance along the riverbank, gesturing for her to sit. He took a place beside her, holding her hand and smiling for, despite the subject of their talk, this was very pleasant, sitting together, surrounded by family and friends on a sunny day. He told her everything Tuck had said about the Flemish knight, Giselbrecht van Zottegem, and the fact he was connected to the Hospitallers.

"It's a shame Sir Richard-at-Lee wasn't still alive," his wife said, mentioning the old knight that had befriended them when they were outlaws, before he was executed for his part in the Contrariant revolt. She picked up a small twig and threw it into the river, and they watched as it sailed languidly past and was lost to sight around a bend. "He could have sorted out a pardon for you. Or at least helped you find out more about the treasure. Do you think his sergeant-at-arms, Stephen could help you? He's no baron, or nobleman admittedly, merely a sergeant."

Robin shrugged, smiling as he watched Little John and Will helping his sons hold the fishing poles into the river. "I don't even know what rank Stephen might hold now. He had some trouble with them before, remember? Their Grand Prior, Thomas L'Archer, tried to do away with him. There's a new head of the Hospitallers here in England now though, and Tuck seems to think Stephen has been welcomed back into the fold by those in charge in Clerkenwell. He's been given a place in a preceptory called Eagle, which is a funny name but it's in Lincolnshire apparently."

"Go, then," Matilda said, squeezing his hand and gazing earnestly into his eyes. "Go and speak with him – Lincolnshire isn't too far from here."

"Come with me," Robin replied, excited by the prospect, but she shook her head emphatically.

"Don't be silly. I have to take care of the boys. Or do you think they might come with us too?" Her face seemed to glow with some inner light as Robin stared at her, his heart full of love for her and their beautiful boys. "Besides, who knows what you might find in Clerkenwell's records, and where that might take you?"

He leaned into her and they kissed, until small arms grasped Robin around the neck and little Henry almost pulled him into the river, screaming with laughter as Arthur came and hugged him too, and Marjorie's dog barked excitedly.

"We've got a bite!" Little John roared then, handing his fishing pole to Arthur and suddenly everyone grew serious as they watched the child manfully struggling to land what turned out to be an even bigger carp than the one Will had caught and cheers filled the little clearing.

This was the life Robin had dreamt of when they were on the road from Scotland back home to Wakefield. This was all he had ever wanted.

Somehow, he had to win a pardon, and live the life that should be his, even if that meant riding all the way to Flanders and back.

CHAPTER TEN

"The old band, back together!"

Robin grinned at Little John as they, alongside Friar Tuck and Will Scarlet, rode southeast, towards the settlement called Eagle. All were looking forward to seeing the Hospitaller sergeant-at-arms, Stephen, again. He had served the old knight, Sir Richard-at-Lee, and made friends with Robin's outlaw gang when their lives became intertwined with the two Hospitallers, having a series of adventures together. Stephen eventually joined forces with them when Sir Richard was hanged after the Contrariant rebellion and, although the sergeant was even more dour than Will Scarlet, he was a loyal friend, a hardy fighter, and a welcome addition to their group before it disbanded.

"You've kept in touch with him over the years, Tuck?"

The friar nodded at Robin's question. "Somewhat. When he was first sent to the preceptory at Eagle he sent me a message. We've been corresponding intermittently ever since. He's always interested to hear about our escapades." He glanced around at his companions. "I get the impression he does not lead a very exciting life at his preceptory."

Will gave a snort of laughter and guided his horse around a large hole in the road, a result of the recent dry spell. "Old Stephen won't like that," he noted. "He likes a good fight."

"Like you," Tuck said.

"Aye, I suppose so. We've had enough excitement over the past few years that I've not found myself getting too bored with life as a farmer, but if Stephen is stuck pottering about a dusty old preceptory all his days, well…"

"Good," John piped up. He looked absolutely enormous that day, for he'd bought a new horse that was even larger than his old one. With his unruly long hair, grizzled beard, and padded leather gambeson, he was a truly formidable figure. They all werc, in truth, and it made Robin feel a little more secure as they started their journey. John Coterel's threat against him really did now seem more of a warning than an actual statement of intent – if Robin and John left the Coterel gang alone, they would be left alone in turn. Or so Robin told himself, and his fears abated with the presence of his stout, heavily armed companions.

Matilda and the boys' farewells rang in his ears but Robin did not miss them too badly yet. He had, of course, spent many a long month hiding out in the greenwood when he and Matilda first became lovers ten years ago, and again when their oldest son, Arthur, was born. It was not a wholly new experience for him to be away from his beloved family, if an unfamiliar one in recent years. This journey would not take too long though, and, God willing, once it was all over, he would be a free man again and he could forget about the Coterels.

The Hospitaller preceptory in Eagle was only around sixty miles away, the road taking them past Sheffield which all four men knew quite well, before they came to lands unfamiliar to them. The weather on the first day was fine and sunny, but the second saw them soaked by a fine drizzle that did not let up. The damp continued on the third day as they finally made it to their destination, the tower of All Saints' Church guiding them past the ash, elm, beech, and willow trees that grew in abundance all along the road.

"Stephen doesn't know we're coming, does he?" John asked as they approached the manor, and a couple of young servants spotted them, sprinting immediately away, towards the complex of buildings. "You didn't send one of your letters to him to let him know?"

Tuck shook his head. "How could I? We'd have made it here before any messenger."

Their sudden appearance had excited quite a bit of interest, and no wonder. It wasn't every day that four armed horsemen rode into Eagle, and, although the preceptory there was mostly used to help the sick and infirm, it was under the auspices of a military order. The Preceptor was a

Hospitaller knight, and Stephen, of course, a veteran of many battles.

By the time Robin and his friends had ridden into the courtyard of the preceptory four men wearing red surcoats with white crosses strode out to meet them, all armed with spears and shields. Leading the way was a powerfully built, middle-aged man, wearing a black felt cap and a black woollen cape with the white Hospitaller cross on its left shoulder. He was armed with a sword but had not drawn it. Despite that fact, he exuded a tangible air of command as his steely gaze bored into the four newcomers.

"Hold!" the man in black, evidently the preceptor, called out in a clear, hard tone. "My name is Sir Simon Launcelyn. State your business here. We were not expecting visitors this day."

"We're here to see our friend, Stephen," said Robin, smiling and gesturing towards one of the soldiers in the red surcoats.

For a moment the Hospitaller sergeant-at-arms stared at them, squinting into the drizzle, and then he burst out laughing. "Robin? And Tuck, is that you? And Little John, and the angry man himself, Will Scarlet!"

"Not as angry as you," Will retorted with the ghost of a smile. "Good to see you again, old friend."

"Robin?" The preceptor barked, staring from one rider to the next. "Little John? Will Scarlet? And the bold friar, Tuck? Then these must be the outlaws we've heard so much about! God's blood, Stephen never ceases talking about his adventures with you men. I'd almost began to wonder if you were even real people."

"I don't talk about them that much," Stephen protested. "Besides, there's not much else to do around here other than relive past glories."

"That's true enough," the preceptor admitted. "But enough of this chattering. I assume you men have not come here to cause trouble. No? Good, then come inside out of

97

this damned rain and you can speak properly with my sergeant."

The two young servants who'd ran from the gates to raise the alarm were summoned and they took the four horses off to be rubbed down and watered while Robin and his companions went into the preceptory with the Hospitallers.

Introductions were made all round and then the other soldiers in surcoats excused themselves and went back about their own duties, leaving Stephen and the preceptor with the four travellers in the ground floor of the preceptor's dwelling house.

"Very nice home you have," Little John complimented the preceptor who shrugged, unimpressed.

"It's all right," he said. "There used to be a moat around the whole place but it's become filled in over the years. The site belonged to the Templars until they were disbanded and we were given their properties. Comfortable enough, but we are working to make them better."

"Well, we spent some time at Haltemprice Priory around Christmas," John told him. "I would say your property here is on a par with that fine place."

Robin watched the bailiff, amused to hear John talking so grandly to the preceptor. The big man had certainly grown more confident conversing with the upper classes since his days as an outlaw.

"Would you have a library here, Preceptor?" Tuck asked then, apparently eager to continue their mission.

"We do," Sir Simon told him. "Although, like the rest of the place, it's not very big, and there's not much you'll find of interest, Brother Tuck."

"Perhaps," the friar said, tilting his head and smiling enigmatically. "Perhaps not. We are looking for information on a Flemish knight who, it's said, was connected to members of your Order."

Stephen glanced at the other three visitors, eyebrows raised in mock astonishment. "What's this?" he demanded. "Something has interested Tuck so intensely that he can't even wait until refreshments have been served before he turns his attention to it? How things have changed since I knew you."

The friar shook his head. "Have no fear, Stephen, I'll heartily partake of any, and all, food and drink Eagle Preceptory can provide."

"Of course he will," Scarlet murmured, sharing an amused glance with John.

"But, while we wait, we might as well get down to business," Tuck went on, not at all put out by the gentle ribbing. "I'm keen to get to the bottom of this mystery."

Robin tried to catch the friar's eye, to let Tuck know that he might want to hold his tongue. Did they really want everyone in England knowing what they were about? If word got out…He realised how absurd he was being. If it was so easy to find King John's treasure someone else would have done it by now. The reason for their visit here really did not have to be a huge secret.

"What mystery?" Sir Simon asked, leaning forward on his seat, eyes glittering with interest. "Did you know about this, Stephen?"

"No, lord."

"Oh. Well, carry on, Brother Tuck. What brings you men here to my preceptory?"

Now Tuck did look to Robin, and the concern in his expression made it clear that he was belatedly wondering if he should have spoken so freely. Robin nodded reassuringly, looking towards the doorway as a woman came in. She was of hefty build and easily carried a number of pewter cups on a trencher, along with a jug of wine. All conversation ceased as the drinks were poured and shared out, and then a second woman, this one tall and rake thin, brought food for the men.

The preceptor thanked them, as did the others, which they accepted with broad smiles and left the room, the thin one casting admiring glances at Robin.

Eagle Preceptory might not have been as large, or as grand as the likes of the Hospitaller site at Clerkenwell in London, but it must have been doing well for the wine was fragrant and delicious, even to the men from Wakefield who were all ale drinkers. The food was also fine, with strong cheese, roast pork, bread and butter, and even some nuts and fruit to fill eager mouths and bellies.

As they ate, Tuck explained their mission in detail to Sir Simon who listened intently, offering comments and questions here and there, as did Stephen who was clearly as interested in the whole affair as the preceptor.

"So this Flemish mercenary was not actually a Hospitaller?" the preceptor asked when Tuck had finished explaining everything they knew.

"I don't believe so," Tuck conceded. "But one of the sources I found made clear mention of the fact Giselbrecht van Zottegem was close friends with a Hospitaller knight from Aachen."

Stephen nodded at that. "Aachen has one of our commanderies there. I believe it was only officially founded about twenty years ago, but our Order certainly had at least one property there around the time of King John. Did you find out the name of this Hospitaller from Aachen?"

Tuck shook his head. "That was not listed." He gave a heavy sigh and rubbed at one of his ears. "You know what it's like searching old records. Very seldom do they give you all the information you want."

"True," the preceptor agreed sympathetically. "You usually find just enough to tantalise you, but not the exact thing that would make your task easy."

"We, well, Tuck, had hoped your library might have some more information that could help us," Robin said. "Since we're friends with Stephen, we thought it might make it easier for us to get permission to search your archives."

"Can you read?" Sir Simon asked, not unkindly.

"Only a very little," Robin told him.

"And the rest of you?"

John shrugged. "About the same as Robin, which isn't a great deal. And certainly no Latin, or other foreign languages."

"Then it will just be the two of us, Brother Tuck, searching the library for what you need. We have the old Templar documents, as well as some of our own Hospitaller ones that were brought here when we took control of the property." He finished his wine and smiled, plainly happy to have this task to complete. "If you're finished your meal, we can get started right now. Stephen? You could come and help us search the records, but I think you should remain here, and entertain our guests."

The sergeant-at-arms smiled. "Of course, my lord."

"Then follow me, Tuck. We may have a long day ahead of us, and my eyesight isn't what it used to be."

The pair left and Robin felt a real surge of hope as they headed for Eagle's archives. He did not have a clue what the library might look like, or what it would contain, but seeing Tuck and Sir Simon – both a similar age, and with long years of travel and experience behind them – steadfastly setting about their task made Robin glad. If anyone could help them find King John's treasure it would be those two old warriors.

"More wine?"

Robin gave a start and looked up as Stephen held out the jug to him. "Aye, don't mind if I do," he said, happily refilling his cup. The wine was more sour than the ale he preferred, but it was making him feel very pleasantly relaxed. What better way to spend an afternoon than with these old friends and some free drink? "Fill us in then," he prompted. "What have you been doing for the past five years or so?"

The serving women came in to clear away the remnants of the meal, refill the wine jug, and bring fresh water for the men to clean their hands. Robin pointedly ignored the admiring glances from the tall one, and the smirks of Will and John.

Stephen, it turned out, had been welcomed back into the Hospitaller fold when the new Grand-prior of England, Leonard De Tybertis, took control. His predecessor Thomas L'Archer had wanted Stephen dead, but his governance of the Hospitallers in England had been so poor that he was deposed. Stephen was a well-known and well-respected sergeant-at-arms and there were not so many of them serving in England at that time that the new Grand-prior could afford to leave him out in the cold. Serving at the Order's base in Clerkenwell for two years, he had then been given the position there at Eagle, to help Sir Simon with the running of the preceptory. It was a fairly prestigious post, for the old Templar properties were seen as vital for the Hospitallers' growth, and Stephen proved a great asset.

"It's pretty bloody boring though," the sergeant grunted as he came to the end of his story. "A great life for the sergeants who were never active soldiers, and the servants, but for me?" He tapped his sword. "I miss the days when I carried this beside Sir Richard-at-Lee and fought for the glory of God."

Robin examined him, seeing a man who looked fit, lean, and dangerous. But Stephen was no longer a youngster – he must have seen fifty or so winters, and Robin suspected the Hospitallers didn't want men as old as that serving on the front lines. Not too many of them, at least. Besides, there was always the threat of marauding outlaws in England, as Robin knew all too well, and the preceptory needed an experienced soldier like Stephen to help protect the place, and the sick people it housed there. From what the sergeant had said however, there had been no trouble in Eagle the entire time he'd served there.

"This has been the most exciting day I've had in years," Stephen said. "I almost hoped you lot were coming to rob us when the servants raised the alarm. But enough of me! What have you three been up to these last few years, Robin? I expect Tuck and the preceptor will be in the library for some time, so come on – let's hear about your miraculous return from the dead!"

CHAPTER ELEVEN

It was dark outside by the time Friar Tuck and Sir Simon returned from their search of Eagle's records. Candles had been lit – something a Holy Order had in abundance was candles – and, although no one had said so, Robin assumed they'd be allowed to stay the night at the preceptory.

"Did you find anything?" John asked eagerly as Tuck came into the room, closely followed by Sir Simon.

The friar's face was pale and drawn and he rubbed at his eyes, visibly tired from their hours of delving into old records. He did not look unhappy or downcast though, and smiled as he sat and accepted a cup from Will Scarlet.

"Nothing of great interest so far," the preceptor said, also taking a seat. He too was clearly worn out but had been drawn in by the mystery that had been laid in his lap. "We have found one lead that might go somewhere useful, however." He ran a hand through his iron-grey hair and nodded determinedly. "Tomorrow, Tuck, we'll return to the library and follow that trail, hopefully to a satisfying end."

Robin felt his heart swell as he sat there in the dwelling house of Eagle Preceptory and looked around at the men who had vowed to try and help him. Of course, they all wanted to find the mythical lost treasure, but his friends would never have set out on this journey had they not hoped to win Robin a pardon.

Then there was the preceptor. He looked utterly drained from his day's work. How far would Sir Simon go to discover the location of King John's crown jewels? He was not beholden to Robin in any way – even Stephen was not as close a friend to the young archer as Tuck, John, and Will. The Hospitallers had offered Robin the hospitality of Eagle however, and he had no doubt they would both do whatever they could to help him and his companions.

Now it was time to rest though, and after some more food the travellers were given blankets and allowed to sleep right there in the dwelling house. The preceptor went to the upper floor where his bed was, and Stephen went off to his own usual bed elsewhere in the complex.

Tomorrow could not come fast enough for Robin as he lay down and closed his eyes, willing sleep to come. They were very near to discovering something important, he was sure of it!

* * *

It was barely even dawn when Robin awoke, confused, wondering where the hell he was as he peered around groggily at the unfamiliar surroundings. The sight of Little John, mouth hanging open as a loud snore escaped from it, reminded Robin of their location, and their reason for being there in Eagle.

People were moving around outside and he guessed it was the sergeants and lay members of the preceptory starting their day. Religious orders always liked to be up as early as possible Robin knew, although Friar Tuck did not quite follow the same rules. He was lying near John, a seraphic smile on his face as he slept on contentedly.

Robin glanced at Will, expecting him to be sleeping too, but Scarlet was wide awake. He grinned nastily at Robin and then sat up and shouted, "Wake up you lazy bastards!"

John and Tuck both scrambled upright, eyes wide in shock, hands scrabbling for their weapons before they caught sight of Will and Robin in fits of laughter.

"You dirty oaf!" John cried, pointing a finger at Scarlet who spread his hands wide, shaking his head innocently as though he'd done nothing wrong.

"God have mercy on your soul, Will Scaflock," Tuck grumbled sitting down and scratching at his tonsure before yawning widely. "You'll burn in the fiery pits of hell for that."

It truly was dawn then, as a cock crowed nearby and Robin went to open the door for one of the serving ladies who knocked politely. She brought them fresh water for washing and drinking, and towels to dry their hands and faces, before leaving and returning with some food for them to break their fast.

As a farmer, and even a monk for a short time, Will was used to being up so early and he set about the bread and cheese with gusto. It took the other three a bit longer to fully come alert and, by the time they came to eat, Will had already finished.

"I wish I could read Latin," Robin told Tuck as they chewed their food. "It's frustrating sitting around while you and Sir Simon do all the work."

"Hopefully it won't take us much longer to find what we're looking for," the friar reassured him. "Why don't you three tour the preceptory before morning Mass? Meet the people who live and work here. See how a preceptory operates."

There was nothing else to do so, when the Preceptor came to fetch Tuck and take him to the library, the others went with Stephen for a walk around Eagle.

It was an overcast day, with heavy, portentous clouds rolling in from the east, but the rain held off until mid-morning and by then the visitors had been to Mass and then returned to the preceptor's dwelling house.

"D'you think they'll find anything today?" Will asked as they sat down, looking through the unshuttered windows at the idyllic preceptory grounds, the air damp but warm.

The door burst open then and Sir Simon strode in, face flushed, a proud smile on his weather-beaten although still handsome face. "We have news," he announced, as Friar Tuck came in behind him, a thick, leather-bound tome in his hands.

Robin felt a flush of excitement as the book, which was large and heavy, was thumped down on the table that

106

resided against one wall except for at meal times. Tuck looked back at them, smiling, eyes twinkling merrily as he nodded and said, "We do indeed have news."

"Your friar found it," the preceptor admitted happily, standing beside the book and gesturing for the others to come and see what had so excited them. "I think this is the breakthrough you men were hoping for."

Robin was first to the table, with John and Will close behind. All three looked at the book expectantly, and Tuck pointed to a line on the page. "There," he told them. "It says Giselbrecht van Zottegem was in charge of escorting King John's baggage train when they were struck by a wave in the Wash and England's crown jewels were lost."

"Interesting," John nodded. "This confirms what you were told by the woman collecting reeds at Longa Sutton."

"It does," Robin agreed.

"Incredible to think a Flemish knight was guarding the English king's wealth," Will murmured. "I mean, to be employed as a mercenary fair enough, but to be trusted in such a high position?" He glanced at the preceptor. "Is that common?"

"I wouldn't think so. I must admit I'm not sure, but, like you, I think it seems strange. King John must have trusted this Giselbrecht van Zottegem a great deal."

Tuck was bobbing his head as he listened to them, but he drew their attention back to the old book by tapping his finger on it. "That's not the exciting part," he insisted. "This is the exciting part, right here. It says that after the treasure was lost, and the king died a short time later, Giselbrecht van Zottegem returned to his home in Flanders."

"So what?" Will asked, brow furrowed.

"He asked for an escort back home, but he did not go directly there. He went to Aachen first."

Robin was just as confused as Will. "What has this got to do with anything, Tuck? Why would the Hospitallers even have a record of this?"

"Because it was Hospitallers who escorted him to Aachen!" Tuck gushed. "That's why they kept a record."

John turned to Sir Simon. "Was this Giselbrecht fellow a member of your Order?"

"We didn't find anything to prove so," the preceptor said. "I doubt he was a secret, high-ranking Hospitaller knight."

"Then why did your knights escort him to Aachen?" John persisted. "And why did he even go there if his home was in a different country?"

"Why he went to Aachen I cannot say. But I think it likely that he hired, or somehow persuaded members of my Order to escort him there."

"And that's the thing," Tuck cried triumphantly. "Why would he need an escort? He was already accompanied by his own soldiers – Flemish knights who were so skilled in battle that our King John hired them as his guard. Why would such a force need even more numbers?"

At last Robin understood what the friar was hinting at, and he felt a shiver raise the hairs on his neck. "They were carrying something valuable. So valuable that it demanded a large detachment of knights to guard it on the road to Aachen."

"The treasure!" John said in a low voice, tugging thoughtfully at his beard, perhaps picturing the Flemish knights and their escort of Hospitallers riding halfway across Europe with a cargo that was now utterly priceless thanks to the legendary status it had acquired.

"Would this not be in your records?" Will asked Sir Simon doubtfully. "Seems like something that important should have been written down by your predecessors."

"It's not in the library here," the preceptor replied with certainty. "We searched. But this is just a minor outpost, with records brought here from other preceptories. Don't forget, this was actually a Templar property until fairly recently."

"Besides," Tuck said. "Something like this would have been kept secret by Giselbrecht van Zottegem. He would hardly have told anyone he'd collected the missing treasure and was now making off with it, would he? The Hospitallers would have stopped him."

"Not if it was in their interests to help him," Robin noted.

"How so?" Stephen asked defensively.

"Well, maybe they were paid a goodly sum to escort the Flemish knights to Aachen. Or perhaps the particular items of treasure Giselbrecht van Zottegem was carrying were of such a nature that a holy order of knights wanted to see it kept safe."

Everyone fell silent, pondering Robin's suggestion until, after a long moment the preceptor asked incredulously, "Are you suggesting that, amongst King John's crown jewels, the Flemish knight found…" He trailed off, shaking his head and frowning before finishing with, "The Holy Grail?"

The other men began chattering excitedly, talking over one another, regaling their companions with what they'd heard about the mystical chalice, or cup, that was said to have been used by Christ himself at the Last Supper, and then passed into the keeping of Arthur, the Once and Future King.

"Well, no," Robin admitted a little ruefully when it became quiet enough for him to be heard again. "The Holy Grail hadn't even crossed my mind. I just meant there might have been some other relic that the Hospitallers would have been glad to escort to Aachen."

The preceptor eyed him dubiously, as if he didn't quite believe Robin's denial. The thought of claiming the Holy Grail had obviously fired the grey-haired knight's imagination, so Robin did not try to dampen his enthusiasm. Sir Simon had been a great help to them so far, and who knew what further aid he might grant to them as their quest progressed?

Stephen knew the preceptor far better than Robin or any of the others, and he fixed his master with a warning look now. "You're not…"

"Why not?" Sir Simon demanded. "We're hardly needed here, are we? How long have you served here? Years. And I've been preceptor even longer, yet how many times have we been called upon to protect Eagle and its inhabitants?"

"Well, never," the sergeant-at-arms admitted. "That's why it's so bloody boring here."

"Exactly!" The preceptor stood up and paced back and forwards in the middle of the room, hands clasped as he murmured to himself. "No one will miss us," Robin could hear him saying. "No one will even notice we're gone. And we'll be back in no time. It's long been said that Joseph of Arimathea brought the Holy Grail to these lands – it makes perfect sense that it would have passed to our kings for safekeeping!"

"What's happening?" Little John asked, clearly confused.

"What's happening?" Sir Simon parroted, stopping to gaze up at the giant bailiff. "Why, we've decided to accompany you on your quest, my good man, that's what's happening."

"We have?" Stephen asked, a slightly dazed look on his face.

"Accompany us? Where are we going?" It was Will who spoke up then, as irritable as ever, even when addressing a knight. "What the hell are you talking about?"

"Forgive me," the preceptor returned, eyes travelling across Stephen and his guests before finally alighting on their leader, Robin Hood. "I thought you intended to see your search for King John's missing treasure through to the end, wherever that might lead you."

"That was our plan," Robin hedged. "But we had no idea what that might entail." In truth, the whole scheme now seemed insanely hopeful, and more than a little naive.

Riding around England looking for something that no one had seen hide nor hair of in over a century! It was mad.

Not as mad as Sir Simon it seemed.

"Well the trail leads from here in Eagle's library, to Aachen," announced the preceptor, steely gaze boring into Robin. "And I mean to follow that trail. Think of it! A quest to retrieve lost royal treasure. It's like a tale from an Arthurian romance, don't you think? Will you join me, longbowman? Or will you return to your home in Yorkshire empty-handed, wondering for the rest of your life what might have been?"

Every eye was on Robin now and his mind spun with the possibilities, and, more pertinently, the dangers that a journey across Europe would pose. He was no seasoned traveller. He'd barely even left England, for his home in Scotland had been close to the border. What did he know about traversing foreign countries, dealing with different people and cultures? He was a simple yeoman from Wakefield, by Christ! He was doing well if he could communicate from people in the next town over, never mind folk from Flanders or Aachen.

"I don't know," he mumbled, his usual self-confidence deserting him. "How long would we be away? My wife – all our families, friends! – will be expecting us back in Wakefield soon. And we haven't packed enough provisions, or gear, for a journey halfway across the world."

"Pah, it's not that far," Sir Simon grinned, reaching out and slapping him heartily on the back. "I've been much, much further away than the Holy Roman Empire. We can be in Aachen in a few days, assuming your horses are up to it. And as for gear – what gear do you need? I saw you when you first arrived, with longbows, packs of food, tents, and skins for ale or water." He chuckled, nodding to himself as he began pacing the room again like an animal, caged but ready to be set free after long months in captivity, his imagination burning with thoughts of treasure, and the Holy

Grail, and King Arthur. "Oh yes, I think you have enough gear, and anything else we can provide from Eagle's stores."

Robin looked at Stephen, silently asking the sergeant if the preceptor was mad. In reply, Stephen's mouth twitched and he came close to a smile. It seemed he was coming around to Sir Simon's suggestion.

"As the Hospitallers escorted Giselbrecht van Zottegem to Aachen a century ago, so they will now escort you, Robin Hood, and your friends," the preceptor announced, raising a finger in the air and sending a soft prayer for success skywards.

"God is good," Stephen intoned. "Let it be so."

Tuck and Will had both travelled to different countries in their youth and seemed happy enough to accept this continuation of their quest. Little John had never been further than London however, and was biting his cheek, apparently as uncertain about it all as Robin.

"Well? Shall we do this?"

Robin stared at Sir Simon, going over the reasons why they should not sail for Aachen in his mind and realising that the only thing stopping him agreeing to the journey immediately was his reluctance to be parted from Matilda and the boys for an extended period.

As though reading his mind, Stephen said, "We can send one of our servants to Wakefield. Let all your kinfolk know that you won't be home for a few weeks yet, and not to worry."

"Will your farm be all right?" Robin asked Will, still somewhat hopeful of finding a way out of this.

"Aye, Elspeth knows what's what," Scarlet nodded. "And, when we send the messenger, I'll suggest that she hires a couple of labourers to help out while I'm away. There are always people happy to pitch in around the farm for a bit of extra pay."

"John?"

The bailiff shrugged. "You know yourself, Robin, that things have been quiet lately. I doubt I'll be missed. And my boy is a grown man now. Amber might not be overjoyed about me going off again, but she has plenty of friends to keep her company and make sure she's safe."

Nodding, Robin looked at Tuck, wondering if the portly clergyman might offer a sensible objection to them all heading across the sea.

"I'm a Franciscan friar," Tuck said, tapping his pectoral cross with a blissful smile. "It is my job to go abroad, carrying the word of God, and ministering to the needs of all. Even people in Flanders need the assistance of a wandering friar, I'm sure."

Now they all turned to Robin, leaving him nowhere to hide. They demanded his decision, and he had to give it.

After a long, silent moment, he shrugged and reached out for one of the cups of wine on the table. "It seems we're going to Aachen, then," he said, and drained the cup in one go.

CHAPTER TWELVE

They did not set off on their travels immediately. For all the Preceptor's claims that no one would miss them, there were still things to be taken care of before they set forth from Eagle. Sir Simon's subordinates were told about what was happening and exhorted to maintain order and discipline while he and Stephen were gone. The preceptory was not entirely self-sufficient, but the staff knew their business and things like food deliveries would not be interrupted simply because the commander was away for a time.

Robin didn't ask Sir Simon if he would inform the Hospitaller Grand Prior about his decision to sail for Flanders. It was none of Robin's concern how the Order conducted their business, or what the politics of the situation might be. The preceptor had offered to travel with them, and that was enough. Had Sir Simon not joined their party, Robin knew their quest for the missing treasure would be over already. The presence of a knight and a sergeant-at-arms would give their group a much-needed air of authority as they moved through strange, foreign lands, the red surcoat and white cross telling everyone that they were Hospitallers. It would, Robin hoped, deter robbers from attacking them. Robin, John, Tuck, and Will might look tough, but they did not have the gravitas or military presence that Sir Simon and Stephen would provide.

The serving ladies who'd been bringing them food and drink were tasked with filling the travellers' packs with supplies. Stephen was given permission by the preceptor to take money from Eagle's coffers for they would need it to cover tolls, travel, lodgings, and perhaps even bribes for foreign officials. There would be expenses both foreseen and unforeseen and Stephen made sure to bring enough that they would not run short, God willing.

They spent another night in Eagle and then, when the sun came up, a messenger was dispatched to Wakefield, and the six travellers set off.

"We shall ride for Boston," the preceptor told them, guiding them along the southwestern road. "Outside London, it's one of the largest ports in England. Wool, iron, and lead are all traded from there, with furs and even falcons coming the other way. We should have no trouble finding passage to Bruges from there."

"Bruges?" John asked. "I thought we were going to Aachen."

"We are," the knight confirmed. "But no ships sail directly there. We'll be able to find passage to Bruges easily though. And, since our road from there to Aachen takes us past Giselbrecht van Zottegem's old castle, I think we should visit. See if we can find any more information there."

"Where is his castle?" Stephen asked.

"Laarne, near Ghent. The current masters may be able to help us, especially if they are actual descendants of Giselbrecht."

Robin swallowed as he heard all that. Bruges, Aachen, Ghent, Laarne – places he'd never heard of until now, never mind visited. And on top of that, he'd never been on a large ship in his life, and had heard all sorts of stories about how dangerous and uncomfortable they were. If they didn't sink, you would probably spend the entire time aboard bent over the side puking.

"You look a bit green there, Robin. Not looking forward to sailing? Me neither." Little John rode beside him, bearded face drawn.

"You'll be fine," Tuck assured, overhearing them. "It won't be a small boat we go on. Those are the worst, you feel every wave."

"He's right," the preceptor called back. He'd assumed command, as his military rank and social standing allowed, and Robin had been content to allow the more experienced

115

man to do so. "We'll have to find a ship big enough to take our horses. It should be a pleasant journey, calm, and over fairly quickly. Don't worry about it!"

Robin and John glanced at one another, trying their best to be reassured. The day was bright and sunny with barely a breeze and that did lead Robin to think that sailing in the coming days might be relatively safe. Had it been stormy his fears would have risen.

With the weather being warm and dry, they decided to camp out that first night, setting up camp and taking turns on watch, very much like a military operation. They reached the port town of Boston early the next day and Robin was impressed by the size of the place. Sir Simon had compared it favourably with London, in terms of the port at least, and it appeared to be a fair enough comparison to the young archer.

The sounds, sights, and smells of the busy town were a tad overwhelming for most of the travellers, more used to a rural way of life. Sir Simon knew his business though, and he guided them through the bustling streets towards the port. When they made it there, he told them to wait for him at a tavern while he and Stephen found a ship to carry them across to Flanders.

Robin examined the preceptor as he stood before them, outlining his plans and commanding them not to get drunk while they waited. He was a friendly man, but as hard as iron, and Robin could see his manner was irritating Will Scarlet, but Robin found it reassuring to have someone along on their trip that could guide them with experience and wisdom. Clad in chainmail, a red surcoat with large white cross emblazoned across the front, shield carried on his back in the same colours, with sword and dagger hanging from a fine belt around his waist, Sir Simon looked truly impressive, even without the helmet which had remained with his horse in the inn's stable.

Stephen was dressed similarly to his master, although his gear was not as finely made or expensive as the preceptor's. The sight of them passing drew wary or admiring glances in their direction and Robin knew it would be very foolhardy or brave robbers who'd attempt to hold up their party once they reached Flanders.

The four friends were not troubled as they sat in the inn – a large place called, fittingly, The Ship – for the staff and patrons were obviously used to seeing different faces coming and going every day. Sailors, merchants, dock workers, soldiers, pedlars and more bustled around the building, drinking wine and eating food before moving on. The sight of four more armed, well-built men barely raised an eyebrow in Boston.

It did not take long before Sir Simon and Stephen returned, the crosses on their surcoats blazing brightly in the sunshine as they came in through the front door. The preceptor gestured frantically at them.

"Hurry up," he called. "We've found a ship, but it's about to cast off. Bring the horses, come on!"

There was a mad dash then, as all six men fled the inn, collecting their mounts and the two pack horses from the stables and charging towards the docks, the preceptor ordering people to get the hell out of the way as they ran. Robin felt himself grow breathless quickly and realised it was down to the anxiety he was feeling. In a very short time he would be on a ship for the first time, and he would be leaving the country he'd spent most of his twenty-seven years in, voyaging to lands he could not even begin to imagine.

It was, frankly, more terrifying than facing an army, or hiding in the greenwood from a group of the sheriff's soldiers intent on killing him.

The haste of their departure gave him no time to dwell on things though, as they came to the ship Sir Simon had found for them, and the sailors quickly took control,

117

expertly moving their horses on board. The men followed, and Robin felt his legs grow weak as he went from hard, dry land, onto the gently swaying deck of the great vessel.

"All right?"

He peered up at John and drew in a deep, calming breath. "Aye. You?"

"Well enough. Let's hope this doesn't take too long."

"You'll be fine, you pair of big babies," Will Scarlet chuckled, ushering them along behind the confidently striding preceptor. "Just try not to throw up on me when we get under way, eh?"

"I'll make fucking sure I do," John retorted, but his threat only drew more laughter from Will.

Robin did his best to focus on what he had to do, and what was happening around them on the ship. The former did not take long, for all they had to do was walk to a section near the front of the vessel and sit with their backs against the side, looking out at the docks, or, as Robin and John did, focus closely on the crew as they went about the business of casting off. This latter task was interesting, and diverted the inexperienced sailor's fears at least for a time.

The horses were not around for they were berthed below the deck, out of sight and safely secured so they wouldn't get injured if the sea became choppy. Men were easily visible though, for the ship seemed to have a crew of about thirty or forty sailors. Robin noticed some of them were armed with swords, while spears and axes were stored around the deck. He tried not to think what those might be for. The crew all knew what they were about and moved quickly and efficiently, calling out to one another while ropes were tightened, planks of wood clattered, and other noises Robin could not place filled the air alongside the ever-present shriek of gulls.

"How long will the voyage take?" Friar Tuck asked the preceptor, who looked completely at home on the deck.

"About three days," Sir Simon said happily. "Depending on the weather, of course. Maybe four. But this ship, the *Rodecog*, looks to me a good, fast vessel."

"Three days!" Little John demanded, voicing Robin's own displeasure. "I had no idea we'd be stuck on this thing for so long!"

"Calm down," Will told him, speaking seriously, no hint of the gentle mockery the men often addressed one another with. "You'll be fine. All we have to do is sit here, maybe drink a bit of beer, tell stories, sing, and sleep. That's it. All things you're good at, John." He did smile then, but it was reassuring – the smile of a man looking after a friend.

"He's right," Stephen added gruffly. "I was frightened the first time I had to get on a ship, but I soon realised sailing was more boring than frightening. At least we have calm weather. I'd suggest getting some rest – it'll be hard riding across Flanders if you're not used to covering long distances on horseback."

The short conversation had masked everything else that was going around them, but Robin grasped the side of the ship spasmodically as he felt the whole thing lurch and somehow become even less stable.

They were under way, and there could be no getting off this floating deathtrap until they reached their destination.

Little John's eyes were closed but Robin forced himself to breathe slowly and deeply, hand grasping the hilt of his sword as though he might fight off his fears. He looked out at the docks as they drifted inexorably away, a seemingly massive gulf separating the young archer from dry land. He saw a small boy standing on the docks, waving to the ship as it departed and laughing in delight. The child reminded Robin of his own sons and that shamed him. How could he sit there cowering like a mouse, when even a tiny boy would love to take his place on board the majestic ship?

The vessel – a cog, as the preceptor told them – was not designed to be rowed. Instead, it had a single mast with one sail that the crew seemed to be able to use to guide the ship once they were under way. Robin did not attempt to figure out how things worked – he knew he would only frighten himself with a belief that something wasn't operating correctly. So, he left the sailors to their well-worn tasks and gazed out at the land as it moved slowly past.

"Enjoying it more now?"

Robin glanced around to see Tuck smiling at him while chewing on a piece of bread.

"I suppose so," Robin agreed. "We're not that far from land. If anything happens to the ship we can just swim to shore."

Tuck laughed through his bread. "We're sailing along the River Haven just now, but soon it'll open out, and we'll be into the North Sea. We won't be near land then."

Swallowing, Robin turned back to the riverbank, wondering if that would be the last time he ever saw England. He tried to reassure himself, to remind himself that dozens, hundreds, of ships travelled all around the world every single day, and only a very few ever sank. He was probably safer on board the *Rodecog* than back at home where the Coterels wanted him dead.

Sure enough, as Tuck had warned, the land soon began to widen out and the nearby banks of the River Haven gave way to open sea. It was a dizzying sight, and awe-inspiring to realise that he, Robin Hood, was now no longer in England. He wished Matilda and the boys were there to see it, and, with that thought he realised the wonder of the whole thing had taken the edge off his terror and he was, incredibly, enjoying himself.

Not all the companions were in such fine spirits, however. Little John's feet scrabbled on the wooden deck and, desperately, the huge man grabbed hold of the bulwark and dragged himself up. Instinctively, Robin and the others pushed themselves away as John's mouth opened and, with a massive roar, the bailiff vomited over the side of the ship.

"Ah, God above," Stephen grumbled, face twisted sourly.

"I know, can't take him anywhere," Will chuckled, shaking his head and eyeing Robin questioningly. "I thought it would be you that puked first. You feeling all right?"

Robin laughed and stood up, patting John sympathetically on the back. "Aye, I'm fine. In fact, I could even take a share of that bread Tuck's eating."

The suggestion of food was clearly too much for John, and he threw up again, and again, until, at last, he slumped down on the deck once more, back against the bulwark, and groaned what sounded like Robin to be a prayer for mercy.

* * *

That first day seemed to pass Robin by in something of a haze. He enjoyed looking out at the water, waves frothing and rippling in the sunshine. They saw the occasional ship, but none came close enough to make out details. Eventually, the novelty wore off when there was nothing for the eye to focus upon other than water and sky, and Robin sat with his companions doing as Will had suggested, singing, telling tales, and quaffing beer, of which the ship seemed to have an inexhaustible supply for it was the sailors' main drink.

The second day passed much as the first had done, although at one point they sailed into a fog and John – who had managed to get over his seasickness – spent the whole time praying loudly until they came out the other side. The sailors did not seem perturbed by the big man's behaviour, having seen it all before.

The preceptor and Will checked on the horses occasionally, making sure the animals were comfortable. Robin came down once for a look below decks and was pleasantly surprised to discover the horses apparently happy and unbothered by the unfamiliar position they found

121

themselves in. They were fell fed and taken care of by a young sailor who told them this was his job, and sometimes the ship carried as many as ten horses, importing them to England from Swiss and French breeders in particular. The main cargo the *Rodecog* was carrying to Flanders on that trip was wool, though, which was a major export from Boston's port.

Sleeping had been an issue for most of the six companions. The preceptor and Stephen, experienced old soldiers, were able to sleep anywhere, and at a moment's notice. Robin had thought he would be able to do the same, having spent many a difficult night trying to rest in the greenwood of Barnsdale, but sleeping on board a continually swaying ship was a completely new experience for him and he found that even the gentlest of rocking motions made him feel queasy and on edge. As a result, he, John, and Tuck did not get much sleep the first day and were cranky and irritable on the second.

"This is boring," John grumbled as they sat nursing cups of beer and staring out at the featureless horizon. "Stephen was right."

"I don't know how the sailors can do it, day after day, year after year," Robin concurred. "I'd go mad if this was my life."

"They're busy," Will protested, pointing at one man who was expertly doing…something with a length of rope, and another pair who were scrubbing the decks even though the decks looked spotless to Robin. "They repair the sails, make sure the ship isn't leaking, cook meals, steer us in the right direction, keep watch, and all sorts of other tasks. Besides, it's not always calm – it gets pretty fucking exciting during a storm, trust me!"

Robin shuddered, sharing a worried frown with John, and then he thought of one of the jobs Will had just mentioned. "Keep watch?" he asked. "Keep watch for what?" An image of some gargantuan, tentacled sea-monster filled his mind and he reached down instinctively for his sword.

The answer was, however, more prosaic but hardly less frightening.

"Pirates," Scarlet said.

"Away out here in the middle of nowhere?" John demanded.

"I guess so. I dunno, I mostly sailed in ships with a lot of soldiers – no one was ever stupid enough to attack them. What d'you think all those weapons stacked against the bulwarks are for? Spearing fish?"

Robin had, naturally, heard of pirates. But, having never been to sea, he knew very little about them and, in truth, had thought of them as something of an exaggerated story to make adventure tales more interesting.

"Why didn't anyone mention pirates before we left Eagle?" John asked, looking a little grey of complexion again.

"Why would they?" Will returned levelly. "Pirates are a natural hazard, just like robbers on the road between Barnsdale and Nottingham. I expect Sir Simon didn't think he needed to mention them. I certainly didn't." He shrugged almost apologetically. "I wouldn't worry about it too much. We'll be safely in the port at Bruges by this time tomorrow."

Robin nodded, even managing a smile as he stood up and stretched out his neck. Ships might be a good way to move around the world quickly, but they were far from comfortable.

"I suppose you're right," he said to Will. "I'm worrying about something that will never happen."

"Never say never," John groused, and his words turned out to be prophetic, for a shout came from the front of the *Rodecog* right at that moment, and the sailors around them suddenly began calling out, and, most worryingly, running to gather the weapons that were stowed around the ship.

"What's happening?" Robin asked as the preceptor and Stephen hurried over to them, closely followed by Friar Tuck who'd been offering spiritual guidance to some of the sailors.

"I'm not sure," Sir Simon said, frowning deeply.

"I am," Tuck told them grimly. "Get your swords, and longbows ready, lads. The watch has sighted a pirate ship."

"This is all your fault, John," Will Scarlet called over his shoulder as he ran to collect his longbow from where it was stored with his horse below decks.

"My fault?" John retorted, hurrying after him, Robin right behind as they too went to collect their weapons. "How do you work that one out?"

"Aye, of course it's your fault, you big daft bastard," Will shouted. "You should never have said you were bored!"

CHAPTER THIRTEEN

"How can you tell they're pirates?" Robin asked, genuinely curious. There was a ship sailing directly towards them from the southwest, but it looked exactly like any other one they'd seen on the horizon since they'd left English waters.

The captain of the *Rodecog*, a burly sailor with a luxuriant dark moustache, glanced quickly at Robin and then returned his gaze to the vessel that had caused so much consternation. "For one thing, it's coming straight for us, rather than making damn sure to avoid a possible collision," he said. "And second, look at the flag it's flying."

Robin had very good eyesight, and it seemed so did the captain despite being ten or fifteen years older.

"It's black."

"Indeed." The captain looked at him then, and around at the preceptor and the rest of the passengers. His eyes glinted and the hint of a smile tugged at his mouth. "I've heard you men talking to one another," he told them. "I've heard you being called Robin, and you, John. You're Tuck, and, if I've not gone mad, a friar. And, finally, you're known as Scarlet."

"So?" demanded Will, eyes narrowing dangerously.

"So I'm not sure who the Hospitallers are, but I think you four are from the infamous Robin Hood gang. Am I right?"

"What of it?" John asked. "Seems a strange time to be having this conversation when we're about to be attacked by a ship full of crazy bastards!"

The captain gave a hard smile. "I've heard Robin Hood and his men are experts with those longbows you all carry. Do you know what's could be useful to a ship like this when pirates are about to attack?" He nodded as understanding came to Robin. "It seems God has blessed me this day, and our would-be killers are going to get a nasty surprise."

Robin felt his anxiety rise again throughout the rest of the afternoon. It seemed to take forever for the pirate ship to come closer, despite it being smaller and, to Robin's eyes at least, sleeker and more manoeuvrable.

"This is just like that time we stood in the Earl of Lancaster's army waiting for the king's soldiers to attack us," Will Scarlet noted dourly.

"At Boroughbridge," John murmured in agreement.

"This is worse," Robin said. "At Boroughbridge we could run away when we were losing."

They stood beside one another at the bulwark feeling like condemned men being taken to the gallows. They had removed their bowstrings from the pouches that protected them from the weather and fitted them to the longbows for the enemy vessel was now almost upon them.

"Maybe a storm will blow up and carry the bastards away from us," John said hopefully. "Have you prayed for that, Tuck?"

"No, but I will now," the friar replied tightly, closing his eyes and murmuring softly before looking beseechingly towards the sky and kissing his pectoral cross.

The captain of the *Rodecog* walked over to them then, mouth a hard, thin line as he looked them up and down before nodding in satisfaction. "I won't lie to you, lads," he said. "This is going to be difficult to survive."

"What will happen?" John asked, curiosity replacing his trepidation, at least for a while.

The captain sat down on a trunk used to store rope and folded his arms across his chest, staring towards the pirate ship as it grew larger with every passing moment. "They'll demand we let them board," he told them. "If we were to do that, they might let us all live."

"That's not so bad then," Friar Tuck said, smiling as though his prayer had actually worked.

"Maybe, but chances are they'd simply force us all over the side, into the sea, to drown." The captain stood up and shook his head bleakly. "They are here to take all our valuables, our weapons, your fine armour, Hospitaller, your horses, my cargo, and even my ship."

"Then we have no choice but to fight," Robin growled, running a hand across the goose feather fletching on one of the arrows tucked into his belt. "To fight, and to win."

The captain nodded slowly. "Indeed, and I hope your aim is as true as the stories people tell about you. You can take some heart from the fact that we've been in this situation before." He swept a hand around at his crew, who were armed with the weapons that Robin had seen stacked around the decks. "I won't lie to you, though. The pirate ship appears to have many men on board and they will fight like demons to take control of the *Rodecog*."

"Then we must send these demons back to hell," Friar Tuck cried, loud enough for everyone on board to hear. "Almighty God, guide our arrows, and our blades, and grant us victory this day!"

His words brought some cheers from the nervous crew, and Sir Simon patted Tuck on the back in appreciation. "Well said, brother," he smiled. "Truly inspiring. You'd have made a fine Hospitaller."

"Are we all ready?" Robin asked. "We all know what we're about? Are we ready to die?"

"No, we're fucking not," Little John replied. "But we're ready to kill every last one of those ugly whoresons sailing towards us."

"That's what I like to hear!" Robin laughed, raising his bow and sighting along the arrow. "Ready to loose," he cried.

"Be prepared to take cover," Stephen warned, gripping his longsword and shield. "Some of the pirates may have missile weapons as well."

"Our ship is higher in the water than theirs at least," Robin noted. "So we have that advantage."

"God grant it is enough," Sir Simon said, and his eyes were blazing with righteous anger. He was very clearly relishing the chance to do something more exciting than potter about in, and administrate, the preceptory in Eagle.

Robin's eyes roved across his companions, seeing Sir Simon's fire reflected in all their expressions, and the fear that had formed in his guts was replaced with a hard resolve, and a desire to teach these pirates a lesson they would never forget.

"Blood of Christ." The *Rodecog*'s captain stood nearby, shading his eyes with his hand as he watched the enemy ship come closer. "If I'm not mistaken, that is Klaus Hopfer."

Robin's companions did not seem to know who Klaus Hopfer was, any more than he did. They looked blankly at the captain, and out at the burly man perched arrogantly on the pirate ship's bulwark, long blonde hair and beard seeming to blaze in the sun.

"Who?" Will Scarlet asked.

"He's one of the most infamous pirates operating in the North Sea," the captain replied dully. "Unless there's another man who looks just like him, that—" he pointed with his sword "—is him."

The crew around them began muttering, throwing one another bleak, frightened looks.

"Fuck him," Will Scarlet spat. "He's just a man. He can be killed just like any other."

"Well, he hasn't been so far," the captain returned in annoyance. "And he's well known to be bloodthirsty, and utterly merciless. Oh, God." He ran a hand across his face, calm demeanour deserting him for the first time since the voyage had begun. "Lord, help us."

"Pull yourself together," the preceptor commanded, raising himself up proudly and displaying his red heater shield with its prominent white cross, showing it around to the captain and his crew. "We have God on our side, and this pirate will soon discover that."

Robin wondered what exactly Klaus Hopfer was supposed to have done to earn such a fearsome reputation. His appearance had unmanned the entire crew, and, as Robin knew from past experience, low morale could prove the undoing of any force, even if they outnumbered their foes which, in this case, they did not.

The situation appeared dire.

"Can you take him?" Little John leaned down and murmured into Robin's ear. "If you could, it would even things up."

The ships were still far apart, and the constant motion of the *Rodecog* would make it almost impossible to accurately shoot a longbow. There was more chance of sending an arrow flying wildly into the sea than striking a target as small as a single man at this distance.

"You'll only get one chance," Will advised. "If you miss, they'll take cover until they're close enough to board and our bows are useless. And if you don't take your shot soon, they'll see we have the bows and hide out of the way."

Robin felt his palms grow slick with sweat and he glanced around at their ship's crew. Most looked petrified, faces drawn, eyes darting between their neighbours and the oncoming ship, many even muttering desperate prayers for help.

"Surrender!" A booming cry floated across on the wind and everyone gazed at the huge, blonde man who rode the pirate ship like some golden god of old. His English was heavily accented, but understandable as he went on. "Surrender your ship, and I will let you live. Fight, and every one of you will die horribly!"

The *Rodecog*'s crew were staring at their captain, practically begging him with their eyes to simply give in, and let Klaus Hopfer have the ship.

"Take your shot, Robin," Friar Tuck said in a low, almost soothing voice. "You can do it. Remember your shot when you won the silver arrow from the sheriff?"

Robin did remember that. There had been an arrow in the bullseye of one of the targets at the sheriff's tournament, and the crowd thought the man who'd landed it there would be the winner of the valuable silver arrow. But Robin had stepped up and, miraculously, shot his arrow directly through the shaft of the one in the bullseye, taking the enormously valuable prize and giving rise to a multitude of songs and stories about his legendary archery skills.

That had been a one-off. A fluke. And that target had been completely stationary, as had Robin. Here, his friends expected him to hit a man on a moving ship, from a moving ship, at this distance? It was simply not possible.

"Do it now," Will urged. "Before you lose the chance. None of us can make the shot, you're the only one, Robin."

Time was fast running out.

Wiping the perspiration from his palms, Robin lifted his bow, took a deep breath, held it in, and drew back the arrow until he felt the string reach its very limit. He aimed at the great blonde man sailing so brazenly towards them, silently begged God to guide his missile, and then let fly.

There was a snap as the bowstring became slack, and the arrow with its white feathers tore through the air. Time seemed to slow to an almost complete stop for Robin as he watched the arrow, and then its heavy iron point smashed into the cheek of Klaus Hopfer and the pirate captain was thrown backwards from the bulwark in a spray of blood.

A huge cheer erupted from the *Rodecog*, as wails of disbelief and anguish came from the enemy vessel, and the pirates either scattered for cover or ran to their fallen leader, as though they might help put his destroyed head back together.

The pirate ship was close enough now that Robin could make out the eyes of the men on board as he calmly nocked another arrow to his longbow. He could see them bare their teeth in rage, some showing feral grins as they imagined the plunder that was soon to be theirs, and he could see how they wielded their swords expertly. He could also see that the majority of them wore only leather gambesons rather than more substantial armour, and he sighted along his arrow again, this time at a huge, barrel-chested man standing at the forefront of the pirates as the ships came close together.

"Ready, lads," Robin called, voice surprisingly level. And then he let fly again, with a cry of, "Loose!" He saw one of the pirates collapse with an arrow protruding from his guts, and hesitated only for long enough to see John's arrow take another man in the shoulder. Tuck's shot skidded off a pirate's helmet, and Will's missed its intended target but struck another of the massing pirates in the chest.

"Well done, men!" the preceptor cheered, as Robin and his friends quickly nocked more arrows, sighted, and sent another deadly volley across the water. The ships were now so close together that each missile could hardly fail to find a home in an enemy, killing or severely injuring them, and Robin let out a great war cry as he grasped a fourth arrow.

There was a massive thump then, as the two vessels slammed into one another, and Robin watched in horrified fascination as ropes flew up into the air, iron grappling hooks on each end that thudded down on the *Rodecog*'s deck and were drawn tight against the bulwark.

"Prepare to be boarded!" the captain bellowed, legs spread wide as he held up his sword and beckoned towards the men who wanted to steal his ship and his life from him.

"One more!" Will Scarlet cried, planting his foot on the bulwark and straining at his bow before loosing another arrow into the neck of a pirate, sending the man screaming back in terror, blood pumping from the gaping wound the missile had carved in his flesh. John and Tuck performed

131

similar, lethal feats, but the time for long-range weapons was over.

"Draw your swords," Sir Simon roared, raising his shield and parrying the point of a sword that was intended to skewer Robin in the side. "The bastards are on board!"

Longbows were discarded and the four friends from Wakefield drew their swords, breath coming fast, eyes flickering all around as they tried to take in everything that was happening. Men were falling over, sliding on the damp wooden deck or tripping over ropes, trunks, and other men, but the preceptor and Stephen led by example, expertly using their shields to defend themselves and others, while hacking and thrusting with their blades at any who came too close.

Robin cried out as he saw the glint of steel in his peripheral vision and lifted his sword just in time to bat aside a pirate's weapon. With his left hand he grabbed the attacker, his massively overdeveloped archer's muscles straining as he flung the pirate into the bulwark. The man's head struck the solid wood and his mouth sagged open, but he never had a chance to take another breath as Little John's sword pierced his gambeson and took him in the heart.

Momentary panic filled Robin as he suddenly remembered that there was nowhere to run from this maelstrom of death and dying – they were trapped there in the middle of the sea, perhaps hundreds of miles from firm, safe, grass, and…He saw Friar Tuck fall, his sword smashed down by the blade of an enormous pirate, and instinct took over once more. Launching himself across the deck, Robin's sword pierced the huge enemy's bicep, tearing it wide open. There was a tortured cry as the pirate realised what had happened, but then Tuck, still on his knees, lifted the man's ankles and tipped him right over the bulwark to fall, screaming, into the sea between the two ships.

Something struck Robin hard in the side of the head then and he lurched sideways, stars exploding in his vision as he felt his legs giving way. He desperately tried to stay upright, to lift his sword defensively as someone struck him again and then he was falling, and suddenly it was no longer sunny, and he was plunged into cold darkness.

* * *

Fear filled Robin when he opened his eyes and everything remained black. Memories of the ferocious, bloody battle flooded his mind, and he realised he was dead. He wondered if his friends had survived and felt great sorrow that he would no longer be with them as they continued their quest for King John's lost treasure.

He noticed tiny pinpricks of light sparkling overhead, and the sounds of creaking ropes and wood reached his foggy brain, mingling with speech that slowly became intelligible.

Groaning, he tried to sit upright, abandoning the idea immediately and slumping down once more as a wave of pain and weakness washed over him.

"You're awake! Praise be to God!"

"Tuck?" Robin tried to open his eyes again but even the meagre light from the distant stars seemed too much for him to take and he screwed them shut once more. "What happened? Did we win?"

"Aye, we won," the friar confirmed, but he did not sound jubilant.

"The others? Will? John?"

"They made it through unscathed. Stephen has a wound on his right arm where a pirate's sword sliced through his leather bracer, and Sir Simon damaged his shoulder, but they'll survive. Here, do you want some water?"

Robin grunted and felt a skin being placed against his lips and slowly upended. He sucked the water down, tiny sips at first, but then a final long pull before Tuck snatched it away, admonishing him.

"You don't want to be sick. You took a nasty blow to the head."

"More than one, I think."

"Could be," Tuck admitted. "I only saw the one that put you down and out of the fight. Luckily Will was there to deal with the skinny bastard before he could finish you off, and the battle didn't last much longer after that." The friar heaved a long, heavy sigh and Robin knew he was wondering why men did such brutal things to one another.

"What's happening now, Tuck?"

"The pirates gave up," said a second voice, and Robin recognised it as the captain of the *Rodecog*. "They realised they were beaten and scrambled back to their own ship before it was too late. They've gone, and I doubt they'll be back any time soon. You and your friends gave us the advantage we needed."

Robin opened his eyes again and was relieved to discover he felt rather better. He saw Sir Simon standing over him, smiling almost paternally, as though he was proud of Robin and his friends. "Well done," the knight said. "Taking out their leader was quite the feat."

"It's true," the captain confirmed, as Robin was helped to sit up by Friar Tuck. "Killing that bastard Klaus Hopfer gave us the advantage. What a shot! I still can't believe you made it! Truly, God was guiding your hand. A miracle!" He shook his head in astonishment, laughing at the audacity of anyone even attempting such a shot with longbow from a ship. "On top of that," he went on, "we have forty crew on the *Rodecog*, and there must have been close to fifty on the pirate vessel. The battle would have turned out differently if you and your friends hadn't evened things up before the dirty whoresons even had a chance to board us!" He slapped his thigh and cackled nastily, staring out into the darkness as he relived his favourite moments of the battle. "Those longbows of yours, and your accuracy with them, completely destroyed their morale and gave us a real advantage."

"Glad we could help," Robin murmured and even managed a smile. "Where are John and Will? I thought you said they'd come through the fighting safely, Tuck."

"So they did," the friar nodded. "They're below decks with Stephen, making sure the horses are all right. Poor beasts must have been terrified trapped down there with no place to run while the fight raged above them."

"I know how they felt," Robin admitted with a shudder. "I'm glad I can now say I've fought in, and won, a battle at sea, but I never want to go through it again. It's bad enough nearly being hacked to pieces on dry land, without adding the motion of a ship to the experience."

"Well, Robin," the captain said with a bow and a broad grin. "You have my thanks for saving the *Rodecog*. You all do, and if you ever change your mind and decide you would like to defend my ship on every journey, I'll pay you handsomely."

"No thanks," Robin replied and his companions gave similar, if more crude, replies.

"Ha! Well, help yourselves to my beer, friends. We should be in Bruges soon enough!"

CHAPTER FOURTEEN

The *Rodecog* arrived in Flanders the next day, after all six companions had enjoyed a good night's rest. Even the swaying, rocking motion of the ship could not keep them awake after their exertions during the battle, and they were all more used to being at sea by then. The beer that the overjoyed captain had plied them with in thanks for their saving his ship helped too, although it did not make Robin feel particularly fresh when he disembarked and was reunited with his horse.

"We should find an alehouse," Little John suggested, and Tuck agreed, rubbing his tonsured head and squinting irritably up at the summer sun as though it had personally forced cup after cup of beer down his gullet.

"Alehouse?" The preceptor shook his head, one eyebrow raised in disapproval. "We're on foreign soil now, lads. We need our wits about us."

"But I don't have my wits about me," John protested. "I feel like shit."

"Hangovers soon wear off, I find," Sir Simon returned primly, before he shook his head, smiled, and suggested they all ask the *Rodecog*'s captain for another cup of his beer before they set off along the road to Giselbrecht van Zottegem's castle in Laarne.

So, a short time later, suitably fed and 'watered', and with some of their English coins changed for local currency, the six men took to their horses and set off along the road, leaving the bustling port of Bruges, with its melting pot of different languages, peoples, and cultures, behind.

It was hot – hotter than it had been in England during the recent drought – but there had been plenty of rain recently and the ground was lush and green while the rivers and streams they passed, although not swollen, were far from dried out. Robin drank in the sights as they rode, feeling his sense of adventure grow.

"Are you enjoying the ride?"

Robin turned, startled from his reverie by Sir Simon. He returned the Hospitaller's smile, nodding emphatically. "I am. As a boy I'd never hoped, or even thought, to see any lands outside England. It's humbling to realise just how big the world is, and how…" He trailed off, shaking his head. "Beautiful it is."

"Indeed," Sir Simon agreed. "And so few people get to experience it. Travelling is simply not something most folk do. The lower classes are expected to work hard for their lord, and that doesn't include time to go riding or sailing off across the world."

"Aye, but even the nobles rarely journey beyond their own lands," Robin said. "I doubt someone like our sheriff, Sir Henry de Faucumberg, has come here to Flanders."

"Probably not, unless it was part of an army or some diplomatic delegation. Make the most of it, my young friend, for you might never get the chance to visit these lands again!"

Robin found himself captivated by what he saw there in the lands of the Flemish, and he imagined the long-dead knight, Giselbrecht van Zottegem, making this same journey from Bruges to his castle in Laarne. Some of the trees and bushes were like those Robin knew from home, with oak, silver birch, and blackthorn being sighted regularly, but there were others that he had never seen before, which surprised him. There were also birds that he was unfamiliar with, including an odd brown and white one with dark speckles and orange eyes. Sir Simon told him it was called a hazelhen when Robin asked, but he didn't ask many more questions like that because he did not want to display his ignorance too much. He was content to take it all in, basking in the warmth, and the unfamiliar but very pleasant surroundings.

The settlements they passed through were also similar but slightly different to those the travellers were used to seeing in England. The houses, while mostly constructed from wattle and daub and having thatched roofs, were different in shape and style so that John murmured something about feeling as though he'd ridden into a different world completely. The incomprehensible speech of the Flemish only made that suggestion seem more real to Robin.

They were not troubled in any way – six powerfully built men, armed and armoured, riding large horses, were never to be taken lightly. The English knew it, the Scots knew it, and, clearly, so did the Flemish. Force of arms was a universal language, and the fact that Sir Simon and Stephen wore the livery and devices of the well-known Hospitallers meant the travellers were viewed with even more respect and, no doubt, fear as they rode through the towns and villages on the way to Laarne.

They stopped for a rest and a meal at a little village with a church dedicated to 'Sint-Joris', which Tuck said was simply Flemish for Saint George. The priest met them with understandable trepidation, but, luckily for the expedition, Sir Simon was able to converse quite well in the clergyman's own tongue.

"Just as well we brought him along," Little John murmured to Robin and Will as they stood outside the church watching the preceptor and Tuck meet with the priest.

"Aye, he seems to know what he's doing," Will agreed. "Must be widely travelled."

"Oh, he is that," Stephen agreed. "He's been all over Europe and the Holy Land. He's a very clever man, picks up things like languages very quickly." There was an obvious note of pride in the sergeant's voice and Robin wondered how Sir Simon measured up to Stephen's previous master, Sir Richard-at-Lee.

"Why has he been stuck away in Eagle then?" Will asked with characteristic bluntness. "Rather than being given a prominent position in a more important preceptory?"

"Politics," Stephen growled. "You know how it is, Will. Same crazy reason why I was ostracised from the Order for so long. Sir Simon's a better man than the likes of that bastard Thomas L'Archer, but because he annoyed someone powerful he's been made to rot in Eagle."

"Well, he's been a Godsend for us," Robin noted, and Stephen almost preened at the praise of his master and friend.

"You say that," Will chuckled, lowering his voice as Tuck and Sir Simon turned away from the priest and began walking back to them. "But we wouldn't be here at all if it wasn't for the Hospitaller!"

"Are you not enjoying yourself?" John demanded.

"Oh, it's fine, just fine. Apart from nearly being murdered by a fucking shipload of pirates."

"There are no pirates here," the preceptor announced, face crinkling as he smiled at them. "The priest will allow us to rest and take some refreshments before we continue our journey." He pointed to the northern side of the church. "There are stables at the back there. If you men will take the horses around and meet Tuck and me inside, I shall converse some more with the priest, see if he knows anything about our quest." With a wink, he turned away and led the friar into the church, following the bent, retreating figure of the priest.

The stables were small but very familiar, being constructed in much the same fashion as English ones, and being outfitted the same way. There was not enough space for all eight horses, but there was an overhanging roof that would allow those that couldn't fit inside to at least stand in the shade to drink from a trough and graze in contentment.

Again, the church was small and, to Robin's inexpert eye, like the ones at home. The priest had a small room at the back which was probably used to store vestments and communion wine usually, but now played host to the six travellers from abroad.

Sir Simon introduced each of them to the man who was old and wizened but whose eyes suggested a keen intelligence undimmed by the passage of decades. He could not, apparently, speak any English and certainly not the rough dialect of North Yorkshire, so the preceptor conversed with him while the others enjoyed cups of wine or water, ate fresh bread, and shared their own salted meat with the priest whose remaining teeth were barely up to the job of chewing it. He did his best though, clearly relishing this unexpected visit from strange travellers.

They did not tarry for long in the little church, finishing the frugal but pleasant meal and enjoying the respite from the afternoon sun before preceptor and priest rose to their feet and headed outside. The others followed and thanked the old man with bows and smiles as he went to each, shaking their hand and blessing them in turn. By the time they were outside and riding along the road once more Robin felt quite buoyed by the short stop.

"He was a nice old fellow, wasn't he?" Little John opined to no one in particular.

"That's what you think," Will said. "If you could speak Flemish, you would have known that he was calling you a stupid big twat."

Robin, and even Sir Simon, burst out laughing at that, the knight's teeth flashing in the sun.

"Ah, lads, you've no idea how much I've missed riding out with a group of soldiers, enjoying one another's company and, aye, the silly banter." He patted his horse's neck and looked around at the rolling fields being worked by serfs in wide-brimmed hats. "This is living, my friends. Not being cooped up in a cold stone hall day after day, surrounded by the old and infirm."

"Like Stephen?" Robin asked, drawing more laughter and a very crude insult from the grizzled sergeant-at-arms.

"Stephen's all right." The preceptor grinned, reminding Robin very much of Sir Richard-at-Lee.

"I'm starting to think I'd have been better off back in England," Stephen grumbled. "It feels like I'm riding around with a troupe of minstrels, or court fools. But enough of this – did the priest tell you anything interesting, Sir Simon?"

A wagon was taking up the road ahead, slowly trundling along, an old woman guiding it while a similarly geriatric ox did its best not to expire before reaching their destination. Sir Simon, at the head of their small column, led the way onto the grass and around the Flemish traveller, the others following in his wake. When they were past the woman, who glared at them warily, the preceptor shook his head.

"Nothing new, no," he admitted. "The priest has been living there in that village for decades, but they have no library – not one with old records at least – and he had not heard any rumours about Giselbrecht van Zottegem."

"Maybe he just didn't want to tell a bunch of Englishmen," John suggested.

"I don't think so," the preceptor said with a firm shake of his head. "He seemed genuine to me. Don't be disheartened though – we're on the trail of a great secret. Why would some rural priest know anything about it?"

"True enough," Tuck agreed. "How much longer until we reach Laarne then, Sir Simon?"

"Now that was information the priest was able to provide. We have thirty miles to go, so we'll arrive there tomorrow."

"And then what?"

Robin could hear the uncertainty in Will Scarlet's voice, and he understood it. Were they to simply turn up at this castle, a rather disparate and motley group, and ask the present occupants if they knew where King John's missing treasure was? That hardly seemed like it would work.

"We shall find out when we get there," Sir Simon pronounced, as cheery and hopeful as they'd been since they set out from Eagle.

Robin and John shared a look, and the bailiff shrugged. This truly was a mad venture, but they'd come all this way and could hardly give up now. At least Flanders seemed to be a hospitable, welcoming country, where travellers were safe.

"The priest in Sint-Joris did give me one piece of advice," Sir Simon spoke up again. "The present incumbent of Laarne Castle is indeed a descendant of Giselbrecht van Zottegem."

"Well, that's good, right?" Robin said. "He might know something about his ancestor."

"Aye," Sir Simon said. "He might. But whether he'll be happy to see us or not is another matter."

"What do you mean?" Robin asked.

"The current owner of Laarne Castle, Gerard van Rasseghem, had close ties to the Knights Templar." The preceptor looked at Robin, earlier cheery expression replaced now with a grim frown. "Considering seized Templar property near Laarne was recently given to the Hospitallers, I fear we might find ourselves as unwelcome visitors when we reach the castle."

"How unwelcome?" Will demanded.

"Who knows?" Sir Simon returned. "But I would suggest we don't let down our guard while we're in and around the castle, and do not tell him we are searching for valuable treasure."

"What do we tell him then?" Will asked, growing visibly irritated.

Sir Simon pursed his lips, thinking hard, and then he gave a slight shrug. "We'll say we're looking for an old book – Hospitaller records. The burial place of an important

142

old knight has been lost to time, and the Grand Master wants us to find this old book because it contains a record of the gravesite."

"And why are we here then?" said John.

"You are mercenaries I hired to protect me on the road to Aachen, where the book was supposedly taken. No other Hospitallers could be spared from their duties, so I brought you along."

"You think this Flemish baron will believe such a story?" Will Scarlet was visibly incredulous.

"Why wouldn't he? Listen, religious quests like this are undertaken all the time, pilgrimages and so on. Don't worry, Scarlet, I know what I'm doing, just let me take the lead."

Will opened his mouth, face turning red, but then he closed it and simply shook his head in disgust. Robin sighed, feeling his friend's trepidation. Their journey here had been eventful, but he'd believed they were on the right track, and things were now progressing smoothly. With the worldly-wise Sir Simon Launcelyn at their helm, conversing in Flemish and guiding them expertly from place to place, they stood at least some chance of discovering the treasure they sought. Or so Robin and his friends had tried to convince themselves.

Now, though, as they rode towards Laarne, six men in a land full of hundreds of thousands of strangers, Robin did not feel quite as safe as he had just a few moments before.

"If this Gerard van Rasseghem hates you Hospitallers, why don't you take off those bright red surcoats, and paint over your shields with green or something?"

Sir Simon and Stephen turned disbelieving stares on Little John, so obviously outraged that Robin feared one or both might even attack his big friend.

"What?" the bailiff asked defensively. "Seems obvious to me. The last thing we want to do is get on the wrong side of some Flemish nobleman in his own bloody castle!"

"Even when the Templars were being tortured, and burned alive at the stake, they did not renounce their faith, or their loyalty to their Order." The preceptor spoke calmly with a visible effort. "I will forgive your words, because you clearly do not understand what it means for one to become a Hospitaller as Stephen and I have done."

John muttered an apology, but Will Scarlet said, "Things didn't turn out too well for the Templars, did it? I don't see what harm it would do to take off your surcoats. You don't have to renounce your Order, just don't make it so obvious what you are."

Robin held his breath, wondering what he should do if a fight broke out between his travelling companions. He understood the preceptor's position, but Will had made a good point, and both were so stubborn that a conflict seemed quite possible.

"I will not lie about who I am," Sir Simon replied at last, face held rigid. "If we took off our surcoats, what would we tell the people at Laarne Castle when they ask who we are? We would have to make up some false backstory for Stephen and I, and that I will not do." He shook his head and his haughty expression softened as he looked from Will to the others. "I'm sorry, lads, but we will simply have to trust Gerard van Rasseghem will behave with honour and offer us the hospitality we deserve."

"Chivalry," Stephen murmured thoughtfully. "That's a big thing here in Flanders, and in the Holy Roman Empire in general."

"Chivalry?" Robin repeated.

"Aye," the sergeant-at-arms nodded. "The knights in these countries take their chivalric code seriously, or at least they're supposed to. Some of them, particularly the younger ones, are a law unto themselves right enough."

"Put a weapon in the hand of any rich young noble arsehole and you're bound to get trouble," Will grunted.

"Indeed," Stephen conceded. "But that's why the powers-that-be push this idea of chivalry. It's a way to make knights behave with honour and respect, protecting the weak rather than taking advantage of them."

"And you're hoping the knight who resides at Laarne Castle will treat us well because it's his duty," Robin said. "Rather than turning us away, or worse, because his Templar friends were destroyed, their holdings given over to your Hospitallers."

"That's what we must pray for," Sir Simon said.

"Then that is what we shall do," Tuck stated loudly, and as they continued on their way towards Laarne he began to recite the *Pater Noster*, exhorting with his eyes the others to join in.

CHAPTER FIFTEEN

They arrived in Laarne early that morning, after spending a comfortable enough night camping in a wooded area just a few miles away from the castle. Their arrival in the area was noted – how could it not be? – and riders came to meet them on the road, demanding to know their business. Sir Simon had spoken with the soldiers confidently and respectfully and they'd been granted an escort to the castle. Robin watched the men escorting them, trying to gauge their friendliness towards the foreigners, or, perhaps, hostility. He could see no real emotion reflected in the Flemish soldiers' faces however – they sat atop their horses, stern faced and seemingly indifferent to Robin and his companions. Their weapons and armour were polished to perfection, their horses immaculately groomed, and the overall impression was one of professionalism. They were something of a contrast to Robin, John, Will, and Friar Tuck, who all wore various bits of gear and clothing gathered over the years, with no uniformity between their own outfits never mind with one another. Still, Robin felt sure he and his friends could take the Flemish group if it came to a fight, especially with the proud Hospitallers alongside them.

It would not come to a fight though, he hoped. Why would it? If it did there would be many more soldiers in the castle to deal with, and the small party of Englishmen would have no chance.

He forced his mind away from such thoughts and tried to enjoy the ride towards Laarne Castle, looking at the scenery, and at the farm workers who watched them pass. It was not long before their destination came into view, the road towards it wide but flanked on both sides with well-tended trees and bushes.

Little John whistled in appreciation, for it was a hugely impressive building, this iteration having been built only thirty-five years or so before. There were round towers with pointed roofs, and a great square keep, and the whole castle of pale grey stone stood out against the blue sky and greenery around it, creating a powerful impression of strength. As the company of riders drew nearer, Robin realised there was a moat around the castle, its still waters glittering in the sunshine, quite beautiful yet somehow menacing at the same time.

More soldiers guarded the gates and the entrance at the far end of the moat, watching grimly as the horses thumped across the bridge that led them into the castle courtyard.

Will appeared visibly uncomfortable as they were led in and the gates were closed behind them. Robin and the others did their best to mask their feelings but it was difficult, for Laarne Castle was an imposing place, and the hard eyes of the Flemish soldiers did not appear welcoming at all.

The leader of the riders who'd brought them there spoke briefly with Sir Richard and he translated for the rest of the group.

"We've to wait here. The steward will fetch us when he's ready."

"How long will that be?" Will asked sourly, eyes darting around at the high stone walls and towers that effectively penned them in like cattle.

"I've no idea," the preceptor admitted as stableboys appeared and took their horses away to be taken care of. "I suppose we'll find out."

Thankfully, they were not made to wait for very long, as a stooped old steward appeared some time later and bade the travellers follow him. They'd not been offered refreshments or any other courtesies, but Robin had no idea what the usual etiquette was for these situations in Flanders. Was it a slight, or was it entirely normal behaviour? He had no idea, and Sir Simon's cool demeanour gave no hint of how he was feeling.

They were taken along a high-ceilinged corridor with exquisite paintings and led into an airy chamber with windows that showed more of the countryside surrounding the castle. Robin took it all in, hugely impressed, and wondered what it would be like to live in such a place, guards and servants at one's beck and call. He smiled, feeling only a very little jealousy as he thought of Matilda and his two boys, knowing he would rather have them than any grand castle. A twinge of homesickness made him swallow and he turned his gaze inwards, towards a heavy oak table that sat before an enormous, but unlit, fireplace, and the man seated there.

Gerard van Rasseghem was not a young man, perhaps in his early sixties, and he did not have the look of a warrior despite coming from the line of a man who'd been a renowned mercenary. The Lord of Laarne appeared to be of average height, but almost painfully thin, with hollow cheeks and protruding, blue eyes. Those eyes held an intelligence, even cunning, that immediately put Robin on his guard. Van Rasseghem might not be physically imposing, but the visitors would need to be careful what they said around him.

"Welcome," he said then, in accented but clear English. Robin was glad that they would not need to stand, mute and ignorant, while the nobleman and Sir Simon conversed in Flemish. That removed at least a little of the anxiety the big archer was feeling.

"Thank you, my lord," the preceptor said, once more assuming command of the small group automatically. "We thank you for your hospitality in this—" he looked up and all around, gesturing expansively with his hand and smiling "—quite incredible castle of yours."

The Flemish nobleman's mouth did twitch and his head tilted back which Robin took as a good sign. He was pleased by the Hospitaller's flattery, although not enough to break into an actual smile.

"It is a man's duty to offer travellers hospitality," Van Rasseghem said. "Besides, it is always interesting to hear news from England, which I assume you will share with us over a meal?"

"Of course, lord," replied Sir Simon happily. Clearly he was pleased with how things were going, but Robin had spent most of his life mistrusting noblemen, and he was not quite ready to trust the Flemish baron.

"That is good," Van Rasseghem said, idly fingering some sheets of parchment that were on the desk before him. "But before that, why don't you tell me why you are here in Flanders. I trust you did not come to my castle specifically?"

Sir Simon hesitated and cast Robin an uncertain glance before his smile returned and he spoke to their host again. "We are on our way to Aachen," he said. "To the Hospitaller commandery there."

"I see," murmured Van Rasseghem, evidently a master of masking his emotions as so many politicians were. His face betrayed no hint of whether he disliked the Hospitallers or was indifferent to them.

"In truth," the preceptor forged on, visibly drawing himself up straighter, "we are following in the footsteps of a descendant of yours."

Now the Lord of Laarne did show a real interest, thick grey eyebrows coming together in a frown. "Really? Who?"

"Giselbrecht van Zottegem."

"My great-grandfather." Van Rasseghem stood up, practically unfolding his long, slender limbs from the chair and walking across to gaze out of the windows, his back to them. "Why are you interested in him?"

Robin wished he could see the man's face and guessed he was purposely hiding it so his emotions could not be read.

"We discovered that your great-grandfather had been a mercenary hired by our own King John," said the preceptor.

"It was recorded in old records. Giselbrecht van Zottegem was part of the king's own personal guard."

"This is correct," the Flemish noble confirmed, turning to look at the Hospitaller, chin held up, hands clasped before him. "What of it?"

He really does speak superb English, Robin thought, and wondered again if being so honest with the man was truly in their best interests.

Sir Richard may have felt the same doubts, but it was too late to do much about it now. "We uncovered some evidence that your great-grandfather may have travelled with a group of Hospitallers who were in possession of an old book. They came across the sea from England, perhaps to here, or, as we believe more likely, to the commandery in Aachen."

Robin was glad Van Rasseghem did not have his back to them now, for he saw curiosity plainly written on the older man's face.

"Really?" the nobleman asked, walking stiffly back to his desk and seating himself once more. "What is so important about this book?"

"One of our most respected knights, Sir Richard Thornton, died sometime around the year 1200. The problem is, no one now knows where he was buried. He did great things for our Order, and the new Grand Master would like to find his grave, and make sure Sir Richard's place in history is properly memorialised." The preceptor paused, head tilted, palms up as he continued. "We believe the book your great-grandfather's group was carrying contains a record of Sir Richard's burial site."

"Well, this is fascinating," the baron said. "But why would my great-grandfather, and a party of Hospitallers, be protecting a simple book?"

"Oh, they were not protecting the book, my lord. The Hospitallers were from Aachen, it just so happened that they were carrying the book with them when they returned to the commandery after serving in England."

"Then why did you not ride straight to Aachen? Why stop here at all?"

"Laarne is on the way to Aachen," Sir Simon said simply. "I'd hoped you might let me search your family library to see if there's any record of your great-grandfather coming here with the book."

"I assume you must have some strong evidence of all this, or you would not have travelled all this way with your…" He paused and cast a critical eye over Robin and his friends. "Companions," he finished in a practised, neutral tone.

Robin wondered then just how they appeared to this Flemish baron who was obviously hugely wealthy and enjoyed a social status far above any of the travellers. He glanced at Will and John, and down at himself, and was relieved that they all wore good quality clothes in good repair. They may not be noble knights living their lives by a code of chivalric honour, but they were no paupers either. Only Tuck wore simple, cheap clothing, and that was what a wandering friar was supposed to wear.

"We did not find a great deal of evidence, I must admit," Sir Simon was saying candidly to their host. "Some hearsay, some hints here and there, and some records hidden away and probably lost in the archives for over a hundred years. But it was enough for my Grand Master to send me here, searching for the truth. Our Order really would like to find the burial site of Sir Richard Thornton."

"I see. Well, you must tell me more then." Before the Hospitaller could answer, Gerard van Rasseghem raised his hand, silencing him. "No, I would speak properly with you on this matter. First, though, I must do my duty as a host." He clapped his hands and his steward appeared through the door a moment later, suggesting the man had been standing outside the whole time, waiting to be summoned. "Take our guests to clean off the dust from the road. They will join us for dinner this evening."

Will, Tuck, and John all grinned at one another, pleased at the thought of dining in the grand castle rather than chewing salted meat on the road again. They filed out of the room, all six following the steward who, unlike his master, could walk very fast. As they left, Robin saw van Rasseghem watching with interest, eyes hard, jaw set firmly. It did not seem to be the expression of a gracious host – to Robin it seemed as if they were being sized up, almost like a wolf stalking prey.

He suppressed a shudder and went out into the corridor behind his friends, doing his best to convince himself he was imagining things.

* * *

They did not just dine with Gerard van Rasseghem and his wife and retainers that evening, they were also given quarters to spend the night in, and were even taken hunting the next morning with the Flemish nobleman and some of his staff.

Robin decided that he was mistaken in thinking their host was not quite as friendly as he seemed, for he was jovial and open and seemed to genuinely enjoy the company of the English visitors. He mainly conversed with Sir Simon, who did well to explain the reason for their quest without playing up the possibilities of what they might find at the end of it, but the baron did not ignore the other, lower socially ranked members of the group.

"We were worried you might not be very welcoming," Will said to him with characteristic bluntness as they moved through the undergrowth on foot, stalking deer. "We heard you didn't like Hospitallers."

Robin rolled his eyes at John, irritated by Will's admission. Why cast a shadow when things were going so well? But Scarlet wanted an answer, and, as usual, he would damn well seek it out.

The Lord of Laarne turned hawkish eyes on Will, and Robin could see in them a man just as stubborn of character as his friend. "Why do you say that?" he asked coolly.

"You're said to be good friends with some Templars," Scarlet replied with a shrug. "You didn't like what happened to them, and you didn't like the Hospitallers being given the Templar properties when they were disbanded."

"'Disbanded'," van Rasseghem repeated in a disgusted tone. "Destroyed, more like." He spat on the foliage beside him, shaking his head as he moved after the two soldiers he'd chosen to take point on the hunt that day. "You were misinformed. It is true that I do not like what happened to the Templars, for they were honourable men, and Christendom is worse off without them. But I do not blame the Hospitallers for it. It was hardly Sir Simon's fault what happened to them, or his sergeant-at-arms there."

Stephen gave a nod when the Flemish noble glanced back at him. "True," he grunted. "I had Templar friends. It was evil what happened to them."

Gerard van Rasseghem turned back again, doing his best to tread as silently as the soldiers who were leading them deeper into the woods. "I am not a great admirer of the Hospitallers," he said to Will. "For I believe they might have done more to support their fellow knights. But I would not turn away your party simply because of that. What kind of man would that make me? We live by a code of chivalry here in Flanders, and I take it very seriously."

"Thank you, my lord," said Robin respectfully, hoping to smooth over any ill-feeling Will's unnecessarily direct question might have caused. "We greatly appreciate your kindness, and your hospitality."

That seemed enough to mollify van Rasseghem, although Robin could hardly tell if the man had been annoyed or not. He was a hard one to read, and the cultural and language differences did not help.

They enjoyed the hunt though, and found themselves back at Laarne Castle by mid-afternoon with plenty of game, and the praise of the Flemish nobleman who declared himself greatly impressed by his guests, in particular the skill Robin, Will, and John displayed with their longbows.

That evening they were guests at the baron's table once more, being served exquisite foods, some of which Robin had never even seen before. Some he enjoyed immensely, others he could not bear to even put in his mouth and, with grim fascination, watched Sir Simon and Tuck quickly devour them.

"I've had my steward go through the old records," van Rasseghem informed them when they'd finished eating and were enjoying cups of very fine Flemish beer. "There is nothing there, I am afraid, about my great-grandfather travelling with Hospitallers, or escorting any book to Aachen." He tilted his head and shrugged apologetically. "I am sorry. I would have liked to discover more for you, and perhaps find out where this trail would take you. But there is nothing."

Sir Simon looked annoyed for he'd asked to check the records himself rather than some lackey of the baron's doing it, but he masked it well and Robin shared his disappointment. The Hospitaller had hoped to find a diary or letters in Laarne Castle that recorded what the old mercenary had been carrying to Aachen. Some clue as to what they were chasing, and where it had ultimately ended up.

"Don't be downcast," Tuck murmured. The friar was sitting on his left side and noticed how despondent Robin looked. "We're no worse off than before we came here, and far better fed!"

Robin felt his spirits rise. "You're right," he admitted. "This is all just part of the adventure."

CHAPTER SIXTEEN

The next morning was not as sunny as it had been up until then. There was a fine smirr of rain that hung across the land like a shroud, although it was still warmer than Robin was used to after living in Scotland for so long.

"I am sorry I could not be of more help," Gerard van Rasseghem told them as they made ready to continue their journey to Aachen. "I trust you will return here on your way home, and let me know the result of your quest. It is simply a book of records you are searching for, yes?"

"Yes, my lord," Sir Simon said, and Robin was a little surprised at the ease of the untruths the knight had told in Laarne. It seemed noblemen could be just as good at lying as those on the lower rungs of the social ladder, although he knew he should not be shocked by that. He had dealt with enough rich men over the years to see how duplicitous they could be. That thought gave him pause, and he examined van Rasseghem's hollow face, wondering if perhaps the Flemish lord was also hiding something.

Farewells were said and the six friends rode off, heading along the tree-lined avenue that led towards the main road to the southeast. They were all smiling and refreshed after their time at Laarne, but, as they neared the main road, Friar Tuck suddenly cried out, his pack coming loose and falling onto the road.

"You can't have tied it on properly, you oaf," Will called, as Tuck reined in his mount and nudged it back towards the pack and its spilled contents.

"Indeed," the friar agreed sheepishly. "You all ride on. I'll gather this lot and catch up with you."

"Are you sure?" Robin asked. "I'll stay and help if you like."

Tuck waved a hand and dismounted with a heavy thump. "No, it'll only take a moment. You carry on."

155

The other five looked at one another and then, fearing no danger since they were still in Gerard van Rasseghem's lands, they rode on, following the track until they reached the main road, turning left and continuing at a steady pace.

After a time, Robin glanced over his shoulder to see four other riders turning into the road that led to Laarne Castle and an uneasy feeling came over him. "Slow down," he called to the others. "Let's wait for Tuck." As he spoke, anxiety building, the friar suddenly appeared, cantering towards them, safe and well, and Robin grinned in relief.

"You tied your pack on properly this time, you daft old goat?" Will chuckled as their friend rode up alongside them and the whole group began to move again, trotting eastwards, to Aachen.

"I did," the friar assured them. "But did you see those four horsemen that just rode up to the castle there?"

Only Robin had been looking back, and he nodded. "I did. What about them?"

"Well, as they passed me, one of them said, 'God grant you good day, brother'."

"So what?" said John.

"He spoke in English. And, by his accent, I'd say he hailed from Derby, or somewhere nearby."

"What a strange coincidence," Sir Simon said, smiling. "To come all this way across the sea, and meet men from close to our own homes!"

Robin thought more about it as they continued along the road, the earlier sense of unease growing within him again.

"What's up?" Little John asked, apparently reading his thoughts. "You look concerned."

"Well, don't you think it's strange that four other English travellers are going to Laarne Castle at the same time as we were there? That doesn't strike you as bizarre?"

John thought about it, and looked at their other companions. "I suppose so," the bailiff admitted. "What do you think it means?"

Robin shook his head, irritated for he was really not sure why the appearance of the other riders had put him on edge.

"How do you know they were all Englishmen?" Will asked. "Tuck said only one of them spoke. The others could just be men of Flanders, escorting the foreigner to their lord."

There was not much more to say on the matter, so they proceeded mainly in silence, huddled into their cloaks as it continued to drizzle for the rest of the morning. The land remained mostly flat, and Robin found himself growing a little tired of the lack of variation in the scenery. Fields being worked by serfs of all ages including very young children, small settlements, and flora and fauna that now, after just a few days in Flanders, did not seem so exotic and interesting any more.

A thought struck him as they rode across a narrow bridge that led towards another village of wattle and daub houses. "What if someone else is looking for King John's treasure?" he asked out loud.

"What?" Will demanded. "You mean that, after over a century two separate groups somehow stumble across the same evidence that leads them to Flanders at the same time? Come on, Robin, how likely is that?"

"About as likely as Tuck meeting other Englishmen riding into Laarne Castle just as we were leaving," Robin returned.

"Anything is possible," the friar said. "Although I highly doubt anyone could have followed the same trail as we did, Robin. It was sheer luck, or divine intervention perhaps, that brought us here."

"You didn't recognise any of the riders?" Robin asked, a kernel of doubt growing within him.

"No," Tuck said.

"Did you?" Will asked Robin. "No? Well then, stop worrying so much."

Sir Simon voiced his agreement with Will Scarlet, but then added a second concern of his own – one which mirrored Robin's earlier thoughts. "We were not granted access to van Rasseghem's library," he noted. "I do wonder if that steward could have found something and not disclosed it to us."

"So van Rasseghem might send men of his own to Aachen," said Stephen gloomily.

"Oh, come on!" Little John chuckled in disbelief. "Now you're saying we don't just have one other group hunting the same thing as us, but two? It's ludicrous. This treasure has been missing for a hundred years, and chances are it's all sunk beneath the sand back in England. There's no way a load of people have just suddenly decided to start looking for it here in Flanders after all this time."

It did seem unbelievable Robin had to admit. "Fair enough," he said, smiling at his huge friend. "But let's speed up a little, eh? Just in case there are other people heading to Aachen on the same quest as us. Won't do any harm, and we'll be home quicker."

The others thought about it and eventually all agreed with his suggestion.

"How far is Aachen then?" Will asked as they urged their horses to a canter.

"Over a hundred miles," the preceptor called back. "Four days riding. The Lord of Laarne gave me specific directions so we'll avoid the larger towns and cities like Brussels. I think we would only draw unwanted attention to us in those places. Not all knights follow the chivalric code, and there's more chance of us running into bandits near the more densely populated areas."

"Will that take longer than following the busier roads?" Robin wondered.

"A little longer, aye," Sir Simon conceded. "But I think it will be safer."

Robin accepted that without comment, but the idea of van Rasseghem sending them on a longer route than necessary seemed strange. They could be overtaken, should someone else leave from Laarne at the same time and take the faster route...

He pushed aside such bleak thoughts and did his best to enjoy the ride now that he was growing more used to the physical side of it. His body did not ache as much as it had for the first few days of the journey, and he felt like the horse was responding to his guidance even better than it ever had in the whole time he'd owned it.

The miles passed quickly, and the rain was left behind as it grew sunny once more and again Robin thought about the four riders – Englishmen, he was sure – that had greeted Tuck at Laarne. Who were they? What was their purpose at the castle? Tuck had not recognised the men, true, but there was something about them that set Robin on edge, something that had raised his hackles when he saw them.

Ah well, there was no point in contemplating it further he thought, whistling a hymn to the Magdalene that the others recognised and joined in with. They would be in Aachen in a few short days, and, God willing, they would find what they'd travelled all that way to retrieve: King John's treasure, and the means to win a pardon for Robin.

* * *

The four riders at Laarne were met by the baron's guards and escorted to meet Gerard van Rasseghem, just as Robin and his companions had been a couple of days before.

"More travellers from England?" van Rasseghem asked his steward, who had brought the four men to his audience chamber right away, for he was greatly interested in hearing their story.

"Yes, lord," the steward said.

"It does seem too much of a coincidence," van Rasseghem murmured thoughtfully.

They were standing outside the audience chamber, listening to hear if the newcomers gave anything away when they thought they were alone. Thus far, not a word had passed between them, however.

"What do you think is going on, my lord?" the steward asked. "These four claim to simply be passing through. They did not mention your great-grandfather to me when I asked the reason for their being here."

The baron shook his head and turned to look out the window over his estate. "First the Hospitaller and his gang of ruffians, now these four who look even more disreputable. Do they really think I will just give them all the information they demand, so they can ride to Aachen and find some valuable item belonging to my great-grandfather?"

"They do not know we found what we did in the castle archives, lord," the steward said, lip curling in an unpleasant smile. "The Hospitaller and his lot will travel to Aachen with no idea you have sent men with orders to get there before them."

"Indeed." Van Rasseghem smiled grimly. "Still, although the castle library gave us some idea of what my great-grandfather was doing a century ago, I would dearly like to know exactly what he was escorting to Aachen. Damn it, why was that not recorded? I simply do not believe it was a book and nothing more, that was a bold-faced lie."

The steward shook his head, unable to answer his lord. Whatever had been taken to Aachen all those years ago must have been incredibly valuable, or at least important, to have been kept a secret even within Giselbrecht van Zottegem's own familial records that were stored safely in his castle.

"It has to be something connected with England," van Rasseghem muttered. His curiosity had been piqued by the mystery, and he had no intention of allowing foreign rabble to journey through his emperor's lands and steal a treasure that should rightfully belong to the Lord of Laarne. At that very moment his wife, Lady Elisabeth, was in the castle library, searching the records for any more information that might shed light on the mystery.

"Come," said the baron, beckoning to his steward. "We shall speak with these new Englishmen, and see if we can discover any more about the matter."

Van Rasseghem led the way, reminding himself that, whoever these men were, they were probably not fools, and more than likely dangerous warriors, just as the previous six he'd entertained clearly were.

"Gentlemen." He greeted the English travellers who bowed deeply to him as he appeared and took his customary seat at the great table before the fireplace. "Welcome to Laarne Castle. What brings you to my lands?"

"We come bearing news, my lord." The man who spoke was the smallest of the four, with narrow shoulders and intelligent, green eyes. He was the leader, thought the Flemish baron, and the other three his brutish guards, sent to protect him on his journey to Flanders.

"News?"

"Yes, lord," the man replied, visibly relieved that van Rasseghem spoke fluent English. "We have heard that a wolf's head – an outlaw – called Robin Hood has journeyed here to Flanders, seeking some valuable artifacts. He is travelling with his friends, and two Hospitallers of ill-repute."

"Indeed?"

"Yes, my lord. We would like to find this man, Hood. Have you heard of him?"

Gerard van Rasseghem burst out laughing at that, and his steward shared his mirth, visibly irritating the Englishman.

"Forgive me," the baron said. "You ask if I have heard of Robin Hood. I have not only heard of him, but he has just this morning left this very castle."

The newcomer started, and shared a look of dismay with his three comrades. "He's been here?"

"He has. You must have just missed him! Did you not pass him on the road?"

"The only man we saw, other than your own guards, was a heavyset friar, my lord."

"That is one of Robin Hood's companions," van Rasseghem replied, thoroughly enjoying himself. Life had not been this interesting for a long while! "Friar Tuck. How you missed the rest of them I do not know."

"Damn it," the visitor cursed, fists clenching spasmodically. He shook his head, and his eyes glazed over as he began muttering to himself as though he were alone in the audience chamber.

"Sir!" Van Rasseghem barked, interrupting the man's inaudible monologue. "You have not come all this way for nothing, I assume. What is this fabulous thing Robin Hood and, I assume, you, are hunting? Spit it out, man. I think you owe me answers in return for my hospitality. By Christ, you have not even given me your name yet."

The man accepted the rebuke calmly although the harassed look did not fade from his youthful features as he gave another bow to the Flemish nobleman. "My apologies, lord. We're searching for the lost treasure of King John, England's ruler before his passing in 1216. I'm sure you'll have heard of him. You may not, on the other hand, have heard of me, yet." He flashed a self-deprecating smile. "My name is Matthew," he finished. "Matthew Coterel."

CHAPTER SEVENTEEN

The road from Laarne Castle to Aachen was pleasant enough, but Robin and the others did feel that it was unnecessarily rural and, as a result, not well maintained.

"Was there really any need for us to take this route?" Will Scarlet grumbled as they passed yet another tiny settlement on the third day out from Laarne. "The people in these places act like they've never seen a stranger before."

"They look like they've grown straight up out of the ground beside the wheat and barley crops instead of being born like normal folk," John said with a wry chuckle. As if to confirm his assertion a middle-aged farmer looked up from the field that bordered the road and his face, grimy, weather-beaten and heavily lined, creased in a frown. "See? He's more plant than human!"

"At least he's not trying to rob us," Tuck said, his tone one of mild rebuke.

"Oh, I mean no harm to these people," John replied hastily. "I just mean that this road we've taken seems to have carried us further out of the way than I'd expected."

"You're damn right," Will agreed. "No inns, barely a stable or an alehouse. It's almost as if that Lord of Laarne sent us this way as a joke."

"Or to slow us down," Robin murmured, feeling his previous fears bubble to the surface again.

"I don't know about that," Tuck said. "I thought he was a fine host."

One of the other farmers lifted a rustic-looking hat from his head and rubbed at a sweating, bald scalp, glaring at them as they passed. Robin ignored him, understanding the fear he and his friends must engender in these simple people living out here miles from even a decent sized town.

"He was a fine host," Robin agreed. "But that doesn't mean he wasn't up to something."

His companions rode on in silence for a while and he wasn't sure if they were fed up with him worrying so much, or if they were beginning to think he might be right.

"Well, we shall reach Aachen tomorrow," Sir Simon told them. "Remember, our destination is the Hospitaller commandery there. Even if Gerard van Rasseghem has sent men ahead of us to beat us to the treasure, they'll surely not be granted the run of the commandery by my brother knights."

That thought brought some comfort to Robin and he even managed a smile at yet another farmhand, this time a stooped old woman who did not return his jovial nod, instead turning away to spit on the ground instead.

"We'll have to camp out again," Stephen said. He had been unusually quiet, Robin thought, since they'd reached Flanders. He had always been bluff, taciturn, and even downright rude at times, but he seemed to be more tired than any of the others after their time on the road. "That's one thing I miss about Eagle: a decent, comfy bed, and a roof above me."

"We'll find a warm welcome in Aachen, Stephen," the preceptor assured him, rolling his shoulders as though he too was feeling the effects of travelling so many miles. "At least it's been dry and pleasant, although I think we should set up camp soon. Look – clouds are coming in from the west and I'd rather not build up our tents in a downpour."

The other men eyed the heavy clouds that were rolling in, gravid with the threat of rain, and voiced their agreement with the preceptor's suggestion. Being so far from civilisation there were plenty of potential camp sites, so they chose a stand of trees set back from the road, with a narrow stream nearby. Two of them saw to the horses, the Hospitallers erected the tents, and Tuck set up the iron cooking tripod while Stephen collected kindling for a fire.

Before long slices of bacon were frying, the smell making everyone's mouth water. They all sat, eagerly watching as Tuck cooked the meat to perfection before dishing it out. Thankfully the rain held off until they'd all eaten their fill. They had arranged the three tents so the entrances faced one another with the fire in the centre, and they sat sheltering as they chatted, dry, with full bellies, and aleskins in hand. Even Stephen declared himself content as the light failed, leaving the flames of their camp fire to cast cheery, dancing shadows across their faces.

"I'm not sure even your commandery in Aachen will be as comfortable as this," Tuck drawled as he tried to dislodge a piece of bacon from between his teeth. "This is how a wandering friar should spend each night."

"Pfft. Why don't you live in a tent back in Wakefield then?" Will demanded.

"Well, Wakefield's weather is more extreme than here in Flanders," the friar smiled, refusing to let Scarlet goad him. "Or I would."

They sat talking for a long time, discussing the progress of their mission, and how they hoped things might go when they finally reached Aachen the following day.

"I still wonder who those English riders were that passed Tuck at Laarne," John rumbled, bass voice almost making Robin glance up, fearing thunder.

"Who cares?" Scarlet replied. "None of our business, and, as long as they keep well away from us there'll be no issues."

"But aren't you curious?" John persisted. "Even a little?"

"No."

"Well, I am," Stephen said. Now that they had dismounted and been able to rest awhile he seemed to be getting back to his old self again. "The more I think about it, the more I think they might prove important."

"How?" Tuck asked, reaching out of his tent and rinsing off his pan and cooking utensils in the steadily falling rain.

"I don't know," the sergeant shrugged. "But as Robin said at the time, it can't just be a coincidence that they were riding into the castle as we were riding out."

They sat for a time, the rain pattering on the leather tents and the undergrowth around them, the air smelling fresh and clean, everyone secure in the belief there was not another person within miles of their camp.

"What?" Robin had noticed Tuck's face, pensive now, screwed up as though he was concentrating hard on something other than the orange flames that reflected from his eyes. "What are you thinking about?"

The clergyman looked up at him and pursed his lips. "I'm starting to think I might have an idea who one of those riders was after all," he said. "The one who greeted me in English."

"You know him?" Stephen asked with keen interest.

Tuck shook his head. "Not 'know', but there was something strangely familiar about him. It's been on my mind since they passed me." He seemed to become entranced by the fire again before, at last, he lifted his aleskin and took a deep pull. A small, almost dainty belch escaped his lips and he softly begged his companions' pardon before nodding, and once again meeting Robin's gaze. "I know what it is," he said. "The rider reminds me very much of a man I met once when I was visiting York."

"That's not far from Wakefield," Scarlet chimed in happily.

"Indeed. This was years ago, I was escorting Bishop Baldock to Parliament." He paused, lost in his memory of that time, before saying, "I saw a man, of medium height and build, with a pronounced hook nose, and hard eyes. Distinctive looking fellow."

Robin watched his friend, waiting for him to marshal his thoughts and continue.

"I am almost convinced that the man I saw here in Flanders was the same man I saw at Parliament but," he

166

shook his head, brow furrowed. "But the man I met in York was about the same age as the rider at Laarne, and that must be twenty-odd years ago now."

"A relative then," John said.

"Aye, perhaps," the friar agreed, still frowning into the campfire. "That would make sense. They both had the same eyes, hooked nose, and build. Perhaps they're father and son, or cousins."

The rain continued to drum against the tents as they waited for Tuck to go on, but it seemed he had finished. Eventually, Robin asked, "Who was the man you met in York? A member of Parliament?"

"That I cannot recall. Perhaps he was just accompanying one of the Members, as I was."

"But who was he?" Will persisted, visibly trying to mask his impatience. "What was his name?"

"James," the friar said after another long moment of contemplation.

"James what?" said Will.

As Friar Tuck searched his memory, Robin felt a sinking feeling in his guts and somehow he knew the answer even as the churchman gave it.

"It was Coterel," Tuck breathed at last, looking up and meeting Robin's eyes. "Yes, it was, I'm sure of it. James Coterel."

* * *

The remainder of the evening was spent filling in Sir Simon and Stephen on everything that had happened before Robin and his companions turned up in Eagle Preceptory. They explained the Coterels' extortion and other criminal enterprises across England and, eventually, both Hospitallers agreed that they had heard of the gang. Almost everyone had after all, although they'd never been any threat to Sir Simon or the people in his charge.

"I do not place much stock in gossip," the preceptor said loftily. "But it does seem as though these Coterels have earned their terrible reputation."

"And they threatened you?" Stephen asked Robin.

"Aye, warned me, and John and Scarlet, to keep our noses out of their business, essentially. The sheriff too."

Sir Simon muttered an oath. "It's ridiculous that such criminal scum can work their way into positions of power. I mean, an outlaw attending parliament! Preposterous!"

"Corruption runs rampant all through Britain," Stephen noted gloomily. "We all know that. The wealthy look out for one another, and damn the rest of us."

"That's all very well, but why would one of the Coterels come to Flanders?" Will stood up, almost catching himself on the tent and just managing to right himself before stumbling into the crackling fire. The combination of ale and exhaustion was obviously taking a toll on him. He disappeared into the gloom behind his tent, utterly swallowed up by the night before the sound of splashing could be heard as he emptied his bladder. "Could it be Tuck, and Robin, are letting their imagination run wild again?"

"Maybe," the young longbowman admitted reluctantly.

"Let's just agree it's true," John said. "Let's say one of the Coterels is really here in Flanders with three guards. What are we going to do about it?"

"What can we do?" Stephen wondered.

"Nothing," said Tuck. "Until they make a move against us. We're hours ahead of them, assuming they are following us. And besides, there's only four of them, and six of us."

It seemed clear to Robin that the Coterels had sent one of their family members after them, and to come such a vast distance, they must have a very good reason. Somehow the gang had discovered his purpose in travelling to Flanders, and wanted to follow him to the lost treasure of King John, undoubtedly taking it for themselves should Robin and his friends somehow locate it. Or, and this was even more worrying, those men had been sent to kill him.

"We need to be extra careful from now on," said Sir Simon, voicing Robin's own thoughts. "We still have the upper hand. We're going to a Hospitaller commandery, and the knights and sergeants-at-arms there will side with us over some outlaw scum, or even the Lord of Laarne's soldiers." He nodded to himself, unbuckling his sword belt and placing it within easy reach as he lay down within the tent. "I would suggest we take turns on watch just in case anyone does try to attack us, and then, on the morrow, make all haste for Aachen."

"Suits me," Will Scarlet agreed, and the others added their voices in support of the knight's plan.

Robin was given the second watch and so he lay down and covered himself with his blanket, rolled up cloak for a pillow, dry and warm. As he closed his eyes and allowed sleep to overtake him he tried to imagine how things would go when they reached Aachen but found it to be impossible. There were too many things he did not know, too many possible outcomes, and it was all playing out in lands that were completely alien to him. The most incredible part was that none of them knew if the treasure they were hunting was even in Flanders. It was far more likely to have been swallowed by time and tide back in the Fens of England.

They had come this far though, and Robin meant to see it to the end, no matter who tried to stand in his way.

* * *

Matthew Coterel was not exactly happy about the meeting he'd had with Gerard van Rasseghem. He'd told the Lord of Laarne that Robin Hood and his companions were in Flanders searching for lost crown jewels – valuable treasure! He had expected van Rasseghem would be so excited by the possibilities that the old man would send men of his own with Matthew to hunt down both Hood and the treasure. Yet the Flemish nobleman had not seemed at all interested, which struck Matthew as strange. Rich men were always looking to add even more wealth to their holdings, yet Gerard van Rasseghem had barely blinked when told just how incredibly valuable the missing treasure was – the Crown Jewels of England, by Christ! How could that not stir the blue blood of any baron?

The Lord of Laarne quickly seemed to become tired of Matthew's company though, barely glancing up at the other three men who travelled with him. Some perfunctory hospitality was offered – a frugal meal and some bland wine – before the steward bade them farewell and ushered them firmly out of the castle.

It had not only been surprising, but quite galling as well. As a member of the Coterel family, a powerful force in English affairs both legal and illegal, Matthew had expected a warmer welcome from a fellow nobleman. To be turfed out within a few hours of their arrival in Laarne was both unexpected and unpleasant. As Matthew told his three guards, he would have liked to give the old bastard van Rasseghem some lessons in manners, with his fists, or perhaps even his sword.

Still, their visit to the castle was not entirely wasted. They asked about Robin Hood's group, and the lean old nobleman had given them valuable information, telling them exactly which route the six riders were taking to reach Aachen. Apparently van Rasseghem had provided the details of that route himself, advising them to avoid the bigger, more populous settlements so as to avoid trouble or arousing unwanted interest. The old baron was quite happy to provide Matthew with the same directions he'd given Hood before sending them on their way.

Matthew had told the old man quite explicitly that he was no friend of Hood, claiming to be a representative of King Edward III, chasing the outlaw and his friends who were going to steal the lost crown jewels for themselves. Van Rasseghem might have accepted all that as true, it was hard to tell if he even cared, but he certainly seemed content for Matthew to hunt Hood across Flanders. Perhaps the old man found it amusing to set two parties of Englishmen against one another in a deadly conflict, who knew? Who cared? Matthew had the means to locate his quarry, and he meant to make the most of it by catching Hood's group before they could get to Aachen.

He and his men rode hard from Laarne, following the directions they'd been given closely, trusting that they hadn't been sent on a wild goose chase in the wrong direction completely. As the Flemish lord had said, the route took them along quiet roads, past sparsely populated villages where there were more sheep than people, and they made good time.

"Must we really ride this hard?" one of his guards had asked around mid-afternoon. They were all sweating, and the horses were tired, unused to travelling so fast.

"Aye, Gregor, we must," Matthew had called. He was the leader, despite being the youngest. The other three men were in their twenties or thirties, experienced fighters although not expert riders, at least over long distances. Neither was Matthew, and his body was protesting their speedy ride that day, but it was absolutely necessary if they were to find Hood. "If the bastards reach Aachen it'll make our task much harder. The Hospitaller's there will welcome Sir Simon with open arms, maybe offer him reinforcements, and we'll likely never have a chance to kill Hood and that big oaf of a bailiff."

"I'm bloody exhausted," Gregor gasped, hardly audible over the thundering hooves and clanking of tack as they sped past a glowering old peasant woman who'd turned walnut brown in the sun.

"Hood's party have no idea we're coming after them," Matthew said. "They'll be riding at a normal pace, so we'll soon catch them. We'll rest up soon, all right?" His tone was clipped, but he did not mean to sound harsh. He understood his guard's protests, and he had no intention of angering any of them, for he was quite friendly with all three of them.

When his uncle, John, had asked Matthew if he was up to the task of tracking down and killing Hood he had been eager to prove himself. He'd personally chosen the three men with him, having known them all for years, drinking and fornicating their way around England when he was younger, barely able to grow the moustache that he was now so proud of. Gregor, Peter, and Roger were broadly built, tall, and trained to use the swords they all wore. Most importantly, they were loyal to Matthew for he took care of them, making sure they shared his money, drink, and women. When they had ever found trouble, his three companions had come together to deal with their foes savagely and without qualms. They were the ideal men to accompany Matthew on his hunt for Robin Hood, a known outlaw who could be killed by any man without legal consequence.

They'd visited Wakefield first, of course, and pretended to be old friends of the infamous longbowman. It was apparently no secret that Hood had gone off with his friends to a place called Eagle, supposedly to visit some other old acquaintance of theirs – a Hospitaller sergeant-at-arms named Stephen.

Matthew wasted no time in buying provisions for the journey and headed directly to Lincolnshire in pursuit of Hood. When they reached Eagle, Matthew had gone to the preceptory alone, asking to speak with the sergeant. It was a bold move and showed the bravado of the young Coterel, but he had seen no other way to find out where Hood was. He had not even had to go to the main buildings for there were servants working in the gardens and one of them, in return for a few coins, happily told him that Stephen, and the preceptor, Sir Simon Launcelyn, had left for the port at

Boston that very morning in the company of four Yorkshiremen. For a few coins more, the servant told Matthew that the preceptor and the others were going to Aachen searching for King John's lost treasure.

"Treasure? Are you sure?" Matthew had demanded, thinking the servant was lying, perhaps trying to be funny. But the man was married to a serving wench who took food and drink to Hood and the others and had overheard their conversations and their plans to sail for Europe.

When Matthew and his men reached the port in Boston it once again proved a simple matter to discover where Hood's party had sailed to, for the Hospitaller knight had gone about the place openly asking for passage to Bruges for six men and eight horses. A large man wearing armour and clad in a bright red surcoat emblazoned with a white cross was hard to forget and Matthew was somewhat surprised that Hood and his men were moving around so openly. Clearly they did not fear pursuit, but, in fairness, why would they? The only reason Matthew was hunting the wolf's head was because he and his friends had crossed the Coterels.

It would have been sensible for Matthew to simply wait for Hood to return to England, but his burning desire to prove himself to his father and uncles had driven him across the sea and along the road in Flanders at breakneck pace. He would catch Robin Hood, and he would show not only his relatives, but everyone in England, that he was a force to be reckoned with.

"Let's stop now," he called, allowing his horse to slow down. "There's a stream there where we can replenish our waterskins, and let the animals drink their fill."

"Praise God," said Gregor, grinning as he followed his young leader off the road and down a slope towards the stream. "How about something to eat as well, and perhaps a nap?" He slowly dismounted and bent to splash cool, clean water on his face, upstream of his horse which was drinking thirstily.

Matthew and the others followed him down and they all refreshed themselves, washing the dust of the road away and then refilling their waterskins.

"D'you think we've almost caught up with Hood?" Roger asked, flopping down on the grass and staring up at the near-cloudless blue sky.

Peter answered, for he was the oldest and the most experienced, having once been a high-ranking soldier in the Earl of Lancaster's army. He'd travelled more extensively than the others, picking up a smattering of other languages and, although subordinate to Matthew, he was essentially the one guiding them. "I'd say it would take Hood's party four days to reach Aachen at a normal travelling speed, if the Lord of Laarne's directions were correct. So they'll reach their destination tomorrow. At the speed we've been riding however, we must be almost upon them. Another couple of hours and we'll overtake them."

Matthew sat down on the hard ground and took out some salted meat. Chewing on it, he looked up at the sun.

Peter read his thoughts. "It will be night soon," he confirmed.

"Then we must be careful," noted the young Coterel. "We want to sneak up on them, catch them unawares. If they hear us coming we'll lose the element of surprise."

"And we really do not want that," Roger growled, practically collapsing on the riverbank. Of the four, he was the heaviest and most muscular but also with a paunch and a jowly face gained from years of overeating and indulging in ale. "There's six of them, and only four of us."

Matthew nodded, chewing his beef thoughtfully, staring unseeingly into the rippling waters of the stream.

"Are you sure you want to kill Hood here on the road?" Gregor asked. "Don't you think it would be better to let them lead us to the missing crown jewels, and then ambush them?"

Matthew had wondered that himself but, in all honesty, he did not for one moment think Hood's party would find Softsword's treasure. It had been lost forever in the Wash, and the search for it was nothing but a fool's errand. He shook his head, popping the last of his salted meat into his mouth and slowly masticating it with little relish for it was not particularly appetising. "No," he said. "The treasure is buried in the marshes back home, so we can forget all about it. This is the best chance we'll ever have of catching Hood's group unawares, out here in the middle of nowhere, with no witnesses to report what we've done. It's not just a wolf's head we're going to kill," he reminded them. "One of his friends is a bailiff, one a friar, and one a nobleman – a knight. We can't get caught disposing of them."

He lifted his waterskin and took a long pull, almost emptying the thing.

"Then we should rest for a time," Peter suggested. "Eat and drink as much as we like before moving on, being careful not to let them spot us when we finally catch up."

"Indeed," Matthew said, refilling his waterskin at the stream. "Let's rest, and then, in a few hours when it's as dark as it's going to get, we'll find them, and we'll put an end to their insane quest for King John's lost treasure!"

CHAPTER EIGHTEEN

"Wake up!"

Robin's eyes fluttered open and he strained to make out who was leaning over him. A momentary panic filled him as he remembered he was in a tent in a strange land, and he scrabbled for the sword which lay beside him.

"Calm down, for fuck sake, it's your turn on watch."

The panic drained out of him as he saw Will Scaflock's smile in the darkness.

"Come on, or you'll wake John."

Robin shook his head, an embarrassed grin on his face as he followed Will out of the tent he was sharing with the bailiff. The fire was still burning, but much lower than when they were sitting around it earlier, drinking and telling one another stories. There was a chill in the air for, although it was the height of summer, it was a cloudless night, and a crescent moon added her pale light to that of the small flames as Robin held out his hands to warm them.

"Quiet?" he asked Will and Stephen, who'd taken the first watch together.

"As a tomb," the sergeant replied, using a rather unpleasant analogy, thought Robin.

"Not quite," Will argued, voice low so those asleep would not be disturbed. "We heard what sounded like footsteps a short time ago, over there, to the north." He gestured towards a cluster of trees just a short distance away from their camp. "But they came to nothing. Must have been a fox or maybe a wolf, drawn by the smell of our bacon."

"A wolf?" Robin asked, anxiously staring out into the darkness.

"Aye, but they won't bother us," Stephen assured him. "Not as long as you keep the fire burning low, and stay alert."

There were wolves back home in England, but they usually stayed away from humans. Even when Robin had lived in the greenwood as an outlaw he had never been troubled by the beasts. Flanders was a different place, however. Although it was smaller than England, it was not an island, and dangerous animals like wolves and bears would, Robin assumed, be more abundant since they could roam hither and thither, travelling from Flanders to France, and all the other lands that made up the Holy Roman Empire.

"Tuck and his damn bacon stinking out the place," he muttered, still peering into the gloom that surrounded them, eyes resting on every strange shadow before moving on again when he was sure it wasn't a dangerous animal or a human lying in wait.

"You'll be fine," said Stephen. "Just don't fall asleep, or we'll all be fucked." He smiled and waved goodnight, crawling into his tent where Sir Simon was peacefully sleeping.

"He knows better than that," Will assured the sergeant, patting Robin on the back. "Wake John in a couple of hours, all right?" With that he slithered into his tent and roused Friar Tuck who soon came out and sat groggily by the fire, yawning and scratching the back of his neck, tonsured hair sticking out at wild angles. Robin couldn't help but smile at him.

"What are you laughing at?" the friar demanded irritably.

"Nothing," Robin lied, turning back to stare into the darkness. The pair fell into a bored silence, not wanting to chat for fear it would disturb their friends' rest, and knowing they must not get too comfortable and fall asleep.

Tuck stood up eventually, stretching out and doing his best to smooth down the meagre hair on his head. Then he nodded to Robin and began trudging slowly around the camp. For a bulky man the clergyman could move

177

surprisingly quietly and soon Robin began to daydream, imagining finding King John's treasure, what it would look like, what it would feel like in his hands, and, ultimately, how England's present king, Edward, would rejoice when it was returned to his keeping.

The sound of a dry twig snapping came from somewhere to the left and he slowly turned, expecting to see Tuck. Frowning, he realised the friar was patrolling on the other side of the camp and slowly, carefully, he drew his sword and stood up, pressing himself against a tree trunk while he tried to catch the friar's attention.

"What is it?"

"I heard movement," Robin murmured to his friend who had managed to step across to stand beside him, barely making a sound in the process. "Over there. Listen."

They stood utterly still, senses straining, and Robin heard the soft hiss of steel rubbing against leather as Tuck drew, not his trusty cudgel for once, but his sword. If something was big and brave enough to be stalking them there in the wilderness it would need more than a simple cudgel to deal with it.

Suddenly, Tuck's arm shot out into the darkness, and Robin followed the pointing finger to see a huge black shape silently gliding between a pair of trees. Icy calm filled him and he gripped his sword fiercely. That had been no wolf, for wolves did not walk upright on two legs.

His mind raced as he desperately tried to figure out what to do. Should he wake the others? Doing so would certainly alert whoever was watching their camp, and possibly urge them to attack immediately. On the other hand, he and Tuck could not simply stand there and wait for something to happen.

"Wake them," he hissed into Tuck's ear, and then, without waiting for a response, he moved forwards, doing his best to keep to the shadows where the dim firelight did not reach. He moved even quieter than Tuck had done, stepping lightly, instinctively avoiding twigs and fallen branches as he closed the gap between himself and the man he'd seen behind the trees.

He cursed inwardly for his friends were far from silent as they came awake, scrabbling for weapons, muttering, and fighting with the flaps of their tents to escape into the open where they could defend themselves from the nocturnal lurkers. Focusing completely on his own task, he stared straight ahead, moonlight showing him the way. He was sure his quarry had not moved from behind the tree he was aiming for, and he readied himself to strike as he carefully moved around it to the left.

Some sixth sense screamed in his head right at that moment and he lunged forward, bringing his sword around in an arc. He felt it bite home but there was no scream of agony, and no give in his blade. He had not struck human flesh and bone, he had hit the tree, and the force of the blow rang along his arm.

"Die!"

The black shape had gone around the trunk of the birch in the opposite direction and it came for him now, filling Robin's vision like an enormous bat. He bared his teeth and raised his sword which – thank the Magdalene! – had not stuck fast in the bark of the tree. There was a ringing clatter and sparks flew in the darkness as his attacker's blade was parried, and Robin pushed himself forwards, bringing up his knee. He felt it hit something, and his foe grunted, bending over at the perfect angle for Robin to slam the pommel of his sword down into the back of the shadowy figure's head.

Breathing heavily, Robin stood still, staring at the unmoving enemy attacker and trying to work out what the hell was going on. Back at the campfire his friends were calling out, moving away from the fire in pairs, swords glinting as they walked. Little John was coming towards Robin, grim-faced and clearly in the mood for a fight.

"What's happening?" the giant bailiff growled. "Who's this bastard?"

"No idea. I didn't recognise him. Wait, what's that?" He paused, turning his head to where... "The horses! They're at our horses!"

They ran then, sprinting into the darkness to where they had pegged their mounts for the night. It was not far but, by the time Robin reached the spot, he realised a stranger was climbing onto his own horse.

Roaring an incoherent cry of rage, Robin sheathed his sword and put on a burst of speed, reaching deep within himself to move faster than he'd ever done in his life. He threw himself forward as the horse with its unknown rider broke into a trot, and his hands closed around a leg and a long cloak.

"Let go you stupid bastard, you'll get us both killed!" The rider's shout came in plain English, not Flemish, and a flash of understanding came to Robin. The four men they'd passed at Laarne had come after them. This one must have panicked when he realised his companion had been caught by Robin and decided to escape the area by stealing one of the horses!

Ignoring the rider's desperate exhortation, Robin gripped harder, holding on for dear life as the frightened horse gathered speed, quickly leaving the camp behind in spite of its double load. Again, the cry of, "Let go," came, and Robin could see the rider was trying to take out a knife from where it was sheathed at his waist. If he managed it, Robin would be unable to defend himself from its vicious blade.

Screaming in defiance, he dug his fingers into the rider who let out a wail of pain and flailed his arms, trying to dislodge the tenacious young longbowman who was proving to be unbelievably strong thanks to his countless hours at the archery butts. An elbow caught Robin on the side of the head and he closed his eyes as a wave of nausea washed over him, and then he felt his fingers sliding, the strength leaving them.

There was another cry from the rider and Robin found himself rolling down a hill, utterly disoriented, as the horse added its own terrifying scream of fear. Before he could make sense of it all Robin felt himself strike something hard, and freezing cold, and then he was suffocating and the panic returned, this time much, much worse.

He was in water, so deep that his feet could not touch the bottom, and it was so pitch black that he had no idea where the surface was.

* * *

"Where the fuck is he? I thought you said he was here?" Will Scarlet stamped about the campsite, sword held menacingly before him as he searched for the enemy warrior who'd first attacked Robin by the trees.

Little John, frowning deeply, nodded and bent to examine the ground. "He was here, look. You can see where his body flattened the grass."

"Then where is he now? Did he rise from the dead, like Christ himself?"

"Enough of that sacrilege, Scarlet," Tuck barked. "It's quite obvious the man was not killed, only knocked out cold. He's got up when no one was looking and made his escape."

"Along with the rest of the filthy whoresons," said Stephen, striding back to the camp behind Sir Simon. "They're all gone."

"Bastards!" Will hissed in fury, still not ready to sheath his sword. "What about Robin then? Where the hell is he, and his horse?"

John shook his head. "I don't know." His voice was so low that he was hardly audible. "I ran after them but I wasn't

181

fast enough to keep up. They went through the trees there, and then I lost them at the river."

"At the river?" Sir Simon asked portentously. He had shoved his own sword back into its scabbard and took a seat by the fire, staring deep into its flames. "Then there can be only one explanation for your inability to find him. I hope he can swim."

There was a heavy silence then, as the five remaining men tried to imagine what had become of their missing friend. Robin could swim, of course, he'd often enjoyed sunny afternoons with them, and Matilda, diving into the Calder back at home. But he had not been wearing a heavy sword or gambeson then. Would the weight of those drag him down to the riverbed?

"We have to go and look for him again," John said, almost frantic with worry as he pictured Robin drowning there in that foreign land, leaving behind his wife and children in Wakefield.

"Right," Sir Simon agreed, pushing himself to his feet, visibly exhausted after their night of broken sleep. He gestured to John, Will, and Tuck. "You three go and search for your friend. Stephen and I will break down the camp and make ready to move on. We can't stay here in case the attackers return for another try at us."

There were no arguments and John led the way to the river which they had not even known was there when they picked the spot to set up camp. They were pleased to see that the other horses were safely tethered where they'd been left, only Robin's was missing, and they picked up the pace when they were mounted upon the skittish beasts.

"Sun will be up soon," Tuck noted as they approached the river. "It's starting to get light."

He wasn't wrong, and the improving visibility allowed them to see just how wide the river they'd been camped so close to actually was.

182

"God help him," Will breathed as they grew closer and stopped on the bank, gazing down at the dark waters. "If he's fallen in there we might never find him."

"None of that talk!" Little John turned on Scarlet, shaking with rage and all the pent-up emotion of everything that happened in the past few hours. "We'll find him! And he'll be fine once we get him dried out and warmed up. Just like Tuck was that time he was shot by Gisbourne and ended up in the River Don."

Will held up his hands in apology. "You're right," he conceded. "Robin leads a charmed life. He'll be fine. Come on, we better get looking for him. He might be lying on the bank, too tired, or cold, to call out for help."

"Look for the horse too," Tuck advised. "If we find that, we might find Robin as well."

John sat staring at the water and running a great hand through his grizzled beard and long hair, as if he couldn't figure out what to do, or where he should start.

"He's not going to be upstream," Will said, grasping him by the arm. "So let's check down this way. Tuck, you look in the water, I'll look at the water's edge, and you look along the bank, John, in case he's managed to climb out. All right?"

Tuck nodded and John nudged his horse to a walk, the big bailiff's head swivelling as he searched the heavily sloping riverbank. He tried to understand what had happened, picturing Robin's terrified horse stumbling blindly down towards the river before finding itself submerged. And that was the ideal scenario, for if the horse had fallen badly on hard ground it would likely have broken limbs and, even if it survived the cold water, it would need to be put down. As for Robin, where on God's green Earth was the young archer? How far could the water have carried him?

John glanced at the river momentarily. It did not look particularly fast flowing, but he knew there might be hidden currents and turbulence, not to mention things like reeds concealed beneath the surface, all of which could prove lethal.

The silence was suddenly split by a shocking, high-pitched cry and the three friends turned wide, startled eyes on one another, fearing they were hearing the last moments of the young man who'd come to them a decade before as little more than a frightened boy and ended up as their leader.

"Barn owl," Tuck grunted, shaking his head and forcing a smile as he urged the others to move on and keep their eyes peeled.

"See anything?" Will called after they'd travelled a fair distance.

"No," Tuck replied grimly, never taking his gaze from the water for a moment.

"Nothing," said John, who was feeling despair building within him. It might be summer, but the river would be almost freezing, especially during the night. And it would be extremely deep too. Falling into it would make the limbs seize up, and panic could quickly overwhelm even a strong swimmer. Should the current draw them into the centre rather than closer to the bank, well...

They continued to search for some time, until the sun came up and the land was bathed in light. Still they saw no sign of Robin, his horse, or the enemy warrior who'd stolen the animal.

Sir Simon and Stephen appeared, having packed the others' belongings and brought their horses along.

"No sign?" the preceptor asked. "We expected you back at the camp before now. Thought we should come and find you before we became separated. Remember, there's men out there hunting us, so we need to be careful."

"Let them find us," John snarled.

"Aye," Tuck agreed. "They won't catch us unprepared, like they did in the middle of the night."

"What are we going to do?" Will asked. He'd reined in his mount and was standing with his hands on his hips, his usual stoic demeanour replaced by slumped shoulders and a distinct aura of despair around him.

"We must go on to Aachen," Sir Simon stated levelly.

"And abandon Robin?" Scarlet demanded, outraged.

"Aye," the Hospitaller nodded. "I'm sorry, Will, but you've been searching for some time and found nothing. We can't stay here forever."

"We could keep searching."

"How far should we go?" the preceptor argued. "This is the River Meuse. It's hundreds of miles long. We could ride along it for days and never find Robin."

Even Stephen looked unconvinced. There was a powerful bond of loyalty and brotherhood binding the friends together, and the thought of simply riding on and leaving Robin to his fate did not sit at all well with them.

"Look, we have to be realistic," Sir Simon continued, acting the part of the military commander. "There's a good chance Robin has drowned. If so, there's nothing we can do for him even if we do find him. If God has seen fit to save him, what will he do?"

John's fists had clenched as he heard the preceptor speak so baldly of his friend drowning, but he held his temper in check and tried to answer the question, dismounting and walking to stand by the river as he thought about it. What *would* Robin do?

"It depends on whether he still has his horse," Tuck murmured, continuing to scan the river and the surrounding area.

"Not really," John said. "Whether he does or not, he'll only have two choices: try to get back to England, or try to find us."

They all digested that, knowing John was right.

"So we should remain at the camp we were at last night?" Will asked uncertainly.

"No chance," Stephen spat. "Those fuckers, Coterels or whoever they are, that attacked us will come back and try to finish what they started. We could never rest easy there now."

"And Robin will know that," John observed, walking back up the riverbank to his horse, rubbing its face and murmuring affectionately to it.

"So we go on to Aachen," Sir Simon concluded. "As I suggested. That's where Robin will go if he's able."

"And we watch out for four other riders," said Stephen darkly. "We have a score to settle with them."

Will Scarlet jumped down from his horse, wandering across to stare down at the shore of the river. "Maybe not four," he called, nudging something with his foot. "Looks like we don't need to worry about one of the bastards any more. He's dead."

CHAPTER NINETEEN

Robin fought the urge to open his mouth and scream for help as he felt the weight of his sword pulling him down to the riverbed. He realised his bowstring, in the little pouch he carried, would be utterly soaked, and angrily pushed the thought aside. How was that important, when he was literally dying? He thought of Matilda, seeing her in his mind's eye, smiling at him, arms opened to embrace him, and he thought of his sons, Arthur and Henry, and his parents, and desperately wished he could see them one last time, to tell them all how much he loved them.

Something struck him on the top of the head and, enraged by that and by the fact he was drowning, he kicked upwards, fury propelling him in what he prayed was the right direction. Despite the sword, and his sodden gambeson, his powerful legs and archer's shoulders worked in unison as he fought savagely for his life. Suddenly, he broke free of the water and gasped, desperately dragging in a breath before the current pulled him under again.

He pushed down his panic and his fear. He had his bearings now – he knew where he must swim towards, and so he urged already exhausted muscles to guide him back to the surface. This time when he broke free he saw the riverbank and forged towards it, swinging arms and legs as hard as he could. They were not fluid, powerful strokes, for his strength was ebbing with every moment his body was in the freezing water, but his silent prayers to the Magdalene must have been heard, for a sudden eddy caught him up and pushed him straight towards the shore. He felt his arms strike hard ground and, sobbing in relief and joy, he stood up, hobbling onwards for fear he might still be swept away if he did not manage to get completely free of the river.

Dripping wet, and shivering from cold and shock, he collapsed onto his knees and curled into a ball, trying to get warm without success. He gave thanks to God, Mary

Magdalene, and all the saints, but his teeth were chattering so hard he could not form the words and he closed his eyes, fear rising again as he knew he was still not safe. He could not think straight, and did not have the strength or energy to get up and seek help.

His friends were somewhere nearby, weren't they? Or had he been swept so far downriver that they were left miles behind and would not be able to find him? Could he allow himself to fall asleep, as his body craved, or would he expire from the cold if he didn't try to get warm and dry?

"Magdalene, help me," he prayed through blue lips, shuddering so hard that he feared he might hurt himself. That thought prompted a sardonic laugh – he would be dead soon, what did it matter if he broke a limb or two here on the shore?

He could not remember feeling so helpless in all his life. And then he recalled that word, 'hope' that had become his motto when he was imprisoned in Nottingham Castle by Sir Guy of Gisbourne, beaten half to death, with seemingly no chance of survival. Tuck had adjured him before that time to never give up hope, and, although he came close – very close! – he had remained steadfast and, miraculously it seemed, Will Scarlet had appeared at his cell to rescue him.

"Hope," he whispered, praying that he would find the help he needed. It seemed impossible, stuck on the shore of this great river, in the middle of nowhere. His eyes closed and he began to fall asleep, which amazed him – how could anyone sleep when they were shaking as much as he was? He knew it was a bad sign, that he should fight it, but he did not have any fight left in him.

There was a sound behind him, of footsteps, and he thought with dark humour that it was probably one of the men who'd attacked their camp, come to finish him off. Of all the people to discover him, it would be an enemy!

And then he felt something nudge his back and somehow he found it in him to turn his head. At first he could not believe what he was seeing, but, as his horse lay down by his side and he felt the animal's warmth flow into him tears welled in his eyes, so overcome was he by the horse's loyalty and friendship. It might not be a miracle, but it felt like it to the young man who slowly ceased shivering and started to believe he might actually survive this latest adventure after all.

* * *

"Where is that bloody fool?" Matthew Coterel stood on the bank of the River Meuse, hand up to shield his eyes from the sun as he scanned the water and the land all around them. "Surely Hood and his mates didn't capture him."

"No chance," Peter returned emphatically. "Roger would never let himself be taken."

"Well, where the fuck is he then?" Coterel demanded in frustration. "If he was killed when we attacked, where's his body?"

The third remaining member of the little group wiped sweat from his brow and upended his water skin into his mouth, slurping greedily, eyes closed as the sun beat down upon them. "I told you," said Gregor. "He grabbed one of their horses and was riding it away from the camp. Maybe the beast went mad with fear, scared of the noise and of being mounted by a stranger. We've all seen horses react like lunatics, sometimes for no reason at all!"

Matthew chewed his lip and rolled up the sleeves of his tunic. It was hotter there than it was back in England, and he was not particularly enjoying it. Perhaps if they were sitting in one of the Coterel gang's alehouses, enjoying cool drinks and the attentions of the whores his family employed he wouldn't mind the baking heat so much. Stuck out there in the open though, with one of their number missing, was not at all how Matthew had envisaged their journey turning out.

"What the hell do we do now then?" Peter asked. "I was confident of facing anyone when there were four of us. But three?"

Matthew did not know what to say. He agreed with Peter; their party had seemed complete – secure and formidable – when Roger was with them. Now? Not so much.

"We must find him," he decided. "Or at least try before moving on."

"We have been trying," Peter said plaintively, heat and frustration getting the best of the big warrior.

"Then try harder! Come on, stick together. We've been going slow up until now, doing it methodically. We should move faster." He mounted his horse and waited for his companions to follow suit before trotting along the riverbank, moving downstream from where Robin Hood's camp had been, and the last place they'd seen their friend.

"He wouldn't have come this far."

Matthew was becoming irritated with Peter but, before he could reply, he saw a dark shape on the shore of the Meuse and unconsciously slowed his horse, afraid to go on, but knowing he must.

"What's that?" Gregor said, jumping heavily onto the grass and hurrying down the sloping river bank.

Matthew watched, a tight knot in his guts as he watched Gregor approach the dark bundle.

"It's him."

"Dead," said Peter, and it wasn't a question as he too dismounted and made his way to the corpse. The sun had dried the body completely but it was already showing the effects of decomposition and Matthew swallowed the bile that had come up as he saw the cloud of flies around his friend.

"Looks like some wild animal's found him before us," Gregor noted, seemingly more curious than upset by his comrade's fate. "Or birds maybe."

"Alright, that's enough," Matthew said, hoping his voice did not waver. He had seen death before, had even killed men, but the sight of one of his closest friends lying there, discarded on the shore for animals and insects to feast upon, was a lot to take in, especially after a near-sleepless night. He had to put on a hard front for the other two though. A leader could not afford to show weakness. "Search him for his valuables, and let's get going. Maybe say a prayer over him, ask God to take him into his arms or…whatever."

"No valuables," Peter reported, swatting at flies and standing up, wafting a hand in front of his face.

"What? Where are they?" Matthew demanded, feeling like an idiot even as he spoke.

"Someone must have found him before us," guessed Gregor. "Taken his purse, his sword, knife, and anything else he had of worth."

"And the crows have taken his eyes," Peter finished and Matthew suspected there was a hint of amusement in his voice. Peter had not disliked Roger, but these men he'd befriended and chosen to follow him there to the lands of the Holy Roman Empire were killers, and their sense of humour reflected that. Peter and Gregor had known much brutality and death during their lives, as had poor Roger, who now knew it better, and more intimately, than any of them.

The three were soon mounted again, now with a spare horse since Roger would no longer be needing it.

They had escaped the wrath of Hood's friends during the night, dismayed that their sneak attack had been discovered, and even more dismayed by the ferocity that their targets had defended themselves with. Once Matthew and his two men were safely far away from the camp, back at the place they'd decided to rest before mounting the nighttime raid, they had waited for Roger to appear. At sunrise, with their comrade still missing, they'd made their way carefully back to see what Hood's party were doing. Matthew refused to get too close so it was difficult to make much out, and then the Hospitallers and the others had disappeared out of sight near the river.

It was clear now that Hood and his friends had discovered Roger's body and, like vultures, stripped it clean of anything useful or valuable. It was sickening.

A sudden thought struck the young Coterel and he turned to Peter and Gregor. "Did you see Robin Hood at their camp this morning?"

They all thought back to the red-hued woodland scene they'd viewed from within the thick undergrowth.

"I don't believe so," Gregor replied. "You said he was the biggest of their group, apart from that massive, hairy-arsed bailiff." He shrugged. "I don't think I saw him there. Could be wrong though."

"I never saw him either," Peter agreed. "Never thought much of it at the time."

Matthew took out a little comb and brushed it through his moustache, trying to make sense of everything. It did not take long.

"Roger stole Hood's horse," he said, mostly to himself as he sought to create a timeline of events. "Hood chased after him"—

"And they both ended up in the river," Peter broke in.

"And, just like us, they looked for their friend before leaving the area, no doubt to continue on to Aachen."

"Do you think they found Hood?" Peter asked.

Matthew thought about it, staring at the river, wondering how deep it was, and how dangerous it might be. "I doubt it," he said with some relish. "Roger would have fought hard, we all know that. And that water, freezing cold at night, would have been tough to swim in." His mouth twitched in a bitter, hateful smile. "I think Hood suffered the same fate as Roger."

"Then where's his body?" Gregor asked uncertainly.

"They had two spare pack horses. I doubt the friar that was with them would allow them to abandon the body." As we've just done, Matthew thought guiltily. "He would have demanded they take Hood's corpse for a proper Christian burial, wouldn't he?"

"Perhaps," Peter shrugged. "Or perhaps Hood survived. Or, then again, maybe he died but his mates couldn't find him and they went on without him. What else could they do?"

Matthew wished he could fly overhead like the bird of prey that was soaring above them right at that moment. He was no expert in such birds, especially in a foreign land, but he guessed it to be a kite or a buzzard, perhaps waiting for the men to ride away so it could come down and pick the flesh from poor Roger's bones. If Matthew could fly like that, he might be able to see Hood – alive or dead – and perhaps see where the Hospitallers and the rest had gone.

"What now?" Gregor asked. "It's too hot to sit around here."

Matthew considered. They would find out the young archer's fate eventually. So either Matthew led his men back to England, or they continued to follow Hood's friends until they could confirm that he was truly dead.

"We'll continue along the road to Aachen," he decided, with a final, quick salute to the dead man on the shore. "Let's go. We're already at least an hour behind Hood's men, and we've no idea where they'll be going after they've visited the city."

He urged his mount into a canter, accepting the fact that there were now only three of them, and eager to make up the ground between the Hospitaller-led group ahead. Their horses' hooves kicked up a cloud of dust as they picked up speed, still following the course of the Meuse as they headed back towards the eastern road.

"Wait! What's that ahead?"

Matthew squinted against the harsh glare of the punishing sunshine, trying to follow Peter's pointing finger.

"It's a rider," Gregor cried in excitement, hand falling to his sword hilt. "It has to be Robin Hood!"

Matthew felt his blood begin to thunder in his veins as the man on horseback ahead turned, noted their approach, and kicked his heels into his horse's flanks, guiding the animal off the road and into a patch of dense undergrowth that swallowed them up. Gregor had been right – Robin Hood had survived his plunge into the Meuse, but his life was now Matthew's.

"Three against one, lads," he whooped, drawing his sword and brandishing it in the air. "Come on, let's pay the bastard back for what happened to Roger!"

* * *

Robin had felt quite happy after he awoke on the shore and gave thanks to God for allowing him to live another day. Some of his food – bread mostly – had been ruined when the horse's saddlebags were submerged in the Meuse, but the salted meat would be fine after a rinse in a clean stream, and his water and ale-skins remained intact, and his weapons would be fine when the sunshine dried them out.

The horse seemed completely unharmed after its swim and it gladly let him mount it. He had no idea how far the river had carried them but he guessed it must be quite far, for his friends would surely have searched for him. The fact that they'd not found him suggested the current had taken him quite some distance. With that in mind he was unsure which direction to ride. Continue south along the Meuse until he reached a bridge, or should he head north again and hope to catch up with his friends? The river was a sizeable one, so there were bound to be bridges all along it at regular intervals. And whatever one he crossed, as long as he kept riding eastwards he'd be able to find Aachen.

Doubts assailed him then, as he imagined his friends, distraught at his apparent death, simply turning around and going back to England, while he wandered these lands, lost and confused.

He hoped Sir Simon would keep leading them to the Hospitaller commandery in Aachen though, so that was where Robin would go. If he got there and his friends had not visited, he would know they'd returned home and he would do the same. It was a daunting prospect, but God had saved him from the river and he would not allow despair to dampen his spirits. He had his horse, he had food, he had his weapons, and he had his wits and a little money. All would be well.

He thought it would be sensible to return north, and rejoin the road he and his companions had been on before they were attacked. It was possible John and the others were still there, searching for him and, if not, he may catch up with them soon. Pushing his horse fairly hard, he soon came to what he believed was the correct road, crossing the bridge and once again marvelling at how wide the river below was. He was extremely fortunate to survive his dip in those waters and he gave thanks yet again as he made it safely to the other side and strained his eyes for signs of his friends on the horizon ahead.

Looking around, he saw this section of the road was flanked by thick, lush undergrowth, with trees set further back. Insects flew languidly past and small birds foraged beneath bushes, adding colour to the sea of vibrant green. He spotted a roe deer pushing out of the foliage ahead but it quickly disappeared, alarmed by his approach. That was a good sign – even if he somehow became lost, he could hunt for food with his bow.

Almost as soon as he had come to his wits after waking from falling in the river, he had removed his hemp bow string from its pouch, finding it completely soaked – almost useless in such a state – and allowed it, and the pouch, to completely dry out in the sun. The simple act had given him a sense of security, for, as good as he was with his sword, it was far safer to fight murderous enemies from a distance.

His jaw tightened at the memory of the previous night's trouble. It was incredible to think the Coterel gang had sent men all this way just to kill him. What kind of madness drove people like that? He thought then that perhaps the criminal group had found out about Robin's quest for the lost treasure and that had given them an added incentive to follow him so far. He hoped the bastards had not injured any of his friends but pushed that bleak thought aside, instead focusing on what he would do if he was to cross paths with the young Coterel and his friends.

There were a fair number of travellers on the road, some of whom nodded in greeting or called out as he passed. Most averted their eyes, seeing the sword scabbarded at his waist and deciding it was safer just to pretend he wasn't there. If he thought he could converse with them, somehow make them understand him, he would have asked if they'd seen his friends, but he feared alarming the travellers and causing more trouble so he held his peace.

He had stopped pushing his horse so hard once they crossed the bridge over the Meuse, not wishing to blow the animal out. It had served him faithfully and probably saved his life, so he wanted to treat it with kindness. They trotted at a regular pace, and stopped whenever they came across a stream or a spring, drinking to avoid any bad effects from the continual sunshine. Had it been under different circumstances, Robin would have thoroughly enjoyed the journey.

They approached another stream and Robin's stomach rumbled loudly. He decided they would stop there for a proper rest, have something to eat, and allow all the stress of recent hours to drain away in the cheery burbling of the stream.

He was just guiding the horse off the side of the road when the sound of pounding hooves came from behind and he turned, wondering what he might see. Some part of him hoped it would be his friends, but he thought it far more likely to be soldiers, natives, travelling to Aachen. He felt a thrill of fear when his eyes focused on the three riders galloping towards him and immediately recognised the man at the front, hateful eyes boring into him from above a dark moustache and an unmistakably hooked nose.

"Coterel!"

Robin's mind reeled as he tried to decide what to do. His immediate instinct was to draw his sword and ride back to meet the bastards, to repay them for all the trouble they'd caused. There were three of them though, and he was alone. He was also no expert in fighting from horseback.

He had far more experience at using the undergrowth to his advantage, picking off attackers from the shadows of the greenwood.

Snarling a hateful oath, he kicked his heels in and lurched forward, his horse charging into the dense foliage, somehow picking a path through it until the road was left behind and they were swallowed up by the trees.

Now, Robin thought, they were in his domain. This might be a foreign land, but he was completely at home within the woods, and the Coterels were about to find out why the people of Yorkshire called Robin Hood the 'Forest Lord'.

CHAPTER TWENTY

As the party of five followed the road to Aachen, passing more settlements as they neared the city, Little John was plagued by the fear that they should not have given up so quickly on finding Robin. What if their enemies found him? They would search for their own missing comrade, wouldn't they? And they may very well stumble upon Robin if he was still alive.

The image of the man Will Scarlet had found on the shore of the River Meuse came to John then. The horrifically pale face, the unseeing eyes that stared up at the sky, and the bloody hole in his skull that must have been made by the horse he'd stolen as it thrashed about in the water trying desperately to stay alive.

Served the fucking arsehole right, John thought savagely, wishing he could have been the one that had dealt that mighty death blow rather than a panicked horse.

It was a good sign that the dead man had washed ashore though, and not that far from where John and the others had been searching. If the current had carried him there, it might have done the same for Robin. And, if Robin had not been kicked by the horse, maybe he was still alive. The big bailiff tried to put himself in his friend's position – washed ashore, soaking wet, freezing cold, exhausted, and lost, perhaps without his horse and the supplies of food and drink the beast carried in its saddlebags.

Robin was as hard as the iron nails John had once crafted when he'd been a blacksmith. If he'd survived the river, he would make it to Aachen and be reunited with his friends. Or so John tried to convince himself. It would be difficult, but if Robin could find his horse things would be so much easier. The horse was the key, really, since it had the supplies, as well as Robin's longbow. Even if the men hunting them found him, if Robin had his bow and a few arrows, he would have a chance to escape.

He'd survived death once, maybe he could do it again...

"There it is." Sir Simon smiled and pointed ahead, bringing Little John back to the present.

He saw an impressive pair of round, stone towers in front of an even bigger three-storey building. Both were equipped with battlements, and archerslits for defenders to protect the city, and a moat ran between them, providing yet another obstruction to unwanted visitors.

"The Ponttor Gate," said Sir Simon. "Gerard van Rasseghem told me about it. Remarkable, isn't it?"

Tuck and Will both agreed, visibly impressed by the gatehouse. It would take a lot of soldiers to break through such a structure, John knew, and shuddered at the thought of being thrust into such a situation, ordered to attack the gates while archers hid behind the stone walls and shot arrows at will. He wondered if such a scenario had ever played out and hoped no commander would be so stupid as to waste his men in such a pointless assault.

"Should we expect trouble from the guards?" Will asked, ready, as always, for a fight.

"No," Stephen told him, with a fraternal smile. They were almost like brothers, John thought, looking forward to the next time they could knock out an enemy's teeth. "We're not doing anything wrong, and they should respect the Hospitaller livery Sir Simon and I wear. So keep your weapons sheathed, and your tongue still, alright, Scarlet?"

"If you say so," Will grunted. "It's not like they'd understand me anyway."

"That's true," Tuck agreed happily. "Even I can't understand what you're rambling about half the time, and I'm as English as blood pudding!"

"Aye? Can you understand this?"

John laughed as Scarlet made an obscene gesture at the friar who merely shook his head and turned away, chuckling to himself.

"You know they eat blood pudding here as well?" Sir Simon asked, smiling as their horses trotted closer to the magnificent stone gates to Aachen. "It's not quite the same as what we have in England, but the idea is the same."

"I could go some blood pudding right now," Tuck said wistfully. "Maybe we can find some at your Hospitaller commandery."

"Maybe," Sir Simon nodded. "Now please, let me do the talking. No offence, lads."

"None taken," Will returned, in a tone that suggested otherwise. He did, however, do his best to appear slightly less belligerent than usual.

The gate guards eyed them with interest as they drew closer, although they did not seem hostile. They stood up straighter and thrust their chests out, but John believed that was merely pride, as soldiers prepared to meet others of their kind. The proud Hospitaller knight and his sergeant-at-arms with their red surcoats and stern gazes led the small group towards the archway where one of the guards held up a hand and barked what John assumed was a command to halt.

They dismounted, following the Hospitallers' lead, and stood within the space between the two archways. John was more impressed than he had been already as he saw a great portcullis on the inner archway, and a statue of the Virgin Mary gazing out, undoubtedly to protect those within the city. It all looked sturdy and imposing, rather like the gate guards themselves.

There was a brief conversation between Sir Simon and a guard, while two more soldiers walked along, inspecting John and the others. None were as big as the bailiff, but they did not look worried by his prodigious size. He assumed they had a whole garrison of troops to back them up if the visitors started any trouble, and he offered the nearest guard a cheery smile as the man examined his weapons and gear. The man flashed a grin in response and the bailiff guessed this posting was an easy one, mostly just ejecting drunks from the town of an evening, rather than facing invading armies.

Before long they were waved through and John noticed the soldier that had spoken with Sir Simon took something shiny from the Hospitaller and shoved it into his purse as the six Englishmen led their horses through the second, larger archway and on, into Aachen itself.

"All good?" Will asked when they had left the Ponttor gate behind.

The preceptor turned to him and nodded, but he had a pensive look on his face. "What? Oh, yes, no problems getting access to the city, and a few coins made the guard captain more willing to chat openly with me."

Tuck frowned. "Chat openly? About what?"

"Well, he asked if we were going to the Hospitaller commandery, of course. I told him we were, and he said another group of riders had come to the city yesterday, also heading to the commandery."

"Is that unusual?" John wondered with a sinking feeling.

"I imagine so," the preceptor replied thoughtfully. "Or he wouldn't have mentioned it. You see, the other riders were not Hospitallers."

John shared a dark look with Will.

"The bastards that attacked our camp?" Tuck asked, voicing his friends' fears.

"I don't think so," Sir Simon mused as they moved past tall, colourful, and somehow endearingly quaint houses and workshops. "The captain said these men were not, to him, foreigners."

They absorbed the information, trying to make some sense of it. Was it important, or simply a coincidence?

"They were not merchants or bureaucrats," the preceptor said, just as John was about to suggest it. "The captain thought they looked like soldiers."

"Livery?" Stephen asked.

"They wore none that the guard recognised."

A market was on their right, and a young boy with a little dog ran across to them, bright-eyed and happy, trying to sell them ripe red apples from a basket. Sir Simon took some in return for more of the local coins that he'd exchanged back at the port in Bruges, and the boy ran off again, smile even wider than before. The preceptor passed them out and John gladly took one, biting into it and discovering with some relief that it was just like the apples he was used to in England. For some reason he'd half expected it to taste different.

"I fear those four riders could mean trouble for our mission," Tuck said when he'd worn his fruit down to the core and tossed it into some well-tended flowerbeds as fertiliser.

"How so?" John asked, taking small bites of his apple, savouring the sweet flavour.

"Where do you think they might have come from?" the friar asked with the air of one who's worked out a difficult conundrum.

"You believe they came from Laarne Castle," Will stated. "You think Gerard van Rasseghem sent them here to ask the Hospitallers about King John's treasure."

"I do," Tuck confirmed.

"But how could van Rasseghem have found out about the treasure?" John wondered. "I don't think any of us mentioned it to him."

"No, but he could have found something in his castle's records," said Tuck. "And not mentioned it to us."

"So that's why the wily old shit sent us here on a roundabout route, as Robin suggested," Stephen growled. "A route that slowed us down, while his own men rode along the main road and reached here a day ahead of us."

"And he also sent the men who attacked us along the same route behind us," John guessed. "But why?"

"Why?" Sir Simon chuckled mirthlessly. "Isn't it obvious? He wants the treasure for himself." He breathed a long sigh and waved away another trader who was trying to sell them meat pies that really did not look at all like the ones John was used to eating back in England. "I'm sorry, lads, I fear my idea to visit Laarne was a bad one, and it's not worked in our favour."

Friar Tuck reached out and patted the knight reassuringly on the back. "You had to tell van Rasseghem something, or we couldn't have got any information from him."

"We didn't get any information from him," Will noted darkly.

"Because he is no friend to the Hospitaller Order," Tuck noted. "But we still had to ask van Rasseghem if he knew anything about his great-grandfather's trip to Aachen, for we don't know if his journey ended here in this city. It was worth the risk, even if it did not turn out to our advantage."

"That's an understatement," Will muttered, and Sir Simon nodded sorrowfully.

"Look," Stephen spoke up, clearly annoyed by the criticism of his master. "Van Rasseghem's men are not Hospitallers. There's no guarantee the knights or sergeants at the commandery here in Aachen will help them with..." He trailed off waving his left hand vaguely. "Whatever they're here to find out."

"What are we hoping to find out here anyway?" asked John, who, in truth, could not stop thinking of Robin, wondering if he should turn back and go searching for his missing friend. Although the arguments against such a course made sense, he also felt like a traitor for riding away and leaving Robin to his fate. "Are we really expecting that the Holy Grail was brought here by some Flemish knight a hundred years ago, and the Hospitallers here not only know about it, but will hand it over to us?"

"Put like that," Sir Simon laughed drily. "It does seem fantastical. Ludicrous even."

"You can say that again," Will murmured.

"But this is the quest!" the preceptor concluded, his excitement evident again as he walked straighter, and with great purpose.

"Exactly," Stephen agreed, nodding firmly. "We don't know what we'll discover, but the only way to find out is to follow the trail where it takes us."

John let out a breath and held his tongue. He was wondering if it was even worth finding the lost treasure – the whole point, for him, was to help his friend win a pardon. With Robin gone, the treasure meant little to John. He did not want to bring the mood down any further though, so he remained silent as the Hospitallers led the way through Aachen.

"Don't worry," Tuck said, walking close to him and looking up with a determined expression. "Robin will find us. God will guide him."

"Then I'll pray to God," John replied.

* * *

"God's bollocks, watch where you're going! You almost took my head off with that branch." Matthew Coterel had ducked just in time when Peter, who was riding ahead of him, pushed back a branch and let it ping back as he passed. "It's bad enough trying to keep up with Hood without worrying about getting my teeth smashed out, or worse, by my own man."

"Sorry," Peter grunted, focused completely on the bent undergrowth that their quarry had left behind as he tried to flee. "I think we're going to have to leave the horses and continue on foot. The brush here is too thick. There's brambles and all sorts."

"Then how the fuck did Hood make it through? Can his horse fly?"

"Maybe," Gregor said from the back of the group. "It can run and it can clearly swim. Maybe it can fly as well."

Matthew didn't bother replying to such a stupid comment, but it did seem as if Hood and his horse had somehow managed to pass through briars and bushes that should have held them up, if not halted their progress completely. "Have a care," he warned his companions. "Hood lived in the forest for months. Years. He'll know things that we don't."

Bearing that in mind, the three dismounted, making sure to peg their mounts to the ground so the beasts wouldn't wander off and leave them stranded there in the wilderness without their supplies.

"He must have left his horse somewhere too," Peter murmured as they walked in single file. There was evidence of someone, presumably Hood, having passed this way before them so they were sure they were on the right track, but none of the men were trained trackers, and they could not tell if the trail they were following had been left by a man on foot, or a horse.

"Maybe we should stop looking for Hood then," Gregor suggested. "And go back to find his horse."

"Why?"

"Well, if he's left out here without food or water he'll be as good as dead."

Matthew wondered if he'd made a mistake in bringing Gregor along. He'd never realised how stupid the big man was until now.

"He knows how to survive in the forest," Peter said over his shoulder, rolling his eyes at Matthew. "Now keep your voices down or he'll hear us coming. Remember, he has a longbow."

I wish we did too, Matthew thought, kicking himself for not bringing a skilled archer along with them. It was not ideal to be blundering through the woods chasing a man who might be able to pick them off at any moment without them even seeing where he was. There was no point fretting over it now though.

They pushed on in silence, or at least tried to. It proved impossible to walk without stepping on dried out twigs, or stumbling over thick tangles of grass, or cursing in pain when thorny brambles tore their skin. By contrast, they never heard a sound from the man they were hunting and, eventually, Matthew pulled Peter to a halt and stepped in front of him, staring down at the ground.

"What exactly is it you've got us following?" he hissed, shaking his head as he met Peter's gaze. "There's nothing there. No bent grass, no snapped brambles, nothing."

"Well, look around." Peter gestured. "This is the only possible path. The foliage is too thick for him to have gone anywhere else without leaving an obvious trail."

"I told you, he's a skilled woodsman. He can probably get past things we wouldn't expect anyone to be able to."

"How? He's not a fucking ghost."

Matthew sighed in exasperation. "I don't know. He might have climbed a tree and shimmied along a branch before dropping down on the other side of that bush." He pointed at an ancient oak tree as he spoke, one that would not look at all out of place in an English forest, tracing an imaginary line up its trunk and along a thick branch before waving his hand at an unfamiliar shrub.

"He might have done something like that ages ago then," Gregor noted. "In that case, we've passed him, and he's behind us."

All three spun to look back, swords dragged hastily from scabbards and held up defensively as though they expected Robin Hood to come charging out of the dappled shadows to attack them. There was no one there, and they stood stock still, looking around or eyeing each other fearfully.

"Maybe this wasn't such a good idea," Gregor said, and, although Matthew agreed, he would not admit it.

"He's one man, by Christ! And, although he survived going into the river, it can't have been pleasant. He'll be exhausted, perhaps suffering injuries, broken bones, whatever. Come on, let's just kill the lowborn turd and get this over with."

His speech might have been uplifting if it hadn't been delivered in a breathless, anxious tone. Matthew was frightened, and wishing they'd not allowed themselves to be led into that thick, mysterious woodland. Even the trees seemed to loom threateningly overhead and, when a great grey bird took noisy flight, he almost fell on his backside as he jumped in fear.

There was a longbowman somewhere nearby, and he would not hesitate for a moment before taking any chance he could get to tear them apart with his arrows.

"Come on," he practically shouted, shoving Gregor aside and then shouldering his way up behind Peter. "I want this over with before it gets dark and we can't find our way back to the horses."

They moved on, treading as lightly as possible, but some unknown bird seemed to be following them. Matthew heard the low, ululating song long before he realised it was keeping pace with them. When it let out its oddly un-musical vocalisation right in front of them he stopped, jaw clenched, staring up at a stand of trees. They were heavy with foliage and he could not make out any birds at all.

"What's wrong?" Peter asked softly.

Before Matthew could answer, he saw a great dark shape unfold itself within the branches of the tree directly in front of them, and then came the terrifying snap of a bowstring. His reflexes had kicked in before he knew what was happening, and he fell to the ground, arms covering his head.

The instinctive movement saved his own life, but there came a sickening sound of metal hammering into human flesh, and a monstrous roar of agony filled that claustrophobic little clearing within the greenwood.

Gregor dropped to his knees, eyes bulging so much it looked like they might pop right of their sockets. He was staring at his bicep, which was torn wide open, red, wet skin ripped apart to reveal the white bone beneath. Blood covered his whole arm and Matthew saw bits of flesh splattering the greenery beside them. It was a truly horrific scene, but Matthew knew their attacker must have more than one arrow, so, without a care for loyalty or friendship, he threw himself behind the whimpering Gregor, crouching low, using his comrade as a human shield.

"Help me!" Gregor screamed, kneeling in shock and making no attempt to hide from the archer in the tree. "Matthew, help me! What will I do? Please, I need a bandage! Peter!"

Matthew could not see Peter, who must have at least had the sense to take cover. He prayed the more experienced older man would remain calm and work his way forward to the tree, where he could defend them from Hood before the wolf's head did any more damage.

"Shut up, you fucking halfwit," he shouted at Gregor. "Pull yourself together."

"But my arm—"

There was another snap from overhead, followed by a thud, and a grunt. Matthew peered up from his prone position on the grass and blinked, trying to make sense of what had happened. It did not take long for him to realise he was seeing the blood-soaked head of an arrow protruding from Gregor's back, having torn straight through the man's torso.

"Get the bastard, Peter!" Matthew roared, closing his eyes and trying his best to hide behind Gregor when the man collapsed, dead, on the ground. He did not pray often, but he did then, desperately begging God, the Virgin Mary, the saints, anyone, to save him from the wrathful longbowman in the trees. When he opened his eyes, still muttering to any higher power that would listen, he saw Peter. His friend was not working his way around the tree Hood was hiding in, and neither was he climbing up it to deal with their attacker. Instead, Peter was doing much the same as he was himself: crouching behind the thick trunk of a maple, unwilling to leave cover for fear the expert marksman above would put an arrow in him.

Matthew waited, arguing with himself over whether he should remain where he was and hope Gregor's corpse would stop another missile from hitting him, or make a break for it and finding more substantial cover to shelter behind.

He decided to stay where he was, listening for movement and staring anywhere but at his dead comrade's body despite being pressed right up against it. The smells of sweat, leather, and blood filled his nostrils and he swallowed, almost gagging, righteous anger slowly replacing his terror.

How dare this wolf's head, this lowly yeoman, attack them? And Hood hadn't simply attacked them, he had actually killed two of Matthew's closest friends! It was outrageous! Who the fuck did the whoreson think he was to use such violence against the notorious Coterels?

"I think he's gone."

Matthew still did not move. He lay there for a while longer, listening, trying to decide if Peter's assertion was correct.

"He has. He's gone."

"How? I never heard him climbing down from the tree," Matthew protested. "Are you sure?"

"Aye, I'm sure. I can see where he was standing. He's gone."

Slowly, Matthew got to his feet, staring anxiously at the oak tree.

Peter was pointing at the huge oak limb their nemesis had stood upon to shoot at them. "He wedged his body between the branches so he could use his longbow."

"And somehow managed to disappear without us even noticing, or hearing." Matthew was slowly coming to the conclusion that this whole thing had been a really bad idea.

Peter did work around to the far side of the oak then, still holding his sword up defensively although it would offer scant protection against another of those terrible broadheads Hood was using. "He might be a far better woodsman than us, but he's no wraith. I can see where he jumped down from the tree and made his way off to the west. He's gone right enough."

They did not attempt to chase the archer any further. They'd learned their lesson: the forest belonged to Robin Hood. Matthew still intended to find the hedge-born scum, but they would do it in a setting that gave them the advantage. Where they could bring swords to bear, and not fear the cowardly long-range attacks of a bowman.

"Strip Gregor of his valuables," he said to Peter. "He won't be needing them anymore. And say another prayer."

"If you think it'll help him," Peter replied dourly. "I'm not sure any of us will be going to Heaven though."

They remained there for a time, one searching through the clothes of the dead man for money and weapons, the other staring up at the massive oak, wondering at the skill of the archer who'd so brutally stolen the life from Gregor.

"One thing puzzles me," the young Coterel admitted when they turned, leaving their friend's body for the woodland animals, and began making their way back to where they'd tethered their horses.

"What's that?"

"We were at his mercy. Why didn't he kill us all when he had the chance?"

"I don't know," Peter muttered. "But thank God he showed us mercy, for we were sitting ducks."

Matthew knew his friend was right. Hood could have easily slaughtered the three of them, but something had stayed his hand. They had badly misjudged the magnitude of this mission, not taking into account Robin Hood's skill with a longbow, and his ability to overcome seemingly insurmountable odds.

Perhaps it was time Matthew admitted he was not up to this task, and returned home to England with Peter.

CHAPTER TWENTY-ONE

Robin had slipped down from the oak tree, using his enormous upper body strength to lower himself silently to the ground while still grasping his treasured longbow. He hurried away through the undergrowth, instinctively moving past obstacles and avoiding anything that would betray his position. He went towards his horse – not directly, but in a roundabout fashion to throw off pursuers – and tried to calm his racing mind.

He had meant to kill all three of the Coterel gang members. They were right there, at his mercy, too afraid to run away and too afraid to climb up the tree to reach him. Yet he had only dispatched one of the men before making his way down to the forest floor and disappearing like a wraith into the greenery.

Angrily, he thought back to what had actually happened. The chase had made his blood thunder and the rage build within him so that, when he'd hidden his horse and made his way around to the oak tree to set up his ambush, he'd been eager to slaughter the three men hunting him. He'd climbed the rough old trunk and immediately found the perfect branches to position himself within, allowing him to set his feet and also support his front and back so he'd be able to balance and put all his strength into his arrows.

It had kindled many memories in him, for he'd not stood in a tree with a longbow like that in five years or more. It had all come back naturally though, as he steadied himself and waited for Matthew Coterel and his lackeys to come blundering through the woods like winded boars. They'd moved gracelessly, despite doing their best to be stealthy, and Robin had smiled as he sighted along the first of his arrows at the leader, Matthew Coterel.

The hunters had approached the oak tree without bothering to look up, too stupid to understand the danger they were in, blundering into the forest as though they were swaggering through the urban streets of Derby or London. The sight of their swords reminded Robin, as if he needed a reminder, that these men, total strangers, were coming to kill him. Had, in fact, tracked him for many miles, and already attempted to murder him and his friends as they slept peacefully at their camp.

Focusing his righteous fury, he took a deep breath, aimed at the foremost of his hunters, and let fly.

He was as good a shot as he had ever been, for he practised regularly, and taught others how to use a bow. Even when he'd lived in Scotland he had hunted and maintained his archer's physique. It was not a hardship to him for he enjoyed it, and in all honesty, he was quite proud to be spoken of as England's greatest longbowman. He had no idea if that was true, perhaps there was someone better than him living an unremarkable life in some backwater village that no one had ever heard of, but the minstrels sang songs about Robin Hood's incredible accuracy with a bow, and he intended to show the Coterel gang members that he'd earned that praise legitimately.

His arrow had been loosed with power and precision, but the man he was aiming for, Matthew, had dodged out of the way just before the missile hit him, so the iron head tore through the flesh of another man's arm rather than taking Coterel himself in the heart. Standing on a branch in a tree rather than on solid ground meant it was awkward to draw a second arrow from his belt, nock it to the string, aim, and release. That one had lanced through the air without deviating from its intended course, striking the injured hunter with such force that it punched straight through the man's armour and his torso.

It had all been done instinctively by Robin, his years of experience and training allowing him to act and react without conscious thought, his movements fluid and easy. Grimly satisfied with his handiwork, he reached for a third arrow, eyes fixed on the cowering figure of Matthew

Coterel. Before Robin could draw the arrow from his belt however, the branch he was standing on had bent alarmingly, almost throwing him out of the tree completely. Desperately, he'd tried his best to regain the solid footing he'd had originally, but it proved impossible. Before his enemies noticed his plight and found the courage to attack him, he'd slipped down from the branches and lost himself within the undergrowth, making his way back to the waiting horse. When he found the animal he hugged its long head close, relieved to see it.

Would the Coterels think he'd let them live because he wanted to be merciful? Would they see that as a weakness they could exploit? Or would they think that Robin was toying with them, as a cat would do with a captured mouse?

Robin hoped the latter but he led his horse away from Matthew Coterel and his sole remaining companion and tried to focus fully on reaching the road without being noticed.

It did not take too long, as he moved quickly, trusting that his pursuers would take some time to gather their wits and plan their next move before leaving the cover of the trees. He did not expect them to simply come hurtling through the undergrowth, blindly searching for him. They would not be stupid a second time, not after seeing what he could do with the longbow. He'd be safe for a while he guessed, so he allowed himself to lead the horse quickly back around to the road and, when they reached it, he kicked his heels in and pushed the beast to a gallop.

As far as he could tell, the Coterels did not carry bows, had probably never practised with the weapon, so could not kill him from a distance if they suddenly appeared in front of him now. They'd need to step out into the road and try to hit him with their swords, and that would be a foolhardy thing to do.

As he expected, there was no sign of them, and the thundering hooves of his horse soon carried him far to the east, surely miles away from Matthew Coterel and his remaining guard.

The sun remained high overhead in a cloudless, stunningly blue sky, and his horse was lathered in sweat by the time Robin headed off the road again and down to a stream. He drank the cool, refreshing water like a man who'd been lost in the desert for a week, and the horse did the same, replenishing precious stores that had been lost in a constant lather of perspiration.

Would the two men who'd been hunting him continue to do so? Or would they decide they'd lost enough of their friends and go home before Robin dispatched them too?

He had no idea.

Shaking his head sadly, Robin filled his waterskin to the brim and led the horse back to the road. He'd truly hoped to live a life of peace when he returned to Wakefield.

He should have known better.

* * *

The Hospitaller commandery in Aachen was rather more impressive than the one back in England, at Eagle.

"These people really like to build big buildings, don't they?" John asked, marvelling at the sight of the religious Order's complex of structures set near the very middle of the city.

"Aye, and from stone too," Tuck agreed.

The friar had seen places like this before, John knew, on his travels when he was younger and acting as a bodyguard to important clergymen, but even he openly admired the commandery's walls and gates, and the larger keep-like structure behind those defences.

Sir Simon and Stephen smiled proudly, preening almost as if they'd built the place with their own hands.

There were guards here too, for it was a busy, cosmopolitan city with lots of travellers, and many ne'er do-

215

wells who would take advantage of an undefended building, robbing any and all valuables they could find. And John guessed a Hospitaller commandery would have plenty of precious relics behind its doors.

It was beginning to get on John's nerves that he couldn't understand what Sir Simon was saying when he was conversing with the people in those lands, and he had to stand beside his horse, again, wondering what was happening as the preceptor's frown grew deeper with every unintelligible sentence he shared with the guards.

They were waved through before long, and one of the guards hurried ahead of them to let the people in the main body of the commandery know that visitors were there.

Will looked almost as fed-up as John felt. It had been a long journey to get there, Robin was missing – probably dead – and now Sir Simon told them that there had been four other men visiting the commandery the day before.

Gerard van Rasseghem's men, undoubtedly. The Lord of Laarne's soldiers were a full day ahead of them.

"Are they still here?" Tuck asked, but the preceptor shook his head. They'd left just a few hours after arriving in Aachen.

"Then they must have found what they were looking for," Stephen noted grimly.

"Let's hope whatever it was, is still here," Will said, and his tone was as portentous as the sergeant-at-arms'.

Tuck caught John's eye and the clergyman shook his head, reading his thoughts. John had been about to tell them all that he was sick of this stupid 'quest', that it was all for naught, and that he had no intention of racing van Rasseghem's men to take possession of this mythical lost treasure. He held his peace though as he saw Tuck's gesture, deciding to wait and see how things went there at the Hospitallers' headquarters.

Inside, the commandery was not quite as impressive as the exterior. It was as bland and functional as a religious place should be, even a military one. Or so John thought. The stone walls kept out the harsh afternoon sun and for that at least the travellers were glad, wiping sweat from their brows as they were shown inside and told to wait for the Commander, or his representative, to come and meet them.

A lay sergeant, an elderly man with a head as bald as an egg and a thick grey moustache brought them jugs of cold water, and beer which he told them, relayed via Sir Simon of course, was brewed right there in the commandery. John, Tuck, and Will all went directly to that latter jug, eagerly helping themselves to what proved to be a light-amber coloured drink, made from local wheat in some process John could not begin to imagine but certainly enjoyed the results of.

"God's bones," Will breathed as he took a long mouthful of the beer. "This is delicious. You'll have to get the recipe from them, Sir Simon."

The preceptor nodded distractedly, apparently far more interested in what his counterpart there in Aachen would tell them about yesterday's visitors from Laarne than how the wheat beer was made.

They were not made to wait long before the commander came into the chamber. There were benches and chairs all around, suggesting this was often used as a meeting room for the Hospitallers and their charges, and the commander quickly found a seat.

Introducing himself – in accented English, John was pleased to see – as Sir Hans von Horstmar, he nodded to each of them in turn before naturally looking to Sir Simon as the one he'd mainly be conversing with. John watched as the pair made introductions, examining the knight who was perhaps forty years old, tall, straight-backed, with close-cropped brown hair and craggy features. He did not look particularly friendly to John, but neither did he look unwelcoming, or put out by their presence.

"We are searching for a very old, and very valuable English treasure," Sir Simon readily admitted to the commander once the niceties were out of the way. "The crown jewels, or what remains of them, of King John."

The Aachener's eyes narrowed and he leaned back on his seat, visibly taken aback but nonetheless interested. "Oh?"

"Indeed, Herr Ritter," Sir Simon said, giving the man his rightful honorific of 'Sir Knight'. "We have come all the way from Eagle Preceptory in England with our companions here, following the trail of the lost treasure."

"And it led you here?"

Sir Simon explained everything to the commander, telling him how their party members had been brought there by hearsay, and from the records in the library at Eagle. "Giselbrecht van Zottegem came here, to Aachen, with something so valuable that it was guarded by many of our brother knights. We've come to see if your library can prove as useful as the one back in my own preceptory, and guide us along the next step of our quest."

"You were told that four men were here yesterday, also seeking to view our records?"

"We were," Sir Simon nodded. "Perhaps naively, I told the Lord of Laarne something about our quest and now, apparently, he's sent men of his own to beat us to the lost treasure."

Von Horstmar gave a crooked smile at that. "You do not think it naive to then come here and tell me even more of the tale?"

"We are brother knights," replied the preceptor with a slight tilt of his head that made him appear even more earnest than usual. "Hospitallers. I would hope I could trust you, Herr Ritter."

"But you are not searching for the old king's treasure to benefit our Order."

Sir Simon pursed his lips and nodded. "We are, or at least were, hoping to find it to return it to the present king, Edward, in order to win a pardon for a friend of ours."

The commander looked at Tuck, Will, and John expectantly.

"Not them," Sir Simon said. "Another. We were attacked beside the River Meuse by unknown assailants and our friend has gone missing."

The German knight took all this in with a deepening frown, finally shaking his head regretfully. "I'm sorry, brother. This all sounds deeply intriguing. Attacks, subterfuge on the Lord of Laarne's part, and some enigmatic hoard of valuables. I would like to help you, I really would, but I do not have the men for it."

John examined the man's face as he spoke, and guessed the commander thought them all mad. Good, the fewer people that believed in the existence of the treasure, the better. At least they wouldn't need to worry about soldiers from Aachen trying to beat them to the finish line!

"We wish to search your records," said Sir Simon. "We're hoping to find some clue here."

"You think van Rasseghem's men found it before you?"

"I fear so," the preceptor agreed. "But if we can find it too, we may yet overtake them. Did the soldiers from Laarne access your records?"

"They did," the commander admitted a little sheepishly. "I was not here, but my steward let them visit our library. They said they were searching for an old book with information on some descendant of van Rasseghem's."

John rolled his eyes at that and Sir Simon looked at him ruefully.

"You may have full access to our library," the commander said kindly. "And I will have a sergeant assist you. As you say, we are Hospitallers. I would be happy to help however I can, especially if it means stopping that old weasel van Rasseghem from growing more wealthy."

"You know him, Brother?" Tuck asked.

"I do," von Horstmar returned with a sour expression. "Had I been here yesterday his men would never have been allowed to enter, for he is no friend to our Order."

"That has become all too clear," Will noted dourly.

"Go on, then," the commander barked, standing up and gesturing towards the door. "I presume you, Sir Simon, and the friar, will be the ones searching the records? Good, let's go. I will take you there and leave you to it." He smiled at John, Will, and Stephen. "You may rest here. I will have refreshments sent in, although, I warn you, they will be frugal. We are a religious Order after all." His wink gave John hope that the food and drink, when it came, would not be quite as frugal as suggested.

* * *

Little John did not love the slices of ham the commander had ordered a sergeant to bring them as they waited for their companions to search the library. It looked nice enough, but had been cooked in some strange oil or butter, and the taste and smell were both unfamiliar and unpleasant. He did help himself to some summer berries, and good, old-fashioned buttered bread, while taking it easy with the wheat beer. Stephen and Will did not share his dislike for the ham, wolfing it down greedily, although sharing his reticence to drink too much of the beer. They might be amongst friends now, but God knew what the rest of the day might bring. There had been enough nasty surprises over the past few weeks to make them all wary.

They'd only just finished their repast when Tuck came back into the chamber, followed by a pensive-looking Sir Simon Launcelyn, who was chewing his cheek and staring unseeingly at the floor.

Behind them, Hans von Horstmar hurried in, staring from Tuck to Sir Simon. "What's wrong?" he asked. "I was told you must see me."

"Bad news, Commander!" Tuck burst out, red-faced. "The Lord of Laarne's men did find what they were looking for in your records."

"And?"

"The bastards ripped out the page with the information," Sir Simon said, visibly distraught, although whether it was the loss of the lead they needed to continue the trail that had upset him, or the destruction of such an old record, John was not sure.

"They what?" Apparently the commander shared his English counterpart's outrage, balling his fists and glaring almost murderously at Sir Simon.

"It's true," Tuck said, eyeing the cleared plates of food sorrowfully.

"How dare they?" von Horstmar cried. "To come to my Commandery and wilfully damage Hospitaller records? I will have van Rasseghem's balls for this!"

"That would be good," Sir Simon said vehemently. "But it won't help us just now. As things stand, our quest for the lost treasure is over. We have no idea what to do next."

"You're assuming van Rasseghem's men found anything at all," Will Scarlet broke in, as sceptical as ever. "What if they tore out that page to make it seem like they'd found something important? Maybe they didn't find anything at all, but wanted to sidetrack us, or put us off continuing."

"Or maybe they found the treasure itself," John suggested. "All the way here, we believed it was brought to Aachen for safe-keeping. Perhaps van Rasseghem's men found it here and smuggled it out without the Hospitallers noticing."

All eyes turned to the commander, but he shook his head firmly. "Unless the treasure really is a book, those soldiers did not find it here. My sergeant was in the library with them and he did not see them either leave the room, or do anything other than look through the records."

"Fair enough," John shrugged.

A thoughtful, angry silence settled over the group for a time, and then von Horstmar let out a low oath in German and smacked his hands together in fury. "Whatever their motives, they have damaged Hospitaller property, and ruined a valuable historical record. It is..." He paused, searching for the right word. "Unconscionable," he finished, rather to John's surprise. The man spoke excellent English, which suggested he was a true scholar and made his rage over the torn book more understandable to the barely literate bailiff.

Again, silence fell across the men in the room and then Will said, "Well, what are we going to do now? Follow van Rasseghem's men? If we can find them, we can take back that page they ripped out, and shove it right up—"

"We need to be able to read the thing, Scarlet," Stephen interrupted with a rueful smile. "Although I like your idea of finding the flea-ridden curs and making them pay for what they've done."

Sir Simon sat on one of the chairs and looked up at the ceiling, utterly deflated. John wondered if he was praying silently, for he remained withdrawn and silent for quite some time. It was a marked contrast to the enthusiasm he'd shown during the rest of their journey. Perhaps this was one setback too far, even for the idealistic preceptor.

Little John gave a heavy sigh. When Robin had not been around in the 'old days', it had always fallen to John to lead the gang. He could be relied upon to keep a cool head, and look at things rationally, without allowing emotions – especially rage – to cloud his vision, unlike, for example, Will Scarlet.

It seemed he would need to take up the mantle of leader once again.

The quest was over, and it was time to return to England. But first they had to make another attempt to locate Robin. Dead or alive, they simply had to discover their friend's fate – John could not return to Matilda and the children without the truth.

Before he could open his mouth however, one of the Hospitaller lay sergeants appeared in the door, breathless, wide-eyed and obviously bringing exciting news to share.

CHAPTER TWENTY-TWO

John immediately stood up, staring expectantly at the sergeant who was a small man with short grey hair and delicate fingers which he clasped before him. He's come to tell us Robin has turned up, the bailiff thought, hope rising and bringing a lump to his throat.

The sergeant spoke directly to the commander, who smiled almost triumphantly as Sir Simon broke into a wide grin.

"What is it?" John demanded. "What did he say?"

"Excellent news," the preceptor gushed, looking around at all the Englishmen. "The sergeant has found a second copy of the record that van Rasseghem's men ripped out and stole!"

Tuck gave a bark of joyous laughter, and both Stephen and Will nodded at one another happily. John felt disappointment that his friend had not come to Aachen, but he did his best to hide it, not wishing to ruin everyone else's excitement.

"Where is it?" Tuck asked, looking at Sir Simon who directed the question to the sergeant.

The man gave a reply and the preceptor nodded, translating for the others. "It's in the library. In one of the books that are chained to the shelves so no one wanders off with them."

"How did your sergeant know it was there?" Stephen wondered.

"He copied it out himself," von Horstmar told them. "We make copies of some important, or particularly old documents. Some go to other Hospitaller libraries, or royal libraries in some cases, while others remain here. Luckily, this sergeant thought your record important enough to make a duplicate."

"Ha! Well done, that man!" Tuck beamed, offering the sergeant a salute. "Can we see it then?"

"Of course," von Horstmar said. "Come on. Why don't we go down and find out what hidden knowledge this tome contains?" He signalled to the sergeant who bowed slightly and turned away, leading the whole group to the library.

John had been in plenty of buildings like this one back in England, and he saw that the design of the place was very similar to the ones he was familiar with. The library was protected by a massive door and, inside, it had the fusty smell that all such places seemed to have. As they walked, he looked at the books on the shelves, doing his best to read the titles on the spines, but they were all in Latin or some other foreign language and he had no idea what any of them said.

The section with the chained books was against the rear wall of the large chamber and they hurried towards it, a sense of great expectation building even within John. This was what they had travelled all that distance to see, from Eagle to Aachen in the Holy Roman Empire. Whatever this great leather-bound volume contained, it would either make or break the friends' quest. Would it contain the key to unlock the next stage of their journey, or would it turn out to be meaningless and prove the end of the road for them?

The little sergeant went straight to the book he wanted, having already laid it out for inspection. John wondered how many such books the man had read, and copied, over his lifetime. Dozens. Hundreds. A thought struck the bailiff then: if this mighty tome contained some really earth-shattering piece of text, why had the sergeant not brought it to anyone's attention when he first copied it out? That put a dampener on John's enthusiasm, but he stopped with the others, impatiently waiting as Sir Simon and von Horstmar stood side by side and bent to inspect the section that the sergeant had left open for them.

"Well…" The German knight was first to finish reading and he leaned back, still staring down at the page with its spidery lines of script. "I did not expect that."

Sir Simon finished a moment later and he was frowning as he turned to Tuck. "It's in Latin, would you like to read it too, brother?"

They all waited for the friar to take his turn and then both he and the preceptor looked at von Horstmar.

"What is *Untersberg*?" Sir Simon asked.

"That is the part I was not expecting," the German admitted. "It is a mountain."

"The text says Giselbrecht van Zottegem went there after coming here. Why would he travel to a mountain? What's there?"

The commander shook his head. "It is a famous mountain in this country, but it is simply that: a mountain. There is nothing there that I know of that would draw a Flemish nobleman to it, especially if he was carrying, or perhaps escorting, valuable treasure that rightfully belonged to the king of England."

The preceptor turned back to the book, re-reading the Latin script as though he might draw out some hidden meaning.

"You said Untersberg is famous," Tuck said to the commander. "Why?"

"Well, first and foremost it is a pleasant place to visit. Or so I've heard, I never have visited it myself. But there are said to be spectacular views from the top of the mountain." He shrugged. "Noblemen and women who have too much money and not enough work sometimes go there. It is close to Salzburg, so quite easy to get to on main roads."

"What else, lord?" Stephen asked.

"Well, there are many…legends, surrounding Untersberg. Even the name – 'under the mountain'."

"Under it?" John repeated.

"*Ja*," von Horstmar confirmed. "There are many stories about dwarfs, wizards, demons, and other fantastical creatures living beneath the mountain. There are deep caves there, and people sometimes go missing in the area, said to have been abducted by the mysterious beings."

"Demons?" Tuck murmured.

"So it is said," von Horstmar smiled, although it was no longer the pleasant, easy expression of an hour before. Now the commander looked pensive to John, maybe even a tad frightened.

Perhaps to dispel his own uneasiness, the knight moved the talk onto a separate legend, one that was far less disturbing than dwarfs that kidnapped unwary travellers. "Apparently one of our old kings or emperors lies within the mountain in a throne room, surrounded by his knights. When his beard has grown around his marble table three times, and when the ravens have stopped circling around the summit, he will return for the final battle between Good and Evil. Sometimes it is said to be Karl der Große – Karl the Great – and other times it is claimed to be Kaiser Rotbart."

"We have a similar legend in England," Tuck noted. "Only it's King Arthur who's said to be sleeping somewhere, ready to come to our aid one day."

"I wish he'd bloody hurry up," Will grunted and John smiled in agreement.

"Every country has a mythical hero," the Aachener chuckled before growing serious again. "Untersberg has more than its fair share of strange tales around it though. I simply do not understand why the old Lord of Laarne would go there with your King John's treasure. Do you know what that treasure actually consisted of? Not a book, I presume."

Sir Simon and Tuck shared a glance and the Hospitaller shrugged. "The usual things. A crown, gemstones, gold and silver coins."

"And a sword connected to the legend of King Arthur," Tuck added.

John was glad that no one mentioned the Holy Grail. Their quest had drawn enough unwanted attention already, without the people of Aachen believing they were hunting for one of the greatest relics in all Christendom.

"Why take such items to the mountain?" von Horstmar asked, evidently baffled by it all.

"To hide them?" Stephen guessed, and, to John, it seemed a sensible suggestion.

"Maybe," Sir Simon agreed with his sergeant-at-arms. "If there's a network of caves beneath the mountain maybe they would be a good place to hide treasure. It was stolen from England after all."

"So they took it to Untersberg to hide it," said Tuck. "Until people forgot about it, and about the Flemish knights that had been escorting King John when the treasure was supposedly swallowed up in the Fens."

"In that case, Giselbrecht van Zottegem may have intended to return for it at some point, but never got around to it." John rubbed his eyes which were growing tired from the lack of light in that windowless section of the library.

"But, thanks to us, his great-grandson's soldiers are now on the way to retrieve it," Sir Simon sighed.

"Indeed, and van Rasseghem will no doubt claim the treasure is his by right, since it was once in the possession of his great-grandfather." Von Horstmar's face twisted in distaste. "I would rather it was returned to England, than let that Hospitaller-hating *Schweinehund* get hold of it."

"As would we," Sir Simon agreed. "So we should really be on our way if we're to have any hope of overtaking those soldiers before they reach the Untersberg. Would you be so kind as to write down directions to the mountain, Herr Ritter?"

"I do not know the exact way there," the German knight told him. "But I do know how to get to Salzburg, and you can easily find the path from there. I will write it down for you, and I will also make sure your supplies are fully replenished, and your horses will be ready, fresh for the road to the Untersberg."

They all thanked him profusely for his help and, when he'd taken his sergeant's quill pen and ink and written clear directions to Salzburg on a piece of parchment, they left the library and headed out to the courtyard.

John's sense of adventure had been tickled by the talk of the mysterious mountain. In recent years he had enjoyed dealing with elements of what most people would describe as 'supernatural'. Those experiences, alongside Tuck and Will Scarlet, had proven frightening it was true, but also incredibly interesting. Untersberg promised to be another exciting and extremely unusual adventure.

He just wished Robin could be there to share it with them.

Von Horstmar came to bid them farewell as they took their horses – thoroughly fed, watered, and rubbed-down – and headed for the commandery's outer gates. Their saddlebags were bursting with foods that would not perish too quickly in the summer sun, and skins of wheat beer and water.

"South-eastward, lads," Sir Simon called, grinning, plainly excited to continue the journey, and Stephen smiled back at him, sharing his enthusiasm.

"One thing the commander never mentioned," John said, glancing back to wave to the knight as they passed through the gates and walked out into the main part of town one more. "How far is it to the Untersberg?"

"Not that far," said Sir Simon cheerily. "We should be there in a couple of weeks or so."

"Two weeks?" Will demanded, even before John could voice his own dismay.

"Four hundred miles or so," the Hospitaller told them, and his voice took on a defensive note. "That's not all that far. The Holy Roman Empire is a huge place, lads. We'll be there before you know it."

John stopped walking and so did Will. Both looked at one another and shook their heads. "This is too much," the massive bailiff growled.

The others in the party also stopped now, gazing back at them in surprise. Even Tuck appeared eager to get going.

"Two weeks is too long," John said firmly. "That's a month's round trip, and that's only to get back here to Aachen. We'd still have to get home to England. And none of that takes into account how long we'll be at the Untersberg!"

"Or if one or more of our horses is lamed and can't continue," Will added angrily. "John's right. We came here thinking we wouldn't be away from home for too long, and it was all going to be worth it because we'd find the treasure and take it to King Edward to win Robin his pardon."

"But Robin isn't here anymore!" John put in. "And riding another eight or nine hundred miles to hunt for some damned treasure that might not even exist is just madness! Our families are at home waiting for us to return. There's work to be done and, quite frankly, I'm sick of riding around in this heat while people try to kill us."

"Well said," Will congratulated him. "Couldn't have put it better myself."

The preceptor looked sadly at them, but he nodded in understanding. "I get what you're saying, and I don't blame you. Perhaps I've become so wrapped up in the excitement of the quest that I've forgotten you men have lives to get back to. This has been just the kind of thing Stephen and I really needed after so many long, boring months at Eagle." He shrugged. "If you've decided to go back to England, I won't try to change your mind. You go with my thanks for coming this far, and for allowing us to share in the adventure in the first place. I will continue on to the Untersberg though, with Stephen, and, if you wish, Tuck, you will be most welcome to join us."

Tuck looked torn, and John felt sorry for the friar. He knew Tuck had been thinking of the Holy Grail ever since the mystical chalice was first posited as one of the items Giselbrecht van Zottegem had been escorting to Aachen, and the friar was clearly upset at the thought of having to give up the hunt at this stage. So near, yet so far…

"You go on with them," Will said to their tonsured old friend. "You have no wife waiting for your return and, as you said yourself, a mendicant friar is supposed to travel, spreading the Lord's message." Scarlet smiled warmly, if a little sadly.

Tuck handed his reins to Stephen and walked to Will, reaching out to shake his hand. Scarlet laughed gruffly and drew the friar into a rough bear-hug, and then it was John's turn. He thought there were tears in Tuck's eyes as they too embraced, neither man speaking, at a loss for words for once.

"Shall you go straight home?" Sir Simon asked. "Or try to find out what happened to Robin?"

John turned to Will and shrugged. "I think we should at least attempt to find out what we can about Robin," the bailiff said with a heavy heart.

"I'd like to know what happened to him too," Stephen piped up, grinning. "Maybe we should ask him."

Irritated by the sergeant's incongruous levity, John opened his mouth to berate him, but he turned as he did so, looking back towards the Hospitaller commandery where he saw what had made Stephen so happy.

"Robin!" Will Scarlet shouted in pure joy.

* * *

The reunion changed everything. They could not stand in the street blocking the way with their horses, so they walked on and found an inn. Their mounts must have been surprised to find themselves stabled again so soon after leaving the commandery, but the men needed to have a proper discussion. Sir Simon did suggest they return to the Hospitaller's headquarters since it was nearby, but the others felt the commander had done enough for them and might not appreciate them returning so soon, expecting more free hospitality.

Tuck was very happy to discover the inn sold the German version of blood pudding and soon the reunited friends were in the common room discussing all that had happened since Robin was separated from them.

He told them how he'd found himself half-drowned on the bank of the Meuse and likely been saved from freezing to death by his loyal horse. He then recounted the tale of Matthew Coterel and friends chasing him into the woods and how that had turned out, admitting his disappointment at not being able to finish off the final two enemies.

"I knew you were heading here, of course," he finished. "So I simply followed the road, pushing my horse so I could catch you up before you moved on again."

"We did search for you," John said guiltily.

"Aye, but we found no trace of you," Will added. "We found the body of the bastard who'd went into the water with you though."

"Two of them dead then," Robin grunted. "Hopefully the two that are left decide they've had enough and fuck off back to England."

"Speaking of merry old England," the preceptor said. "John and Will had just decided to return there before you arrived, Robin. What say you now, lads?"

"You can't go home," Robin told them, aghast. "Not after coming all this way. Tell me what you found out at the commandery here in Aachen. I assume you did find something?"

It was his turn to listen then, as the others told him what they'd been doing since the events at the River Meuse.

"Well then," he said when the story was over and he'd taken in the news about the Untersberg and its eerie mythology. "We can't give up now. John? Will?"

Robin could see the conflict in his friends' faces. It seemed they had made up their minds to return home to Amber and Elspeth, and his return, although very welcome, placed his friends in something of a dilemma.

"The thought of riding for weeks doesn't appeal to me, Robin," Little John admitted. "Neither does the idea of being away from home for such a long time."

"Exactly," Will agreed, before breaking into a smile. "But now that you're back with us we have a real reason to find that bloody treasure, don't we?"

"Indeed!" Sir Simon roared, visibly overjoyed at the prospect of continuing to the Untersberg together again. "And come on, Will, admit it: you want to know what we'll find at the mountain, don't you?"

"Aye, I do," Scarlet nodded. "Things are never quiet back in Wakefield, but this whole adventure is beyond anything I've ever been a part of."

"John?"

The big bailiff met Robin's gaze and let out a heavy, theatrical sigh. "All right," he said. "I'll come too. I can't ride home on my own, can I?"

"Then it's settled," Tuck said, making the sign of the cross and looking up at the rafters as he asked God for his blessing on their continuing adventures together.

"What are we waiting for then?" Stephen demanded. "Let's get moving. We still need to catch up with van Rasseghem's lot, or they might find the treasure before us."

"That bastard has a lot to answer for," Robin stated darkly as they trooped out of the inn and headed for the stables to collect the horses. "If it wasn't for the Lord of Laarne we wouldn't have been attacked at our camp by the Coterels, and we wouldn't be in a race with his men to find the lost treasure."

233

"Agreed." Sir Simon handed the stable-hands some coins and led his mount into the courtyard. "It would be nice if we could repay him for the trouble he's caused us."

"The best way is to find the treasure before his soldiers do," Tuck said, grunting as he hauled himself up into the saddle and wiped sweat from his shaved crown.

"Nah, the best way would be to knock his fucking teeth out," Scarlet argued, checking the two pack horses were safely tethered before mounting up himself.

"I agree," said the preceptor. "But there's little chance of us being able to do that, so let's just do as Tuck says, eh? Are we all ready? Let's ride, lads. To the Untersberg!"

"To the Untersberg!" Robin grinned, and the companions cantered out onto the open road once more, filled with renewed hope, and the burning desire to see a successful end to their quest.

CHAPTER TWENTY-THREE

"God help us, will it ever stop?"

Tuck chuckled although even he cowered a little as another blinding fork of light lit up the darkened sky and, shortly after, a terrific rumble of thunder filled the air. "You should be used to it by now," the friar said to Robin. "It's not like this is the first storm we've encountered on our journey."

"This one feels like the worst," the big archer replied. He did not like to show fear, even to his friends, but he hated how helpless he felt as the sky cracked and rumbled as though it might come crashing down on top of them at any moment. It was truly terrifying, and really made Robin appreciate the power of nature like never before.

"Anyone would think you'd never been in a storm before," John said, apparently not frightened at all. He was gazing up at the clouds and the fir trees in the hills around them, an almost beatific smile on his face, clearly enjoying the spectacle. "Considering how much time we spent living in the forests of Barnsdale and Sherwood, I'm surprised you don't feel at home in this. I know I do."

"We didn't have storms like this in Barnsdale!" Robin retorted as another fork arced out of the sky. "At least not every fucking day, like here."

"It's not every day," Will laughed.

"It's not far off it!"

"Many places have more extreme weather than England," Stephen told him. "Spain, Rhodes, here. You get used to it. To be honest, it's quite beautiful, don't you agree?"

Robin gaped at him. The bluff sergeant-at-arms rarely spoke so appreciatively about anything.

"Beautiful or not," Sir Simon grumbled. "It's holding us up. We need to reach Salzburg as soon as possible."

"How far away are we now?" Robin asked. "It feels like months since we left Aachen."

The knight nodded, flinching slightly as a leaf, grown heavy with collected rain, tipped and emptied its contents onto his bare neck. "We're only a day or so from Salzburg," he said. "And, from there, a few miles to the mountain."

"Can't we just go straight to the Untersberg?" John asked. "It would be quicker."

"You want to head to the mountain without any idea of what you're doing? Which side to enter? Which tunnels are safe to go through? Which tunnel might lead to the treasure?"

John smiled sheepishly and drained water from his beard as the rain continued to splatter against the leaves around them. "I never thought of that," he admitted. "I've never climbed a mountain before."

"I'd like to question the locals in Salzburg about the myths too," Tuck said. "I've always been interested in folklore. I'll bet the people living beside the mountain will have plenty of interesting tales to tell."

"A load of bollocks they've made up to entertain gullible visitors," Will said.

"Ha, no doubt that will play a part in it," the friar agreed readily enough. "But as long it's interesting, I'll be happy to listen."

"Bollocks," Sir Simon repeated, grinning at Scarlet. "You do have a direct way of putting things. Rather like Stephen here."

"Aye, they're a pair of sour faced wankers," said John, dodging the blow that Scarlet aimed at his head.

The storm continued to dump rain upon them, thunder booming and lightning flashing for another half hour before it finally rolled past and the sun came out. Steam rose from the tree-lined road as the riders began the journey once again and, so intense was the sunshine that it was impossible to tell that there had been such a heavy downpour just a short time before.

"It's so different to England," Robin said, taking in the almost monotonous sight of hundreds of similarly shaped spruce, fir, or pine trees covering the hills everywhere he looked.

"That's what happens when you visit different lands," Stephen told him. "You should see Rhodes if you think it's different here."

"Maybe one day," Robin replied, never intending to leave England again once this quest was finished.

They stayed at inns, or camped out if no sizeable settlements were nearby when they stopped to rest each night. The ubiquitous conifer trees offered extra protection against the elements and hid their tents, and horses, from other travellers so they were not too worried about being attacked again as they slept. Still, they did take turns on watch – even when they were staying at an inn – and kept their weapons within easy reach all through the night, just in case the Coterels or some local bandits came for them.

They were not molested at all, however, and, when they reached Salzburg at last the sense of impending danger that had followed them ever since the River Meuse was beginning to fade. It seemed the Coterels had given up the chase or at least lost their trail, and the only other real enemies – the soldiers from Laarne – were ahead of them. Robin and his friends had not passed them on the road, or seen any sign of them, and the people in the settlements they visited were happy to confirm the Flemish warriors had passed through a day or so before them.

As they neared Salzburg the land seemed to level out, although there were mountains in the distance. They had covered hundreds of miles, climbing hills, crossing bridges, and ferries that took the horses over rivers in ones or twos, but now their destination lay before them. The road, as expected, grew more crowded as merchants, traders, mercenaries, farmers, and all sorts of other folk flowed in and out of the city.

"Keep your eyes open for the riders from Laarne," Robin advised as they were forced to slow their pace on another bridge just outside Salzburg. "We've pushed the horses to try and close the gap on them, so there's a chance they're nearby. It would be better if they had no idea we were so close."

"You think they'd attack us?" Will asked. "Let them try!"

"They'd probably not do anything out in the open," Robin replied, looking at Sir Simon. "I expect there's some kind of militia, city watch or the like, operating in Salzburg?"

"Oh yes," the preceptor confirmed. "We can't afford to get into a public brawl with van Rasseghem's men. I'd suggest we keep to ourselves, find a good inn, and you lads can rest while I go out in the city to find a guide that will lead us into the Untersberg."

"Alone?"

"One of you may escort me. We shall be safe enough, I think. Hospitallers are generally well respected in this part of the Holy Roman Empire."

"I like that plan," Tuck stated. "Hopefully we can find an inn that does that blood pudding like the one we had in Aachen. I've grown rather partial to that."

"You? Partial to food?" Will pretended to be amazed, and Tuck flicked an obscene gesture at him.

"I forgive your vicious words, Scarlet, for it is written, 'He who ignores fools lives a longer, happier life'."

Sir Simon's brow furrowed and, after a time he said, "I don't remember that being in the Bible."

"It's not," Tuck admitted. "I never said it was. I just said it was written, and so it is, in the journal I've been keeping to document this quest of ours. I wrote out that mantra to remind myself not to get dragged down to Will's level whenever he spouts any of his nonsense."

The other men laughed, and Robin bent over his horse's neck, overcome by mirth as he saw the outraged look on Will Scarlet's ruddy face.

"That must be the Untersberg," said John, before an argument could develop. Robin followed his pointing finger to the largest of the enormous mounds that utterly dominated the skyline ahead despite being miles distant.

"It's big," said Stephen.

"That's an understatement," Robin breathed. He had never seen anything like it before. It was far, far bigger than any of the hills or mountains he'd seen in England or Scotland. So big that he could hardly take it in. It would take days – weeks maybe! – if one decided to travel around the whole thing. His mind tried to imagine how such a monstrous edifice could have been created but he could not begin to fathom the forces that would be required. And it was not the only such mountain for there were others beside it, not quite as huge, but still enormous. Robin squinted and raised a hand to shelter his eyes from the sun, gasping as he did so. "Is that…. snow on top of it?" he asked, astonished to see slivers of white around the summit of the Untersberg.

Snow, in the middle of summer!

"God is great indeed," said Tuck at the sight, blessing himself and kissing the cross around his neck, echoing Robin's own awestruck musings.

"I can see why so many myths and legends have sprung up about the place," Will said, apparently forgetting his earlier annoyance. "It's magical."

"It is that," Sir Simon agreed wholeheartedly, taking a piece of linen from his pouch and using it to wipe beads of sweat from his forehead. "But it will also be dangerous, especially to men like us, who have no experience in exploring such a place."

"Dangerous?" John asked. "You mean because of the dwarves and demons?"

The preceptor did not laugh, or even smile, as Robin had expected. It seemed Sir Simon feared there might be some truth in the old legends. He did shake his head though.

"No, I did not mean those things in particular. I was simply thinking of more mundane dangers: getting lost, falling from a great height, drowning in an underground lake, getting trapped in a cave or a crevice, or freezing to death from cold. As Robin noted, that looks like snow on the mountain, as incredible as it seems."

"And we can't forget the soldiers from Laarne." Stephen grimaced, touching a hand to his sword hilt menacingly.

"As if the mountain wasn't dangerous enough on its own," Will grumbled.

"God will watch over us," Tuck promised confidently, and Sir Simon voiced his agreement.

Robin looked around at the party and felt his heart swell with pride. Enemies, be they demonic or corporeal, would find their match in Robin and his friends.

And yet, he could not help but feel a little thrill of trepidation – fear, even – as they approached Salzburg and the brooding presence of the ancient, legend-haunted mountain. What would they find there? King John's lost treasure, or something far darker?

His mind quickly turned away from the mysterious and back to the city before them. Smells came to him, of cooking meat, summer flowers, the river they had just crossed, and other, less pleasant scents that always accompanied a large grouping of people and animals.

"This place is incredible," said Will, shaking his head at the sight of an actual castle within the city, high atop a hill. "That's like the one at Nottingham, but much more impressive."

"It's like something from a story," John said, and his voice was low, as though he was fatigued by all the amazing sights that assailed them.

"Well, now it's part of your story. Another chapter in the legend of Robin Hood's gang." Sir Simon smiled at them and then dismounted to deal with the guards at the city gates. They were quickly waved through and led their horses along the bustling streets towards an inn one of the guards had recommended.

The place was rather like the one they'd rested at in Aachen and they were soon safely ensconced in the common room with mugs of the rich local beer, their horses stabled, and platters of food brought to them by a pair of buxom, blonde women.

"God be praised, these are delicious," Tuck exclaimed as he chewed the food.

"King's Chicken," said Sir Simon. "That's what the serving wench called them."

Robin dug in and could only agree with Tuck's glowing review of the flavour.

"We should get the recipes of all these wonderful dishes before we go home," the friar declared. "What's in these? I detect saffron, ginger and..." He sniffed a piece of the chicken, shaking his head as he did so.

"Anise," Sir Simon offered. "And eggs."

"Cooked in lard," said Will who had been too busy shovelling the food into his mouth to speak before then.

"Write that down, Tuck," Robin told the friar. "And you can make this for us back in Wakefield."

"He's no cook," John mumbled, bent over his own dish, eyes focused intently on it. "He's far better at eating meals than making them."

"That's not true," Tuck returned defensively, washing down the last of his chicken with a swallow of beer. "Many a time in the greenwood you enjoyed my pottage. But if you insist, we could give the recipe to your Amber. She does make the best pies in Wakefield."

John straightened, grinning proudly. "Aye. That she does," he agreed, before leaning down to devour the rest of his meal. "That she does."

"I'll go out in the city when we're finished," the preceptor told them when the serving girls had taken the main course away and brought a second consisting of a creamy almond pudding dusted with sugar. If anything, it was even tastier than the King's Chicken.

"I'll come with you, if you don't mind," said John. "I'm getting pretty fed-up of sitting around indoors while you go about talking to people." He held up a huge hand, smiling to offset what might have been considered a criticism. "I know, none of us can speak to the locals so you have to do it. But I can come along too, can't I? I'd like to see more of the city."

The knight nodded jovially. "You're welcome to join me," he said. "And anyone else that wants to."

"I'm not sure that's a good idea," Robin protested. "We need to keep our presence here a secret. Remember, we don't want van Rasseghem's men to know we're almost at the Untersberg, and I don't really want to make it easier for the Coterels to find us either. So you and John go and find out what you can about the mountain's folklore, and hire a guide to take us there if you can."

Sir Simon accepted the younger man's instructions with good grace, Robin was glad to see. The Hospitaller might be the highest-ranking military man in their group, and the only one who could speak the language of the locals, but Robin felt it was time to lead again. It had been his quest to start with, and he was the one who needed the missing treasure to win a pardon. They would do things his way, when possible.

"Very well," the preceptor said when they'd all completed their meal and were sitting back, pleasantly sated, with mugs in hand and smiles on their faces. "Shall we go, John?"

The bailiff nodded, groaning and patting his belly as he got to his feet. "Maybe we shouldn't have eaten so much," he said.

Sir Simon chuckled. "We'll soon walk it off. Come!"

"Take care," Will cautioned as they headed for the door, every eye in the place following John who was forced to stoop or crack his head on the ceiling beams.

"We shall. Don't be starting any fights, Scarlet!"

* * *

John pushed his long hair back from his face and blew out a long breath. "It's bloody hot again," he said to the preceptor. "I don't know how you can wear that long surcoat and chainmail. You must be melting under it."

"Discipline," Sir Simon replied sternly. "A Hospitaller must always look smart."

"Are you saying I don't?" John asked, teeth flashing from within his grizzled beard. He was only wearing his trousers and a tunic that was too small for his huge frame, revealing glistening muscles and hairy arms. He knew he did not look smart, but he didn't care. Better to stay cool than collapse from heatstroke.

The knight only replied with a smile of his own and led the way down the street towards one of the main commercial areas of the city. John had been to London before and he thought Salzburg was about as busy although, for some reason – perhaps all the fir trees in the surrounding lands – the air seemed cleaner. Many of the buildings were painted bright colours as well, and flowers of various hues bloomed all around. It really was a pleasant place to visit and John was glad he'd asked to accompany the preceptor.

As they walked, Sir Simon spoke with men and women selling their wares from market stalls, almost all of them wearing black which, apparently, was how peasants were expected to dress in those lands. John heard the name 'Untersberg' mentioned a lot, and the preceptor would point in the direction of the mountain before moving on. He did not look unhappy so John assumed they were being directed towards someone who could guide them rather than being fobbed off or otherwise turned away.

They came to a drinking establishment, Salzburg's equivalent of an English alehouse thought John, and Sir Simon jerked his head towards the door, silently beckoning the bailiff to follow him inside.

There were no pretty blooms growing in wooden pots outside this place, and the interior was just as gloomy for the windows were small and the swarthy denizens glanced up from their drinks with expressions of distaste as they saw the newcomers. John glared back at them, marking the ones who held his gaze as potential troublemakers – people did not usually return his hard stare, but those who did were generally too drunk, stupid, or dangerous themselves to fear the enormous bailiff.

Sir Simon ignored the black looks and went directly to a plump, red-faced woman that John took to be the alewife, if they had those in Salzburg.

A conversation ensued as John refused to turn his back on the alehouse's patrons, standing with his hands by his side, as straight as he could manage in the low-roofed building, silently daring anyone to have a go if they reckoned themselves hard enough.

"Here."

He glanced back and saw the Hospitaller handing him a cup of wine. Or at least he thought it was supposed to be wine, although it tasted more like vinegar when he took a sip. A couple of the other drinkers chuckled knowingly as his mouth twisted at the sour taste and he smiled back sheepishly.

"Come over here," said the preceptor, tugging John's tunic sleeve as he led the way to a bench in the corner. A small, wiry man with long brown hair that was receding at the front sat on the bench nursing a cup of the horrible wine, and he watched them as they approached, nodding in greeting as Sir Simon and John sat down opposite him, their combined weight making the wooden bench creak alarmingly. The bailiff shifted position so his backside was directly over one of the legs – the last thing he wanted was for the bench to snap and deposit him and the knight on the floor while the alehouse patrons pointed and laughed at them.

Another conversation was struck up, this time between the small man and Sir Simon. It seemed this wiry fellow was one of the locals with extensive knowledge of the Untersberg, and experience in taking people there to explore it. For a fair price of course.

The man did not look as dangerous as some of the other patrons. His eyes were clear and intelligent, and he did not have the swollen belly or fleshy nose of a sot, although John knew those were not always totally accurate methods of judging how much a man liked a drink. Still, the guide appeared clear-witted and, as Sir Simon explained their needs to him, he nodded enthusiastically and replied in clear, sober tones.

"What's he saying?" the bailiff asked. "Is he up for guiding us?"

"*Ja*," the little man said, blinking as he smiled. "I will be happy to guide you to the holy mountain."

"You speak English," said John and Sir Simon together.

"You might have said so before now," the preceptor added, a little put out.

The guide shrugged, still smiling. "When would you like to leave? Do you have everything you will need? Many times people want to visit the Untersberg, but they do not bring the proper clothing, or supplies."

"What clothing?" John asked, confused.

The guide examined him with a critical eye. "You are wearing only a thin tunic with the sleeves rolled up."

"And? It's bloody summer. What would you have me wear? A winter cloak, gloves, and a hood?"

The guide chuckled, showing off clean white teeth. "The mountain is cold, Englishman. Have you not seen the snow on the top, even now, in this fine weather?"

"Aye," John said. "But that's on the top. We're not going up the top. We're not here to take in the views." He paused, looking apologetically at the preceptor, wondering how much of their story Sir Simon had told to the guide, and kicking himself for not being discreet.

"You wish to go into the caves," the guide replied. "Do you think it is warm in the deep, dark recesses of the Earth? Where the sun does not reach, even on days like this? Where black things crawl and flop and—"

John gaped at him, horrified, and Sir Simon chopped his hand down in the air, silencing the little man.

"That's enough of that," the preceptor commanded in annoyance. "You can tell us all about the folklore of the mountain on the way there. You're simply frightening my friend with that talk just now."

"Frightened? A giant like you?" The guide chuckled again, and John imagined there was a hint of madness in the man's eyes. Maybe he'd seen something in the mountain that had affected his mind. One of those crawling, black things...

"Where did you learn to speak our language?" Sir Simon asked, tactfully moving the conversation along in a less eldritch direction.

"I know lots of languages."

"That's interesting, and exceedingly rare," the preceptor noted. "But not what I asked."

Laughing softly, the guide said, "I was a servant in the Teutonic Knights."

Sir Simon leaned back, greatly interested now. "A Soldner," he stated.

"*Ja*, a Soldner."

"What's that?" John wondered.

"A servant," the guide told him. "At first, I was a volunteer, but they recognised my worth and employed me as a tracker and an esquire. I've travelled all over the world you know, probably seen more places than even you, Hospitaller."

"Perhaps," Sir Simon smiled. "Dare I ask why you are no longer employed by the Teutonic Knights?"

"Nothing untoward," the guide grinned. "I just became homesick, and decided to come back here to Salzburg. I grew up here, exploring all the mountains and trails nearby. It made sense for me to offer my services to travellers who needed a guide to the area."

"You earn much from doing this?"

The little man shrugged at the bailiff's question. "Enough, *ja*. The only kind of people who can afford to spend their time exploring far-off lands are people with money and free time. It is not serfs coming here looking for my services, it is people like you, my cheerful *Jötunn*. People with enough money to buy proper clothes and equipment for a visit to Untersberg."

"*Jötunn?*" John repeated, turning to Sir Simon in confusion. He merely shrugged.

"Giant," the guide translated. "The *Jötnar* were mythical beings before Christianity came to these lands. Come. If you want to get started we should buy the things your group will need." He drained his wine cup and immediately headed for the door. John and Sir Simon gaped at one another then, not bothering to finish their own turgid drinks, hurried after the little man.

"Wait," Sir Simon called after him as they went out into the blinding sunshine once more. "There are six of us in our party, and eight horses. You will need someone else with you, to look after our mounts when we go into the mountain."

"That is fine," the guide called back, striding purposefully past blooming flowerpots, intent on a destination obviously well-known to him.

"Slow down," John shouted, tired from the heat and humidity. "And one more thing!"

"What?" the guide asked, not bothering to slow at all.

"What's your name?"

"Ymir!" came the cackling reply, as though the man's own name greatly amused him.

CHAPTER TWENTY-FOUR

Back at the inn, Robin and the others enjoyed rather too much of the local food and drink while they awaited John and Sir Simon's return. The serving wenches brought them beer refills and platters of sweetmeats, cheese, and smoked sausage continually, fluttering their eyelashes at the men and giggling at jokes and compliments. Robin did his best to remain sober, but it was such a comfortable inn, and the atmosphere so inviting that he was rather drunk by the time the preceptor struggled in through the door with John at his back.

"What's all that?" Will Scarlet demanded, inanely amused by the armful of cloaks, trousers, and other items Sir Simon was carrying.

Robin laughed with his friend, their mirth doubling when Little John came in also heavily laden with what seemed to be winter clothing.

"Supplies for our trip to the mountain," the preceptor retorted irritably. "Have you lot just been sitting here downing wheat beer all day?"

"Bastards," John put in, eyeing the empty mugs and platters jealously. He unceremoniously dumped his bundle on the floor and gestured to one of the serving girls, using the universal sign language for 'drink', thumbing his own chest and then nodding towards Sir Simon.

"Untersberg is very cold inside," the preceptor was telling the bemused, and rather inebriated, companions. "So we brought you all warm clothing. There's a cloak and a thick pair of trousers for each of you amongst that lot, along with gloves, hats, and blankets. We also have candles, and lanterns to collect before we leave."

Robin struggled to understand what was happening and wished he hadn't taken so much beer. Or perhaps he should have drank even more. He wasn't sure, but nodded to the serving girl for a refill just to be on the safe side.

"Have you at least secured rooms for us to spend the night?" John demanded, glaring around at the others.

"Of course we have," Stephen replied defensively. "We're not idiots."

John grunted noncommittally at that and sat down, finishing half the mug of wheat beer he'd been handed in one great pull.

"Did you find a guide?" Tuck asked, still munching away on slices of bratwurst.

"Aye, we did," John said, and to Robin he looked much happier now that he'd had a mouthful of beer and a seat indoors, away from the stifling heat of Salzburg's streets. "Strange little fellow, but he seems to know his business."

"He'll come for us here at dawn on the morrow," Sir Simon told them. "So I'd suggest you all curtail your drinking for the rest of the evening, or you won't be fit to travel. Get your new clothes stowed safely in your packs as well. You'll be sorry if you forget them, the guide was adamant that it was freezing cold in the mountain."

They sat in companionable silence for a while, sipping drinks and lazily watching the serving girls and the other patrons of the inn. After a time it started to rain, the sound of heavy drops pattering on the ground unmistakable through the inn's open doors. The temperature dropped and a wonderful cool breeze blew inside just as there was a rumble of thunder.

"Storms aren't so bad when you're safely indoors with a beer," Robin averred, getting up to walk to the door, watching the weather change dramatically in the space of a few heartbeats.

"Did you find out anything about the soldiers from Laarne?" Stephen asked Sir Simon. "Has anyone seen them here, lord?"

"We never had a chance to really ask around," the preceptor admitted. "I'm not sure it matters anyway, to be honest. We must assume they reached Salzburg before us, and have gone on to the mountain. All we can do is try to catch up with them before they locate…What we're looking for."

"Or, if they find it first," Robin said, coming back to sit with them again. "We'll have to take it from them."

It was not a particularly pleasant prospect. Gerard van Rasseghem's men would not relinquish their prize without a fight, and it would likely be a fight to the death. Robin took a deep breath, steeling himself for what might be on the horizon in the coming days. Even a pardon was not worth a single one of his friends dying. They would have to tread carefully and hope to persuade the Laarne men to give up the treasure without a fight, should they find it first.

"Is there a church nearby?" Tuck asked the preceptor.

"Aye. We passed one just along the street. Impressive place too. Are you thinking of visiting?"

"I am," the friar confirmed. "Would you like to join me after you've had some food? Yes? We can pray together for the success of our mission to Untersberg."

"I'll come too," Will Scarlet said.

"And me," Robin put in, thinking the fresh air and walk would do him good, and it certainly couldn't hurt their quest to petition God's aid.

A short time later, when the storm had passed and the sun was beginning its descent into the western horizon, the companions – all except John who stayed behind to guard their belongings – left the inn to pray at the local church. Later, they returned in fine fettle to the inn and enjoyed a night of unbroken rest, looking forward to the morning, and the next stage of their adventure.

* * *

"Why do you laugh every time someone says your name?" Will Scarlet's brows were drawn together, although Robin wasn't entirely sure if his friend was irritated or simply squinting because of the sun. Both, probably. It certainly was strange how their new guide interacted with them.

"Ymir is not my real name," the little man admitted to Will. "No one in Salzburg calls me that. I find it amusing when people like you call me Ymir."

"If it's not your real name, why use it at all?" Stephen persisted. "Seems mad to me."

"It's a joke," 'Ymir' grinned. "It is the name of a famous *Jötunn*. A giant, from ancient mythology."

"But you're small," Will observed.

"That's the joke!" Ymir said, and laughed again.

"Good one," Stephen muttered, shaking his head.

"Almost as funny as people thinking your name is Little John because you're so big," Robin said to the bailiff who was riding to his right along the broad trail that would take them to the fabled Untersberg.

"Aye, that's always hilarious too," Will grunted, clearly as unimpressed as Stephen by the low-quality banter.

"Ah, you men are too serious," Ymir opined, shaking his head sorrowfully. "Let me tell you all about the old gods, and the giants."

Robin wasn't sure he cared to hear the man's stories, but, as Ymir spoke on he found himself drawn into the tales. Some of the names were familiar to him for the old gods and goddesses once worshipped by the people of the Holy Roman Empire were clearly analogous to those of pre-Christian England. Wotan, Donar, Tiwaz, and Frea had direct counterparts in the Anglo-Saxon pantheon, as Tuck pointed out.

The friar was very interested in Ymir's stories, as were the others, except Sir Simon who listened with distaste, as though he felt it sacrilegious for God-fearing men to talk about heathen things. It helped the miles pass quicker though, and the brooding mountain grew ever bigger as the morning wore on and Ymir led them closer to its monstrous bulk.

They did not pass many other travellers, although they saw plenty of people working in the fields and woods including shepherds in great floppy hats and wooden shoes, hunters with bows and small, energetic dogs, woodcutters, fishermen, children collecting baskets of summer fruit, and farmers taking their wares to and from Salzburg and the surrounding rural homesteads.

The sky remained blue and almost cloudless right up until they reached the foot of the mountain. There they stopped to rest, allowing their horses to drink from one of the many crystal-clear streams that flowed down from Untersberg, while the men ate some bread and cheese from their packs. Robin felt somewhat hungover from the previous day's carousing, and he could see some of his companions were suffering too.

Their guide, Ymir, had brought another man along with him when he came to collect them at the inn. This man was called Ludwig, and he was tall and overweight, and sullen with it. He did not join in with the banter at all as they rode from the city to the mountain although, to be fair, it was highly unlikely he could understand a word of what was being said.

"Giants are all very well," Robin said to Ymir as they relaxed in the shadow of the Untersberg. "But we'd heard there were dwarves living inside this mountain."

The guide nodded thoughtfully, his usual good humour slightly dampened. "Many people have claimed to see them," he said. "Little men, mostly. It is said they were the ones who dug all the caves and tunnels, but it is also said that they steal folk away, never to be seen again, carried off to live as slaves inside the Untersberg."

"If they're never seen again, how do these stories get reported?" Stephen asked sceptically.

"Every so often one of the abducted people will escape, and come back to tell their tale." Ymir shuddered slightly. "One man turned up at his own funeral, a year after he'd

253

first gone missing! They are usually the same age as when they were stolen away, even if ten, or a hundred, years have passed here outside the mountain. Time does not work the same for the dwarves as it does for the rest of us."

Robin felt horrified at the thought. To be forced to live as a thrall for years, only to escape and find all your loved ones had died decades ago and you were alone in the world!

"I've never met any of the folk who escaped," Ymir admitted. "But I know people who have. I've also personally heard strange sounds in the mountain. If you listen carefully, you might hear whispered voices and footsteps in the depths of the shafts and springs."

Looking up at the towering rock Robin shivered, finding it easy to believe there were strange beings living inside it. What did they do all day? Would they try to abduct Robin and his friends, or did the dwarves only target lone travellers?

"If they're so small," Will Scarlet piped up. "Why can't they just be fought off? I'm trying to imagine being attacked by men as small as children." He shrugged. "Doesn't seem very likely. If a dwarf tries to make me a slave, I'll be folding his fucking back."

The others laughed at Scarlet's evocative threat, but Ymir looked stricken, turning to stare fearfully at the mountain, as though the dwarves might be listening to their conversation. "They are small, it is true," he agreed. "With large heads, clever eyes, and grey skin. But they can work magic, and there are many of them. A family working in one of the farms nearby reported seeing four hundred of the little people passing silently in the night, and disappearing into a crack in the mountain."

Will swallowed, and Ymir nodded.

"Yes, my friend. If we meet a dwarf, it is better to try and befriend them than to attack them."

"Fair enough," Will mumbled, and he too eyed the Untersberg with trepidation now. "I don't want to get on the wrong side of anyone who can work magic."

"God will protect us," Sir Simon stated flatly. "If such a thing as dwarves exist, they are His creations, just as all things are. He has guided us this far, He will see us safely to our goal if we place our faith in Him."

Tuck nodded. "Indeed. I wouldn't be too concerned about supernatural creatures – it's the soldiers from Laarne I'm more worried about."

"They should be the ones afraid of us," Will returned venomously. "But you're right, Tuck. The longer we tarry here, the farther ahead of us they're getting."

"Aye, let's get moving," Robin said, standing up and replacing his things in his pack. "Where are we entering the mountain, Ymir?"

The guide pointed to an opening in the Untersberg some way above. "We will go in there, and my friend, Ludwig, will camp in the woods over there with the horses." Again, he pointed, this time to a forested area half a mile distant. "He's trustworthy, and will make sure the animals are safe for our return. If the men you are hunting come by this way, they will not see him or our mounts."

"You've thought of everything," Little John said in admiration.

"I'm an expert," Ymir replied levelly. "You hired me to do a job, and I will do it. Now, are we all ready to move on? Good, then get what you need from your saddlebags – clothes, weapons, candles, and so on – and let us head inside the mountain."

* * *

Robin felt like a fool carrying a winter cloak up the side of the great mountain along with the rest of his pack. It was warmer that day than he could ever remember it being in

England, with a cloudless, blue sky, pretty blooms dotting the grass around, and white sheep roaming free on the lower parts of the slope. A perfect summer's day, and he was labouring under the added weight of a heavy cloak. Madness.

It was not an easy climb and he checked back continually on his friends, who were all older than he was. Tuck in particular, well into middle-age and carrying some extra weight thanks to his famous love of food and drink, was a worry for Robin, but the stoic friar did not complain any more than the others, and rather less than Will and Stephen. Robin understood the grumbling, for the Untersberg was incredibly steep in places and they were forced to scrabble up at times, grabbing handfuls of turf or weeds to haul themselves onto flatter ground.

They passed a surprising number of caves and crevices in the side of the mountain, and the friends pointed them out, wondering just how many places there could be to stash things away from prying eyes. And, more worryingly, how the hell would they find what they were searching for when the men who'd supposedly brought the treasure there had so many hiding places to choose from.

Despite the worries and hardships, the hike was made somewhat easier by the stunning scenery. They took rests often, simply sitting and gazing out at the glorious alpine views, most of them having never seen such a landscape before, or climbed to such a height. It was exhilarating for Robin, and the others voiced their wonder or just stared in silence, drinking in the incredible sights. If ever a man doubted the reality of God, the views from the Untersberg would soon prove His existence, Robin thought, wishing he had Matilda and the boys beside him to see what he was seeing.

The members of the group had all grown fatigued during the journey from Aachen to Salzburg by the sight of so many similar conifer trees, hills, and mountains. Exotic and beautiful at first but slowly losing their lustre with each mile travelled. Robin had not been the only one openly wishing to see more of the alder, birch, oak, hazel, hawthorn, and rowan that characterised the beloved greenwood of merry England. Now, though, seeing the landscape from so high up, all thoughts of Barnsdale and Sherwood were forgotten. The trees, rivers, fields, and distant mountains all hammered home just how incredible the world was, and Robin felt truly blessed to be experiencing such a view.

And then they entered the Untersberg, walking through the opening as though swallowed up by some great, dark beast, and almost immediately the temperature dropped. They moved deeper into the tunnel, the roof of which was so high that even John did not need to stoop, and it grew colder still. There was no need for the extra cloak just yet, but now Robin understood why Ymir had made them bring the thick clothing and blankets. They also had a pair of lanterns which were lit by candles, illuminating the gloomy, damp interior just enough for them to see where they were going.

"How long do you think we'll be in here?" Sir Simon asked the guide.

Shrugging, Ymir admitted he was not sure. "Maybe a few hours. Maybe a few days?"

"Days?" Robin breathed, wondering how they could stay there for so long, away from the fresh air and sunshine. God, even the frequent thunderstorms would be preferable to being cooped up in the dark for days on end.

"I have no idea where the thing you seek is," Ymir said. "I have explored all the caves near here, and never seen anything valuable." He sidestepped a stagnant pool of water on the floor and warned the others of its presence. "If there really is something hidden in here, it must be a long way inside. To find it, we may need to walk for a long time."

"Don't worry," John told his friend. "We bought plenty of candles for the lanterns. We'll never be in darkness."

"That's reassuring," Robin admitted. "But let's up the pace a little, eh? I'd rather not be in here for too long."

"How do we know this is the right tunnel?" Will called. He was at the rear of the group, head swivelling constantly as he made sure no enemies – or dwarves – were creeping up behind them. "If there's lots of caves and tunnels, what makes you think this is the one we need to be exploring, Ymir?"

"There are many tunnels," the guide said. "But this is the longest, and the deepest. If anyone wanted to really hide something they would do it in here."

That made sense to Robin. The lost treasure may not be in that tunnel, but it was the best place to start their search. Sir Simon had not told the guide what, exactly, they were searching for, just that it was valuable, and large enough to be noticed unless it was purposely hidden. There was possibly more than one item as well. From that vague but truthful description, Ymir had immediately decided that this tunnel should be searched first.

Robin glanced at Tuck, noticing for the first time that the friar's breathing seemed somewhat laboured. They had all been panting heavily as they climbed the side of the mountain in the sunshine, but, after resting, the men had moved into the tunnel apparently refreshed.

"Are you all right, old friend?" Robin said, speaking softly.

Tuck looked at the young archer and swallowed. It was clear he was not all right, and he did not try to claim so. "Not really," the friar admitted, and his voice was hoarse, the words forced out between heavy breaths. "I think it's the air in here. It's not good for me."

Robin nodded, trying to hide his concern. Tuck was stoic, dependable, and as hard as iron, but he'd seen more than fifty winters now. Perhaps bringing him along on a climb into an enormous mountain had not been wise.

"Let's stop for a rest," he suggested, noting with mounting concern the friar's look of obvious relief.

"Rest?" Sir Simon demanded, rounding on them from the front of the group where he was walking with Ymir. "We had a rest not long ago. We've hardly moved from the mouth of the tunnel, by God. Are you tired already? A fit, young man like you?" His tone was light but his eyes could not mask his irritation. "If we keep stopping we'll never reach the treasure."

"He wants to halt so I can catch my breath," Tuck spoke up, sitting down on a large rock formation, wincing as he realised it was damp. "To be honest, lads, I'm not sure a rest will do me much good."

Will Scarlet was by his side immediately, deep concern in his eyes as he examined the friar. "What's wrong? Do you feel unwell?"

"Not unwell," Tuck said, shaking his tonsured head slowly. "But I'm having a hard time breathing."

"That happens to some people," their guide said, coming to look at the friar as well. "The air is not fresh within the tunnels, and it only gets worse the deeper in you go." He looked at the preceptor. "I hate to say it, but perhaps we should leave the friar and go on without him."

It was a mark of the concern they all felt for the clergyman that no one argued against the suggestion. Even Tuck did not speak up to defend himself and proclaim he was up to the challenge ahead, sitting and gazing down at the rock floor dolefully.

"He can't just stay here," John argued. "It's too dark, too cold, and what if the soldiers from Laarne come this way and stumble across him? We don't know if they're ahead of us, or behind us, but we know they're coming to the Untersberg. Besides, it's fresh air Tuck needs."

"You're absolutely right, John," the friar conceded, rising to his feet once more and taking another wheezing gulp of air. "I'll return to the tunnel entrance, and setup my tent in a hidden spot nearby. I'll wait there for your return."

Robin did not like it, not at all, but he could see nothing else for it. Clearly, Friar Tuck could not continue deeper into the stygian depths, and, as John noted, they did not know if Gerard van Rasseghem's men were ahead of them. They could not afford to spare anyone to escort Tuck back to setup camp.

"I'm a big boy," the friar said to Robin, smiling reassuringly. "Don't worry about me. As the air gets fresher, the better I'll feel. I'll sit on the side of the mountain with my food and drink and enjoy the sun. Don't worry about me, it will be you lot doing the hard stuff."

Sir Simon came and grasped Tuck's hand, pumping it vigorously. "Be careful then," the preceptor commanded. "Watch your footing as you go. Take one of the candles to light your way back. It should be alright unless the wind picks up outside. You have your flint and steel, if it does go out? Good. Then fare well, my friend, for now."

"Don't go rolling down the mountainside then," John said, reaching out and grasping the friar in a bear hug. "A man of your size could do a lot of damage if you smash into one of the farms at the bottom of the slope."

Tuck laughed hoarsely. "May God forgive you, John Little, for mocking an old man."

Robin felt a lump in his throat. He could not remember Tuck ever referring himself to as 'old' before. It was unpleasant to hear.

"Let's get moving then," Sir Simon said, turning and gesturing for Ymir to lead the way once more. "You take care, Tuck. We shall see you soon."

And, with forced jocularity, the friar bade them all goodbye and began the hike back to the outside world, and, hopefully, restorative fresh air.

CHAPTER TWENTY-FIVE

There was a noticeable shift in the mood of the group as they continued further into the tunnel. Robin felt a rising, unsettling claustrophobia, as the unbidden thought came to him of just how many tons of rock were pressing down upon them. What if that unfathomable weight was to collapse the tunnel, crushing them all to death?

The tunnel had not collapsed yet, he had to remind himself. It had stood there for hundreds, maybe thousands of years, so why should it suddenly fall upon them now? Still, it was easy to think rationally, but hard to make one's mind accept those sensible thoughts.

They were all dismayed by Tuck's departure too, although it was not really mentioned. Hopefully the friar's breath, and vigour, would return when he went out into the sunlight and rested on the grass, looking out over the peaceful alpine scenery.

Thoughts of those wonderful views made Robin wish he was outside too. The gloomy tunnel was barely lit by the lanterns – one carried by Sir Simon, the other by Will – and it was all too easy to imagine things were hiding in the darkness where the light did not reach. Ymir had stopped telling tales of the grey-skinned, large-eyed dwarves some time ago, but Robin still felt as though he was being observed by those mythical cave dwellers. He felt the hair on his neck rise more than once, but when he looked into the shadows he could see nothing. He never took his hand from the pommel of his sword unless he needed to steady himself or climb over a rocky obstacle.

He knew he was not the only one suffering from superstitious fears. Only Sir Simon's eyes glittered with religious fervour as they walked further and further into the seemingly endless darkness. The strength of his faith carried the pious knight onwards, and Robin felt guilty to be so fearful.

It was not, of course, only creatures from legend that posed a threat to the party hiking through the tunnel. Where were the soldiers sent by the Lord of Laarne? If they had found a guide as experienced as Ymir – and apparently there were a few of them offering their services in Salzburg – they were surely in the tunnel ahead of them. If the two groups met, it was likely there would be a fight, and Robin did not like the idea of that. He preferred to take on enemies in the familiar environs of the greenwood, or at least out in the open where he could see what was happening. Being attacked by a man with a longsword in the cramped, damp, and dark confines of the tunnel would be like something from a nightmare.

"Look." Ymir held up a hand, halting them all, and he bent, sniffing, eyes fixed on something on the ground.

"What is it?" Stephen asked, staring ahead rather than down at the tunnel floor, ever ready for trouble.

"A spent candle," their guide said. "And it smells fresh."

"Van Rasseghem's men," Sir Simon growled. "Come on. We can't let them steal the treasure."

They all hurried on, Sir Simon practically leading the way as Ymir tried to guide them past obstacles with his keen, experienced senses.

"If the soldiers are ahead of us," Will said from the rear of the group. "They'll have to come back this way to get out of the tunnel. Maybe we should just lay an ambush for them, and take the treasure from them when they pass."

"The tunnels here split off in places," Ymir shouted over his shoulder, making Robin cringe as the voice echoed off the walls and seemed to return to them from different directions in a most unsettling manner. "If the men ahead of us find this 'treasure' you seek, they might also find another route out of the mountain that does not come back this way."

"God, guide us," the preceptor murmured, staring ahead. Robin could not see his face, but he could feel the intense desire to find the lost relics emanating from his armoured back like a physical force. It was disconcerting – the Hospitaller knight's desire to find King John's missing treasure seemed to intensify the further into the mountain they hiked. In fact, now that Robin thought about it – he had plenty of time for introspection after all – Sir Simon's connection to the quest had deepened with each mile that had passed since they left the port in England.

It had been helpful, and Sir Simon had undoubtedly brought them this far, for without his grasp of languages and knowledge of other cultures and peoples, Robin and his friends would have been utterly lost. Now, however, as the preceptor urged them onwards as though leading them into battle, it seemed like the quest was no longer about returning the treasure to King Edward and winning Robin a pardon. It had become something else. Something far deeper, and more intensely personal for the knight.

"Is that…ice?" Little John's exclamation startled Robin and his eyes widened in amazement as he saw what the bailiff was gazing at.

To call it 'ice' was a monstrous understatement, for Robin had never seen anything like it in his life.

"It's a stalactite," Ymir told them, grinning proudly as they came up to the glittering spire of ice that hung from the tunnel ceiling. "There are many of them within all the caves in the mountains here."

John stood next to the stalactite and touched it gingerly. "It's cold," he reported, drawing a snort of derisive laughter from Will.

"Of course it is, you bloody lackwit. Ice generally is!"

Robin smiled, approaching the great frozen spike. The lanterns' light reflected from it, showing him that it was really just like the icicles that were common on winter nights back in England. Never had he imagined one could be so huge though. It was as big as a man. As big as Little John!

"Come on," Ymir said. "We're in the colder sections of the tunnel now. You will see lots more of these, and ones that come up from the ground, rather than down from the ceiling."

They moved on, Ymir's words quickly proving correct, as dozens of stalactites filled the tunnel now, glittering in the yellow light, looking to Robin like beautifully carved sculptures, crafted by the hand of God. Or, perhaps, sinister battlements, designed by the mythical dwarves to defend their gloomy tunnels…

Like the ubiquitous conifers that populated seemingly every hillside on the road to Salzburg, the stalactites, and the ones that bizarrely sprouted upwards from the tunnel floor – called stalagmites by Ymir – soon grew tedious to Robin's eye. Special, almost magical at first sight, the sheer number of them quickly became tiresome, especially since their presence marked a distinct drop in temperature, as well as a deterioration in stable footing. The warm cloaks and gloves were needed, and what had been a fairly simple hike up until then, became a slow, potentially treacherous journey, where every step had to be carefully taken. The thought of slipping and falling face-first into one of stalagmites made Robin shudder and he wondered how much longer the icy conditions would continue.

"Hopefully not much further," Ymir answered, and it was clear their guide had no real idea, having never trekked as far into the tunnel as this.

"Wait!" Sir Simon, at the front of the group which had now formed into single file as the way grew narrow, stopped and hissed at those behind him. "Listen."

Robin was in the centre of the party and he felt the claustrophobia rise within him as he was trapped there with no way out of the tunnel. He forced himself to breathe slowly, closing his eyes and listening to whatever it was Sir Simon was drawing their attention towards. At first he heard nothing, just water dripping from the ceiling, forming the centuried stalactites and stalagmites around them, but then there came, from an indeterminable distance away, a harsh scraping noise.

"What is it?" Stephen growled. "An animal?"

"No animals live this far underground that I know of," Ymir responded, a touch of alarm in his tone.

"The dwarves?" Robin asked, and he felt the panic again as he realised he would not be able to wield his sword within the narrow tunnel should they be attacked.

"I doubt it." Sir Simon murmured, walking on again and exhorting them to move as silently as possible. "It's far more likely to be the soldiers from Laarne. They must be working on something ahead – perhaps they've found the chest that the treasure was stored away in a hundred years ago."

Robin thanked God as they started to move again and the tunnel widened out once more, allowing them to walk three abreast in the places where they were not forced to move around obstacles. The sounds of scraping grew louder and the idea that it was some wooden chest being broken open did not quite ring true to Robin. It was not the hollow thumping of timber he could hear, it sounded more like a heavy stone being dragged, or rolled, across the rock floor of the tunnel.

Immediately, his mind went to the story of Christ's resurrection. He pictured the risen son of God hauling away the great boulder that had sealed his tomb, and understood then what they were hearing.

"They're clearing stones away from a hidden chamber," he said softly. "They may have found the treasure right enough, but it's locked away from them, for now."

"Then we have time to get there and stop them taking it," Will Scarlet spoke up excitedly, drawing his sword from its scabbard and moving faster so he was walking beside Sir Simon at the head of the group.

265

If he were a dog he'd be straining at the leash, Robin thought with a grim smile. He looked then at John and saw the huge bailiff was calm and prepared for anything as usual, staff in hand, eyes fixed on the inky blackness that beckoned them forwards with promises of battle, and glory, and the lost treasure they'd travelled so many miles to retrieve. Stephen was well used to the stress of battle, and his face betrayed no emotion as the tunnel widened out even further, so wide, in fact, that the light of the lanterns was almost completely swallowed up.

Despite the gloom, Robin could sense a change in the air, could sense the vastness of the cavern they were walking into.

"Have a care," Ymir warned, holding up his arms and waving them backwards, like a bird trying to reverse. "There is a drop here. We will need a rope."

"There's one," said Will, holding up his lantern to show the others a sturdy length of rope fastened around a massive stalagmite.

"The soldiers must have climbed down it," Robin guessed. "That's handy for us."

Sir Simon was staring into the darkness, face tight with anxiety and John went to stand beside him.

"What's wrong?" the bailiff asked.

Pointing, the Hospitaller shook his head. Robin peered down and saw a dim light moving around below. It was not very clear because it was within a smaller cave or tunnel that fed off the vast, main chamber.

"They've moved the rocks and made it into the cave where the treasure must be hidden. We need to hurry!"

"Hang on," John cautioned, not moving to follow the preceptor as he went to Will and grasped the rope. "We don't know what we're up against. We were told that four men visited Aachen and ripped out the page of the book, but there might have been more of them that didn't go into the commandery and slipped into the city in ones or twos fearing a large group would attract unwanted attention from the local militia."

"What would you suggest then?" Sir Simon snapped irritably. "Wait here until we can see how many enemies we face? It could be too late by then – the cave they've gone into might lead straight back out to the mountainside, and we'll stand here waiting while they make their escape with the Grail!"

"Grail?" Ymir demanded. "I thought we were looking for some rusty old treasure. Do you truly believe the actual Holy Grail is here in the Untersberg?"

"I do," the preceptor replied, eyes wild in the dim light. "Why else would a mercenary from Laarne travel all the way here to hide what he had? This," he raised his arms and his eyes upwards. "This is the heart of the world. This mountain, this Untersberg. Is that not one of the legends you people tell about the place?"

Ymir nodded. "Indeed. Wise men, holy men, have proclaimed it so. If someone had a holy relic they wanted to hide safely, this would be the perfect location."

Sir Simon smiled ecstatically, still staring up into the impenetrable darkness. "You have all been wondering why someone would bring old swords and a few gemstones halfway across the world just to hide them away here in this mountain. I am telling you now that Giselbrecht van Zottegem somehow came into possession of the Holy Grail. Whether he found it amongst the king's treasure in the Wash, or the Hospitallers he was travelling with already had it, he escorted it here so that it would be safe forever."

"Safe from what?"

"Safe from evil," the preceptor returned vehemently. "You all know what happened to the Templars, don't you? The powers-that-be destroyed them so they could seize their wealth. And you must know that the Templars were rumoured to have found the Grail. That's why they were really disbanded. That's why so many of them were tortured

267

and burned at the stake. Powerful kings wanted the Grail. And somehow, Giselbrecht, and the Hospitallers he rode with, got hold of it. What else could they do with it, but hide it here for future generations to find, and utilise?"

Robin gaped at the knight, astonished by what he was hearing. He had no idea these thoughts were roiling within the preceptor's mind. No wonder the man had been so quick to volunteer his services; to guide them across the sea, from England, to Bruges, to Laarne, Aachen, and thence to Untersberg's tenebrous depths.

"Think about it," Sir Simon continued, half-begging, half-demanding. "Why else would anyone come here to hide something?"

Robin had thought about that. A lot. "Because it would never be found by anyone," he replied. "It would lie here, safe and untouched, until it was needed again."

"Exactly!" the preceptor laughed triumphantly.

"Listen," Will Scarlet broke in, shaking his head at the back and forth between Robin and the knight.

"I don't hear anything," said John.

"That's what I mean. The sounds, and the lights, from the cave below have stopped."

"They're gone!" Sir Simon wailed, and immediately started climbing down the rope, quickly traversing the twenty feet or so to the rock floor below. "Come on, sergeant!" he barked at Stephen. "Get down here, and bring the lantern. That's an order. The rest of you can do what you like, but I will not let the Grail be taken from me while I stand here, so close to holding it!"

Stephen followed his superior's order without hesitation, as expected of a Hospitaller, climbing nimbly down the rope with one of the two lanterns. "Come on then," he said to the others. "You're not turning back now, are you?"

"He's fucking mad," Will Scarlet avowed, watching as Sir Simon headed towards the gaping black maw that had swallowed up what they all thought to be the soldiers from

Laarne and whatever treasure had been concealed within the mountain for a century.

"Maybe he is," said John. "But we have to follow him, or go back the way we came." He looked at Robin, as did Will, expecting him to lead as he had done when they were outlaws in distant Barnsdale.

"I'm not giving up," Robin grunted, reaching for the rope and letting himself gingerly over the edge. "Come on, Ymir, lead the way. Let's find these crown jewels, or the Holy Grail, or whatever the hell is in that cave!"

* * *

This section of the tunnel network was not filled with stalagmites or stalactites the way other parts had been.

"It almost looks like someone carved out this tunnel by hand," Little John observed as they hurried after the two Hospitallers, the faint light ahead slowly growing closer with each hurried step. "Look at the ceiling," the giant bailiff practically demanded, pointing upwards and almost tripping over a dip in the floor. "Those look like tool marks."

"You're as mad as the preceptor," Will huffed, holding up his lantern to reveal another slight dip in the floor that might have made one of them trip. "How could anyone have cut out a tunnel as big as this? And why bother?"

"I think the Untersberg more than deserves its reputation as a mysterious place," said Robin, peering upwards and feeling himself forced to agree with John's assertion: it did look like tool marks on the walls and ceiling, as if this tunnel had been carved from the living rock. By whom? Regular men like them? Dwarves with strange powers? Or some titanic race of giants who dwelt there in the hidden, dark places of the Earth?

When they climbed down the rope and headed towards the entrance to this tunnel, Robin had paused, his attention

269

drawn by something carved into the wall that had been momentarily lit up by the lantern as Will passed. He had called his friend back and, together, they'd examined the motif that was crudely etched into the rock. Neither Robin, Will, John, nor Ymir had ever seen such a design before, but they all agreed it held some religious or mystical significance. It was plainly a marker, telling those who understood its meaning, that this tunnel led to something important.

Stephen seemed to be moving slower than his master, for the four men caught up with him without too much trouble. Sir Simon's lantern could be seen some distance ahead, bobbing up and down as he tried to move as quickly as possible, hunting the men from Laarne.

"Did you see the carving on the wall back there?" John asked the sergeant, breathless from the chase and the lack of fresh air so far underground.

"Aye."

"Did you recognise it?"

"No. But Sir Simon did."

"Well?" Scarlet asked irritably. "What the fuck was it?"

"I don't know," the sergeant responded in a similar tone. "He smiled when he saw it, muttered that this was the place, and charged into the tunnel here."

"Did you know he was moon-touched?" Will asked.

"No," Stephen said, before hastily adding, "I mean, he's not. He's just filled with religious fervour. He really believes we're going to find the Grail down here. Maybe we will. It has to be somewhere, right?"

"Not really," John countered. "I don't think the Bible says the Grail was magic or anything, does it? It was just a cup. After a thousand years it would have been broken, or turned to dust."

"Dust?"

"Aye," Robin agreed. "Christ and his disciples were normal workers – fishermen, carpenters. They'd have been drinking from wooden cups, not some fancy golden chalice like noblemen."

"And a wooden cup wouldn't survive all these centuries," John noted. "So I really doubt we'll find the Holy Grail here, especially in a damp environment like these tunnels!"

"We'll see," Stephen murmured, visibly torn between agreeing with their common-sense arguments, and his master's bold claims. "Either way, we need to hurry up, and catch Sir Simon before he's ambushed by whoever is ahead of us. Come on, Scarlet, get that light up and move quicker."

Muttering to himself, Will did as he was asked and, leading the way, practically ran after the distant light that was Sir Simon, simultaneously warning the others to watch their step.

"Look!" Scarlet slowed, staring at what looked like a shelf in an alcove that had been carved into the wall.

"Something was here," Robin said, joining his friend and examining the strange shelf. "Look, there's a circle in the dust."

"The Grail!" Stephen cried. "It must have rested here until van Rasseghem's men found it. Look, there on the wall, another of those strange symbols is carved into the rock."

Suddenly a roar echoed back along the tunnel, quickly followed by the familiar ring of steel on steel. As the group threw caution to the wind and raced after Scarlet, Robin shouted to Ymir who was bringing up the rear, "You can go back! Go back to Tuck, stay out of danger!"

"I'm not missing this for anything," the guide called, eyes as wide as his smile, although he did allow more of a gap to form between himself and the others who had drawn their weapons as they ran.

"Die, you bastards!"

Robin's foot slipped and he breathed a curse as he tried to catch up with his friends. The shout from Sir Simon was accompanied by another clash of sword blades, and then a crunch that Robin knew from past experience was cartilage. He guessed the knight had headbutted whoever was attacking him and was amazed at how the sound had carried through, and even been amplified by, the tunnel.

When he reached the others he was greatly relieved to see that the tunnel had widened out once more. His eyes quickly took in the scene, noting this new area was more like the others they had travelled through, more natural looking, with mineral deposits on the floor and perhaps on the ceiling although it was too high up to see properly. Besides, he thought, mentally kicking himself, he wasn't there to sightsee – not right now at least.

"I warned you there might be more than four of them!" Little John shouted, bringing up his sword as a man clad in a helmet and what looked like a cloak made from a wolf's pelt tried to skewer him.

Robin stared, dismayed to see they faced eight enemies, all armed and powerfully built. Sir Simon was giving a good account of himself, holding off three of them with expert flicks and thrusts of his sword, but Robin knew that could not last forever. Praying he reached the knight in time, he let out a war-cry and threw himself at one of the soldiers. His shout did enough to distract the man before he could stab Sir Simon, but it also allowed the enemy to swivel and parry Robin's somewhat wild swing.

The young outlaw thought he recognised the soldier from their visit to Laarne, but before he could think more about it he was on the back foot, desperately trying to stave off a wave of attacks that sent pain shooting through his forearm. His foe was incredibly strong!

He was not as young, or as fast as Robin though, who neatly sidestepped his enemy's next strike and brought his blade around in an arc, slicing it deeply into the back of the man's thigh. There was a scream of pain as the injured soldier collapsed, unable to support himself on his leg which was already coating the back of his breeches with blood. A momentary pang of guilt filled Robin – why was he fighting? Why were any of them fighting? Robin did not even know if the treasure was in the hands of these soldiers, and neither did he know if it was worth killing or dying over!

The madness of it all did not matter at that moment, as the downed enemy bared his teeth in fury and took a wild swing, crawling on the cave floor after Robin like a monstrous spider, utterly intent on killing the man who'd probably made him a cripple forever.

Robin's attack had put Sir Simon's other two attackers off balance and they fought more defensively now. The Hospitaller, seeing this, took the opportunity to lash out, brutally kicking the soldier on the floor hard in the face. Robin saw the man's head jerk backwards and more than one tooth flew out of his mouth, and then Sir Simon was taking on the other two with his sword again, the enemy on the ground silent and unmoving as his lifeblood pumped out onto the tunnel floor.

The chamber was so dark, and the grunting, shouting, clattering of metal, and other sounds of fighting reverberated off the rock walls. It was all so disorienting, and the smell of blood filled Robin's nostrils so he imagined he could taste it in his mouth, bitter and metallic. Another shriek of pain echoed around the chamber and immediately Robin felt a lurch of fear in his guts for he knew whose throat it had been ripped from.

"Will!"

Casting about, Robin saw his old friend lying on the ground, staring up at a man who was about to deliver a death blow. Again, the young outlaw flung himself bodily across the chamber, slamming himself into the soldier before the man could bring down his sword on Will's head.

A voice rang out in a language Robin did not understand then, seeming to come from somewhere high overhead.

Whatever the voice was saying, the soldier who'd just been about to dispatch Will Scarlet stood up and, somewhat gingerly, as though Robin's shoulder-charge had injured him, hobbled away in the direction of the shouting.

"Are you all right?" Robin demanded, reaching down to help up his fallen friend.

"No!" Scarlet bellowed, pointing down at his leg. "The bastards have an archer with them. Look!"

Robin did look, and he was shocked to see an arrow sticking out of Will's thigh.

"Get back!" he roared. "They have a bowman with them! Get behind cover, all of you, now!" He did not take his own advice, at least not immediately. Instead, he glanced around, searching for the nearest place to take shelter from the hidden archer, and then he kicked over the lantern that was sitting next to Will, plunging the area around them into complete darkness. "Douse your lantern, Sir Simon!" he shouted into the void, bending down and feeling for Will Scarlet's armpits. His friend understood what he was doing and lifted his elbows so Robin could drag him backwards, towards the section of wall that would hopefully protect them from enemy missiles.

The fighting was over, and now, from a position of relative safety, Robin and Will tried to make sense of what was happening. The preceptor had taken the advice to extinguish his lantern, but there were other lights at the far end of the chamber and they showed the figures of their enemies scaling a wall there, climbing two ropes although, it had to be said, with some difficulty.

"Ha, a few of them must have been injured," Will chuckled nastily. "They can hardly make it up."

Sir Simon was howling obscenities and threats at the retreating soldiers, demanding they come back and fight with honour, like men, and claiming that God had guided him there to retrieve the Holy Grail for the Hospitallers. Despite his fury he was not, Robin was thankful to see, mad enough to try and cut down the men climbing the ropes. It was impossible to see the enemy archer up there in the darkness, hiding somewhere outside the glow of the lanterns, but they knew he was there, and they knew it would be suicide to break cover and show themselves in the light.

The sounds of the soldiers scrabbling up the wall continued for a time, but then the noise and the lantern-light faded and it seemed the danger was over. Still, Robin and his companions did not move, for fear of the enemy archer who might perhaps still be hiding above, just waiting for them to relight their lanterns, making them easy targets for his lethal arrows. Robin and his friends had not even brought their bows, Ymir assuring them it would just be more to carry and there would be no possible need for the weapons within the cramped, winding tunnels.

At last, Sir Simon's patience ran out and the sparks from his flint and steel could be seen in the gloom. It did not take long for his tinder to catch light and then his candle flared to life and the lantern cast its yellow illumination around the chamber.

Robin looked down at Will's thigh and winced. The arrow was lodged deep in the flesh and it must have been causing his friend immense pain, but, although Will's face was drenched in sweat and as white as a ghost, he did not cry out.

Knowing they would need as much light as possible to try and help Will deal with the missile, Robin took out his own fire-making kit and lit the second lantern.

"Are you all right, Scarlet?" Little John asked, warily making his way across to inspect the wound.

Will stared up at him in clear disbelief. "Oh, aye, never been better. Apart from having a great arrow in my fucking leg, everything is just wonderful!"

"I see your tongue hasn't been injured at least," John replied with a wry smile. "But what are we going to do about the arrow?"

Will's face paled further as he looked down and must have imagined the damage that removing the arrowhead would do to his leg. What else could they do, though? He couldn't walk around with it sticking out of him forever.

It would need to be dealt with before they could move on.

"Leave him here," Sir Simon commanded, striding across to glare at the three of them. He waved his hand dismissively at Will. "We can come back for him once we have the Grail."

"You want us to leave our friend here with an arrow in him?" John returned, rising to his full height and towering over the preceptor who seemed oblivious to the giant's threatening gaze.

"Aye, and do it quick," said the Hospitaller, turning on his heel and striding across to the wall the enemy soldiers had climbed up to make their escape. He already had a length of rope in his hand and was fashioning the end into a loop so he could throw it around the same boulder the Laarne men had used to anchor their rope. "Ymir can stay here with Scarlet, the rest of us will go on."

Robin's mind was racing. He had come hundreds, perhaps thousands of miles, he really wasn't sure of the distance they'd covered since leaving Wakefield, but he knew it was vast. He had not travelled all that way for nothing, and the thought of the lost treasure being carried away by Gerard van Rasseghem's men was thoroughly galling. He desperately wanted to go after those soldiers, and claim the riches that would see him win a pardon from King Edward III.

He looked down at Will and realised his friend was in a bad way. Blood was oozing from his leg and his eyes were beginning to roll as though he was becoming delirious or feverish.

Could they leave Will there with the guide, hunt down the soldiers, defeat them, and then return there to help their wounded comrade?

"We don't have time for all that," he decided, only realising now that Little John had been watching him stonily, praying he would come to this conclusion. He frowned at the bailiff, a tad irritated that John might have feared he would make any other choice. Loyalty to one another had been paramount when they were outlaws living in the greenwood, and it remained so now, no matter what.

"What do you mean?" the preceptor demanded. He had already managed to throw his rope about the boulder on the ledge above and was shimmying up it. When he made it all the way to the top he looked down on them, face red with anger as he gestured at Stephen. "Get up here, sergeant. The rest of you too, hurry now, those Flemish devils are getting away!"

Stephen's gaze moved between his master – his military commander – and the friends who'd taken him in when he'd fallen on hard times and his previous master, Sir Richard-at-Lee had been hanged. At last, his duty to the Hospitallers won out and, muttering a sincere apology to Robin and the others, he went to the rope and climbed up beside the preceptor.

"Stephen is morally, and legally bound to follow your orders," Little John spat, eyeing Sir Simon venomously. "But we're not. We'll not leave our friend here to die just for the sake of a few baubles."

"Baubles!" the knight cried in outrage. "You call the Holy Grail, the very cup used by Christ at the Last Supper, a 'bauble'? Lucifer take you all then, I'll not waste another moment here."

With that, he turned and stalked away with Stephen slump-shouldered beside him. They quickly disappeared from view, the lantern light fading along with their hurried footsteps.

"Holy Grail," John raged. "Even if those soldiers did find some chalice back at that alcove there's no way it's the actual Grail used by Christ. It's not possible! Sir Simon really is mad."

"Maybe," Ymir shrugged, visibly stunned by everything that had happened. "But what are we going to do now?"

Robin let out a heavy breath and stared back at the apparently man-made tunnel that had brought them to where they stood now. "We have no choice," he murmured. "First we have to do what we can about the arrow in Will's leg, and then we'll have to carry him all the way back to Tuck, if we can."

CHAPTER TWENTY-SIX

When they looked closer at the point where the arrow was lodged in Will's thigh they quickly realised that they could not pull it out, not there. They had bandages, but they did not have a fire to cauterise the enlarged wound that would result in the arrow's removal, and they did not really have the skill to perform such an operation either.

"We have to get him to Tuck," said Robin with a horrible sinking feeling as he thought of trying to make it all the way back through those dark, often slippery, tunnels while Will lost blood and strength. "And we must move now, there's no time to waste."

John had taken the lantern and walked around the chamber searching for anything they might use to fashion a crude stretcher. Out in the open, branches would be ideal, but down there in the Untersberg nothing was available. He went to the man that Robin and Sir Simon had killed and stripped off the fur he was wearing, carrying it back to place around Will who was breathing heavily now, teeth gritted as pain wracked his body.

"We'll need to snap the arrow at least," Robin said, swallowing nervously. He knew that, no matter how gentle they tried to be, it would cause their friend immense pain to move the arrow at all, but it was necessary to make sure nothing accidentally caught it as they were traversing the tunnels back to where they'd come in.

"You hold it at the bottom, around his leg," John suggested. "I'll snap it off. It doesn't have too thick a shaft, so hopefully it will break easily."

"All right. You ready, Scarlet?" Robin asked, setting himself firmly into a crouch and grasping the arrow directly where it had entered the flesh. He had wrapped a piece of linen around it already but he was dismayed to see that already saturated with blood. Will did not answer other than with a grunt. "Do it, John."

The huge bailiff knelt down across from Robin and they looked into one another's eyes, steeling themselves for the gruesome but necessary task. Nodding, John took hold of the wooden shaft as Robin tried his best to hold it completely still. They were both strong men but, as the arrow broke off in John's hands, its small snap was drowned out by the terrific roar of agony that erupted from Will's throat, reverberating around the darkened chamber.

"I'm sorry, Scarlet," John gasped, throwing away the broken section of ash wood. "It had to be done."

Robin set about winding more bandage around Will's thigh, pulling it tight but leaving the remainder of the arrow protruding out between the folds of linen.

"Can you walk at all?" John asked, but Will's eyes were closed and he was breathing too heavily to reply. Robin wasn't even sure if the question had been understood.

"You two lift him," said Ymir, taking hold of the lantern. "I'll light your way back through the tunnel. If you get tired, I will swap positions with you, all right? God, if only we had a *jötunn* with us now!"

They made their way back into the tunnel, Robin and John on either side of Will, an arm draped across each of them. He did his best to help them, but he could not put any weight on his injured leg so it was slow going. Ymir went first, pointing out uneven points in the floor so they did not trip and possibly hurt Scarlet even more.

As they walked, Robin tried to focus on the strange tool marks on the tunnel walls and ceiling, imagining how anyone could have dug out this long tunnel, and why. He did not let his imagination stray into the realm of dwarves, or giants, or demons, instead picturing men like him doing the work. It was possible, he knew that, but he could not imagine why anyone would go to such lengths to make a tunnel away down here in the darkness. He suspected he would never find out.

Before he knew it, they were back at the entrance to that man-made tunnel and his heart lifted for it had not taken as long as he'd feared. He realised he was rather exhausted though, for Will Scarlet was not a small man. John was also tired, his hair and beard matted with sweat despite the chill air in the tunnel.

"Let's have a rest," the bailiff suggested, lowering Will to the chamber floor. "I've had to stoop all the way here, bending my legs so I'm at the same height as you, Robin. My thighs are burning like hell."

"Oh, his thighs are sore," Will said sarcastically. "Try having a fucking arrow stuck in one of them!"

"Shut up, Scarlet," John retorted with a grin. "Or you can hobble back to Tuck on one leg, you moaning-faced twat."

Robin laughed, buoyed by his friends' silly banter even as they faced up to this dire situation they found themselves in. "Could you eat anything, Will?" he asked. "Drink?"

"Aye, give me some ale. Maybe if I get drunk the pain will ease a bit."

"Worth a try," John agreed, taking Will's aleskin and unstoppering it before handing it to him. "Might make you less cranky too. Probably not though."

Ymir watched them, unused to the humour of Englishmen, a baffled look on his face.

"Maybe I should run on ahead," the guide suggested. "Find Tuck, get help somehow."

Robin thought about it, but shook his head. "Tuck can't come into the tunnels, we know it makes him unwell. We'll have to go to him. No, remain with us, Ymir, if you would. We'll need you to take our places carrying Will. It's hard going, and we still have quite some distance to go."

Ymir nodded. "No problem. It's my job to guide you through the mountain, and I shall do so."

"Good man," Will told him, trying to force a smile but managing only a sickly grimace. "Thank you."

"What about us?" John demanded. "No thanks for me or Robin? We're the ones carrying you!"

"Thanks, lads. Now, can we get going again? I want to feel the sun on my face before I die."

Robin glanced at his friend in alarm but Scarlet was smiling, doing his best to keep his spirits up in spite of the pain he must be feeling.

"We need to get you up to that ledge again," Robin pointed out. "Can you grip the rope while we haul you up? Are you strong enough."

Will flexed his biceps. "I think so."

"All right. I'll go up first with Ymir. We'll pull you up, while John waits at the bottom."

"Why?" John asked.

"To break his fall if he can't hold on."

John went off on another rant about him being the one to get dropped on but it was all good-natured and, as it turned out, Will's upper body strength was equal to the task of gripping the rope and all four men were soon on the ledge and making their way back towards the place where they'd entered the mountain.

"How d'you think the Hospitallers are faring?" John asked as he swapped places with Ymir, taking the lantern and leading the way, rolling his head and trying to work out the stiffness that had set in from crouching to support Will.

"I'm not worried about the preceptor," Robin grunted, lifting Will a little higher over a lip in the tunnel floor. "He's made his choice to chase wealth rather than looking after one of his men. It's Stephen I fear for."

"Aye," Will agreed. "I like Stephen. One of the few people I do like! Hopefully he makes it out of this damn mountain in once piece.

"Hopefully we all do," John said, and they continued through the gloom in thoughtful silence.

* * *

Stephen felt torn. He hurried along the tunnel behind Sir Simon, knowing that he'd chosen the right path – he was a soldier, a Hospitaller, after all, and it was his sworn duty to follow a superior officer's orders – but he did not like leaving behind his friends.

The sergeant cursed as he tripped over a rock, formed from strange minerals over untold millennia, and wondered how Will Scarlet would make it back to the surface of the Earth. It had been a long, hard journey of several hours through the Untersberg to reach the chamber where they'd been attacked, and that was with everyone able to walk and climb freely. If the arrow that had lodged in Scarlet's leg stopped him from moving properly he would need a stretcher, and maybe some kind of pulley to lift him over the high sections in the caverns. Would Robin, John, and the guide abandon Will to go back and collect materials for a stretcher? Would Will survive until they returned, or would he bleed out?

If Stephen and the preceptor somehow defeated the remaining soldiers from Laarne the sergeant would persuade Sir Simon to go back and help somehow, if it was not too late.

He laughed bleakly, knowing that, of all these scenarios, the most likely outcome would be death for Scarlet, and death for the Hospitallers. How the hell were he and the preceptor supposed to defeat such overwhelming numbers? It was surely impossible. And even if, by some miracle they managed it, Stephen had no doubt the 'Holy Grail' would turn out to be nothing more than a modern cup or, at best, some old thing whose provenance could never be proven. Still, he had sworn his oath when he became a Hospitaller, and he would do his duty, just as he always did, no matter the outcome.

"There they are!"

Stephen came up behind Sir Simon and looked over his shoulder. Ahead, the lanterns of their prey could be seen.

"Remember they have at least one bowman with them," the sergeant cautioned. "They must have heard us coming and could have laid an ambuscade. We must proceed with caution, master."

The preceptor was not so taken with his desire for the grail that he could not recognise the sense in his sergeant's words. "All right," he agreed. "We continue forward, but keep close to the walls, and use whatever cover is available."

Stephen tried to do as he was told, but they were in a tunnel with nowhere to hide, and a lantern that showed their exact position but could not be extinguished or they might fall over an unseen ledge to their doom. It was a horrible situation, and Stephen felt sweat drenching his body as they approached the lights ahead.

From that dimly lit area ahead came a shout, ringing out along the tunnel, becoming lost in the inky blackness behind them, before echoing back in a horribly sinister manner that made the hairs on Stephen's neck rise.

"Halt!" the voice said, in English, although when it continued it was in Flemish.

The sergeant waited, sword in hand, pressing himself as hard against the wall as possible, staring ahead for some signs of the enemy archer. Beside him, Sir Simon did not appear so afraid of missiles striking him down from the gloom, glaring forward indignantly as he barked at the enemy leader, conversing back and forth as though he was the one with greater numbers at his back.

"What's the bastard saying?" Stephen hissed during a brief moment of silence.

"He's asking why we're chasing them, and why we attacked them. Obviously, I told them that they had been the ones who attacked us first, and that we'll let them go in peace if they simply hand over the holy treasure."

"The 'holy treasure', master?"

The knight glanced at him with a wry smile. "You didn't think I'd tell them it was the Grail did you?"

Stephen did not reply. What could one say to such a question. He felt sure the soldiers would know if they'd discovered the true Grail and, if they did, they would hardly hand it over without a fight.

More shouting came from the Flemish man then, answered in turn by Sir Simon.

"They will not give it up," the preceptor growled. "They say they have no desire to kill us, but they will if we pursue them further."

Again, Stephen remained silent, thoughts already turning to the journey back to Will Scarlet and the others.

Sir Simon would simply not give up, however. "Christ will protect us," he said softly, almost to himself. "The Holy Grail must be guarded by an Order like ours, Stephen. It should not fall into the hands of a grasping minor noble from the arsehole of the Holy Roman Empire, do you understand? Are you with me?"

The sergeant listened as his master's voice grew harsher with each word, rising in pitch and intensity, and when the final question came, he did not answer. Could not answer.

"Charge!" Sir Simon Launcelyn roared, eyes blazing with the fire of Heaven as he lifted his longsword and ran along the tunnel towards the enemy soldiers.

Stephen stared, too shocked to move for a moment. He had not expected his master to simply charge such a large group of armed men, especially when they knew at least one carried a bow and wouldn't hesitate to use it. When his mind registered what was happening, Stephen lifted his sword, took a hesitant, terrified step away from the wall, and then threw himself on the hard, rock floor of the tunnel as an arrow flew past him. He did not see the missile, but he felt it grazing his ear, and knew from the terrible stinging sensation that blood had been drawn.

Before he could get back to his feet a second arrow had been loosed. Again, Stephen could not see it, this time because Sir Simon's large frame obscured it as well as the light, but he did see his master stumble and fall to his knees, utterly still and silent in the near total darkness.

"Master!" Stephen cried, crawling forward on his belly, desperately praying any further arrows would go over or around him. "Master!"

No reply came and, by the time the sergeant reached Sir Simon the knight had slumped down, still kneeling on the tunnel floor but bent like a sack of carrots, not upright like the proud Knight Hospitaller he was.

Stephen grabbed him and pulled him down beside him, and then he realised there were two arrows in Sir Simon's chest, and one had pierced the thick cloak, and the chainmail right at the preceptor's heart. The knight's body lay unmoving beside Stephen and the pale light of the lanterns ahead were reflected in the dead stare of his master.

* * *

"This is too hard," Ymir groaned, halting and taking Will Scarlet's arm off his shoulder. He slumped to the ground, clearly too exhausted to care that he was sitting in a puddle of stagnant water that was probably teeming with protozoic parasites. "I'm so sorry, but I can't go on. My legs are aching, my back is agony, and I just need to lie here and sleep."

Robin turned to look at him, holding up the lantern which reflected off the tired guide's face, slick with a sheen of sweat.

"Aye, let's take a rest," Little John said, gently helping Will sit on a drier patch of the tunnel floor. "We're getting there, but it's hard going right enough."

"Are we getting there?" Ymir practically sobbed. "We still have a long, long way to go, my friends, and I do not think I can carry on any further."

Robin bit his tongue, holding back the retort that he might have given to one of his friends, exhorting them to pull themselves together. Ymir had proven himself a loyal comrade, but he did not have the shoulders of a master longbowman like Robin Hood, or the giant arms of John Little. Their guide had given them everything, and he did not need to be rebuked for admitting how tired he was.

"Take a rest, Ymir," the archer said. "Have you got something to drink left in your pack? I still have both ale, and water if you need some. No? All right, well, have some food then, gather your strength. I'll take your place supporting Will for the rest of the way."

Scarlet did not say anything. He did not look at all well, and Robin shared a worried look with John. Had infection already set in to the wound? They were in a damp tunnel, and it might be making the wound worse than it would have been in the fresh, open air. Robin was no barber-surgeon, but he did not need to be to know that Will was in grave trouble.

Slumping down onto a rock, Robin helped himself to a sip of water, not taking as much as he would like, for who knew when they would be able to refill their skins? He ate a chunk of bread and was glad for it, for he believed he could feel strength flowing back into his drained limbs as he chewed. An apple finished his meal and, by then, he was ready to carry on.

Little John seemed to be sleeping though, his fringe covering his eyes as he lay unmoving with his back against the tunnel wall. A moment of panic hit Robin as he feared a second of his friends was terribly ill, but the steady rise and fall of the bailiff's great chest suggested he was simply asleep.

Ymir was still awake, but his face was twisted in an expression of deep unhappiness.

Will Scarlet returned Robin's glance, but his eyes were distant, and the younger man was not sure Will was even seeing him.

They would have to rest for a time longer.

Robin did not feel as exhausted as the other two obviously did, but then he'd been allowed a break from supporting Will, only having to guide the way with the lantern for the last little while. He felt restless, and something made him want to examine their surroundings. He took the lantern and stood beside the wall, using the light to show up details of the minerals and rock. It was fascinating to think all this was down here, and practically no one had ever seen it.

He lifted the lantern and walked a few paces along, eyes scanning the wall, ceiling, and floor, and then his eye was drawn by something in the rock. Squinting, he bent to look closer, trying to work out what the shape was that he could see. With an excited start, he realised it was a carving – the same design or motif that had been engraved at the entrance to the tunnel Sir Simon had proclaimed to be the hiding place for the Holy Grail further back into the Untersberg.

This carving was bigger than the other one, but time and the conditions in that section of the tunnel had almost completely obscured it. Purely by chance had the four men stopped to rest at that point, and purely by chance had Robin's lantern reflected off a section of the carving that caught the light just so…

"Something's here," he exclaimed, putting the light down on the ground and pointing at a pile of rocks beneath the carved symbol. "Look, just like back at the other tunnel we went through!"

None of the others came to help him as he began lifting the rocks away, although they did eye him with curiosity, especially Ymir.

"I've been coming into these tunnels for years," the guide said. "And never noticed carvings like that before."

"You never came this far in though, did you?" John asked.

"I've been as far as this point, *ja*," Ymir protested. "It is annoying. I think of the Untersberg as my domain, but then you foreign men come here and discover things like this that I have never seen before!"

"Well, come and help me," Robin encouraged him. "Let's discover this together, whatever it is."

Ymir sighed, but the lure of this new adventure, this new secret, was too great. He pushed himself to his feet with a groan and, smiling, moved to help Robin remove the rocks, strange insects crawling and slithering away, searching for the safety of darkness once more. John came over as well and, with their combined strength, the pile of rocks was soon shifted out of the way, revealing an opening in the tunnel wall.

"Lantern," said Robin, peering into the darkness, hand outstretched behind him. Ymir gave the light to him and he held it into the opening which was just big enough for a man, although perhaps not a man as big as John, to crawl through.

"What do you see?" the bailiff asked, squinting through the gap.

"It looks like this was carved by men too, like the other tunnel with the symbol outside. I can see tool marks where the rock was cut away." He shuddered as a particularly large spider scuttled away from the lantern then forced himself to put his head further into the new, narrow tunnel. "I'm going to see where it goes," he said.

"Don't be mad," Will Scarlet mumbled, shaking his head weakly. "What if you get stuck? We're in enough trouble as it is."

"I won't get stuck. I don't think it goes very far, and it seems to widen further ahead, so I'll be able to turn around and crawl back this way."

"I'll pray for you," said Will and did just that as Robin took a deep, steadying breath and pushed his great shoulders through the tunnel opening, taking the lantern with him and plunging the other three into stifling darkness. Both John and Ymir muttered prayers too as Robin forged deeper into the tight space. He tried his best to ignore the insects that scattered at the lantern's approach, forcing his imagination not to create images of any of the creeping things being on him…

It did not take long – thank Christ and all the saints! – before he reached the end of the tunnel. It did not open onto another one, simply came to an abrupt end, but there, on the ground, was a long, narrow wooden box with iron bindings and hinges.

Excitement filled him as he looked upon it. This had been placed here in this man-made section of tunnel deep beneath the Untersberg, and hidden by a large pile of rocks. It had to be something important. Something, perhaps, that would win him the pardon from King Edward that he craved…?

"Well?" John called tensely. "Did you find anything? Are you coming back out, or staying in there forever."

Grinning, Robin grasped the wooden box, feeling that it was surprisingly weighty. "Aye, I've found something," he said excitedly. "I'm coming out now!"

There was a pause as the three friends digested Robin's statement and then they demanded to know what had been discovered.

"We'll find out as soon as I get the hell out of here." Using his elbows and his knees, he shuffled himself, the lantern, and the precious wooden box back towards the opening as fast as he could. Any trace of tiredness was gone now, and he no longer worried about insects or other beasties as he had done before. The box filled his mind, practically consumed him as he tried to picture what was concealed inside it. What was so precious that it had been laid in an iron-bound chest, and brought all the way to the stygian depths of the Untersberg? Surely not simple gold, or silver, or even gemstones. Such things did not require a hiding place as extreme as that legend-haunted mountain.

When he reached the opening John grasped the precious wooden box and pulled it out. Robin chastised him, telling the bailiff to take care with the treasure. Ymir tried to help Robin out but he was more of a hindrance and the young archer did not have it in him to tell the guide to leave him be.

At last, they stood looking down at the box which they'd placed before Will so he could see what was happening too. The lantern lent the scene an almost mystical nature, and Robin wondered just what they were about to discover within the old chest.

"Well, hurry up and open it then, before I'm fucking dead," Scarlet grunted, and Robin nodded, staring intently at his prize.

"All right," he said, and bent to examine the box for a means to open it. It was not difficult; there were two simple latches which he flicked downwards, realising he was incredibly nervous as he did so, and glanced up at his watching companions before reverently lifting the chest's lid.

It swung open on two hinges that showed no signs of rust or corrosion and the men strained to look closer at the contents which, as things stood, represented the sole reward for their long, arduous journey.

CHAPTER TWENTY-SEVEN

"That's not the Holy Grail," said Will Scarlet. "Unless they used some strange cups for drinking wine in Christ's time."

"Of course it's not the Grail," John returned caustically. "I already told you all: any cup would have been destroyed over the course of thirteen hundred years. It's long gone. That though…" He gazed into the box which was lined inside with a rich blue velvet. "That looks far more interesting to me than some old cup."

"Just as well Tuck isn't here," Robin noted. "Or he'd give you a smack about the head for your sacrilege. 'Some old cup' indeed." He smiled though, and reached into the chest, gingerly lifting the sole item within.

"It's a sword."

"Well done, Ymir," said John sarcastically. "No wonder you're such a famous guide – you're very observant."

Robin chuckled and raised the sword up so the light fell directly upon it and they could see it better.

"It's broken. Look, the tip has snapped off."

"So it has," said Robin, surprised. Why would anyone bring a broken sword all the way to the Untersberg and hide it away in a chest? It made no sense to him. "King John's treasure was said to include an old sword that once belonged to one of King Arthur's knights," he remembered. "Maybe this is it."

"I reckon it must be," John nodded. "That's why it was hidden away. It might be broken, but it must have some great value, or it wouldn't have been brought here by the Flemish knight and the Hospitallers." He straightened, smiling broadly through his grizzled beard. "Well done, my friend. You've found your treasure, and once we get it back to England, the means to a pardon."

"If we get it back to England," Robin replied, the excitement of his discovery fading as reality struck him. "We still need to get out of these tunnels. Are you ready to move again?" He glanced at Will and saw his friend's eyes were closed, his complexion deathly pale, mouth twisted in pain.

"Aye," John nodded. "Put the sword back in the box and let's get moving. Whoever carries the lantern can take the box as well."

"That's Ymir then," said Robin, reluctantly holding out his prize to the guide. "Be careful with it, please."

Ymir accepted the treasure with great reverence, as though he really was being handed the Holy Grail, and bent to take the lantern in his other hand. "All right," he said.

"Good man," Robin said, patting the guide on the back before turning once more to Will. "Ready?"

"Aye." Scarlet's reply was hoarse, and so quiet it was practically inaudible. He did not say any more and Robin shared a worried look with John before they reached down and each grasped their injured friend under an arm and gingerly lifted him up. Clearly the rest had not done him any good, for he actually seemed weaker than before and was unable to put any weight whatsoever on his wounded leg.

"Let's go then," John said, nodding to Ymir who read the intent in the gesture and set off walking at a brisk pace, holding the lantern up to light their way.

They walked for some time like that, trying to move as quickly as possible but, with Will no longer helping carry his own weight in any way, Robin and John both tired quickly. They were forced to rest more often, and Ymir was too slight of build to take a turn carrying the wounded man for very long at all before he had to swap places with one of the bigger two.

"How far are we from the surface?" Robin asked Ymir during yet another of their resting periods. He had not broached the subject for a while, not wishing to ruin anyone's morale, but Will appeared to be unconscious, and Robin desperately needed to know how much longer they had to go before they saw sunshine again.

Ymir's face told him all he needed to know. No words were necessary.

"God help us," John groaned, putting his head in his hands and sighing with all the titanic weight of the Untersberg.

"I could go on ahead and fetch the friar," Ymir suggested again. "I know he found it hard to breathe, but..." He trailed off and gestured mutely at Will Scarlet.

Robin had thought about this already as they trudged through the benighted tunnel, but he had rejected the idea then, and he rejected it again now. He'd seen Tuck, had heard the friar's laboured, ragged breathing. It was bad enough they might lose one friend there beneath the mountain, he did not want to lose two.

"No, we just need to keep moving," he said, standing up and doing his best to ignore the pain in his own legs. He was at his very limit and he knew it, but what else could they do?

John stood up without a word, massive shoulders slumped, and then disaster struck.

An almighty bellow came from the bailiff, so loud that it even roused Will Scarlet who opened his eyes and cried, "What the fuck?" as John collapsed against the tunnel wall.

"What's wrong?" Robin demanded, hurrying to his giant friend and grasping his arm fearfully.

John looked at the tunnel floor, his face a mask of pain and despair, and nodded. "I stood on that rock," he said. "Didn't see it in this damned darkness. I've turned my ankle."

Ymir sat down again and stared at the ground, encompassing all their feelings in his defeated expression.

Robin had thought they were in trouble already, but now, with John unable to carry himself never mind the dead weight of Will Scarlet, they would need a miracle if this adventure was to end in anything other than terrible tragedy.

Stephen felt utterly bereft. The sergeant-at-arms had failed in his sworn duty to protect his master, for Sir Simon was quite dead, the twin arrows stealing his life and sending him into the waiting arms of Christ and St John, while Stephen was left there alone in the tunnel with only the lantern for company.

The soldiers from Laarne had not come for him – God knew why – retreating into the distance once Sir Simon was dispatched, the sound of their chatter fading along with their lantern-light and their footfalls. Stephen wished the bastards had not gone on without coming for him. He wanted nothing more than to throw himself upon them, tearing and slashing at their flesh with his sword, repaying them for what they'd done to his master.

In truth, he had never been as close to the dead preceptor as he had been to his previous master, Sir Richard-at-Lee. There had not been the deep bond of brotherhood he had shared with the knight he'd met back in Rhodes after Sir Richard's previous sergeant had died during a bizarre adventure that had never made much sense to Stephen when he heard his master recounting the tale. He thought of that story now, remembering Sir Richard's claims of frightening dreams, a murderous cult, and an eldritch demon that…

Pushing those old memories aside, Stephen wondered if he was delirious. If the shock, and exhaustion of it all was playing tricks on his mind. Had Sir Richard ever told him such an insane story? Surely not.

He looked at Sir Simon and, although there had never been as great a bond of camaraderie with the preceptor, they had been friends, and Stephen felt great sorrow at the sight of the hardy old knight, sightless eyes staring back at him. Accusing him of not doing enough to stop the men who'd stolen the Holy Grail from them.

Madness. It was all madness.

He returned the dead stare of his fallen master and then reminded himself of who he was. What he was. He was a sergeant-at-arms of the Knights Hospitaller, not some puling serf! Soldiers died, that was what they were supposed to do, and now Sir Simon had passed into the arms of Christ just like millions of other brave warriors.

Rising to his feet, Stephen bowed his head and said a prayer, commending the preceptor's soul to God, and then, knowing he could not carry the body out of the mountain, he stripped it of its valuables. It felt sordid, almost evil, divesting his master's corpse of its money, mail coat, knives, sword, candles, and whatever else he could find, but he was not about to leave it all there for some random explorer to steal in coming years. If Stephen was to make it home to Eagle Preceptory he would need the money, and the other things should not fall into the hands of strangers.

He had a decision to make then. Go back the way, and hopefully find Robin Hood and the others, perhaps helping them take Will Scarlet back to the sunlit outside world for healing; or follow the soldiers from Laarne who, he assumed, knew of some other way to escape the Untersberg. As he crouched there staring into nothingness the idea of avenging Sir Simon faded. The knight had been offered a chance to save himself by the enemy soldiers, and he had rejected the opportunity. It had been a true moment of madness brought on by a religious mania that Stephen had seen before while fighting with the Order. Stephen did not share in that madness, and he knew that trying to fight so many soldiers would only lead to his own death.

He took a long breath and, with a last, fond farewell to his master, he trotted along the tunnel in the direction Gerard van Rasseghem's men had gone. In his mind, Stephen tried to picture where he was within the Untersberg, and he felt sure that he must be near the outside world. Following the soldiers would – should, hopefully – lead him out to the mountainside far quicker than retracing his steps. At the same time, if the soldiers took a side tunnel Stephen might become hopelessly lost and end up dying of starvation down there, candles used up, his imagination and thoughts of sinister dwarves his only sustenance while he slowly expired.

Terrified by such a dire end, the sergeant started running, glad to see the tunnel did not split off in different directions, at least not in this section. He wondered if the men he was following had a map of the entire cave system, or perhaps a guide who knew the mountain even better than Ymir claimed to. Certainly, the soldiers seemed to know where they were going. That at least boded well for Stephen's survival, assuming he could catch up to them.

He prayed as he ran, taking care to watch his step so he didn't turn an ankle or worse and, mercifully, God must have heard him, for after a time the sergeant heard the sound of men talking over his own laboured breathing. Not long after that he saw dim, yellow lantern-light around a bend in the tunnel and slowed his pace, relief filling his heart.

He took his time from then on, not wishing the soldiers to know he was behind them. Another ambush was the last thing he wanted to run into when he believed he was so close to being free of the suffocating press of the Untersberg. He took some bread from his pack and chewed as he walked, hand on the pommel of his sword although he knew it would be of little use if that damned archer in the enemy group was hiding somewhere in the shadows.

The sergeant's belief that he must be close to exiting the mountain proved correct and soon he knew it was not a lantern he was seeing ahead, but the deep orange glow of the setting sun. Tears filled his eyes, and he realised then just how terrified he'd been of getting lost, trapped within the tunnels forever, and the sight of sunshine made him truly thankful. He had prayed for God's mercy, and it had been granted.

Stopping, Stephen crouched behind a large rocky outcropping some distance from the tunnel exit and remained there, eating more food and taking long sips from his aleskin. He could no longer hear the enemy soldiers and guessed they would be hastily carrying their prize – whatever it was – down the trail, away from any pursuers. They would know they'd killed Sir Simon, but they also knew there were more men tracking them and they would not want Robin Hood and his friends catching up with them.

Stephen waited for a little longer, hearing only the sounds of wildlife coming along the tunnel, and then, slowly, he made his way to the opening, keeping his body pressed as close to the wall as possible. Breathing a sigh of relief, he saw the soldiers, small specks snaking down the side of the mountain in single file.

They were gone, and Stephen was safe.

He prayed for a while, simply giving thanks to God and drinking in the sight of the stunning scenery around the Untersberg. Eventually though, he remembered the sun would soon dip beneath the horizon and he would need somewhere to camp. He stepped further out away from the tunnel and tried to get his bearings. Picturing the subterranean route he and Sir Simon had taken, and all the twists and turns that had brought Stephen out where he now stood, he suspected Friar Tuck must be somewhere nearby, and the wise clergyman would have setup a secure campsite. If Stephen could find him, he would be able to rest properly, and it would be good – so good – to enjoy the companionship of his old friend once again.

He could no longer see the soldiers from Laarne, they were miles distant by now he guessed and so, with no better plan, he looked in the direction he thought the friar must be camped, opened his mouth, and bellowed, "Tuck!"

His shout echoed shockingly back from the rocky mountainside, rolling out seemingly all the way to Salzburg. The sergeant cringed a little, and stared down the trail where the soldiers had disappeared, half expecting them to come running back towards him. He chuckled at that thought. Of course they would not do that. Why would they? They had their Holy Grail, or whatever treasure they'd found, and they were escaping with it. Why would they even think to come hunting Stephen? Especially when they must be just as tired as he was.

"Tuck!" he cried again, cupping his hands around his mouth to direct the sound a little better. "Tuck! It's Stephen! Where are you?"

The echo came again, "you-you-you..." trailing off as he stared at the rapidly darkening mountain and wondered where he should set up his own tent. They had taken their tents off the horses when Ymir led them up the Untersberg, having no idea how long they might be gone but knowing they would likely need a warm, dry shelter to rest in, even inside the mountain.

Friar Tuck did not return his shouts. The mountain was silent as night fell and, sadly, Stephen chose a site to pitch the tent and prepared himself for a lonely night of reliving his master's death.

* * *

Robin felt his eyes closing even as he walked, the weight of Will Scarlet pressing down on him with as much force as all the rock in the Untersberg. He trudged onwards, body and mind numb with a fatigue that he had never felt before in his life. Somewhere in his consciousness he knew that Ymir was not supporting Will – the guide had not been strong enough hours ago, and now...Well, now Robin was doing all the work, as Ymir and Will were dragged along through the tunnel.

Little John had barely stopped apologising for going over on his ankle since it had happened, and Robin had long since stopped telling him not to blame himself. The huge bailiff limped along at the head of the exhausted group, lantern in one hand, precious sword in its wooden box in the other.

They were forced to take maddeningly frequent rest stops, but Robin was coming to believe those were only making them even more tired. Sitting in the gloom thinking about how dire their situation was took a toll on the spirit, while resting weary muscles only allowed them to cool and tighten up so resuming the journey grew harder and harder.

"What time do you think it is?" Little John asked, and had to repeat himself before Robin understood what he was being asked.

"I don't know."

"It must be nighttime, don't you think? We should get some sleep. This is getting us nowhere fast." He halted and leaned against the wall, grimacing. "Maybe when we wake up my ankle will feel better, and I can carry Will again."

Robin did not stop walking, dragging Scarlet past John who was forced to limp onwards, lamp held out although no longer up high.

"Come on, Robin," the bailiff groaned. "I can't go on like this. And neither can you or Ymir from the look of you."

"If we stop now, Will is dead."

"If we don't stop now, we'll all be dead!"

"Ymir, how much further do we have to go?"

The guide stared at him blankly, not answering, just stumbling along, Will's arm draped over his narrow shoulders. Eventually he said, "A mile? Two? Ten? I have no idea."

Miles from the outside world, and even when they made it there, Tuck might not be camping nearby. If they did find the friar, would he be able to remove the arrow from Will's thigh, clean the wound, and bind it? Or was it already too late to do anything for their injured friend?

Robin stumbled and almost fell. Little John was close beside him and held him up, but that was enough. They all stopped and sat on the floor, oblivious to how cold it was.

They were in a tomb. A deep, dark tomb that would claim the life of at least one of them, if not more, and finding the valuable sword would all be for naught.

Robin flopped onto his side and looked closely at Will's leg. The blood seemed to have dried up which he took as a good sign, and then a momentary panic filled him as he thought Will might actually have died and that was why blood was no longer oozing out of him. Will's mouth was slightly parted, and his eyes flickered open as Robin watched. They looked at one another, neither smiling, or saying anything, and then Robin turned away, shamed by his failure to save his friend.

"Tuck!"

Robin jumped at the shout, staring up at Little John who repeated the call.

"What the fuck are you doing?"

John held his arms out irritably. "Maybe we're not as far from the tunnel entrance as Ymir thinks. If Tuck hears me shouting, he might come and help us. If he doesn't, Robin, we're done!"

"You might have warned us before you started bellowing like a fucking bull."

"Sorry," John replied dismissively, and then cried, "Tuck!" again, this time even louder.

No answering cry came, and they all sat or lay there, the candle in the lantern burning low and, worryingly, Robin knew they did not have any more left. When that one went out, they would have to continue on in complete darkness. He wasn't sure whether he should laugh or cry at the absurdity of it all, and, in the end, simply lay there staring at the glittering stalagmites.

It seemed like an eternity passed then as they dozed, despairing of ever seeing sunshine, or grass, or blue skies again, and then a thought struck Robin like a blow and he sat up.

"Stalagmites," he blurted, pointing.

"So it is," John agreed, a worried frown on his face as though he knew his young friend had gone insane. "Well done."

"No," Robin retorted, and he got to his feet, a sudden infusion of energy filling him. "Think about it! We passed this section with the stalagmites and stalactites not too long after we first came into the mountain, remember?"

John and Ymir gaped dully at him, then John nodded slowly. "Aye. I suppose so. It seems so long ago now."

"We must be nearly at the exit! Don't you think, Ymir? Come on, man, get up and look around. You know these tunnels. Do you not recognise this place?"

Their guide pushed himself up with all the speed and grace of a withered old crone but a smile slowly spread across his face as he took in their surroundings. "I think you are right," he conceded, happiness fading as quickly as it came. "But we still have some way to go, and I cannot carry your friend any more. I do not have the strength."

Robin's joy evaporated like snow on a sunny morning and he pressed his back against the wall, fighting despair. He could not carry Will by himself. If they were all to survive this they would need a miracle.

"Saint Mary Magdalene, lady fair and bright,

All Christendom passes through your clear and ghostly light;

You teach men to leave sin and love God aright;

To them who ask for your help make known your great might."

He recited the prayer, one of his favourites and, as he began the second verse Little John joined in, their tired voices growing in power and filling the cramped space.

"Saint Mary Magdalene, may your grace be abundant;

You have delivered many men from prison and drink,

302

Out of all illnesses, and to dead people you have brought life!

For my needs think on me, and may my help quickly succeed."

Now, as they began the final verse, Robin was astonished to see Will Scarlet mouthing the words.

"Saint Mary Magdalene, I make to you my complaint I am sinful –

I need your help before God's throne.

Of those you defend, may none feel dejected,

I ask of you, make yourself known to me, and all my friends like me."

They trailed off, the words reverberating in their heads long after the sound had died away and then, shockingly, the candle guttered and died, plunging them all into darkness.

CHAPTER TWENTY-EIGHT

Robin stared ahead, his vision so black that he thought he must have been struck blind, their prayer to the Magdalene somehow offending God. But then he understood what had happened and fear rose within him. They had sought a miracle, but instead had been met with another disaster!

How could they go on now? Carrying Will Scarlet had been an increasingly difficult task, but without a lantern to guide them, and chase away the shadows that reached out with every perilous step, it would be impossible.

He did not fear for himself – he was strong enough to stumble through the darkness and find his way out once he had a few hours sleep, he was sure of that. Ymir would be fine too. But he was not at all sure Little John could make it through the darkness on his injured ankle, not with all the uneven surfaces they'd have to contend with. And as for Will Scarlet…

Robin found himself completely at a loss, with no idea what they should do next. Praying had been a last resort, and even that had not helped. Anger rose within him then. How could God forsake them? A friar, Hospitallers, a former monk, and Robin himself who had paid for the building of a church dedicated to the Magdalene?

The world was a harsh place though, and God moved in mysterious ways, as churchmen so often said.

From somewhere nearby came the sound of murmuring, and Robin realised it was Will, praying again. He opened his mouth to berate his friend – they had already asked for divine aid and look where it had got them. He swallowed his rage though, ashamed by his own lack of faith, and glad that Will could at least find some comfort by praying in his last moments. Robin wished he could share in that comfort, cold as it was, but fatigue and despair had taken him and he sat with his head down, tears filling his eyes.

"What was that?"

Robin did not bother to look up, or respond to John's hushed question. Hope had faded at last.

"What is it?" Ymir asked, as Will continued drowsily murmuring prayers, prayers he must have learned when he was a monk, for they were in Latin and Robin did not recognise them.

"A noise," John said, and it sounded like he'd pushed himself to his feet, perhaps readying himself for some enemy that could see in the dark and was coming to make an end to them. Thoughts of hateful dwarves came to Robin and gave him a welcome outlet for his frustration. He stood up too, drawing his sword, and preparing gladly to face whatever fell beast was stalking them.

He heard a sound then, an odd murmuring that almost seemed a distant echo of Will's soft devotions. Was that all it was?

"Look!" Ymir was on his feet and Robin was surprised to realise that he could actually make out the guide. The tunnel was no longer completely devoid of light. Following Ymir's pointing finger, Robin could make out a pale orange glow, very dim, but seeming to come closer to them.

"Hello!" John shouted and, for a breathless moment there was only silence, and the light faded once more.

Had they imagined it? Was this some mirage born of sensory deprivation and exhaustion?

And then, "John!" came the reply out of the darkness, and Robin started laughing almost hysterically as he recognised the voice.

Someone had heard their prayers, either God or the Magdalene, and sent them help, and now Friar Tuck – beloved Friar Tuck! – came into view holding a candle, its tiny, flickering flame seeming as bright as the sun to the exhausted friends.

Robin glanced at Will and saw a smile on his drawn face, the same kind of rapturous smile he'd seen on the face of Tuck many times. It made him wonder what had driven

Scarlet to take up the life of a monk, and what that experience had changed within his old friend who'd always been the quintessential warrior before Robin left for Scotland. The tale of what had happened during Will's time at Selby Abbey had been recounted to Robin when he returned to Wakefield, but not in any great detail, and with an emphasis on the action and intrigue of it, rather than Will's own feelings and internal struggles as he found new purpose in his life, and was reunited with his beloved daughter once more.

Robin vowed to ask his friend about it in detail one day, but, for now, they had to get the arrow out of his leg before it was too late.

"Tuck! I thought you couldn't breathe down here. Why have you come back into the tunnel?"

The friar nodded at John's statement. "It was true, I couldn't breathe. But now? I feel fine. Perhaps it was all in my head." He looked up at the tunnel ceiling and gave a small shudder. "The thought of…" He trailed off, bending to place his candle inside the dead lantern, illuminating them all a little better. "As for why I'm here, well, I was asleep and, in my dreams I heard someone calling my name, asking for my aid. It woke me up, and I couldn't shake the feeling that you were all in grave danger down here, so I thought I better be a brave big boy and come to find you. But never mind me. What's happening?"

Quickly, they explained about the enemy archer shooting Will and their seemingly doomed attempt to carry him out of the mountain. Tuck examined the wound, tutting and shaking his tonsured head every so often while Will remained silent except for when the friar touched the arrow, drawing a whimper from the wounded man.

"How are we going to get that thing out?" John asked. "We had nothing that could do the job. We were hoping you might be able to help him if we could get him to you." He looked around. "Not much down here that would do it though."

Tuck thought about it for a moment and then his frown changed to a smile and he began rummaging in his pack. "We're in luck," he said, drawing out a pair of clean, white goose feathers from his belongings. "I carry these with a little pot of ink so I can take notes and document my days."

Will looked at the feathers, and drew in a heavy, anxious breath, understanding what was to happen. There was no avoiding it though, and John held his wounded leg while Robin braced his shoulders and Tuck placed the lantern as close to them as possible.

"Are you ready, Will?" the friar asked gently, his gaze, and his hands, reassuringly steady as he held the two feathers over the arrow.

"Aye," Scarlet breathed, eyes wide, skin deathly pale.

"Here, bite down on this," said John, placing the leather strap of his pack in Will's mouth. "I don't want you screaming like a little girl and deafening us all."

The ghost of a smile twitched Will's lips as he bit down on the strap and closed his eyes.

"Ymir, can you draw the arrow out?"

The guide swallowed and bit his lip, but he nodded and knelt beside Tuck.

"Do it slowly, all right?"

Again, Ymir nodded, not saying anything as he wiped perspiration from his palms onto his breeches and held out his hands to the broken arrow shaft.

"Ready?" asked the friar. "Brace yourself Will, we'll be as fast as possible. Try not to move."

"Get on with it, Tuck," Will grunted, and he turned away, shut his eyes, whole body tensed.

It was a brutal operation for the strap in Will's mouth could not completely silence his tortured cries, and they had to use all their remaining strength to hold the thrashing man down. The feathers were used to gently widen the wound, so Ymir could draw the missile out. There were no complications, the iron arrowhead did not catch on the flesh, coming out easily enough, but it was difficult to see their friend in such terrible pain.

When Ymir finally lifted the arrow free, Tuck hastily cleaned the wound with water and bandaged the wound tightly to stanch the bleeding. Then they all lay or sat on the tunnel floor, drenched in sweat, utterly spent and feeling as though they'd just taken part in a titanic battle.

"How are you, Will?" Tuck asked after a time.

"Sore."

The friar chuckled. "Aye, no doubt. Although in truth the arrow had not penetrated very far."

"What?" John demanded. "We thought he was dying."

"Well, he would have if it wasn't removed eventually. But it was really not that bad an injury. I've seen far worse."

"Not bad?" Will sat up, glaring at Tuck. "You must be joking. That was fucking agony!"

"Of course it was – you had an arrow in you! But, like I say, it wasn't in very deep, and it came out easy. It was a bodkin point, not a broadhead, thankfully. You'll be fine."

"'Fine,' he says! And what the fuck are you giggling at?"

They all turned to look at Robin then, for he was laughing uncontrollably, tears streaming down his eyes. "Oh, God," he gasped. "This has all been too much. Can we please get out of here now? I've had about enough of the Untersberg for one lifetime."

* * *

Tuck's miraculous appearance had given them all a boost and, with his help, they managed to get Will Scarlet safely out of the Untersberg. It was the middle of the night, but the sight of the stars and the moon had them all loudly thanking God for their deliverance.

"The sky has never looked so beautiful," Ymir gasped, dropping down onto the trail outside the tunnel mouth and staring upwards.

It was a warm, dry night, so Tuck ordered them all to simply find comfortable spots on the grass and catch some sleep, promising he'd cover them with tents or extra blankets if the weather turned. Robin had told him the full story of what had happened while they'd been parted from him, so he wanted nothing more than for them all to rest and recuperate. He took another look at Will's dressing and proclaimed himself content with what he saw.

Robin felt full of nervous energy and wanted to sit up, drinking in the sight of the stars, but before he knew it, he'd fallen into a deep slumber and, when he awoke, the sun was up, revealing the full glory of the alpine scene around them.

His mouth was dry and he reached for his pack, taking out his waterskin which was almost empty. There was just enough to slake his thirst but he knew they would need Ymir to lead them past a spring, or a stream, on their way back down the mountainside.

He sat up, wondering how Will Scarlet was. The smell of cooking meat filled his nostrils and he noticed that someone, probably Tuck, had set a fire and was roasting slices of bread and meat over it. Robin's mouth watered as his eyes moved from the food to Will Scarlet who was, praise God, sitting up and talking to Stephen.

"Stephen, you're alive!" Robin laughed and scrambled across to grasp the Hospitaller sergeant by the forearm, dragging him up into a bear-hug, so happy was he to be reunited with another of their companions. "How the hell did you get here? Where's Sir Simon?"

The bluff sergeant returned his embrace with obvious pleasure, but his happiness quickly faded and he returned to his seat on a boulder, staring out over the green landscape that rolled away for miles below their campsite. "I came out from a different tunnel to the one we went in. Since I knew

Tuck was camping somewhere around here, I just shouted his name every so often until he eventually shouted back this morning and I made my way here. It's good to see you all well. Or alive anyway."

Robin waited, a sinking feeling in his stomach as he watched Stephen struggling with what to say next. At last the sergeant met his gaze and in a level tone, explained what had happened to them when they caught up with the soldiers.

"Terrible," said Little John, who had woken up just as Stephen was starting his tale. He limped over to place a hand on the sergeant's shoulder. "Truly terrible news. I'm sorry, old friend. The preceptor was a good man. Our journey home will be a lot less enjoyable without his company."

Aye," Will Scarlet and Tuck both agreed. Robin nodded too, picturing the friendly knight's face, a heavy sadness filling him at the thought of never seeing him again. Then he suddenly realised just what the death of the knight meant. Sir Simon was the only one who could converse with the people in the lands they travelled through – without him, how would they be able to find a ship back to England, or seek lodgings for the night, or buy food, or, well, do anything? It was bad enough losing the companionship of such a noble individual, but in this case, it was something of a disaster. He did not mention his fears at that moment, but he knew the others would share them once the news had sunk in.

"How's your leg this morning?" John asked Will, sitting down and accepting some of the roasted meat and bread from Tuck. "Any better?"

"Not really," Scarlet told him with a wince. "Aches like a bastard. But the bold friar assures me I'll survive so…I suppose I should thank you all for not abandoning me, even when it looked like it was hopeless down there in the mountain."

"Go on then," said John.

"What?"

"Thank us!"

"Thanks a lot," Will replied, screwing up his eyes and making an insincere face at the bailiff who laughed and popped another slice of meat into his mouth.

"Did you see what we found, Tuck?" Robin asked, suddenly remembering the sword.

"Aye, we saw the box," said the friar, nodding towards Stephen. "We opened it up while you were asleep. You realise what it is?"

"I remember you saying a sword had been part of King John's crown jewels."

"Aye. The Sword of Tristan. I'm fairly sure that's what you've got, Robin. It should be more than enough to win you a pardon."

"Anything else?" Will wondered. "I mean, it'll be great if Robin is pardoned, but what about the rest of us? You think Edward will give us some gold or something?"

Robin looked at him, and then he repeated the ridiculous face that Will had made to John moments before, realising his friend was playing with him.

"What do we do now?" Ymir asked, finishing off his own pieces of pork and smiling in thanks to Tuck. "Do you need me to lead you down the mountain, back to the horses?"

The companions all looked at one another. What else could they do? Robin wondered if Stephen might ask them to go in and find the body of the preceptor, but the sergeant remained silent. Apparently he had made peace with the fact that Sir Simon's final resting place would be the Untersberg. It seemed a fitting tomb for a Hospitaller Knight, Robin thought.

It was Little John who spoke up first. "Let us rest here for another day or so," he said to the guide. "By then my ankle will be stronger and I can help get Will to the bottom.

311

Maybe he'll be able to walk himself after another night's rest."

Will did not rise to the bait, chewing butter bread and shaking his head in wry amusement.

"You think we're safe here?" Tuck asked. "I wouldn't want to get into a fight with those soldiers when you two are injured."

"The soldiers are gone," Stephen reminded them. "I saw them go. They have no reason to return. If they knew Robin had found that second secret chamber and the sword was there they might come back for it, but they have no way of knowing."

"Exactly," John nodded. "They believe they got whatever was hidden here by that Giselbrecht fellow. They'll be halfway to Laarne by now with their prize, whatever it is."

Robin looked at Stephen. "Did you see what they found?"

The sergeant shrugged, a dour expression on his lined face. "Sir Simon seemed to think they'd found the Grail. From the way he was talking I got the impression he had seen them carrying it, but I didn't see it myself." He sighed. "Something got him worked into a frenzy, so he must have seen them carrying the Grail, or at least what he – and they – believed was the Grail. We all saw the clean circle in the dust didn't we? In that alcove. So I'm sure they did find a chalice of some kind."

They sat in silence then, the food all finished, enjoying the fresh air, the smell of the campfire, and the sounds of nature around them. The preceptor may not have made it out of the Untersberg alive, but the rest were thankful that they had, and were able to enjoy the serenity and beauty of the mountainside once more.

No one mentioned the Holy Grail again – no mention of whether it might be the real artefact, or whether they should be chasing the men from Laarne who were in possession of

312

it, whatever it was. They had as much right to it as Robin and his friends after all, and probably more, since it had been brought to the Untersberg by Gerard van Rasseghem's great-grandfather.

"We will go home tomorrow, I think." All eyes turned to Robin as he went on. "We have the sword, which Tuck has told us is part of King John's missing treasure. Unless anyone has objections, I say it's time to go back to England."

"No objection from me," Will said, grunting as he shifted his wounded leg. "But without Sir Simon how are we going to communicate with people?"

Robin had been thinking about that, and he turned to Ymir now. "Would you escort us back to Bruges?" he asked. "I know it's a lot to ask, but I'm sure we would pay you handsomely for it. We still have quite a lot of your Salzburg coins left. What do you call them? Pfennigs and groschen?"

Ymir stared at him in surprise before, at last, he grinned. "Why not? I enjoy your company, and I will not be doing anything better in Salzburg. It will be nice to travel again for a time."

"Then it's settled!" Robin replied happily. "We'll spend another night here resting, and then get down the mountain and reclaim our horses tomorrow. From there, God willing, we'll have an open road back to the port in Bruges."

"All right," agreed Stephen. "Right now, I think you and I, Robin, should find a couple of stout branches just in case we need a stretcher to get Will, or John, down the mountain on the morrow."

"Good idea," said Tuck. "And I'll take another look at that wound of yours, Will. Come on, let's see it. It'll want stitching, and a fresh dressing applied if it's to heal properly."

As Robin and Stephen headed for a small grove of trees growing on a flat section of the nearby mountainside they looked at one another and chuckled as, behind them, the sound of Will Scarlet complaining about his rough treatment at the hands of the friar could be heard.

CHAPTER TWENTY-NINE

The following day the six companions made their way safely down the Untersberg without too much trouble. Little John's ankle was no longer as painful, and, although there were some steep sections of the trail, Ymir was able to guide them past the more dangerous sections so they could help Will Scarlet descend without falling and hurting himself more. It was slow going, using the stretcher for much of it, and they were all drenched in sweat by the time they made it down, but they were safe, and Scarlet's wound had apparently not been made worse by the journey.

They found their horses, safe and contentedly grazing with Ymir's quiet friend, Ludwig, and they were all pleased to see their mounts. Robin had secretly feared Ludwig might not prove as loyal as Ymir had to their group, and would sneak off to sell the horses in Salzburg, so he was glad to greet the big man and thank him, a little guiltily, for taking good care of the animals. Ludwig did not manage to muster a smile, and certainly could not understand what Robin said to him, but everyone was content and glad to be on horseback once more, taking the weight from their own feet as they rode northwards, away from the legendary Untersberg.

They did visit Salzburg to replenish their food, drink, and medical supplies. They also visited a barber-surgeon who examined Will Scarlet's leg and made sure it was not infected but, as he told Ymir, Friar Tuck had done a fine job of stitching it and setting the thigh on the way to healing fully.

They saw no sign of Gerard van Rasseghem's soldiers and were soon on the road that would take them back to Bruges. Robin had managed to persuade Ymir to continue guiding them as they made their way back home, and the little man had happily agreed. Ludwig came too, finally cracking a smile as he was paid by Stephen for his services.

The companions were quiet for the first few days, sadness over Sir Simon's untimely death pervading the whole group, but, as the miles passed their smiles returned, and the atmosphere became more hopeful.

"It truly is a stunning country," said Will Scarlet as they setup camp on the seventh night out from Salzburg. He'd been commanded by Tuck, and the barber-surgeon, not to move his leg any more than necessary, so he was allowed to just sit by the fire while the other men did the hard work of pitching tents, foraging for kindling, and making the horses comfortable. He sat there, gazing through the branches of the trees, looking up at the side of a mountain that rose to the west. Of course, it was covered in the familiar trees, but a light mist hung in the air, and the setting sun made it glow an eerie shade of pink. "It's like a different world to England," Scarlet opined as the other men worked around him.

"It is," Robin agreed. He tossed the carcasses of two hares he'd hunted to Scarlet. "There you are. You don't need to move your leg to skin those for our dinner."

Will smiled and set about the task he'd been given. "I'm looking forward to getting home to Wakefield," he said. "But I'm going to miss these lands."

"Me too," Robin concurred. "I'll never forget our time here."

"Not a chance of that happening," said John, coming across to join them now that he'd finished setting up the last of the tents. "The tale of this adventure will be told for a hundred years and more, you mark my words."

"No doubt of that," Tuck said, bringing a panful of water across from a stream that passed close to the campsite. "I've been taking notes about everything that's been happening. Although—" he looked accusingly at Scarlet "—I had to throw away my good feathers. I like to write my journals in ink, not blood."

"You're a good man," Will smiled. He genuinely seemed to be enjoying the journey home thought Robin. Almost dying tended to make a man more grateful for his life, and Will was no exception, although this was far from the first time he had been so close to death.

The others had all finished their chores now, the horses were tethered nearby, fully rubbed down, fed, and watered, the tents were ready to be slept in, and Tuck would soon cook the skinned and butchered hares for their final meal of the day. As they rested, they told stories and jokes, reliving past adventures and possible future ones, and even Ludwig appeared quite happy as Ymir translated bits and pieces of the conversation for him.

The ride homewards was certainly a more relaxed affair than when they had first headed to the Untersberg. Robin had dealt with the threat of the Coterels way back before they reached Aachen, and no longer did the friends need to fear being beaten to the treasure by the soldiers from Laarne. They also did not need to worry about what they would find in the mysterious mountain. Perhaps dwarves, or demons, did live deep within the ancient tunnels, but Robin and his comrades had not seen them and were now safely miles away from the place. They still had a few weeks of riding, and sailing, before they would be back in England, but there was no pressure or need to push the pace any more. They could take their time, allow Will's wound to heal properly, and just enjoy the journey.

That was certainly what they did that night, when the sun slipped beneath the mountains and the moon took its place, pale silver shining down on their camp as they enjoyed a hearty meal and some of the delicious local wheat beer.

When it came time to sleep they had full bellies and were looking forward to a good rest before the road took them another twenty or thirty miles closer to home the next day. They were in the middle of nowhere but there was always the threat of wolves or bears lurking nearby, drawn to them

317

by the smell of their cooking, so they had a rota for one man to keep watch for each hour of the night. Ludwig was exempt from the duty, simply because they were not sure of his ability to remain awake and alert, but Tuck took the first watch and the others crept into their tents, soon falling into a contented sleep.

* * *

Matthew Coterel hadn't stopped thinking about Robin Hood since the longbowman had not only evaded their ambush, but had put an arrow through Gregor. There were three men with Matthew when he left England, and somehow Hood had killed two of them. It made sense that he and Peter should decide to return home after they'd lost Hood's trail on the road to Aachen, especially since neither of them could speak the languages in the settlements they were passing through.

Such was Matthew's hatred though, that he flatly refused to return to England. His family would not appreciate his inability to kill the wolf's head. So he and Peter continued to Aachen and, when they arrived in the city, they went directly to the Hospitaller Commandery, asking if visitors from England had come there recently.

The commander himself had come to speak with them, admitting that, yes, two members of his Order had visited a few days before, but flatly refusing to give them any more information. Angrily, Matthew had raised his voice and placed a hand on his sword pommel, but, within moments they were surrounded by burly soldiers who roughly escorted them out of the commandery, practically throwing them into the street.

It had been galling, but Matthew knew he and Peter could hardly take on the might of the Hospitallers. He also knew that Robin Hood's friends had been there though, and that was useful information. From there, the Coterels went

318

to each alehouse along that street, searching for anyone who could speak English. After much searching they finally found a man and they paid him to come out into the street and translate for them as they questioned passersby, traders, and people working at stalls.

They were quickly told that a group of men had indeed passed that way, heading towards the southeastern gate of the city. Following that trail, interpreter still in tow, they went to the gates where they had to bribe the guards but ended up with confirmation that the Hospitallers and their companions had taken this road days before. It was not possible to find out if Robin Hood had been with them, but it seemed likely, and so Matthew and Peter left Aachen, taking the same road as the Hospitaller-led party.

They asked the interpreter to travel with them, but Matthew did not have enough money to persuade him, or to buy the man a horse. As a result, their progress along the road was far slower than they would have liked, for they had to try and communicate with the people in each settlement they passed using sign language. No one in those little towns and villages seemed to speak English, not even when Matthew tried to bribe them, and he found it humiliating trying to communicate with the bloody yokels by making gestures and holding up fingers to show he was inquiring about a group of five or six riders, two of them wearing crosses on their chests, one of them with his hair in a tonsure. Luckily, Robin Hood's friends were rather conspicuous and were noted in every settlement they passed through, so, although the going was slow, the Coterels were able to track their quarry for days, over hundreds of miles.

They were chased twice, probably because Matthew had been flashing his money around while trying to entice people to converse with them. The men who tried to rob them on the road were clods, poorly armed and clearly expecting to defeat them by force of numbers and brute force, but their mounts were no match for Matthew's and

Peter's. It rankled having to run from such men, but on both occasions they were outnumbered by at least three to one and so they urged their horses into a gallop and quickly left their pursuers behind.

Combined with a number of drenchings during thunderstorms, the whole journey was an unpleasant one and made the already murderous Coterels desperate to find Robin Hood and make him pay for all the indignities they'd been forced to endure since leaving England.

And then, earlier that day, they'd spotted a group of riders heading towards them. It had been sheer luck that they were not mounted themselves at the time, for they'd stopped to eat a meal and rest their horses, so they were able to quickly scurry out of sight into a stand of trees before the approaching riders noticed them. They'd become wary after the two robbery attempts and feared this might be another such attack, so they made sure their horses were well out of sight of the road before hiding behind a thick-trunked spruce and watching as the large group came closer.

Their voices marked them as Englishmen long before they rode past the hidden watchers, for the riders spoke loudly, laughing often, clearly in good spirits. Matthew looked at Peter and they grinned at one another when they heard the names the men were calling one another. "Robin." "Tuck." "Scarlet." "John."

The miles of tracking had been tough, but they had been worth it, for here were the very men they'd been searching for.

They remained pressed hard against the spruce as the group passed, only peering out when the riders had gone by.

"Only one Hospitaller," Peter had noted. "Where's the other one?"

"Maybe he died," Matthew suggested. "I'm more interested in what's in the box on the pack horse. Did you notice it? They had something long and flat in the beast's pack, covered up with a blanket, but still visible."

"You think they found the lost treasure?"

"It would explain why they're all so bloody cheerful."

"Who are the other two men with them?"

Matthew shook his head, still intently watching as the riders moved away into the distance. "Guides probably. Look how much trouble we've had trying to communicate with the locals. They probably hired those two in Salzburg." He nodded, sure that he was right. "If the Hospitaller knight is dead, that would make sense. He was the one that spoke with the Lord of Laarne's guards, remember? That's what the Flemish nobleman told us. Without the knight to translate, they've been forced to hire those men to do it instead."

"Well, now what do we do?"

Matthew had not needed to think about that question at all. "We mount up, and follow the bastards until they stop for the night." He hurried through the trees to their horses, mind racing, excitement building within him. "And then we show Robin Hood what happens to anyone that crosses us."

It had not been difficult to track Hood's party, for they made no attempt to move stealthily, keeping to the main road and continuing to jest with one another and even sing at one point. The Coterels were careful to keep well back, well out of sight and, when Hood and his friends stopped at sunset to set up camp, Matthew and Peter moved off the road and into the undergrowth again.

There, they tethered their horses, and sat down to wait for night to fall, sharpening their weapons, and discussing with some glee what they would do once it was dark.

God had placed this opportunity directly into their lap, Matthew knew. He might be called a criminal by some, but he went to Mass and prayed just like any other man, and now he had been rewarded for his faith, and his tenacity.

They would kill the wolf's head Robin Hood, and take that long, narrow box with its priceless treasure back to

England where the senior members of his beloved Coterel family would hail him as a hero.

Peter slept for an hour or so, and then Matthew woke him, and rested himself. That section of woods was extremely dark thanks to the canopy of foliage, and they expected the soft carpet of old pine needles would mask their footsteps as they walked. They knew exactly which direction to go thanks to the smell from Robin Hood's campfire which, although it would be burning low now, gave off a distinct, strong aroma.

They moved with an abundance of caution, using their hands to navigate the sea of trees, taking their time and stepping gingerly. At the back of Matthew's mind was the memory of Hood's devastating skill with the longbow – the last thing they wanted to do was warn the archer of their approach. The success of this mission rested completely on their not being discovered. They could not defeat all the men at Hood's camp, but they could strike fast and be gone before anyone knew they'd been there.

Matthew's pulse rate quickened as the smell of burning spruce grew stronger and the gentle glow of the enemy campfire filtered through the trees. Would one of Hood's men be on watch? Probably. More than one? It was impossible to know. He would just have to be alert.

It was decided beforehand that Matthew would be the one to do the actual killing, while Peter stood guard, ready to defend his superior if anything went awry. Because it was a warm, dry night, they were hoping that the tents would be open and it would be a simple enough matter to see which one Hood was in. They circled the campsite, keeping to the shadows. The tents were set up in a circular formation around the fire and, from where they stood, Matthew could see that the entrance flaps had indeed been left open at both ends on at least some of the tents.

Nodding for Peter to wait, Matthew steeled himself and moved towards the first of the shelters that was opened to let the air circulate through. He could see someone sitting by the fire, facing the other way thank God, but the guard's shoulders were narrower than Robin Hood's. He slowed and took a deep breath. His heart was racing and his whole body was damp with sweat but he was not frightened, merely excited by the prospect of killing his enemy and stealing the treasure from him.

He peered into the nearest tent but he could see the shaved pate of the friar lying there, a soft snore emanating from his jowly face. Beside him another man slept, but that was a small, gaunt man. Not Robin Hood.

Creeping past, Coterel went to the next tent which also had its flaps open and a thrill ran through his whole body. A longbow lay on the ground just inside the tent and, as Matthew stared, the man sleeping within murmured softly in his sleep and turned his head so the nearby firelight played across his face.

Robin Hood.

Matthew Coterel's lips turned up in a lupine grin as he slowly crept towards the slumbering wolf's head who murmured again, apparently enjoying a pleasant dream even as his doom approached. Then Matthew noticed that there was not another person sleeping in that tent, but there was a long, narrow wooden chest, and his grin grew wider, so wide in fact that he feared someone might spot his teeth gleaming in the darkness and he shut his mouth. He took out his knife, the shining blade dulled by earth before he and Peter headed there, and lifted his other hand to clamp it over Hood's mouth so the wolf's head could not let out a sound when the blade sliced through his windpipe.

Glancing over his shoulder, he saw Peter standing in the shadows, sword drawn, its blade dulled just like Matthew's. Elation flooded him, and he turned back to the man sleeping in the tent, hand clamping down on Hood's mouth.

Somehow, his hand met only empty air and it took a moment before he understood what had happened. Robin

Hood was no longer lying defenceless within the tent – he was kneeling up, glaring at Matthew.

Panic claimed the would-be assassin and he lunged forward with his dagger. It didn't reach its intended target though, as Hood's arm swept up and something struck Matthew's wrist, knocking it aside. The two men came together, Matthew grappling with wild fury but his strength seemed to fade within moments and he felt himself thrown roughly back, out of the tent, the massive shoulders and arms of Hood tossing him as though he were a child.

Matthew lay flat on his back, strangely calm and, when his eyes travelled downwards he understood why the fight had gone out of him. His right wrist had been slashed through deeply, and he thought he could see the bone in the dim light from the fire, as his lifeblood gushed from the open wound. He desperately tried to rise, to use his other hand to close the pink, gaping maw in his flesh, but, as he struggled to move, Robin Hood towered over him, eyes filled with hate.

"You thought to kill me while I slept? You should have gone home when I gave you the chance, Coterel. What kind of evil drives a man to follow another across so many miles? You don't even know me, yet you've done everything you could to kill me!"

"Peter!" Matthew cried out for his friend. Where was he? Why had Peter not already come to his aid?

"Your friend is dead," Hood growled. "Little John just dealt with him now, while you were creeping about behind my tent. All your friends are dead, Coterel, and soon you'll join them in Hell."

"Please. Please help me, Robin. My family will reward you! We're rich. You know who we are!"

Hood's other companions were out of their tents now, crowding around to see what was happening.

"Aye," one of them said. "We know exactly who, and what, you Coterels are."

"Two fewer in the world is no loss," said another of the grim-faced men, coming from the direction Peter had been standing, staring down at Matthew malevolently, a blood-stained quarterstaff in his hands.

"I will pray for your soul," the friar told him sadly. "And that of your dead friend. May God have mercy on you."

"God might show you mercy," growled Robin Hood, placing the point of his sword on Matthew's throat. "But you'll get none from me!"

CHAPTER THIRTY

"Rise. I was told you have something for me. A gift of some sort." King Edward III stared down at Robin who'd been kneeling before him and now slowly got to his feet, head still bowed reverentially. "You are a wolf's head, I believe?"

"Yes, Lord King," Robin admitted. "That's why I've come here."

"Oh?"

"I believe that a man who performs a valuable service for his king may win himself a pardon."

The king's lips twitched and he nodded. "This is true. Are you saying you've performed some valuable service for me?" He grinned widely. "You were here before, weren't you? You and the giant behind you. I've been told about that previous visit. My father apparently liked you both immensely."

"We were here before, yes, Your Grace, and we met your father. He was kind to us. And yes, I think I have performed a service that you will appreciate." He swallowed, eyes dropping down to the flagstones in the audience chamber again. "I hope so, anyway. It took a lot of effort, and the life of a brave Hospitaller knight, to bring us here now."

The king's grin faded but his eyes were sparkling with amusement and interest as he held out a hand, palm up, and said, "Well then, let us hear about this in detail. What have you done, Robert Hood of Wakefield, and why should I care enough to pardon you for your crimes?"

Robin took a deep breath and turned back to where John, Will, Tuck, and Stephen stood. Ymir and Ludwig had not come across the sea with them, travelling only as far as Bruges before heading back to Salzburg with their well-earned pay.

Robin gestured and Little John stepped forward, handing him the long narrow box they'd brought all the way from the Untersberg.

"Oh, this is interesting," Edward said, peering at the wooden chest curiously. "What have you got in there?"

Robin knelt again, this time to open the box. He stared at the old sword, praying that this was what they believed it was, and that the king would be pleased to receive it. He spun the box around so it was easier for Edward to see and held out his hands. "This, Your Grace," he intoned solemnly, "is the Sword of Tristan, which was lost in the Wash a century ago, when King John's baggage train was swept away."

The reaction to Robin's pronouncement was immediate, as the other people who'd come to petition the king that day murmured in excitement, with many suggesting the sword must be fake, and that Robin and his friends were seeking to fool Edward.

"The Sword of Tristan." England's monarch stood up and walked across to gaze down at the weapon on its bed of blue velvet, uncertainty plain on his face. He was only eighteen years old, with the beginnings of a wispy beard, and neatly brushed brown hair that came to his shoulders. He did look rather like his father, but he did not yet have the easy confidence of the old king. Waving to one of his retainers – a tall, well-built man who seemed more like a soldier than a servant – Edward bade him come and examine the box and its contents, saying to him, "Can this possibly be real, William?"

Robin guessed this man must be William Montagu, the king's closest companion and advisor. He stood beside Edward and bent to carefully lift the sword. He scrutinised it closely, touching the broken tip with his finger, running his hand, and an expert eye, across the blade before passing it to Edward. "It looks old," he said. "We'll need to check the records for a detailed description, or perhaps even a picture if we can find one. But my gut feeling is that it's real."

Edward took the weapon and his pleasure was clear as he turned it this way and that, and then gave it an experimental swing or two. "If this is what you claim it to be," he told Robin, "then a pardon shall be yours. But how did you come to possess it, man? Come on, you must tell us the whole story, eh, William?" He crouched to put the sword back in its chest and then sat on his throne again as Montagu sat beside him on a smaller, although still hugely impressive chair.

"Yes, Your Grace, we need to hear Hood's tale. I wager it's a good one!"

"That's settled then. You, Robert Hood, and your companions, will join us for tonight's feasting, and you shall regale us with the story of your adventures."

Robin swallowed, desperately wishing he could refuse. They'd avoided Laarne, but then sailed straight from Bruges to Gravesend, and ridden from there directly to Westminster. So they'd not been back to Wakefield yet, and were all desperate to get home, including Stephen who admitted to missing Eagle even though it would not be the same preceptory without Sir Simon. But what could Robin do? One did not refuse an invitation to dine from his own king!

"Thank you, Your Grace," he croaked, mouth dry, knowing his friends would be just as uncomfortable as he was.

"Good, then go with my steward and freshen up. If you've been to Salzburg and back you will need a good scrub, eh?" He smiled, reminding Robin very much of the previous king. "I will have my people examine this sword, and we'll decide if it truly is what it appears to be."

The steward came to Robin then, escorting him from the audience room along with his friends, all of whom looked sick at the thought of the royal feast, except Tuck, who was grinning from ear to ear at the prospect.

"This way," the steward ordered, striding ahead, feet slapping rhythmically on the hard floor. "You can't attend the king's feast looking like you've been lost in a forest for a year. It's baths for you!"

* * *

"More wine?"

The man holding the goblet could hardly hear over the chattering of noblemen and women, and the minstrels plucking on lutes and gitterns in the corner of the great chamber. "Do you need to ask?" he called back with a tilt of the head and a smile.

Gerard van Rasseghem's goblet was refilled with the rich, burgundy wine and his wife, Elisabeth, poured some into her own cup before setting the jug back on the table and pressing her head affectionately against her husband.

The couple often entertained the great and good of Flanders and beyond, and this evening was another such celebration of life, and wealth. Yet van Rasseghem could not fully enjoy the feast – he'd been on edge for weeks, since the travellers from England came, and he'd sent his own soldiers to Aachen to beat the foreigners to the treasure his great-grandfather had once owned. Treasure that should not fall into the hands of Englishmen, for it rightfully belonged to him. Even if it had once been King John's, the fool had not taken care of it and lost it all. Whoever found it amongst the shifting sands that swallowed it up was the rightful owner, and that had been van Rasseghem's progenitor, Giselbrecht.

Giselbrecht van Zottegem, as Gerard's wife had discovered in combing the archives there at Laarne Castle, had been something of a brutal man in his youth. As seemed to be the way so often, his brutality and penchant for killing

329

contrasted starkly with his near-fanatical devotion to the Church. Although he had not been a member of any religious Order, he had been close friends with members of the Teutonic Knights, Templars, and Hospitallers, fighting beside them in various campaigns across the world and building powerful bonds of brotherhood with many. That had all added up to a desire in Giselbrecht to take his newly plundered treasure from England, to Aachen, escorted by his Hospitaller friends.

Van Rasseghem's wife's delvings in the deep recesses of Laarne Castle's old records had uncovered the truth when she found a secret document written by Giselbrecht von Zottegem himself. Giselbrecht and his Hospitaller escort had indeed gone to Aachen a century before, but they'd not left the treasure there, they had gone on with it, to the mythical Untersberg, even deeper within the Holy Roman Empire and, supposedly, the heart of the world, or some such pious nonsense. There they had hidden it away forever, or at least until the world needed it again.

Gerard would never be able to understand his great-grandfather's decision – why take such wealth and hide it away in a damned mountain, by Christ? But religious zealots often performed apparently insane acts, and it seemed Giselbrecht truly believed the Untersberg to be a sacred site, and the perfect resting place for the treasure he'd found.

Would the soldiers Gerard sent from Laarne be able to follow the trail onwards from Aachen to the Untersberg? Had the Hospitallers recorded their movements a century ago, leaving evidence in the commandery's library, just as Giselbrecht van Zottegem had done in Laarne? There was no way for Gerard to find out, but the fact his soldiers had not returned to Laarne yet suggested they had indeed followed the treasure to its next, and final, location.

Well, either that, or they'd been killed by Sir Simon and his English friends.

Gerard was an optimist though, and he expected the lost treasure to be returned to its rightful place in Laarne Castle. The thought excited him greatly and he took a long pull of his rich, dark wine, the blood pounding in his head. He did not know exactly what treasure had been brought out of England and carried to the mountain, for that was not recorded, but he did know that his great-grandfather believed at least one of the items held great religious significance. The parchment that Gerard's wife's burrowings had turned up spoke of it, and it was not difficult to infer what his ancestor had been talking about when he wrote of a 'holy chalice'.

"Darling!"

Van Rasseghem looked at his wife and saw her eyes gleaming, and not just from the abundance of candles that were placed around the feasting table. "What is it?" he asked, throat constricting as he waited for her to answer. From her expression it was clear something momentous was afoot.

"They're back."

The nobleman turned, following her shining gaze to see the captain of the soldiers he'd sent to Aachen standing in the doorway looking decidedly grubby and tired.

"At last," Gerard breathed, excitement rising although the captain's face was as stony as always, giving no indication to the success or otherwise of his mission.

"Come, then," his wife said, putting her arm in his and guiding him towards the double doors of the dining room, smiling and assuring inquiring guests that they were only stepping out for a moment and would return shortly.

"Is it good news?" Gerard demanded once they were beside the captain who'd noticed their approach and stepped discreetly out of the room to await them. "Did you go to the mountain?"

"Yes, my lord."

The nobleman shared an excited glance with his wife, and they gestured towards a nearby chamber where they could speak in private. Neither asked the captain about his men or, indeed, his own welfare. All they could think about was what had been found in the Untersberg.

When they were within the chamber, the captain reached into the pack he carried and reverently took out something that was wrapped in the remains of an old tunic. Hardly a fitting covering for a valuable, ancient artefact, but it did not matter at that moment. Gerard and Elisabeth watched raptly as the captain pulled back the cloth to reveal a goblet.

"Good God, it's beautiful," the lady gasped, reaching out to take it, before changing her mind and withdrawing her hand in wonderment.

Her description was no exaggeration, for the exquisite cup was made from stone – possibly agate, although Gerard was not certain – and it was set in a gold housing with precious stones inlaid around it.

"Is it the real Holy Grail?" the captain asked softly. "We had to travel many miles, and face many obstacles to recover it. We lost more than one man during the journey. After all that, my lord, surely it is the real thing?"

Gerard's eyes greedily drank in the receptacle, his mind racing. "Of course it is," he said. It was his now, and therefore it was real.

"What will you do with it, lord?"

Gerard tore his eyes from the Grail and blinked at his captain, unable to process the question for a long moment, so consumed was he by his glittering new possession. "Do with it?" he repeated blankly. "Why, I will keep it here in my castle where it belongs."

"But if anyone finds out it's here they'll try to steal it from us," his wife warned. "We can't let that happen."

"You're right," Gerard nodded, mind finally starting to work properly again. He looked at the soldier, wondering if the man could be trusted to keep his mouth shut. "You'll be well rewarded for returning this to its rightful home, captain," said Gerard. "And you will tell no one of the Grail's existence, do you understand? You'll also tell your men that this is merely an old goblet. Somewhat valuable thanks to the materials it's made from, but nothing more than that. They will also be rewarded for their service, but we, and they, will never mention your mission to Aachen, and thence to the mountain, again. Are we clear?"

The captain saluted. "Of course, my lord. I'll make sure your orders are followed precisely."

"Thank you," the nobleman said, thoughts turning back once more to the priceless item in his hands. "We'll hear your full report on the morrow. Before you go, did you find any other treasure in the mountain?"

"No, lord. We were followed, and attacked, by the Englishmen, but we beat them to the Grail, and killed the Hospitaller knight as we escaped."

"Oh, well done, captain! As I say, you will be very handsomely rewarded for your loyalty."

So dismissed, the soldier left the chamber and Gerard and his wife were left alone with the goblet.

"The Holy Grail," murmured Lady Elisabeth, reaching out to stroke the gold lovingly, reverently. "It's ours, and it will remain here in Laarne forever."

"Yes," Gerard van Rasseghem agreed. "We'll hide it away in the library, along with all the records that mention my great-grandfather's part in its story."

"And you're sure the soldiers that brought it to us will keep silent about finding it?"

"Don't worry about them," said Gerard grimly. "I'll make sure none of them ever tell a soul about this."

* * *

"Here, Robin. Take it."

Robin Hood, laughing as Will told the packed alehouse all about being carried out of the Untersberg by his companions, accepted the mug of ale from Little John and hugged Matilda, overjoyed to be home. At last!

The friends had been feasted by King Edward at Windsor, telling him the same story the people of Wakefield were hearing now, while the royal staff checked the provenance of the supposed Sword of Tristan. Old records had been thoroughly scoured by various scribes and, eventually, the broken bladed weapon was pronounced the real thing. The description in the royal records matched the sword Robin had gifted to the king and so, as a reward, Edward bestowed a pardon upon the young archer. He had also been so pleased to recover at least that part of King John's lost treasure, and so entertained by the tale of its retrieval, that he gave Robin and his friends a sizeable purse of coins each to take back to their homes.

When they left Windsor they travelled then to Clerkenwell with Stephen. He reported the death of Sir Simon Launcelyn to his Hospitaller superiors, gifted his purse of coins to their keeping for members of the Order could have no personal wealth, and then, accompanied by Robin and the rest of the friends, returned to Eagle to await a new preceptor being assigned to the property.

After that, the miles flew past as the companions made their way north, to Wakefield. It was not exactly a hero's welcome for them from Matilda, Amber, or Elspeth, but, once furious reproaches had been made, and explanations given, the entire village began a feast in celebration of their safe return.

That feast had lasted for two days, and, when it ended, Robin and his friends continued to be feted in the local alehouse, where the proprietor, Alexander, encouraged the companions to repeat the stories of their recent adventure to eager listeners who came from all the nearby towns and villages to hear them. Alexander did a roaring trade in ale and food, and was more than happy to keep the drinks flowing for the storytellers.

If Robin Hood, Little John, Will Scarlet, and Friar Tuck had been local heroes before, now they were almost mythical in stature. And it helped that they'd got one over on the Flemish Lord of Laarne, Gerard van Rasseghem, by finding the Sword of Tristan and leaving him apparently empty-handed.

Of course, the friends knew van Rasseghem's men had found something, and, when they were at Windsor the king's scholars provided a strong clue as to what that something was.

"The records are not particularly extensive," Edward had told them as he bade them farewell the morning following the feast. "Well, they must have been at one point, but they've become scattered, damaged, or simply lost over the past one hundred or so years. My clerks have been able to find a description of the Sword of Tristan, of course, and some of the other crown jewels of my predecessor, John."

Robin listened intently as Edward went on to describe an exquisite chalice, or goblet, that was once owned by King John. Made from agate, and set in gold inlaid with precious gemstones, it had been one of John's favourite pieces and it had utterly devastated him to lose that particular piece in the Wash. Some even thought it was that terrible loss that had sent him to his grave.

"Was it truly the Holy Grail, Your Grace?" Tuck had asked, wide-eyed.

Edward laughed at the question. "Certainly not, Brother Tuck. It was merely a modern recreation of it, or at least a recreation of what John had presumed the real Grail to have looked like. He had it made himself. Oh, don't mistake me, lads." The king had looked them all in the eye then, his amusement fading. "That goblet is worth a fortune, and I should very much have liked it to be returned to me. Its loss is keenly felt to this day. But its value is purely in monetary terms, and in the fact it was once part of our royal crown jewels. It has no religious significance or value whatsoever, though – it was crafted over a thousand years after the Last Supper."

Robin and his friends believed that goblet was what the soldiers from Laarne had found in the tunnel marked with the esoteric symbol, and what had led Sir Simon to his death. The Hospitaller knight had claimed he'd seen the soldiers escaping with an exquisite cup, one he believed be the Holy Grail, and he had been so caught up in religious fervour that he'd lost his life for it.

It was depressing to think the chivalrous, loyal knight had died for something that held no spiritual value whatsoever, but it was also amusing for the friends to imagine Gerard van Rasseghem venerating the golden goblet, mistakenly believing it to be the Holy Grail.

Robin and his friends did not mention this part of the story when they recounted their adventures to the people of Wakefield. The Lord of Laarne was a powerful nobleman, and it was better for all involved if they had no further dealings with him, or his soldiers.

The tales about the expedition to the Untersberg also never mentioned the Coterel gang members that had stalked Robin and his companions for so many miles. The Lord of Laarne was a real threat, but the remaining Coterels were a far more potent danger, since they were based right there in England.

No one except the friends – and Ymir and Ludwig – knew that Matthew Coterel had been executed by Robin, and that was how it would remain.

That was how it must remain, if he and his friends and family were to continue living peacefully in Wakefield. And, now that he'd been pardoned, Robin Hood meant to make the most of his freedom by living peacefully, and keeping away from trouble.

Although, he had one more thing left to do before he could settle down to a quiet life…

CHAPTER THIRTY-ONE

Sheriff Henry de Faucumberg stood looking out over the marketplace in Nottingham, pleased that the people were, for the most part, behaving themselves. He had stepped up patrols in the city recently to combat a rise in petty thefts and the inevitable unrest that arose from such crimes, and, so far, it seemed to be working. Of course, the sweltering heat of summer had now given way to the onset of autumn and that no doubt helped tempers from snapping the way they'd done during July and August.

He bit into an apple, relishing the tart flesh as he chewed, content that he was doing a good job of overseeing Nottingham and Yorkshire.

"Busy?"

The pair of soldiers that Sir Henry employed as bodyguards stepped between him and the man who'd addressed him. They were both tall men, with craggy faces that bore visible evidence of the fights they'd been involved in over the years, and only a fool would go against them without good reason.

"Aye, I'm busy," the sheriff retorted, tossing away his half-eaten apple. "Doing my rounds, making sure everyone – and I mean everyone – in Nottingham is behaving themselves. Do you take my meaning?"

John Coterel's lip twitched in a mocking, derisive smile. "Oh, I take your meaning, reeve."

"What do you want here then?"

"I would speak with you."

Sir Henry's eyes narrowed, and he peered at Coterel's face, trying to read the man's intention in his eyes. "What about?" he demanded.

"Did you know Robert Hood had recently returned to Wakefield?"

338

The sheriff felt his blood run cold at the question. He should have known the Coterels would not have forgotten about Robin and his friends.

"I did," he admitted, nodding his head ever so slightly. "What of it?"

"It seems he sailed across the sea to some faraway lands, and had great adventures there. When he came back to England he gifted some fabulous treasure to the king and won a pardon in return."

Sir Henry listened, watching John Coterel's face as he droned on. "So what?" said the sheriff when he was sure the man was done speaking, for now at least.

"My own nephew, young Matthew, also sailed to those lands," Coterel growled, jaw tightening as his eyes bored into the sheriff.

"Again, so what?"

"Matthew, unlike Robert Hood, has never returned."

Sir Henry absorbed that information. He did not know that one of the Coterel family had left the country, and neither had he heard that the young man was yet to return home.

"Maybe he got lost. Europe is a big place. Much bigger than this island. Dangerous as well."

"Maybe," John replied stonily. "But he had some fine warriors with him, and none of them have been seen or heard of in weeks either."

"Like I say, Europe is a big, dangerous place." The sheriff shrugged, making little effort to pretend he gave a damn about the missing gang members. The fewer of them plaguing England the better as far as he was concerned. "They've probably got lost, or had some issue finding a ship to carry them across the water. I hear it can be hard to find passage at this time of year." He'd heard no such thing, but there was no point in antagonising John Coterel. "Maybe they'll turn up soon."

"I hope they do," Coterel replied ominously.

"Why did they go to Europe?" Sir Henry asked innocently.

"Family business."

The sheriff did his best to keep the smirk from his face. He had seen Robin and Little John since they'd returned to Wakefield, but they'd not mentioned running into the Coterels when they were abroad having adventures. This was the first he'd heard about any of the gang members travelling in the same area as Robin's group, but he could guess Matthew Coterel's motives for such a journey.

He could also guess what would have happened had the two opposing parties come across one another.

"You didn't know about any of this?" John Coterel demanded, suspicion making him openly rude.

"No, I did not," Sir Henry snapped back. The damned cheek of the man berating him in his own city! "I did not even know Hood and his friends had left Wakefield until weeks after the fact. Contrary to what you may believe, we are not close friends. I sometimes employ John Little as a bailiff, but apart from that I have little to do with them." That was not strictly true; he did think of John and Robin in particular as friends, and Will Scarlet and Friar Tuck were stout fellows he was glad to spend time with when the chance arose. The Coterels did not need to hear about any of that though. "Why are you here annoying me anyway?" he asked, happy to move the conversation along from what he might know or not know.

John Coterel stared at him for a long, deeply uncomfortable moment, as though he could see into the sheriff's soul and judge if he was lying. At last, the gang member turned away and looked into the busy crowd of people buying or hawking wares in the marketplace around them. "I wanted to find out what you knew about my nephew's disappearance," the man replied at last, facing the sheriff boldly again. "I actually believe you when you say you don't know anything."

Sir Henry had a hard time holding his temper. "Oh, I'm glad to hear that," he snarled sarcastically.

"So you should be. If I thought otherwise, things would not go so well for you."

Now the sheriff's guards turned, both frowning, to look at him, silently begging for permission to teach John Coterel some manners. For a moment, Sir Henry wanted to give them free rein to beat the bastard bloody, but, again, he drew in a deep, soothing breath and shook his head.

Coterel must have understood the silent communication that had just played out between the three lawmen and his mouth twisted in another mocking, bitter smile. "I'll be about my business then," he grunted. "Farewell, Lord Sheriff. Perhaps we'll meet again sometime."

"I'll look forward to it," Sir Henry told him with equal ill humour.

Raising a hand in an ironic wave, Coterel started to walk away, two of his thugs coming from the shadow of the city walls to join him. Before he was out of earshot he glanced over his shoulder at the sheriff, whose smouldering glare continued to track him. "Come on," he said to his loutish companions. "I need to send a messenger to Notton. Business has been good there lately, and I'd like to thank the Tanner for all his hard work."

"Damn the smug bastard!" Sir Henry hissed as the crowd swallowed up the gang members. "God, I hope John, or Robin Hood, did kill his shit of a nephew. The day that whole family is wiped from the face of God's green earth will be a great one."

"What did he mean about Notton?" one of his guards asked. "Seemed like he wanted you to hear him saying that, my lord."

"No doubt." The sheriff nodded. With Little John away on his own adventures there had been no-one Sir Henry trusted enough to check in on the good people of Notton. He'd had reports that villagers continued to be targeted by

341

the Coterels' extortion efforts in recent weeks though. In truth, the Coterels seemed to have changed their usual tactics lately – before they'd been happy to openly use violence to get what they wanted. Their approach had softened this year however, and there had been fewer reports of people being maimed or killed by the gang. Instead, the simple threat of violence was apparently enough to extort money and lands from frightened victims. That did not seem to be the case in Notton unfortunately, at least from the dark rumours the sheriff had heard regarding the tanner there. The man was becoming more of a liability with every passing week, as he and his two friends – drunk on power as well as ale – brutalised the villagers, who could only afford to pay a pittance in return for the tanner's 'protection'. Sir Henry had not mentioned it to John Coterel, but he'd heard from one noble associate that the criminal gang was close to withdrawing their operation in Notton, for it was simply not worth the attention being drawn to them.

For one moment the sheriff pondered asking Little John to stir things up with the tanner, and perhaps hasten the Coterels' withdrawal from the village. But even if the massive bailiff did stop the criminal goings-on in Notton, it might prove a death sentence for John, and anyone who helped him.

Sighing, Sir Henry forced himself to calm down and forget about the Coterels and their lawbreaking lackeys. The sheriff had to pick his battles, like any good commander, and this was not a fight he could realistically win.

Still, there would be no harm in sending Little John a message. What the bailiff did with the information was up to him…

* * *

"If we're caught, this won't go down well with the Coterels, Robin. Not at all." Little John pushed aside some brambles, moving past the jagged branches almost in silence, his grace astonishing for such a huge man.

Robin came behind him, also gliding through the undergrowth with practised ease, somehow leaving no trace of his passing.

Will Scarlet and Friar Tuck had travelled there with them, but they'd not come into the forest, instead remaining hidden near the main road with the horses.

It was a dry day, but autumn was in the air, and a fresh breeze stirred the russet leaves in the trees as Robin and John crept along, ever alert for signs of danger, although there did not seem to be guards posted. Why would there be?

"We can't just let the people of Notton be preyed upon," Robin muttered. "When we pull this off it'll solve the problem, at least for a time. You told me yourself, the sheriff sent word that the Coterels are fed-up of Notton and the attention it's drawing to them. This will end their interest here for good, I'm sure of it."

When they'd returned from their adventures abroad, Ivor, the butcher from Notton, came to visit Robin one night. He had a badly bruised face that he told Robin was the result of a brutal beating by Simon Tanner and his two labourers. Ivor had not had the money to pay Simon for the Coterel gang's 'protection' that month, and he'd been assaulted as a result.

"It's not just me either," the terrified butcher had told Robin. "They're targeting every business owner in the village now. If anyone refuses to pay they get beaten to a pulp, or their shop or home gets robbed or smashed up." Ivor's demeanour had been truly pitiful as he'd begged Robin to help the people of Notton. "One of the Coterels visited the other week and he brought men with him. We were all told that if we didn't pay Simon regularly the gang would kill us, and our families. They're coming back in a few days to collect the money from the tannery. Notton has become a living hell, Robin, please do something!"

"But what can I do?" Robin had demanded, feeling helpless.

"The tanner's been heard boasting that he's going to go and live somewhere else. Somewhere he isn't beholden to the Coterels," Ivor had told him then. "He was in his cups as usual, telling his pals in the alehouse his plans. He thinks he's a big man now, can do whatever he likes. Until he sobers up at least."

It only took a moment for Robin to understand what the butcher was saying. Ivor, and the other people in Notton, wanted him to dispose of Simon, and make it look like the tanner had gone off to bully and brutalise the inhabitants of some other poor town.

"I'm no murderer," Robin had said, refusing to simply go to the tannery and start killing the men there. "But I might be able to help you another way."

The butcher had gone home, not entirely happy with Robin's offer of aid, but with at least a spark of hope where previously there had been none.

"You really think this will be easy?" Little John asked, breaking his reverie.

Robin had told him what the butcher had said that night and, between them, they'd agreed to do what they could to somehow help the people of Notton, while not committing murder, or openly crossing the violent Coterels and bringing trouble to Wakefield as well.

"Aye," Robin murmured, stepping neatly over a dried-out branch that would have snapped loudly had he put his weight on it. "Easy enough. They're arrogant. They don't believe anyone has the balls to cross them. And, on top of that, they're fucking stupid."

John grunted in amusement. "That's true. Still, if we're spotted things will go badly for us, and our families."

That dampened Robin's spirits, but only for a moment. "No one will see us," he said. "And we know exactly where we're going. It'll be simple."

Snorting, John ducked down behind a juniper bush and peered out at their destination. "Simple, eh? I've heard that one before."

Robin crouched at his side and took in the view of Notton's tannery. Someone was there, for black smoke poured out of a chimney in one of the buildings. That was only to be expected though. Simon might be a member of the Coterel gang, but most of the money he made from extortion went to his masters, so he still had to make a living there at his workshop.

"Part of me wants that bastard to catch us," said John, gripping his quarterstaff menacingly. "I'd like to give him a proper lesson in violence."

"Don't worry, big man. When we're finished, Simon Tanner will be taught the hardest lesson he's ever had to learn. Come on."

They moved fast, still crouching as they made their way through the deep grass beside the tannery, working their way around to the north. The low building they had expected to see was just a short distance away and they headed straight for it, coming around it at the back. The doors were at the front, and there were no windows at all for it was used only for storage. It was made of wood though, like the rest of the tannery buildings, and would be ideal for what the two men needed. Hastily, they made a small pile of broken branches and old leaves, heaping it all up against the wall of the storehouse.

"Keep an eye out," John said, and took flint and steel from his pouch. He had dried nettles for tinder, and it took mere moments for his expert strikes to yield a spark that caught in the desiccated leaves and bloomed into a small flame. Grinning like some pyromaniac, the supposed lawman put the flame to the pile of leaves and watched, eyes reflecting the glow as the fire took hold.

Robin smiled and the pair stood for a few moments, waiting to make sure the blaze took hold of the wooden wall. It seemed to take forever, the old leaves giving off a nasty smell and pouring oily smoke into the sky that Robin feared might bring someone running before the fire was too big to easily extinguish.

Robin guessed the wood must have been saturated with oils or fats from the tanning process, or from whatever had been stored in the building over the years, for, once it caught, it went up far quicker than he or John had expected. Chuckling nastily the pair ran into the tall grass and made their way back around to the front of the tannery. There they hid, and waited.

It did not take long.

"Fire! Fire! Quick, the storehouse is on fucking fire! Help, you fucking whoresons, grab the buckets and move!"

Although the tanner and his workers were inside the main building, their shouts of fear and alarm easily carried to the sniggering men outside.

"They're going," Robin said, getting to his feet and leaving the cover of the undergrowth. "Let's go."

They sprinted across the open delivery area to the main front door of the tannery and lifted the latch. It was not locked, and, heart pounding, Robin led the way inside. He had his sword in his hand, but no one was around for they were all out the back trying to deal with the fire. Ineffectually it seemed, judging by the frightened shouts.

John moved past him and went to the back wall. There was Simon Tanner's locked chest, just as it had been before. Unlike the previous visit, they did not have the tanner's key to open the lock, but the bailiff was prepared. Leaning down, he took out a pass key – a copy of the tanner's own crude key that John had made himself. He put it into the lock on the chest, jiggled it around, and, with a low click, the mechanism sprung free.

"Told you it would work," John grinned at Robin while hiding the pass key in his pouch again. "Being a former blacksmith comes in handy at times. This lock is a simple one, ridiculously easy to open if you know how."

Robin moved forward, reaching into the open chest and scooping a handful of coins out and into the sack Little John had been carrying in his belt.

"Hurry," the bailiff urged, eyes going to the open back doors constantly.

"Don't worry, they'll be gone for a while," said Robin, although he did try to finish what he was doing as quickly as possible.

"Is that it? Come on then!"

John shut the chest and clicked the lock back into place as Robin hurriedly tied his sack, then they moved back to the front door, glancing anxiously over their shoulders with every third or fourth step.

Robin felt like he was a child again as he and his giant, giggling friend burst from the tannery and raced for the undergrowth. He could remember stealing apples from the orchard to the east of Wakefield when he was a young lad, racing through the trees in terror as the roaring farmer came after him and his friends, threatening to kill them or set his wildly barking dog on them. That was exactly the kind of thrill he was getting here, although instead of a bounty of apples, he carried a large amount of silver coins. And instead of thumbing his nose at some old farmer, he was showing Simon Tanner and the Coterels that they could be attacked just like anyone else, no matter what contacts they had.

"Fire's out from the looks of it," John noted, jerking his chin upwards in the direction of the billowing smoke that seemed to be less pervasive, and less black than before.

"Aye, they've stopped shouting as well," said Robin. "We'll hide here until we're sure they've gone back to their work, then head back to Tuck and Scarlet."

They crouched in the autumn undergrowth and watched the tannery. Eventually, the sounds of thumping, and loud chattering came from the largest building and Robin made to stand up, preparing to make good their escape.

Suddenly, a despairing cry came from the tannery, and Robin dropped down again, desperately trying to make himself as small, and as silent as possible.

Simon Tanner was making no such attempts, and the furious roar that emanated from his workshop was quite something to hear. It rose up, filling the sky like the dark cloud of smoke from his ruined storehouse, and changed from a howl to a shriek.

"Shit, he's discovered the missing money already! D'you think he'll realise it was us?" John whispered.

"Nah. The prick must have dozens of enemies. Everyone in Notton would like to take him down a peg or two. Well, when the Coterels find out Tanner doesn't have their money, he'll be taken down alright."

"Look out, they're coming!"

Robin pressed himself even further into the ground, doing his best to peer through the undergrowth while remaining out of sight. Simon Tanner and his two workers stormed out of the main workshop carrying wooden hammers and knives, faces twisted in rage.

"That fucking blacksmith!" the tanner shouted. "This was his doing! The turd thinks he can rob us and just sneak back to his smithy. Well, I'll fucking show him! And then I'll show the butcher, and that alewife! I'll show them all! Come on, lads!"

"Oh, shit," John murmured. "What are we going to do now?"

Robin's mind raced even faster than his heart had done when they'd been emptying the Coterels' money into his sack. If Simon Tanner found out it was really he and John who'd burned their storehouse and stolen their money, things would not go well. The Coterels' would come to Wakefield, and it would be war. Matilda and the boys, not to mention the families of his friends, and of anyone who got in the gang's way, would be in mortal danger. But they could hardly stand by and let the blacksmith be attacked.

You fool! He berated himself. Killing four of them wasn't enough for you, was it? You had to teach Simon Tanner a lesson as well. And now what?

"Now the blacksmith will get it," John said. "We can't let that happen, Robin."

They stared at one another, lying in the grass, their humorous prank no longer funny, memories of childhood fun transformed into the certainty of terrible, adult violence.

"Come on," Robin said, jumping to his feet and heading east, through the trees that fringed Notton. "We'll leave the stolen money here for now, but we have to do something. This was all my idea – I wanted to help the downtrodden common folk, just like we used to do before I went to Scotland, but it's not worked out as I hoped."

"We had to try and help somehow, but this is bad," John conceded as they hurried along. "Really bad. We'll have to admit to setting that building alight, and you know how much people hate fire. Even a small one can spread and destroy an entire town."

Robin tried not to think of it, but that wasn't the only trouble they faced. The money in the tannery might have been the ill-gotten gains of criminality, but stealing it was also a crime, and the Coterels would not be slow in using their contacts in parliament to make sure Robin and Little John were declared outlaws again.

They had gone all the way to the Untersberg to win Robin's freedom, and he'd thrown it away for the sake of getting another one over the Coterels. It didn't matter that their intentions were good, that they wanted to bring a little bit of justice to some bad, bad men and help the innocent people in Notton.

They were facing total ruin, and on top of that the people here would be left worse off than ever.

CHAPTER THIRTY-TWO

Simon and his two workers made it to the blacksmith's before Robin and John, who arrived just in time to see the smith being punched in the face by the tanner.

"You think you're clever, Alfred? Stealing our money and setting fire to my storehouse? Let's see how clever you are now, you thick bastard! We're going to destroy this place, and remove the last of your teeth. And then…" Simon held up his knife, the blade glinting dully as he did so. "The Coterels will come looking for the silver you stole from them, unless you hand it over now."

"I don't know what you're talking about!" the smith objected, blood streaming from his nose onto his moustache. He seemed dazed from being struck, as though he might collapse. "I never stole anything. I've been here all day!"

Simon and one of his lackeys were standing in front of Alfred, making sure he couldn't escape or lift a weapon, but the third man from the tannery – the small, dark, rat-faced individual – had gone inside the smithy. He brought out a piece of wood that he'd set alight in the furnace and held it up now with an evil grin. "Shall I burn down this stinking shit-hole?" the man asked.

"No, you'll drop that, and fuck off back to your tannery, or things will go badly for you," Little John bellowed, charging out of the trees, quarterstaff raised threateningly.

Robin saw the man with the burning brand, saw him thinking about what he should do, and it was clear he'd decided to ignore the bailiff's command. Snarling something in defiance, the man turned and placed the flaming piece of wood against the side of the smithy. Robin raced towards him, wishing he'd brought his longbow as he saw the wall of the smithy begin to smoulder.

"This bastard has just robbed me, so stay where you are, bailiff," Simon Tanner screeched, brandishing his knife at

351

the smith as he addressed Little John. "You should be arresting him, not attacking me and my workers!"

"I never set fire to anything," protested the smith, slumping back, eyes closed. "I told you; I've been here all day."

"You're fucking lying!" Simon shouted, placing the point of his blade against the smith's neck. "You're the only one that would know how to make a copy of the key to my chest. And you've been giving me dirty looks for weeks now. It's obvious you've been desperate to get back at me."

"Aye, I hate you, Tanner," the smith admitted. "I'd like to beat you to a pulp. But I've made no pass keys, and I did nothing today, other than working here."

Robin ran up to the man trying to set alight to the smithy. He was tempted to draw his sword, but he knew killing the tannery worker would only lead to more trouble with the law. The man saw him coming however and, snarling, rose to his feet, lifting his wooden hammer as he did so.

Robin's momentum carried him inexorably forward and, as his opponent swung the hammer, he tried desperately to dodge the blow. It whistled past his face but caught him on the left shoulder and he cried out in agony.

"Get back," the tannery worker spat, teeth bared as he came for Robin again, swinging his hammer as though he was trying to pound a piece of leather.

Robin found himself off balance, the pain in his shoulder filling him with rage. The rat-faced man laughed gleefully, aiming another vicious attack at Robin's head. Stepping inside the swing, Robin brought his forearm up. Had the hammer struck him his bones would surely have been shattered, but Robin was close enough that it was the tannery worker's wrist that thumped into him, and Robin snapped his head forward, smashing it into the rat-faced man's nose.

The tannery worker fell back against the wall he'd been trying to burn, eyes looking in different directions, and Robin moved away, grimly clutching his shoulder.

"Get up," Simon shouted at the rat-faced man. "Get up, and finish what you started. We're not leaving here until the smithy is burned to the ground. Maybe then the goat-shagger will tell us where he's hid the money he stole from us."

"It can't be far away," the third tannery worker observed, looking around, his slack jaw and lumpen body giving him a distinctly menacing appearance. "The money was only just stolen before we got here."

"So you idiots think I broke into your tannery, carried off a heavy load of silver, hid it somewhere, and then calmly went back to forging that horseshoe in time for you three to turn up here?" The blacksmith shook his head in disgust. "You really are as thick as pig-shit, Tanner, aren't you?"

Simon's face contorted in fury and, as Robin watched in horror, plunged his knife into the smith's body.

"We have to stop this," Little John shouted, running forward again. "Get them!"

Robin gritted his teeth, trying to ignore his own pain as he made once more for the rat-faced fellow who'd retrieved the stave of wood he'd set on fire earlier and was now shuffling towards the furnace to bring it back to life.

The blacksmith's mouth had opened in shock as he was stabbed, but now he reached down to his belt and took out a knife of his own. Roaring like an injured beast, he thrust his blade into Simon's guts and dragged it upwards, massive muscles bulging in his arm as he lifted Simon right off his feet.

Little John ran to the third, lumbering tannery worker who came to his senses and draw back his knife, ready to plunge it into the smith's back. The bailiff's quarterstaff thrust out first, catching the man in the temple. It was not meant to be a killing blow, but the combination of John's enormous strength, charging momentum, and the heavy ash wood were enough to crack the tannery worker's skull, the sound of it echoing sickeningly back from the smithy wall as the man slumped to the ground.

Simon Tanner was bodily thrown through the air by the smith then, landing in the road on his back, torso torn wide open, blood and guts spilling out of him as he quickly expired.

Only the small, dark friend of the tanner remained alive. He had managed to get the length of wood burning and, as Robin and John came towards him, the man lashed out. The smell of burning flesh and hair was carried on the breeze and Robin saw his huge friend's beard smouldering, his cheeks a livid red.

As the bailiff stumbled back, cursing in pain, the tannery worker came forward, swinging the fiery brand and swearing he'd see Robin and John turned into human torches.

Things had gone too far already, and Robin knew they had to finish off this remaining enemy before he did for them. Drawing his sword, he waited for the tannery worker to swing another wild blow with the flaming brand, and then plunged the point of his blade into the man's unarmoured side. He felt the steel scraping against ribs and tried to pull it free, but the tannery worker panicked and, in fright he turned. His startled movement only had the effect of sawing the sword even further into his side, and a wide gash was torn open before Robin managed to draw the blade free.

The man had forgotten the burning length of wood in his hand, and it continued to blaze away merrily as he looked down in shock at the gaping hole in his torso, blood pouring from him. His gaze lifted and he met Robin's eyes before falling to the ground without another word.

Tuck and Will Scarlet appeared at that moment, riding along the street towards them, faces tight with worry.

"We're fine," Robin called, holding up a hand. "Apart from a bruised shoulder, and a singed beard."

"Aye. Bastards," John said, rubbing the affected section of hair and glaring irritably at the dead tanners. "But my beard'll grow back. Tuck, come and check on the blacksmith, will you? He's been stabbed."

"Stabbed? Oh, God help us." The friar dismounted, almost falling out of the saddle in his haste, and ran to the injured smith, cassock flying, sandals slapping against the path. "Let me see it," he ordered. "Come on, lift your apron."

"How did you find us?" Robin asked Scarlet.

"When you didn't come to get us we were worried you'd been caught by the tanner, so we went looking for you. We found the empty chest lying open, and assumed you'd been chased. It was easy enough following your trail here – you didn't try to hide it."

"No, we were in too much of a rush to help the smith," Robin confirmed. "We weren't fast enough in getting here though. Poor Alfred was blamed for the robbery, and took Simon's knife in his belly for it."

"Not his belly," Tuck called. "Just to the side. And praise the Lord, his apron took much of the power from the tanner's thrust."

"Really?" the smith asked weakly. "It hurts bad."

"Well, you've been stabbed. Of course it will hurt. Now lie still and stop complaining."

"What are we going to do about all this?" John muttered as he came out to look back at the smithy.

Robin had been asking himself the same question, and he thought he had the ideal solution. "Take those three." He pointed at the bodies of the men from the tannery. "And hide them."

"Hide them?" John asked uncertainly.

"Aye. The Coterels will come looking for their money before long, and they'll find it all gone, along with Simon and his two workers."

"And they'll believe Simon robbed them?"

"Exactly."

"Will someone tell me what the fuck is going on?" the smith demanded, trying to wipe away the caked blood on his moustache. "Why did those bastards come here accusing me of all sorts? And why are you lot talking about the Coterels and stealing money?"

"We'll explain later," Robin told him. "For now, we better get those three bodies out of the way before someone comes along and finds them."

"It's just as well the smithy is set away from the main village," Scarlet said, going to the smallest of the dead men and effortlessly lifting him onto his shoulder.

"I like how you're taking the lightest load," John said.

"Well, my thigh is still not right," Scarlet returned in a hurt tone. "Now, where are we dumping this rubbish?"

"There's an old well about half a mile to the north," the blacksmith suggested. "It dried up years ago, and there was some local superstition about an old hag putting a curse on it. Nobody goes near it now."

"Well that's handy," Scarlet grinned.

"I know the place you mean," John said, nodding as he thought over the plan. "I remember it. As you say, people shun the place, so it was ideal for a place to camp when we were outlaws." He shook his head as Robin opened his mouth. "It was before you or Tuck joined us."

"I remember it now," Scarlet said. "Come on then, let's get it over with."

Tuck stripped Simon's cloak from his blood-soaked torso, and the friar did his best to bind up the terrible wounds, stopping the blood and gore from leaking too badly before he lifted the dead tanner onto Robin's uninjured shoulder.

John took the biggest of the corpses and they trotted northwards after Scarlet, quickly swallowed up by the trees and bushes, leaving Tuck to take care of the smith.

It wasn't long before they found the well, although it had become almost completely overgrown by weeds and grass. Their swords came in handy to pull the undergrowth back, and then the dead men were unceremoniously thrown in.

"Think that's enough?" Scarlet wondered, staring down into the gloomy well-cum-tomb.

"Aye, no way anyone will find them there," John said confidently. "Even if they're discovered, no one's going to the trouble of dragging their carcasses out. Far too much effort."

"They'll be badly decomposed after a few days anyway," Robin said. "We did strip them of valuables and things that might be recognised, didn't we? Good. Shove those weeds back over the top then, John, and we'll return to the blacksmith's."

They picked their way back through the woods as the dust settled and the reality of what they'd done finally hit them. It was just supposed to be a robbery that day, but it had turned into the deaths of three men, and the unlawful disposal of their bodies. No Christian burial for Simon Tanner or his mates, just an eternity stuck beside one another at the bottom of a cursed old well.

"Good enough for them," Will Scarlet grunted. "Pricks."

"Aye, but I'm still worried about the Coterels," said John.

"Nothing we can do about them now." They reached the smithy and Robin smiled as he saw Tuck and Alfred sitting enjoying a drink together. "Might have known you'd be taking it easy while we do all the hard work," he said to the friar.

"What's more important? Saving a life, or hiding bodies?" Tuck countered, raising his cup in a toast to the smith's recovery. "I've told Alfred all about what we were doing here in Notton today, and that we'll hand back the stolen silver to him, and the butcher, and all the other villagers that were extorted."

Robin nodded. This was not how he had expected things to work out. He'd planned to steal the money and hide it nearby. When John Coterel came to collect the coins and found Tanner's chest empty, there would be all sorts of confusion, and recriminations. The Tanner would deny any knowledge of the theft, but Robin suspected that the Coterels must have heard about Simon's drunken plans to leave Notton to work for himself. They would not believe Simon's protestations of ignorance, and things would go very badly for the Tanner. Especially when the butcher, acting on Robin's orders, would tip off the Coterels as to where 'Simon' had hidden the money he'd stolen from the gang...

It was not a perfect plan, since the Coterels would end up with the extorted silver, but Robin had believed it would lead to the end of the tanner, and most likely the gang's interest in Notton.

Events had not quite gone as expected but, in truth, everything had worked out for the best, Robin thought.

"What are we going to do about the Coterels?" John asked again when the bloodstains and any traces of the earlier fight had been cleared away, and they were finally seated outside the smithy with cups of his ale in hand.

"Nothing," Scarlet told him.

"I agree," said Tuck.

"Fuck them," the smith piped up. "When they come here asking questions, I'll tell them the tanner attacked me and took my money off me, then left the village with his pals, all packed up like they were going away for a long time. The butcher, and the others that have been extorted, will help me spread that rumour around."

John nodded. "That sounds good," he said. "As long as the bodies aren't found."

"What about you, Hood?" the smith asked him. "You're awfully quiet over there."

Everyone turned to Robin as he sat sipping his ale for a long moment, choosing his words carefully. "I agree, the Coterels will spend some time hunting around Yorkshire for the tanner, but they'll give up eventually and hopefully decide Notton isn't worth the hassle anymore."

"And then what?" John asked.

"And then we can worry about them if they become a problem again," said Robin with a shrug. "But for now I think we've solved the trouble here. If the Coterels try to persuade someone else to extort the villagers, well, we can make sure the new man finds out what really happened to the tanner and his pals; that should be enough to put them off." He spread his arms and grinned. "On top of that, I have my pardon, we're all alive and in one piece, and we each have a full cup of ale. What more could a man ask for?"

"Well said," Tuck cried, standing to hoist his cup aloft in salute. "To Notton, by God! And Robin! And all of us!"

"And to getting it right up the Coterels," Will Scarlet added.

"To all of that!" laughed Little John as they raised their drinks. "And to the future."

"To the future," said Robin. "Whatever it may bring!"

THE END?

AUTHOR'S NOTE

The Forest Lord was the first series of books I ever worked on, and *Wolf's Head*, my debut novel, was published way back in 2013. When I was writing those early stories I didn't want to string the series out the way some other authors do when they find a good formula (not naming any names here). Although the four Forest Lord books sold well, and some readers even told me this was their favourite ever version of the Robin Hood legend, I had no desire to keep churning out the books just because they were making me money. "Hang on," I can hear you saying. "You've already written seven Warrior Druid of Britain novels with no end in sight, what are you on about?" The difference is, my Druid stories are entirely my own creation, whereas the Forest Lord tales are, or at least were, based on the Robin Hood ballads and legends. There simply wasn't enough material in those medieval stories to write more than three or four novels. I covered it all within the books up to and including *Blood of the Wolf*, and that was that as far as I was concerned.

However, I couldn't bring myself to show Robin actually dying in that fourth (and ostensibly final) novel, and, on top of that, I continued to write my winter/Christmas novellas like *Sworn to God,* and *Faces of Darkness* using the other characters. So there was always a very dim thought at the back of my mind that maybe, one day, Robin might return to Wakefield and have another adventure with his old friends.

The thought began to take firm root around four years ago when I listened to a podcast about the lost treasure of King John. I'd never heard of the treasure before then (I'm Scottish, don't forget, we didn't learn this stuff at school), but I thought it was a fascinating story. Where exactly was the treasure lost? What caused all those men and wagons to be lost? Had the treasure really all been swallowed up, or had some of it been secretly carried off? No one knows the answer to any of these questions for sure, so the mystery really got my imagination going and, given the period the treasure went missing (1216), I thought it might be an interesting thing for Robin Hood and his friends to talk about and ultimately investigate.

The second thing that sparked my imagination was a thread on the now defunct conspiracy theory forum, Above Top Secret. I used to enjoy browsing that site until 2019 when posters started predicting a terrible pandemic which eventually became the Covid 19 lockdowns. I was so freaked out by how accurate those posters' predictions had been that I stopped reading the forum, but not before I'd read a long, and incredibly interesting thread about a mysterious mountain on the border of Austria and Germany called the Untersberg. So many strange tales were told about this mysterious mountain that I really wanted to use it as a location for one of my books. The fact that I'd actually visited two similar places while on honeymoon with my wife (the Dachstein Ice Caves in Hallstatt, Austria, and Hitler's Eagle's Nest in Berchtesgaden, Germany) even meant that I'd have at least some idea of what hiking up, and exploring the dark interior of such a vast mountain was like.

The combined thought of Robin Hood searching for King John's mythical treasure in the legend-haunted Untersberg was too much for me to resist and that's why I decided to bring Robin back to Wakefield at the end of *The Heretic of Haltemprice Priory*. True, nothing in *Return of the Wolf* has anything to do with the original Robin Hood ballads, but I think I've made these characters mine by this stage and hopefully you enjoyed the story.

When I began researching the lost treasure I discovered a possible reason for what might have happened to the unfortunate baggage train. Essentially, the full moon played a part in affecting tidal forces, causing a rogue wave to wash away, or sink, everyone and everything as they tried to cross the Wash. You can find out more at the link here if you're interested: https://news.txst.edu/research-and-innovation/2022/celestial-sleuth-longfellow-poem-king-john-lost-crown-jewels.html

I was a little worried that Robin and Tuck going to visit the Wash thinking it would have dried up in the sunshine would seem ridiculous to readers. Nowadays we have detailed maps, and the internet to quickly find out what an area is like. But I'll be honest with you – I actually believed that the Wash might have dried up, that's what gave me the idea in the first place. I had no clue it was beside the sea (again, my excuse is that I live in Scotland, not England)! It was only when I started looking into it, and asked one of my readers about the area (thanks Weylin) that I discovered the Wash would never dry up. By then I'd already started writing the book so I decided to just have Robin and Tuck go through with their ill-advised trip anyway. If they seem like idiots, well, so am I!

Incidentally, there really was a drought in England in 1331, that's what initially made me (and the characters) think the Wash might have dried up at all.

Real, too, were the Coterels. This notorious gang genuinely caused mayhem around England during the 1330s, kidnapping people, extorting money from them, raping, murdering, stealing and so on. Nothing was ever really done about them because they had powerful people, and a corrupt system, protecting them. I guess some things never really change…

Next up for me will be the winter novella I'm writing with Matthew Harffy. No title yet, but it'll be published just a few weeks after *Return of the Wolf*, most likely in November 2025, so look out for it. It stars John, Will, and Tuck as usual, but this time they face a brand-new enemy created by Mr Harffy. We think people are really going to enjoy it!

After that, I'll be writing the eighth Warrior Druid of Britain novel at some point, but perhaps before that I might try my hand at the fantasy genre. What do you think? Would you like to see a fantasy novel written by me? Let me know by using the CONTACT ME button on my website at stevenamckay.com, or my social media pages on Facebook and X. You can also sign up to my Email List to keep up to date with all my news and to take part in the giveaways I regularly run (not just for signed copies of my own books either, this year I've given away fantastic signed copies of novels by Peter Gibbons, and Griff Hosker)!

As always, thank you so much for reading my work, I truly appreciate your continued support. If you enjoyed *Return of the Wolf* please think about leaving a rating and a short review to let other readers know, it really is a great help.

Cheers!

Steven A. McKay
Old Kilpatrick,
August 21, 2025

As always, thank you very much for reading this book. If you enjoyed it, please leave a 5 star review on Amazon/Goodreads. And if you'd like to keep up with my news, sign up for my newsletter at www.stevenamckay.com – I regularly give away signed copies of my books, and sometimes I even send out exclusive, FREE short stories.

ALSO BY STEVEN A. McKAY

The Forest Lord Series:
Wolf's Head
The Wolf and the Raven
Rise of the Wolf
Blood of the Wolf

Knight of the Cross*
Friar Tuck and the Christmas Devil*
The Prisoner*
The Escape*
The Abbey of Death*
Faces of Darkness*
Sworn To God
The House In The Marsh*
The Pedlar's Promise*
The Christmas Gift*
The Heretic of Haltemprice Priory*
Swords in the Snow* (w/Matthew Harffy, Nov 2025)

The Warrior Druid of Britain Chronicles
The Druid
Song of the Centurion
The Northern Throne
The Bear of Britain
Over The Wall*
Wrath of the Picts
The Vengeance of Merlin
The Druid's Prey

LUCIA – A Roman Slave's Tale

Alfred the Great trilogy

The Heathen Horde
Sword of the Saxons
King of Wessex

Titles marked * are spin-off novellas or short stories.
All others are novels.

ACKNOWLEDGEMENTS

This section is usually just me thanking the same people. It's no different this time! Huge thanks to Bernadette McDade for her help with the first draft, my editor Richenda Todd, and cover designers More Visual. Biggest thanks to you, the readers, for continuing to buy my books!

Printed in Dunstable, United Kingdom